RELENTLESS GUERILLAS

Autorifle slugs chittered through the air a meter above Grayson's head, and the deeper-throated wham of a hunting rifle popped a geyser of sand near his feet.

"Hold your fire!" Grayson yelled. "We're friends," he continued, holding his arms out from his sides, showing that he was unarmed. "We want to talk."

"It's a trick, Colonel," a voice barked from behind a sand dune. There was a crack and something hot plucked at Grayson's sleeve.

"Hold your fire, dammit!" another voice replied. "Dober, put that thing down!"

"I'm Captain Carlyle, Gray Death Mercenary Legion," Grayson told them. He had to stifle the tremor at the back of his throat, and his knees felt weak. He wanted very much to drop to the sand, out of sight, but he knew that any sudden movement would unleash a storm of gunfire. "We were brought here to help you, not fight you!"

BATTLETECH®

#7

MERCENARY'S STAR

WILLIAM H. KEITH, JR.

A ROC BOOK

ROC
Published by the Penguin Group
Penguin Books USA Inc., 375 Hudson Street,
New York, New York 10014, U.S.A.
Penguin Books Ltd, 27 Wrights Lane,
London W8 5TZ, England
Penguin Books Australia Ltd, Ringwood,
Victoria, Australia
Penguin Books Canada Ltd, 10 Alcorn Avenue,
Toronto, Ontario, Canada M4V 3B2
Penguin Books (N.Z.) Ltd, 182–190 Wairau Road,
Auckland 10, New Zealand

Penguin Books Ltd, Registered Offices:
Harmondsworth, Middlesex, England

Published by Roc, an imprint of New American Library,
a division of Penguin Books USA Inc. Previously published by FASA
Corporation.

First Roc Printing, November, 1992
10 9 8 7 6 5 4 3 2

Series Editor: Donna Ippolito
Cover: Bork Vallejo
Interior illustrations: Jane Aulisio
Mechanical drawings: FASA Art Staff
Maps: Aardvark Studio

Prologue

There who have never seen a BattleMech up close can never comprehend the raw power and mechanical precision of these ten-meter tall, armored giants. The smallest weigh twenty tons and can stride across uneven ground—or leap over it—with a speed and grace that belies their mass and complexity. The heaviest 'Mechs weigh ninety tons or more and are equipped with enough weaponry to defeat a regiment of more conventional infantry.

It is only desperation that could drive unarmed and unarmored humans to challenge these dreadnaughts in open combat, and that is exactly what happened on Verthandi. This planet changed hands in 3016 when the forces of House Kurita defeated the Steiner defenders at the Battle of Harvest in that year. Among his demands, Lord Kurita claimed sovereignty over the seemingly unexceptional Steiner world of Verthandi, located in the border reaches of the Tamar Pact region of the Lyran Commonwealth.

Until that time, Verthandi had been a peaceful world of small villages set among blue-green hills. It was an agricultural world of lumber and coffee plantations scattered over the broad and fertile area known as the Silvan Basin, with quiet resort communities lying along the tropical coast of its Azure Sea.

The capital city of Regis was governed by Verthandi's ruling Council of Academicians, a democratic body elected from among the senior professors of government at Regis University. There was a local militia to investigate the rare crime, but war, politics, and interstellar intrigue were remote from the Verthandians' day-to-day life.

Then House Kurita descended with its iron-mail fist, and life on Verthandi would never be the same.

—Jani ce Taylor, *Shapers of Men and Destiny*,
Avalon Free Press, 3031

MAP OF VERTHANDI
Silvan Basin Area

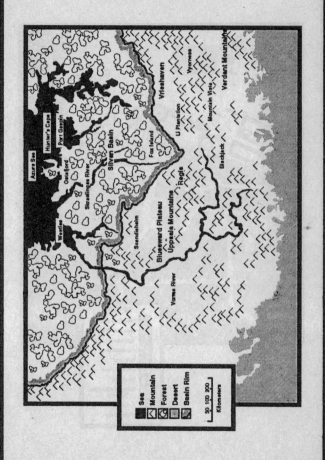

MAP OF REGIS
University Area

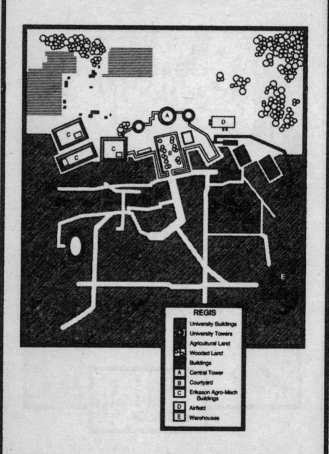

REGIS

- University Buildings
- University Towers
- Agricultural Land
- Wooded Land
- Buildings
- **A** Central Tower
- **B** Courtyard
- **C** Eriksson Agro-Mech Buildings
- **D** Airfield
- **E** Warehouses

Book I

The night sky churned with smoke and fire, reflecting the lurid flames over the dying village. People ran, hastily grabbed possessions clutched to their chests or carried in baskets, their shadows vast and outlandish where the fires cast them across broken pavement. There were shrieks and screams, babbled shouts and imprecations, a smattering of gunshots, all enfolded in the roar of the blaze devouring the village of Mountain Vista.

The MAD-3R *Marauder* turned ponderously, its weapon-heavy forearms dropping into line with its next target. The sign above the building's broad, plate-glass windows proclaimed it to be a farm and plantation supply store. Fleeing civilians overflowed from the walkway in front of the store and spilled out into the street. Engulfed in flames, an overturned groundcar illuminated the panic and sent reflections dancing along the store's miraculously unbroken windows.

The death machine's right particle cannon flared once, the air between gun and target ionized by a charged beam of eye-searing brilliance. One window shattered under the touch of man-made lightning. Then something inside the building—stored bags of fertilizer, perhaps—detonated with a concussion that jarred the pavement under the 'Mech's feet. The remaining windows exploded outward into the street, broken glass, splintered wood, and shards of ferrocrete block cutting through the mob like a vibroblade through unprotected flesh. The building's upper three stories seemed to hang suspended for an instant, then settled one atop the other on the ruin of the ground floor. Rubble and debris rattled against the *Marauder*'s legs a hundred meters away as billows of smoke and dust rolled across the bodies of the silent dead and the shrieking wounded.

Valdis Kevlavic grinned with savage satisfaction inside the heat of his neurohelmet. The *Marauder* responded to his soft urgings, completing its turn and lurching with ground-chewing strides toward the heart of the town. Infrared scanners fed him green-colored images that blurred into white where the heat of multiple fires etched dazzling traces on his viewscreen. Human figures fleeing from the *Marauder*'s wrath became eerie green shadows that ducked, twisted, and flitted across the screen. Kevlavic triggered the Mech's autocannon, felt the solid chunk of fresh ammo carousels snap home, heard the thundering chatter of rapid-fire death from the weapon mounted just above his cockpit. White flashes stitched across the pavement, chewing through those fleeing green shadows with bloody abandon.

This demonstration should please Regis Central, Kevlavic thought. There had been many reports that Mountain Vista was a staging area and refuge for raiders in the Regis area. Many of those shell-torn corpses were no doubt rebel, though Kevlavic cared little whether they were or not. The whole valley from Regis to the Silvan Basin and as far east as the Verdant Mountains would see what resistance to Lord Kurita meant. Mountain Vista's destruction would make other communities think twice before offering shelter or aid to Verthandi's rebel vermin.

Something whanged off the *Marauder*'s tiny, armor-bound cockpit window, leaving a bright-smudged star on the tough plastic. Kevlavic calculated trajectories, swung his machine, and spotted movement on the IR scanner. The sniper was hiding in a shattered church tower, his perch a little lower than Kevlavic's cockpit. The sniper's rifle, an old hunting weapon of some kind, flashed again. Once more, the bullet smeared uselessly across the 'Mech's canopy.

Kevlavic urged the *Marauder* forward.

As his machine loomed over the broken-off steeple, he could see the sniper cowering inside. Scarcely more than a boy, he was obviously terrified, but wore the same camouflaged military fatigues favored by rebels in the Verthandian jungles. The boy threw his rifle down and raised his hands above his head. The 'Mech's external mikes picked up a shrill string of pleas for mercy, of surrender.

Not for the first time, Kevlavic wished that his *Marauder* had proper 'Mech hands as he slowly raised the machine's left forearm to where the heavy, twin-barreled vambrace was less than a meter from the boy's side. Then he snapped on the external speakers. His voice, thunder-loud through the amplifiers, made the sniper cringe. "In the name of the Governor-General of Verthandi and of the military forces of the Draconis Combine, you're under arrest! Climb on!"

The rebel understood. He scrambled across the rubble of the steeple and grabbed the handholds welded to the Mech's metal`forearm. Even an enemy sworn to die rather than surrender would think twice when faced with execution by a 70-ton *Marauder*. Moving slowly and with precision, Kevlavic swung his captive up out of the steeple's ruin and over the street. Crouched there in alleyways, ruined buildings, and anywhere else they could find the illusion of cover, people were staring up at the monster machine silhouetted against the burning town. Kevlavic smiled. *Good*, he thought. *To be effective, terror demanded an audience.*

Slowly, deliberately, Kevlavic's *Marauder* kicked the broken church into rubble, then swept laser fire across people fleeing its collapse. The captive clinging to the *Marauder*'s arm screamed again, pleading with Kevlavic to stop. The church crumbled with a final roar and a billowing cloud of dust.

Kevlavic flicked the massive forearm once, twice. The captive shrieked and clung to the handholds, his legs kicking over empty air. Kevlavic brought the 'Mech's right arm across. The PPC muzzle, still hot from his shot at the farm store, trailed smoke as he moved it. The captive shrieked again as hot metal brushed him, then wailed as he kicked and thrashed down the eight-meter drop to the pavement.

The sniper was still screaming, writhing against the partial immobility of a broken back, as the *Marauder*'s huge foot slowly descended on him.

As many times as he'd been over it, Grayson could not see what more could be done. Devic Erudin's offer was the only one the Gray Death Legion had received during their whole six months on Galatea. Unless he could get work for his unit, he'd be forced to disband so that his men could find other work among the larger, better-equipped mercenary units. Galatea was a hiring center for mercenaries from across the Lyran Commonwealth and beyond. Merc units or their representatives gathered here to look for work, and Galatea was where governments sent their representatives to seek out and sign up mercenary fighters.

The problem was that mercenary units were so common and most could muster full, twelve-'Mech companies or even entire regiments. The Gray Death Legion numbered a mere five 'Mechs upon arriving on Galatea. Only two of these, Lori Kalmar's *Locust* and Grayson's own *Shadow Hawk,* were piloted by combat veterans. As the weeks passed, five more 'Mech Warriors had signed on, and two of them brought 'Mechs of their own, raising the Legion's strength to seven. The unit had been able to hire Techs and support troops, too, then put in the time to drill these troops and to acquire salvage parts to repair and re-equip the 'Mechs.

Renfred Tor, Captain of the jump freighter *Invidious,* had met and recruited a pair of AeroSpace pilots to fly close tactical fighter support for the unit in space or during ground combat. Meanwhile, Sergeant Ramage was transforming the ground troops into a unit well-trained in anti-'Mech and 'Mech-support infantry tactics. Now, the unit numbered just 186 men and women, including all the crewmembers of the aging *Invidious*, the Techs, astechs, and ground infantry they'd brought from Trellwan, and the handful of experienced men they'd been able to recruit here on Galatea.

Grayson knew that it would all be for nothing if he could not find a patron, and quickly. Precious few employers were looking to sign up a unit of less than two full lances, especially a newly organized one with only a single campaign under its belt. After six weeks, Grayson had spent most of the money that the grateful government of Trellwan had awarded him for freeing them from the tyranny of House Kurita's Duke Hassid Ricol. After paying the Galatean port fees and buying salvaged parts for the 'Mechs, fuel, food, weapons, and ammunition—not to mention bribes for port officials, which was the only way to get through the bureaucratic red tape—Grayson barely had enough left to pay the troops. In fact, just two weeks before, he had stopped paying the unit in C-bills and had begun to issue them promissory notes instead. No merchant in Galaport would accept a unit's own notes as payment for anything, and very soon, neither would the Legion.

Grayson had first met Erudin in one of the Galaport strip's innumerable bars. The place was named "Marauder Bill's", though some earlier patron had shot out the "B" in the neon sign, leaving only "Marauder ill's". Renfred Tor had made the first contact with the man and then later brought Grayson along to meet him.

Marauder Bill's—or ills—was typical of a hundred similar establishments within a kilometer of the Galaport gate. Outside, it was all grime-coated, sun-baked, age-peeling whitewash, the cracked façade shimmering in Galatea's desert heat. Within, it was dark and marginally cooler, with the sounds of raucous laughter and conversation punctuated by the clatter of glassware and an occasional drunken fistfight. Erudin had been sitting way in the back, well away from the pools of stagelight in which naked dancers writhed and away from the crowd of heavily armed mercs maneuvering for spaces at the bar and central tables.

Nothing about the man suggested that he might be a warrior. He was a full head shorter than Grayson Carlyle's rangy height, his pale eyes magnified grotesquely by thick-lensed eyeglasses. Those glasses identified him as native of a planet lacking the technology for corneal implants or myopicorrective surgery. *Lostech* was the word that had been coined for such a place, a world that had begun the long fall from civilization to savagery during centuries of unremitting warfare. The word now applied only to those worlds that had lost the most. After all, the whole Inner Sphere of known Space had suffered a similar decline in technology and the destruction of scientific knowledge.

What sort of commission might await Grayson and his mercenary band on a Lostech world?

He kept that thought to himself as he accepted Erudin's hand. "You must be Grayson Carlyle," the man said conversationally enough as he stood up. Though his appearance was bookish, the small man's handclasp was strong, and there was a look of quiet determination about him. "Your pilot here has told me a very great deal about you."

"Well, he's told me nothing about you, Mr. Erudin, so you have me at a disadvantage."

"*Citizen* Erudin, if you please, Captain," Tor said. "He's the leader of a dandy little revolution a few tens of lights from here."

Grayson had cocked an eyebrow at that. "A few tens of light years" suggested the region along the Lyran Commonwealth's border with the Draconis Combine. Such border areas between the various great Houses were always tense enough to keep mercenary units, arms merchants, and whole fleets and armies busy, with planets trading hands along the frontier with monotonous regularity.

"Not the leader, no," Erudin said, seating himself. "I *am* the representative for Verthandi's Revolutionary Council, however. We are fighting against House Kurita, and we need help . . . need it badly."

"I should damn well think so," Grayson had remarked. Just then, they were interrupted by a young lady dressed in more fake jewelry and feathers than clothing, who offered to take their order. Tor had ordered something called lugen coladas for everyone, but Grayson broke in to say he wanted only a glass of ice water, then turned to study Tor's contact as he picked up his tale.

Verthandi was the second of the three-world system of Norn, but the name meant nothing to Grayson. Why should it? There were so *many* worlds . . . Verthandi had once been a peaceful world, Erudin explained, its countryside devoted to agriculture. Verthandi had also been well known throughout much of the Commonwealth for its university at the capital city of Regis.

"That all changed, though," he said. "Ten years ago, there was a major Kurita offensive. . . ."

Grayson nodded. "At Dahlgren, yes." He'd been there himself, though only a boy of ten at the time. That had been the year he'd formally become a Warrior's Apprentice in his father's regiment, Carlyle's Commandos. He could still remember his father's anguish when one of Kurita's Sword of Light regiments had dropped onto the Commandos' rear in the battle of Dahlgren. They'd had to retreat or face annihilation. "The Commonwealth formally ceded a number of border systems when they lost Dahlgren, isn't that so?"

"Verthandi was one of them," Erudin said. "The first thing the Combine did was to establish a naval base on our moon, Verthandi-Alpha. We had been totally reliant on the Lyrans for military support. Outside of a few freighters and merchantmen, we had nothing in the way of ships—not even for a short hop to our own moon."

Grayson nodded again. Verthandi was a Lostech world if its people were that dependent on others for transport and commerce. He knew, too, that House Kurita would not have encouraged them to become more independent, but would have shifted the Verthandians' dependence toward itself. Worlds dependent on them for trade and high-tech gadgetry were unlikely to become rebellious.

Erudin took a deep breath. "The next thing we knew, they'd landed troops, engineers, and heavy equipment. Their surveys had suggested that Verthandi might be rich in certain metals, and they began mining for the stuff." He shrugged. "We'd never paid much attention to such things. We kept to ourselves, governed ourselves. Galactic politics and the Succession Wars were rather outside our grasp, I'm afraid."

Grayson's lips curved, more grimace than smile. "The Draconis Combine does not take well to the idea of self-government. They prefer to help."

"Help themselves, you mean," Tor said.

"That's what it amounted to," Erudin said. "Our planetary forces fought them, but they merely brought in more troops and seized our spaceport and Regis, the capital. They ordered new elections and saw to it that their own people took most of the Council seats. They opened mines in the Southern Desert, working them with people rounded up at gunpoint from various communities. We fought back, of course." His thin shoulders rose and fell in a hopeless shrug. "We fought back. We kept fighting back . . . but when they brought in the BattleMechs, we couldn't keep the fight going. The Dracos burned whole towns, leveled villages. Any home suspected of harboring rebels was burned, and the families of rebels were shot or sent south to the mines.

"The Revolutionary Council finally decided it was time to look for help offworld. I managed to get here by joining the crew of a Verthandian merchant who overtly supports the Loyalist government and the Combine, but who secretly works with us. His ship got me to Gronden, and from there, I was able to arrange passage to Galatea. We'd heard that this was where we would find mercenaries for hire and that I'd be able to buy radios, guns, and other equipment that we need so badly."

The bargirl returned with their drinks. Ice clinked in the glasses as she set them down. "That's five-H fifty for the lugens," she said, "and three twenty-five for the ice water."

"I'll be frank with you, Captain," Erudin said gravely as he counted off the money for the drinks. "The Revolutionary Council sent me here to find a small, battle-hardened unit to serve as a training cadre. Our forces have been scattered . . . Hell, we've been bloody well hammered into the ground every time we've tried to meet Kurita on their own terms. At the moment, we've been reduced to hiding out in the hills and in the jungle, sniping at the Dracos when we can."

Erudin intently studied the glass in his hand. "Sniping is not going to win our war for us. We know that. We need someone our people can rally around . . . someone who can show us how to use what we've got to beat those Brownjackets. I don't care how many BattleMechs they've got, if enough of our people rise up, no 'Mech force in the galaxy could stand against them!''

"Heroic sentiments, Citizen. . . ."

Erudin's face flushed: "I wouldn't expect a *mercenary* to understand."

"Mercenaries fight for causes, too, my friend, but I do have to look out for my people," Grayson said quietly. "What else can you tell me?"

The rest was not encouraging. There were pieces of four Kurita BattleMech regiments on Verthandi. Though only one was known to be at full strength, that still meant the Legion could be facing hundreds of enemy 'Mechs.

The situation was not as hopeless as it first appeared, or Grayson would simply have thanked Erudin for his time and left on the spot. Those four partial regiments were scattered all over Verthandi's northern hemisphere, tied down in garrison details in scores of towns and villages, airfields and mines. The Combine forces were known to muster numerous AeroSpace Fighters, too, but most of those were assigned to the Kurita base on Verthandi's moon. Finally, there were the eight regiments of "Blues," Loyalist militia directed by the Kurita puppet government in Regis. Though they numbered thousands of ground troops, Erudin said that their morale was low.

"There's nothing like a formal blockade," Erudin had explained. "Your ship captain here said you could disguise your DropShip to look like a Kurita *Union* Class freight hauler. If you did that, they might not challenge us at all. I can direct you to a landing spot in the Azure Sea area, where the jungle will shelter you." Once safely down, he continued, they would link up with the Revolutionary Council. The Legion's chief duties would consist of training cadres of Verthandian rebels, particularly in infantry tactics against BattleMechs.

It was not an enviable assignment. The unit was being asked to run a Kurita blockade and then to strand itself on a world garrisoned by hundreds of enemy 'Mechs. They would have to avoid direct contact with a vastly superior enemy army, while teaching the local rebels how to effectively fight back. The fact that they would be engaged in a bloody, fratricidal civil war simply increased the chances that someone would betray them to the Combine forces. Even if they succeeded in their mission, whether or not the Gray Death Legion would ever get off Verthandi depended on the success of what sounded like a ragtag rebellion. Most mercenary units would not even consider such a high-risk, uncertain mission.

The Gray Death Legion, however, could not refuse. *But AgroMechs!* Grayson thought. *How in God's name did these rebels expect to fight with AgroMechs?*

In the end, they'd hammered out an agreement. Though Grayson still had his doubts, the Legion needed the commission. Either that or dissolve the unit, leaving each man for himself on Galatea.

3

Galatea's F8 sun was a tiny white disk against the shimmering heat of early afternoon. In spite of the heat, the starport field bustled with activity, especially near Bay Twelve where a DropShip crouched ponderously in its launch pit. Weaving intricate choreographics between the ship and Bay Twelve's service area were long, low vehicles whose electric motors keened under the strain of provision canisters piled high on their flatbeds. LoaderMechs lifted those canisters to DropShip crewmen, who were busy stowing them.

Bossing the whole scene was the cargo officer and her assistants. They watched to see that each cargo container and load pallet went aboard ship in computer-directed order that facilitated stowage and ensured proper mass balance for launch. Conspicuous in their khaki uniforms and peaked, black-billed caps, two port officials also watched from the blue-black shadows of the ship's hull and made cryptic entries on their handheld computer pads. Except for dark patches of sweat along their spines and underarms, these khaki-clad officials remained immaculate in the heat.

Camouflaged in mottled grays and greens, a 20-ton *Stinger* moved with surprisingly graceful sweeps of mechanical legs and arms across the heat-beaten field toward the Drop-Ship's Number One 'Mech Bay. Four 'Mechs were already on board. Two more remained in the service area undergoing final touch-ups by Techs wielding torches, polyepox, and spraytanks of green-gray paint. Everywhere the men of the mercenary unit to which the ship belonged worked at an unrelenting pace to ready their equipment for final boarding and boost.

Grayson Carlyle doubled-checked the cargo manifest, which ran on interminably: fuel and spare parts; enough provisions to last nearly two hundred people for months; technicians' tools and repair assemblies; seven Battle-Mechs and the small mountain of spares, parts, supplies, and ammo that kept them combat-ready; and the larger mountain of military stores their new patron was shipping outbound with them.

"Everything in order, Captain," one of the port officials said, handing Carlyle a stylus. The gold piping on his collar indicated that he was a lieutenant, and the expression on his face marked him as a bored one. "Your manifest checks and your port fees are paid. All you need now is final clearance for boost."

Grayson glanced up to read the ID badge pinned to the man's khaki tunic. "Right, Lieutenant Murcheson." He scrawled his name across the compad's screen, pressed the enter key, and handed pad and stylus back to the PA officer. "We're just waiting to hear from our patron. My First Officer is working out some last-minute details with him. Can I offer you gentlemen something to drink in the meantime?"

Murcheson manipulated the touch plates that transmitted authorization to Galatean Control Center. "Thanks, no. On duty, y'know." The officer was looking up, squinting against the light of the brilliant sky. High overhead, two men in the basket of a cherrypicker gantry were putting the finishing touches on to a coat of paint that obscured the DropShip's name and numbers. "So, you're going out covert, Captain?" Showing polite interest in response to Carlyle's hospitality, Murcheson's voice was carefully neutral but friendly. The officials on Galatea cared nothing about where a ship bearing supplies enough to start a small war was bound—or why.

Still, Grayson answered carefully.

"Just a fresh coat of paint, Lieutenant. No sense in having *Phobos* show her years to our new employer, eh?"

"Well, if you say so." The man's tone suggested that he did not believe the young mercenary commander, but also that it did not concern him one way or the other. "Request clearance for final boost on the port control frequency when you're ready, Captain Carlyle. And good mission to you—whatever it is."

Grayson watched the PA men walk toward the skimmer that had brought them out from the Galaport Control Tower, then glanced back up at the men on their way down in the cherrypicker basket. The weathered letters that had identified the ship as *Phobos,* Number Two DropShip of the free trader *Invidious,* had been painted out. A new name and ID would not be added until the ship was safely out in space, far from any prying eyes. The PA man had been right. This *would* be a covert flight, and the fewer who knew the ship's new identity, the happier Grayson would be.

He dropped his eyes to the men and women hard at work in the harsh sun, and his hands knotted at his sides. Grayson was not certain that all the security measures in the book would be enough to see them through this mission. The problem was not security, but what awaited them at their destination.

Damn, he thought. *Just what have I gotten us into?* Devic Erudin had better be right about enemy positions on his home world, or the Gray Death's career would likely end abruptly and bloodily with its second campaign.

"Captain?"

Grayson turned to see Sergeant Ramage. The small, wiry, and dark native of Trellwan was one of the men who had joined him when the Gray Death finally left that world. Senior to all of the unit's support infantry in both age and experience, Ramage was Grayson's head NCO in command of the Legion's ground troops.

"Yes, Ram." The sergeant's one Trell name had been even further abbreviated to the inevitable nickname. "How's the boarding going?"

"On schedule, Captain. But some of the boys are a little . . . well . . . worried. There's a lot of scuttlebutt making the rounds."

"If there's anything to tell, I'll pass it on. You might remind them that they're free to stay here if our arrangements don't suit them."

Ramage grinned. "That's one thing we don't have to worry about, Captain! Hell, the thought of being left *here* would be enough to make 'em volunteer to assault Fortress Luthien itself!"

The sound of a ground vehicle brought Grayson's attention back to the field. A tall, attractive young woman in a worn and faded military tunic climbed out, paid the driver, and strode toward Grayson. Grayson's second in command, Lori Kalmar had proven her considerable aptitude for 'Mech combat during her stubborn defense at Thunder Rift on Trellwan. At the moment, however, trouble clouded her face.

"Problems?" he asked.

Lori shook her head sharply. "No. He had the money. Everything is arranged through ComStar. All we need now is final port clearance, and we're set."

So. They were committed. Grayson had never doubted Erudin's word. He'd seen the samples of the light, malleable, gray-white metal, heard Erudin's explanation that vanadium was fairly common on some worlds, but nonexistent on Galatea. A ComStar proctor had already assayed the shipment Erudin and his people had smuggled out of Verthandi, and quoted them an open market valuation of almost a million C-bills. Part of that had gone to buy weapons and military equipment desperately needed by the revolution on Verthandi, equipment that Tor would ship to that world along with the Gray Death Legion. Grayson assured the owl-eyed man that what was left was enough to hire the Legion and Tor's ship. With the final contract signed and deposited with the money at the ComStar offices on Galatea, they had cleared the last hurdle and the mission was go.

Lori was clearly not happy about it, though. For that matter, neither was Grayson. What tormented him still were doubts about the Legion's chances once they grounded on Verthandi. The *Invidious* would have to drop them from the Norn system's jump point, then high-tail for another system, leaving the Legion utterly on its own. If the revolution succeeded, well and good. But if it failed. . . .

Grayson lifted his eyes again toward the brassy, hot sky of Galatea. House Kurita was not known for its leniency toward mercenaries captured while backing an opponent, especially an opponent that dared to rebel against the Lord of the Draconis Combine. The Verthandi contract was, in every sense of the phrase, a win-all, lose-all proposition.

It was a chance, Grayson knew, but that was about all

it was. What would the others think when he told them? Then again, what was he leading them into? Would they even follow? Though no military unit can afford the luxury of democratic organization, mercenary groups usually allowed its members a bit more discussion of assignments than did regular forces. Many a contract had been voided and wars lost because a mercenary army refused the job, even after its leader had arranged the deal. The reason Grayson worried now was that Devic Erudin's proposal sounded less like a job and more like a suicide pact.

Lori seemed to read his mind. "I don't see that we have much choice, Captain."

He smiled, though the expression required effort. Almost . . . he almost reached out to touch her, but the cool distance in her voice restrained him. After Trellwan, he had promised to give her time. *Lori, what's come between us? We were close . . . once. . . .*

He cut off that thought immediately. There were problems enough without agonizing over *that.* He managed to keep his voice light. "You're right. Either we starve on Galatea or we're stranded on Verthandi. But that doesn't make it any easier, does it? Not with our people counting on us."

If it's true that the ideal spy would have trouble attracting a waiter's attention in a restaurant, the nondescript, middle-aged man in a Galatean Port Authority NCO uniform was just such a one. He'd been at Lieutenant Murcheson's side during the talk about port clearance with Captain Carlyle and had said nary a word. Syneson Lon had been alert enough, though, hoping to pick up something that Carlyle might have carelessly let slip about his plans or his destination. He'd been the one to point out to Murcheson that the *Phobos* was very likely headed out on some covert mission, hoping the Lieutenant would mention it and elicit just such a slip from the young Captain. There were people, powerful people, who were keenly interested in the young merc leader and where he might now be headed with his men. Lon leaned now against an angle in the blast pit wall near Bay Twelve, studying the DropShip *Phobos* through compact, but powerful, electronic binoculars.

The spy had already amassed considerable information on Carlyle and his unit. He knew about the aged freighter *Invidious* keeping station at the Galatean system's zenith jump point and about its captain . . . Renfred Tor. He knew about each of the MechWarriors who had signed on with the Gray Death Legion during recent weeks, and was aware of Carlyle's meetings with this fellow Devic Erudin at the Starspan Hotel. Lon still had not learned from where Erudin came, and that worried him. Erudin's homeworld was no doubt where the Gray Death Legion was headed next. So far, the spy's only clue was that the Legion's BattleMechs were being painted in camouflage suitable to a world of jungles or heavy forests.

When the groundcar carrying Lori Kalmar pulled up near to where the Legion's commander was standing, Lon focused the binoculars on her. Kalmar's dossier reported that she was a native of Sigurd, a world in some Bandit Kingdom beyond the Periphery, until she'd met Carlyle on Trellwan. Lon smiled, thinking she was well worth studying with his binoculars.

When he touched a control, the 'nocs focused in on the faces of the man and woman as they talked. He could see that Kalmar looked worried. Though these binoculars were equipped to record the movements of their lips for later study, the spy had become a lip reader himself through long practice. From this angle, he couldn't quite make out Lori's words, but Carlyle was easily visible.

"You're right," he was saying. "Either we starve on Galatea or we're stranded on Verthandi." The words were as clear as if Syneson Lon was hearing them spoken aloud. Smiling broadly, he lowered the binoculars.

So, now he knew exactly where the Gray Death Legion was bound.

4

Even in his father's unit, Grayson had considered staff briefings to be interminable as the various department heads invariably wrangled over points that the young Grayson had found mindlessly tedious. So much of that wrangling had been over money, which had been of little concern to him then. Now that he understood how important a decent cash flow was to a mercenary outfit, he was sorry for not paying attention to those sessions in the briefing room of Carlyle's Commandos. Be that as it may, Grayson still hated staffings.

He'd arranged to be the first one in the *Phobos*'s lounge, which served as his command briefing room. Along with staff meetings in general, he also disliked the formality that many military commanders adopted in such situations. As the nine men and women filed in and took their seats, Grayson remained seated, forcing himself to adopt a casual, relaxed pose. He was aware that much of his unease was due to how little he knew of most of the people now in the Gray Death's leadership core. Except for Lori Kalmar, Sergeant Ramage, and Renfred Tor, the others were comparative strangers. While they studied the contract, Grayson studied them.

Davis McCall was a big, friendly Caledonian with an engaging grin, fierce pride in his Terran-Scots ancestry, and a frequently unintelligible Scots burr. He had brought his own BattleMech to the unit, a 60-ton *Rifleman* affectionately known as the *Bannockburn*.

Next to him was Delmar Clay, lean, dark-haired, and stubbornly untalkative about his past—save that he'd been a member of Hansen's Rough Riders. He still wore the Rough Riders' distinctive green combat jacket, *sans* patches. More important, though, Clay also had his own 'Mech, a 55-ton *Wolverine*.

Hassan Ali Khaled was darker, quieter, and even more reticent about his past than Clay. Once, though, Khaled admitted privately that he had spent most of his life as an *ikhwan*, or brother, of the dreaded Saurimat Commandos of his homeworld Shaul Khala. Grayson had heard of the Saurimat. What Mech Warrior of the Inner Sphere had not? The name meant "Quick Death", and the group had a reputation like that of ancient Terran martial brotherhoods such as the Ninja and the Hashshashin. Khaled piloted the Gray Death's lone *Stinger*.

The two youngest team members were Piter Debrowski and Jaleg Yorulis, an odd pair. Debrowski was a tall, lanky Slav with pale hair and skin, while Yorulis was short, stocky, and black-haired. Though not combatexperienced, they knew 'Mechs, which was why Grayson had decided to give them a chance. He'd assigned them to the Legion's two captured 20-ton *Wasps*.

Seated together at the far end of the table were the most recent additions to the Legion, Jeffric Sherman and Sue Ellen Klein. Only the day before, Tor had found them in a Galaport bar, sole survivors of an AeroSpace Fighter wing that had gone alone into action at the Steiner world of Sevren against overwhelming odds. When their destroyed unit was dropped from the Commonwealth's rolls, they'd come to Galatea looking for work with a mercenary unit that needed fighter support. The best of it was that they'd brought their battle-scarred but fullyoperational *Chippewa* fighters with them. One of *Invidious*'s DropShips could carry a pair of AeroSpace Fighters, and so both had promptly been mounted in the port forward cargo bay of the *Phobos*. Erudin insisted that running the Draconis Combine blockade around Verthandi would not prove difficult, but Grayson was glad those fighters would be along for the ride.

Finally, seated between Captain Tor and Ramage was Ilse Martinez, an attractive, black-maned woman who was Tor's First Officer and senior DropShip pilot. Though she'd been with Tor for the past five years, Grayson had still not gotten to know her well, for she had remained aboard the *Invidious* throughout his campaign on Trellwan. Though she was loud, even brassy, Grayson was willing to trust Tor's assessment that Martinez was superbly competent when it came to handling a DropShip. She had volunteered—if that was the word for her loud insistence—to ferry the Gray Death down to Verthandi past the Kurita blockade.

Grayson watched each of them as they read the contract, feeling a growing sense of inadequacy. He'd been raised in a close-knit mercenary regiment that had been a kind of extended family for him, with his father at the head. Though it always took a while for newcomers to be accepted, they eventually became part of the family, too. Now, Grayson was head of a family of his own. He wasn't comfortable with so many newcomers at once. Nor did they seem much more comfortable with him. That was going to have to change, and change fast, if they were to trust his leadership in combat and if he were to trust them to carry out his orders. This group of strangers would have to be molded into a functioning unit whose members could rely totally on one another. Where to begin?

Papers rustled again as each of the nine set the contract copies aside and looked to Grayson. He searched their faces for some emotion, but found little he could read. McCall was grinning, which was usual for him. Yorulis exchanged some private joke with Debrowski.

Well, Grayson thought, *the speech-making can't be put off any longer.*

"I've told you what I know about our ticket," he began. "It's not a hell of a lot. You can see on your copies of the contracts the terms of our agreement with Citizen Erudin."

"Aye," said McCall. "tha wee laddie's aye neckit deep in fertilizer, frae tha look a' things."

Grayson arched an eyebrow. Not for the first time, he wondered if they would ever be able to understand the big Caledonian over the combat circuit in battle.

"As you say, McCall—I think." There were several chuckles from around the table, and Grayson relaxed a bit. "This looks like a rough one, people. We're supposed to train and organize a rebel army that has spent the last ten years getting kicked back into the jungles of this place called Verthandi. The contract calls for a minimum of 900 hours in-system, with extensions to be negotiated with the Revolutionary Council as the situation dictates. It specifies that we are to avoid contact with the enemy 'if possible', but we all know that's something of an empty promise. If we run into Kurita 'Mechs, we'll have ourselves a fight, contract or no.

"The terms are generous enough. We're being hired to transport Citizen Erudin and the gear he's purchased here on Galatea to Verthandi, then remain there to train his people in 'Mech and anti-'Mech warfare for 900 hours. As payment, Citizen Erudin has posted 150,000 C-bills as advance bond with the ComStar agency in Galaport. We're authorized to draw on that for preliminary expenses, plus another 600,000 CBs, which will be released to us upon completion of our contract period."

"Generous?" A sour look passed over Delmar Clay's face, as he sliced the air with his hand. "Seven-hundred-fifty thousand to be divided among more than 180 people is generous? That's about 4,000 apiece . . . *if* we get back to spend it."

"Ha! We don't even get *that*, Del," Ilse Martinez said. She made a slashing motion with her finger across her throat. "Our expenses come off the top first, remember?"

Piter Debrowski leaned forward, his hands clasped before him as though trying to contain his eagerness. "Hey, it's still more than we'd get sitting in a Galaport bar!"

The youthful earnestness in Debrowski's voice pained Grayson, though the boy was only three years his junior. Debrowski and Yorulis represented a special problem in pulling the unit together. The two of them had signed on together. Both had trained with Lyran Commonwealth line BattleMech regiments, though neither had been good enough to secure one of the rare 'Mech pilot vacancies in their training regiment. After months of repeated tries, each had made his way to Galatea, Yorulis from Morningside, Debrowski from the Commonwealth's capital world of Tharkad. They'd met on Galatea and teamed up in the hope of doubling their chances of finding a pair of open billets.

Grayson noted the barely restrained eagerness in their faces. This was their chance, possibly their only chance, and he could see they were determined to prove themselves. The biggest question, of course, was how they would react the first time into combat. That, after all, was the *final* test for any Warrior.

Grayson leaned back from the table and spread his hands. "I never promised any of you a fortune. If we stay on with these people for more than 900 hours . . . if we actually have a chance of beating the Combine forces cold . . . maybe we can negotiate more. For now, this seems to be the best we could do."

Clay snorted. "Three quarters of a million was all Erudin had with him, and he was out shopping for mercs?"

"He had other expenses, Mr. Clay. His supplies are being loaded aboard the *Phobos* now." Grayson looked around at the others, his gaze resting for an extra beat on Lori who seemed still to be studying the contract printout. "People, this is your chance to back out . . . any of you. If you don't like the terms, if you don't like the assignment, tell me now."

Yorulis laughed. "Sounds great to us, Captain! Count *us* in!"

Grayson swiveled his seat to face the other newcomers to the Legion. "How about you? Khaled?"

So far, Hassan Ali Khaled had made the close-mouthed Delmar Clay appear talkative. His heavily lidded eyes looked almost reptilian. "It is not my place, *Kolarasi*, to advise you. You have my bond. I go where you lead."

The answer was less than satisfactory, but Grayson knew he was not likely to get more from the man. Khaled was decidedly an unknown factor in the unit's ranks.

Let it go, he told himself. He looked toward the far end of the table at Sherman and Klein. "How about you two?"

"We're with you, Captain" Sherman said. Grayson noticed that the young man's hand now covered Sue Ellen's on the table before them. Grayson felt a small, sharp pang inside and stole a quick glance again at Lori, but her eyes still did not meet his.

Romances and BattleMechs don't mix, he thought humorlessly. The relationship between those two would be something he'd have to watch. Or was he still feeling hurt because Lori had backed off from him? He still didn't understand her reasons, except that she'd asked for time. *It's none of my business,* he told himself. *Unless it starts affecting the operation of the unit. Then I'll damn well make it my business!*

"Lieutenant Martinez, how long until you're ready to boost?"

The DropShip skipper grinned. "Any time, Captain . . . once our new employer gets his precious junk stowed aboard. The 'Mechs are all slung and webbed in, and we've topped off our reaction mass tanks. Ten hours, I'd say."

"That's it then, people. Ten hours, if you want to back out. Sergeant Ramage, Captain Tor . . . you've been over this with your people? Good. I'll want a final report for each department no later than T-minus two hours. Now, let's take a look at the Verthandi map. . . ."

In the end, none of the 186 members of the Gray Death Legion chose to remain on Galatea. The prospects of another billet were too lean. Almost exactly ten hours later, the DropShip *Phobos* arced heavenward on a pillar of fire, her course shaped toward the Jump-Ship balanced on softly thrusting ion jets at the zenith jump point of Galatea's star. Passage took nine days.

At the Galatean jump point, the *Phobos* was secured to her docking ring along the rapier-thin length of the *Invidious*'s drive spine. Her crew and passengers remained aboard, though they had access to the slightly less cramped facilities of the aging freighter.

Grayson found Lori in the observation lounge. The slight but constant nudge of the ship's ion thrusters had ceased and the *Invidious* was in free fall toward the Galatean sun, a fiercely brilliant, barely discernible disk 10 AU distant. The sun was visible now that the ship's solar collector had been furled and stowed for jump. Around them, vast powers surged and thrummed, building toward a computer-ordained climax. Somewhere, an electronic voice gave warning of transit in one minute.

Grayson drifted into the small room, catching hold of a stanchion to arrest his movement. Lori hung motionless beside him, clinging to a handhold on the bulkhead. Weightless, there was no down or up. They looked out upon Galatea's sun, whose arc-glare banished the stars even across a billion and a half kilometers.

White light touched her blonde hair with silver. Grayson thought she looked tired. "Hello, Captain," Lori said, but she did not look up at him.

"I hoped I'd find you here."

She sighed. "It's . . . beautiful."

"Lori, what's wrong? You're looking worn to a frazzle."

She did look at him then, twisting her body around the anchor of her handhold. There were circles under her eyes. "Oh, nothing, Captain. Trouble sleeping, I guess."

"Too much work?"

She didn't answer at first. "Captain . . ." She almost reached out. "Gray . . . I don't know if I can face it again."

"You'll do fine, Lori." He hated the platitude even as it passed his lips. He didn't know that she would . . . and neither did she.

Grayson wasn't sure what had happened to Lori on Trellwan, except that it had been a deep, perhaps horrifying shock. He did suspect that it had to do with a critical moment during the battle when her *Locust* had been sprayed with liquid fire. She'd called out to him over their combat frequency and he had heard her, kilometers away. He'd turned from his own battle, hurrying across rugged terrain to where Lori's small band of 'Mechs and troops was holding out against the Red Duke's legions. His arrival had scattered the attackers and ended the battle. The fire on the *Locust* was out, and Lori was safe.

But she had changed. Before that battle, they'd been so close. Afterward, she had become . . . had remained . . . distant. He'd approached her before their boost-off from Trellwan, and she'd asked him for time to sort things out, to heal.

The warning voice gave a ten-second alert. The power feed to the *Invidious*'s jump drive built around them. She released her grip on the handhold, the slight motion setting her adrift into Grayson's arms.

"Gray, I'm . . ."

Jump! Vision blurred, an inner twisting assaulted their senses. Time became timelessness, an endless suspension of now, as space opened around them, a funneling black maw . . .

". . . afraid."

He moved apart from her, his hands still grasping her shoulders. Outside, the sky had changed, the diamond brilliance of Galatea's sun wiped away and replaced by the closer, dimmer glare of a sullen red dwarf. That would be Gallwen, first stop in a long chain of jumps that would take them to Norn.

Grayson swallowed hard, forced himself to draw a deep, even breath as his head cleared itself of the transit effects. Jump affected some more than others, but it was never pleasant.

"We all are," he said, when he could finally speak.

She looked away from him, her shoulder-length hair a swirl of gold in zero-G. *Damn!* he thought. *I'm talking in platitudes again! But what is it she's afraid of?*

He decided to risk confronting her. "Lori, was it the fire? You told me once your parents died in a fire on your homeworld . . . on Sigurd."

"I don't know." Red light illumined tears in her eyes, tears unable to fall in the absence of gravity. "I don't know. I have . . . dreams. I wake up and can't get back to sleep. Captain, I'm afraid I'm going to fold the . . . the next time. I'm just no good. . . ."

His fingers closed tighter on her shoulders as he held her at arm's length. "That sort of thinking isn't going to get you anywhere, young woman! It's only natural that you get the wobbles after the close call you had. But you'll be fine, once you have your 'Mech around you, once you're doing what you've been trained to do. Do you think the rest of us *aren't* afraid?"

Gently, she broke free, drifting back until her hand found the bulkhead grip. "I'll . . . be all right, Captain. I just need . . . time."

Was she upset because he'd gotten too close? Perhaps she thought his coming here had been a romantic advance, a hope that they would get to talking, that she would come into his arms. Well? Hadn't that been why he'd come? He couldn't deny it. And she *had* come into his arms. But what had gone wrong between them?

Perhaps the best thing for now was to keep up this strictly professional wall. She needed time, and he needed an efficient second-in-command. The new MechWarriors, that's where their minds should be focused. How was he going to handle them, weld them together into an effective unit? Yorulis and Debrowski, young and inexperienced. Clay and Khaled, silent and secretive. McCall, a stark individualist unafraid of speaking his mind . . . unintelligibly. As the Legion's Exec, it would fall to Lori to help him bring those people together as a combat team.

"You need sleep," he said, all business. "Talk to Tor's medic. He might have something that'll help you sleep." She started to protest and he sharpened his voice. "That's an order! I can't have my Executive Officer wandering around with circles under her eyes!"

She shrugged and turned away. "Yes, sir. As you say."

He watched her move from the observation lounge, pained by the dullness of her response, concerned that nothing was resolved. Lovely as she was, as much as he would have liked to resume the pleasant closeness their relationship had held before Thunder Rift, the fact remained that he *did* need her first as his Exec. Her depression worried him.

Lori returned to her cramped quarters abroad the *Phobos* without visiting *Invidious*'s sickbay. She had already tried various sleeping drugs, and now detested the dullness they imparted to mind and body, the false sense of well-being, the empty leadenness of the sleep they brought.

Besides, drugs could not change the growing ache she carried within her. She'd admitted to Grayson that she was afraid, but she had not admitted all. Let him think she was afraid of combat. She *did* fear death or injury, as any sane person feared the hell of BattleMech combat. Like the others, she had learned to submerge such fears; you acted, and you let your training and your mental preparation carry you past the numbing paralysis of fear.

She was afraid, but it was a fear of her own feelings and not a fear of combat. The hell of it was, she wanted to be able to confide in Grayson, wanted to recapture the closeness they once had shared, but somehow she could not. There was a barrier between them, and she knew that it was she who had changed, not him.

Lori did not know what the barrier was, though. She was afraid of her own feelings, because she dared not probe too deeply within to examine them. She caught sight of herself in the mirror on the cabin bulkhead, and it was as though she were gazing into the face of a stranger.

5

The *Invidious* materialized in normal space at the Norn system's zenith jump point, 1.28 AU from the star. Norn was a K2 class star, cooler, smaller, and redder than Sol of man's birthworld. Three worlds circled the primary, along with the usual collection of asteroidal debris and cometary junk. Centuries before, Scandinavian settlers had named those planets for the three fates of Norse mythology. There was cloud-shrouded, hot, and poisonous Skuld. There was distant, glacial Urth of frozen ammonia seas and methane gales. And between these extremes of fire and ice was Verthandi, nearly the size of Terra and circling close to the inner boundary of Norn's ecozone. Here, water remained liquid, but its sun's long days and high percentage of infrared made a desert of most of Verthandi's surface.

From the zenith jump point, Verthandi was visible only as a bright, silvery star at an angular separation of 23° from Norn. The *Invidious* hung suspended there, her sensors alert for the telltale flutter of fusion drives or starship power plants. Citizen Erudin had told them that the Combine forces did not routinely patrol the system's jump points, but much could have changed during his months of absence.

As she began her slow slide down Norn's gravity well, the *Invidious* was silent, listening for the emissions and active search signals of Combine craft. There was considerable radio and microwave traffic from the region immediately around Verthandi and from Verthandi's single, giant moon, but the space close to the *Invidious* was clear. Slowly, the ship's jump sail began to unfurl, running out before Norn's streaming wind of light and charged particles. Her transferral net began gathering energy, as transformers converted it to hypercharge and shunted it to her paneled accumulators, readying the ship for her next jump.

"I don't like it," Tor said. He stood with Grayson in the conduit-lined, metal-webbed passageway along the *Invidious*'s spine, close by the locks leading through the DropShip docking rings and into her paired riders. *Deimos* and *Phobos* were commercial inter-system freight haulers, similar in design and capacity to the standard *Union* Class military DropShips of every Successor State, but lightly armed. The weapons had been added to unarmed hulls, and so the *Deimos* and *Phobos* were not as well armored as the DropShips they outwardly resembled.

Using spray gear adapted to zero-G and vacuum, work crews had been painting Combine dragon insignias and a new name and numbers on the *Phobos*'s flanks during the journey from Galatea to the Galatean jump point. They'd worked feverishly, but none of Grayson's staff dared guess how successful that deception would be. Computer ID scans and transponder broadcasts would identify a DropShip approaching a planet long before patrolling fighters could get close enough to eyeball a suspicious vessel. If they were challenged in flight, however, that could get serious. While still on Galatea, Grayson had thought long and hard about whether or not they might need better DropShip weapons, but there'd been no more money to purchase them. Having exhausted their meager resources, he and his men had no future now except for what they could win for themselves on Verthandi.

First, however, they were going to have to run the Combine blockade.

"I can't say I care much for it, either," Grayson said, "but if we can slip past the Dracos, we should be safe enough."

"They'll be patrolling."

"And we'll be looking like a Kurita *Union* Class. They won't be expecting us, but they're likely to put it down to a sloppy schedule. Besides, I doubt that they'll be watching for someone breaking *in*."

Tor did not look happy. "I'll be back. You have the beacon gear."

"Safely stowed. We'll send a coded pulse exactly 900 standard hours after we set down. Don't worry, O.K.?"

"Don't worry, the man says. Right. Well, *Invidious* and me'll be right here, 980 hours from now. At that point, you can tell me what you need . . . or meet me yourself if you have to cut and run." The expression in Tor's eyes showed what they both knew. If it did turn out that the Legion were forced to abandon the system, it was unlikely they would be doing so according to a schedule.

They clasped hands a last time, and Grayson clambered through the docking ring and into the DropShip *Phobos*. Hatches sealed shut with the hiss of pressurization, while the *Invidious*'s intercom announced clearance for release. Then compressed air blasted noiselessly into space, the docking grapples swung free, and the *Phobos* dropped away from her JumpShip's needle shape at three meters per second. Once the spherical DropShip was well clear of the *Invidious* and her delicate, still unfurling sail, thrusters realigned the *Phobos* with the fleck of light that was Verthandi. Her boosters flared into life, and she began to fall toward that distant world at a velocity increasing by nearly ten meters per second with each passing second. Behind her, the *Invidious* had begun the recharge cycle for her jump back into the interstellar void. Captain Tor waited almost three hours before he began transmitting a radio signal toward the waiting Dracos that the *Phobos* was inbound from the Norn system's zenith jump point.

The mournful keening of the jungle ornithoids known as chirmsims carried quite well across the open, grassy, bluesward uplands to the University Gardens. They were loud enough to be heard even above the rumble and clatter of the city of Regis, much closer at hand. From the upper towers of the Administrative Complex, the jungle was visible as a low, shaggy line of black and gray against the green-tinged sky to the north. Governor-General Masayoshi Nagumo took another sip of his drink and scowled at the distant racket.

"Amnesty." Nagumo rolled the word across his tongue

as though uncertain of the flavor. A slight man with heavy, oriental features and a mustache already graying to match the silver at his temples, he wore the severe, utilitarian black of a high-ranking officer of the Draconis Combine. The high-collared uniform's only ornament were the kana symbols spelling out the names of Kurita and Duke Ricol in gold and the black-on-red dragon circles above them. In the cross-draw holster at his belt, he wore a deadly Nakjima hand laser.

Behind him, Olav Haraldssen was struggling to control his expression. His own red and gold uniform was more richly adorned than Nagumo's, but there could be no doubt who was the master and who the servant on that terrace. The crest on Haraldssen's tunic was the emblem of the University of Regis. He was unarmed—native Verthandians were never permitted to go otherwise into the Governor-General's presence—and the terror in his face and posture was plainly visible.

"Your Council is actually suggesting that a writ of *amnesty* be issued for these . . . creatures?"

"My . . . my Lord, it seems the best way. The rebels will never come in, never agree to a cease-fire, unless we offer some promise that they will not be . . . be summarily slaughtered. . . ."

Nagumo whirled to face the First Councilman of Verthandi's Council of Academicians. The planetary leader continued to speak, haste tumbling the words one upon the next. "Of course, the leaders will be taken, handed over to your department for questioning for . . . for whatever it is you want to do with them. . . ."

"Oh yes, my learned friend. The leaders *will* be taken. But do you seriously believe that an offer of amnesty is going to bring those people in out of the jungles? Eh?"

"Lord, we must . . . we must at least make the *attempt* to placate the people."

Nagumo was surprised at the man's boldness despite his obvious fear. Haraldssen's hands were clenched at his side, his tongue flicking across dry lips, but he plunged on in the face of the dragon. What had happened? This man had been chosen because of his haste to welcome Verthandi's new masters. Was he now having an attack of conscience . . . or had someone within the University's hierarchy gotten to him? Might revolt be flourishing again among the University faculty?

Regis University dominated the northern sprawl of Verthandi's capital city, and the Central Tower of the Administrative Complex commanded the University. From the garden terraces halfway up the broad Tower, Nagumo could see not only the distant jungle, but the sweep of Regis itself, beyond the walls of the University. Below him stretched the broad, parklike central Courtyard. From this height, students and faculty moving among the university buildings or passing through the main Courtyard Gateway into the city proper looked minute, mere insects on the pavement.

The government situation here was peculiar, a state approaching anarchy, directed by the faculty-elected Council of Verthandi's principal center of learning. The people seemed to think in abstract notions of learning, culture, and art rather than in terms of power. Nagumo had no personal quarrel with art. He found the University architecture stimulating, enjoyed the haiku of Ihara Saikaku and Matsuo Basho, and numbered among his dearest possessions an original oil painting by Chesley Bonestell . . . but what in hell's name did such things have to do with *power?*

Haraldssen had mistaken Nagumo's silence for encouragement. "The people are restless, have been restless since your forces came here. Harsher treatment will only alienate them further. If we can demonstrate our good faith. . . ."

"Good faith?" Nagumo twisted the words past his teeth. "To dogs and barbarians, jungle scum and bloodsucking vermin? Gah! If you think harsher treatment will alienate them, Haraldssen, you are mistaken. I will *give* them amnesty . . . the amnesty I gave Mountain Vista!"

"Lord . . ."

"Silence!" Nagumo's slight frame seemed to grow, looming over Haraldssen as the Verthandian trembled. "The penalty for resisting the Draconis Combine is extermination! Do you hear me? You, my spineless lap dog, are the ruler of this benighted planet . . . *under my hand!* I charge you to *crush* this rebellion, and that means tracking down these rebels skulking about in Verthandi's swamps and killing them! Not negotiating with them, not

offering them terms or amnesty. Kill them! Kill their families! Destroy the villages that offer them shelter and food! If you fail, Academician, I shall not. If it means eradicating the jungles that give these vermin shelter, so be it, even if the process *ends* all native life on Verthandi!''

"Y-yes, Lord!"

"The raids on Combine garrisons and outposts, the pilfering of supplies and arms from Combine depots will cease. You and your people will maintain the Pax Draconis here, or I will intervene personally. I will burn Regis about your ears, if I must! I will order my BattleMech legions to dismantle your precious University stone by stone, shoot every third person in the city, and send the entire Council of Academicians and their families to Luthien in chains as slaves! *I will have order restored!*''

"Of course, my Lord. You needn't intervene, Lord. I'll . . . I'll issue new orders at once. The rebels will be hunted down and slaughtered, my Lord . . .''

"Then give the orders . . . and follow through with them. This world is Duke Ricol's now, and has been given into my keeping. You will keep the peace in my name and his, or I will dispense with you and keep the peace myself—even if it means hanging every inhabitant and burning every village and farm between here and the Azure Sea! Now get out!''

Haraldssen hurried from the terrace as if pursued by a jungle chirops.

Nagumo watched the Academician go, then nodded to a black-uniformed guard who had stood unnoticed in a corner of the garden terrace throughout the interview. The guard also departed instantly. A moment later, Colonel Valdis Kevlavic emerged from the double doors behind the Governor General, came to attention, and executed a crisp, fist-to-chest salute.

"The man is a fool," Nagumo said, without preamble. "He wants to remain well-liked by the people, while maintaining the privileges of his position.''

"Perhaps it is time to replace him, my Lord." Kevlavic was a large, blond man. The ragged scar that creased his face from the corner of his right eye to the point of his chin pulled the right side of his mouth sideways, creating a caricature of a grin. His eyes, however, were unrelentingly cold.

"Eventually, Colonel . . . but not yet. Not quite yet." Nagumo rested the long, bony fingers of both hands on the ornate guard rail that rimmed the terrace. The jungle animals continued their chorus as the sun westered toward the brown hills on the horizon in a blaze of orange, green, and purple. He admired the beauty of the sunset, letting it sap the fury he had used as a lash on Haraldssen. "How went the campaign in Mountain Vista?"

Nagumo knew the answer already, of course, from Kevlavic's personal reports as well as from his own agents among the Colonel's men. Everyone was watched within the ranks of Lord Kurita's regiments.

"Quite well, my Lord. The town was 80 percent burned and the population driven into the hills. We uncovered quite a large cache of weapons and ammunition in the home of one of the village leaders. The man and his family tried to escape, but we were able to catch them. I had some of my boys make a long, slow example of them and then nail up the remains in the town square, where the locals'll find them when they return. They'll be a long time rebuilding. I don't think the rebels'll find a haven in Mountain Vista again."

"Good," Nagumo said curtly, all the while thinking, *You are as much a fool as Haraldssen. One raid will not change their minds any more than his offer of amnesty. The rebellion will end when they are dead. All of them!*

"We must continue our own campaign against the rebels, Colonel," he went on. "Our plan to allow the local government do our work for us is not progressing well at all. While you were gone last week, three of our garrisons were raided, as were seven Verthandian army posts. Eight Kurita troops were killed, and I don't know how many locals. Their raids are increasing."

"Still, Lord, there seems to be no purpose or direction to those raids. They have no central leadership, no plan or cohesion among their units. They are harassing attacks only."

"And they will cease! Duke Ricol has personally ordered me to end the rebellion here. It will be ended . . . one way or another."

"Yes, my Lord."

"We will take Verthandi in our fists and squeeze until the last drop of blood has trickled through our fingers. The Duke may have need of this world . . . but he does not need the people . . . not all of them, at any rate. Human beings are cheap, easily imported. We will bring in our own if we cannot bend these to our will, eh?"

"Yes, my Lord."

"Good. Now, another matter."

"Lord?"

"Our fleet base on Verthandi-Alpha has reported receiving radio transmissions and IFF codes from a freighter arrived at the zenith point. This visitor was not expected, but claims to be a freelance mercenary hired by the Combine. A *Union* Class DropShip is now bound in-system."

Kevlavic's brow furrowed. "To what purpose, Lord?"

"Most likely Procurement has scrambled things once again and has sent a ship of supplies and 'Mech spares early. Still, it is best to be prepared. Right now, the rebels in the swamps are little more than a nuisance. With outside help, they could begin to pose a real threat to our timetable."

"It might be a Lyran raider, Lord."

"Possible, but unlikely. It might also be a freelance raider, but I don't think that likely either. Any raiding force would have to come with more force aboard than a single DropShip could carry. Still, we will not take chances. If that ship sets down, you will shuttle a force there immediately and take command of local defenses. A DropShip in the employ of hostile forces must not be allowed to lift off again, nor must its crew be allowed to establish contact with the rebels. Understood?"

"Yes, my Lord!"

"Very well. Dismissed."

Colonel Kevlavic saluted smartly, turned on his heel, and strode from the terrace.

Across the savannah, the shrieks of the jungle chirimsims seemed to redouble in intensity, wailing as though the creatures were in pain. At this distance, their eerie calls were mournfully human.

Governor-General Masayoshi Nagumo found the faint jungle noises most pleasant.

====== 6 ======

The straight-line distance from the Norn zenith point to Verthandi was 1.39 AU, a hair over 207 million kilometers. At a steady boost of 1 G, allowing for a midcourse turn-over and deceleration, the trip took 80 hours. On the decks between bunks stacked six-high, the facilities of a DropShip loaded with 'Mechs, supplies, and personnel were too crowded to allow much in the way of training. The fifty-odd men and women aboard spent the time huddled over dice or cards or lay in those bunks reading, trying to sleep, or simply thinking.

The ship's lounge offered the illusion of more space, but not many could fit in at once. It was also the only area aboard the *Phobos* large enough to accommodate Grayson's entire company staff. That meant Legion troops or Techs looking to stretch their legs or use the lounge microfiche reader all too often found the door closed and hung with a hand-penciled sign saying "Staff Meeting".

Held once during each of the ship's 24 standard-hour days, these meeting were Grayson's best opportunity to observe how the members of his staff worked together and with the other MechWarriors of his command. The meetings also served for discussion of alternate strategies and possibilities for the coming weeks, as well as to air worries, disagreements, and objections.

"It's what you signed on to do," Grayson was saying now. His head hurt because they had been around this point a dozen times already. As the hour of confrontation with the Kurita garrison drew closer, the Gray Death's two *Chippewa* pilots were occupying more and more of Grayson's time in these meetings. Their experience at Sevren had made them wary of promises of assistance.

"Look, we weren't told our DropShip would be a pop-gun-mounted freighter," Sue Ellen Klein said. She stood at her place at the conference table, stabbing an accusing forefinger at Grayson. "You say you'll bail us out if we get in deep, but you're going to have trouble bailing yourself out if it really goes down!"

"You may be right," Grayson said quietly, "but you and Lieutenant Sherman are this unit's air-space fighter power, period. I have no one else I can use, and I'm going to need a fighter screen out there ten hours from now. It's a long way back to get replacements. If you didn't want the billets, why didn't you walk on Galatea, when I gave you the chance?"

"I didn't know then we were signing a damned suicide pact!"

Jeffric Sherman spoke from the seat alongside Klein. "We assumed we were signing to provide cover for ground operations, Captain. We're good at ground support, and we'll be an asset to your unit. But a plan like this . . ." He tapped the portable computer screen in front of him. "Pick-up is going to be crucial."

Grayson folded his hands in front of him on the table. How he dealt with this could be critical to the mission . . . and to the future of the unit. The staff knew only too well that Sue Ellen Klein and Jeffric Sherman were the sole survivors of an AeroSpace Fighter wing that had tangled with two full squadrons of Combine *Slayers* over Sevren; that a failed pick-up had resulted in the deaths of their comrades, including Klein's brother. When their squadron had disbanded, Klein and Sherman had become mercenaries, and joined the Gray Death Legion.

Now these two wanted assurances that the Legion's DropShip would not abandon them to the Kurita pursuers.

Grayson spread his hands. "I don't have any answer for you, people. I know you're good at ground support, and I intend to employ you in ground support the moment we set down. But if Combine naval ships close on us, I'm going to need a fighter screen. Agreed . . . if we get caught in a running battle all the way to atmosphere, providing pick-up may not be possible. Things will be happening fast when we hit atmosphere, and Captain Martinez is not going to want to open docking bays to incoming missiles or to take time for complex maneuvers. All I can say is that you have our landing coordinates. Once the *Phobos* is clear of pursuit, break free, and rendezvous with us on the ground." He looked across at Erudin, who had joined this particular briefing. "Do you have something to add, Citizen?"

"Only that if you land anywhere in the polar basin, just stay with your ships. Our people will get to you sooner or later. Combine forces never enter the jungle if they can help it. They tend to get . . . bogged down."

"How is the Gray Death supposed to move 'Mechs through all that mud?" Sue Ellen demanded.

Erudin chuckled. "You'll be meeting a man on our council named Ericksson, and he has a place . . . an island . . . all dry land and full of surprises. As for the rest . . ." He shrugged. "There are swamps, of course, but lots of dry land. Logging is big business around the Azure Sea. There are logging roads and trails all through the Basin."

Grayson frowned at Erudin. The names of the rebel council's members were not good items to share with people who might one day find themselves beating their way through the bush on an enemy-held planet.

Sue Ellen sat down beside Sherman, who took her hand.

There's a weakness there, he thought. *A weak link in the unit. But what am I supposed to say, 'Stop loving each other for the good of the Legion?'*

"Do we have any idea yet what we're facing in the way of space defenses?" Martinez asked.

"Not yet," Grayson told her. "There'll be DropShips, certainly, on the Verthandian moon . . . and Citizen Erudin states that there are AeroSpace Fighters on the planet. He doesn't know how many."

"Great!" Sue Ellen muttered. "We're flying into another bloody, malfing trap . . ."

"That's enough!" Grayson's open palm came down on the table top, startling the room to absolute silence. He let his words hang there for a second, looking at each person in turn. His reaction had been sharper than he'd intended, but there was no going back now. "You two do have a choice. . . . You can fulfill your contracts with the Gray Death—and that means obeying my orders to

the letter—or you can buy out right now. That means you
remain aboard the *Phobos* for the balance of this mission,
in your cabins, relieved of all duties and rank. At our
earliest *convenient* opportunity, we will return you to
Galatea or some other planetary commerce center . . .
and by God, you'd better not get in my way in the meantime!''

Sherman folded his arms. ''You did say you needed
us, Captain.''

''Did I? I need your ships, Mister! They may be your
property, but so help me, I'll seize them as military contraband if I have to and appropriate them as Legion property!''

Klein looked shocked. ''You wouldn't! You have no
pilots—''

''That's *my* concern, Lieutenant. *Your* only concern is
to make that decision, and make it now! Are you going
to work with me, or am I going to have to trample you
under?''

There were further protests, but in the end, Sherman
and Klein backed down as gracefully as possible. They
would obey Grayson's orders, and they would fly the
screening mission as the *Phobos* approached her destination.

When the meeting broke up, Grayson remained seated
while the others filed from the room, his hands pressed
over his eyes. He was tired, so tired . . .

When he opened his eyes, it was to see Ilse Martinez
still standing there. ''Well, *Major*,'' she said. ''You realize those two have a third option, don't you?''

He blinked at her. Her smile and tone of voice were
unsettling; her use of the honorary rank of Major was a
step removed from calculated insult. Aboard the
DropShip, she was Captain, *the* Captain, and naval tradition and protocol dating back to wet navies on old Earth
would not tolerate two people called 'Captain' aboard
any vessel. In such situations, officers such as Grayson
were given an honorary, and temporary, promotion of
one grade. He knew Martinez was using the word ''Major'' like a weapon, as some kind of test, but he had
neither time nor patience for these, interpersonal games.

''What do you mean by that?'' Grayson said curtly.

''Hell, they could sign on with the opposition. They'll

have to if they can't make it back to the ship. Where else can they go?"

"They wouldn't do that," Grayson said, but without conviction. Though he had tried to accurately read the characters of the two fighter pilots, who really knew what another person might do? "Sue Ellen's too bitter about her brother . . . and he died fighting Kurita ships."

The DropShip captain touched her tongue to her lips. Like Tor, she was a native of House Marik's Free Worlds League, and she wore a cosmetic design popular among many in Marik space: blue wings tatooed onto the skin over her eyes. Grayson found the effect sinister.

"Those two are sleeping together, you realize," she said.

The pilot's abrupt change of subject irritated Grayson. "So?"

"God, you *are* young, aren't you? *So,* that's going to be a problem. Two fighter jocks, the only two, and they're more concerned about each other than about your unit or your plan. I don't call that a good situation . . . Major."

"You take care of getting us through the Combine blockade," Grayson said, his headache even worse now. How long had it been since he'd had a decent off-watch sleep? "I'll worry about my people."

My people. How was he to make Martinez a part of the Legion? Or Sherman or Klein? Simply worrying about the unit was becoming a full-time occupation of late. First Lori's fears, and now this.

Moving tail-first and balanced on a flaring stream of light, the *Phobos* neared Verthandi and the planet's lone, giant moon. Long-range radar had already detected the gathering of the Kurita forces as they approached. In a mere ten hours, the Gray Death would have its first encounter with the enemy. And Grayson already knew that his unit was fatally flawed.

A sleek, black JumpShip materialized in the darkness at Norn's nadir jump point, 1.28 AU from the star. Once certain that no other ships lingered nearby, the starship unfurled its sails and began to soak up hypercharge for its next jump. At the same time, onboard computers swung a highly directional dish antenna until it pointed at the amber fleck of light that was Verthandi. A burst of microwave energy lasting less than one ten-thousandth of a second pulsed into space.

Its mission complete, the courier vessel began preparations to return to Lyran space. The Galatean spy's report would reach Verthandi in less than eleven minutes.

Fleet Admiral Isoru Kodo looked up in irritation at the staff Captain who had handed him the report. "Why are you bothering me with this routine garbage?"

Captain Powell stood at rigid attention, her eyes fixed steadily above and beyond Kodo's egg-bald scalp at the harsh and rugged splendor of the airless plain revealed through the curved windows of his office. Verthandi, a gold-edged scimitar knifing through heaven, filled a quarter of the sky, its night side blotting out the stars beyond. Mountains, silver white and raw, thrust themselves from the moon's plain toward the planet's beauty. The moon, Verthandi-Alpha, was a rugged, low-G wilderness, a stark contrast to the life-rich glory of its planet.

Powell brought her inner trembling under control and steadied her voice with words crisp and concise. If the Admiral was not the most forgiving of commanders, neither was he the most exacting. Duty at the Kurita naval base on Verthandi's lone satellite was boring, but still preferable to the constant strife on Verthandi under the iron hand and sharp temper of the Governor General.

"Lord Admiral," she said, "the incoming ship appears to be a *Union* Class vessel, but there are discrepancies." Kodo gave her no encouragement beyond a black scowl, but she plunged on. "The IFF transmission from the starship was in a code and frequency that has been out of date for over two standard years. Further, no starships have been scheduled to call at the Norn system until four standard weeks from now."

"So?"

"Lord, the intruder could be a raider with out-of-date codes."

"Am I surrounded by *complete* idiots?" He spoke the words softly, almost wonderingly, with a slow shaking of the head from side to side. "Don't you think I *know* which codes are current and which are not?" He slapped the computer printout with the backs of his fingers. "Is it possible that *no one* on my staff can use his own initiative, can even think for himself? That starship is an independent freighter hired by the Combine Admiralty to deliver cargo. I notified the Governor General's office hours ago, and they concur with my evaluation.''

Captain Powell's eyes widened slightly at this, but she held any further reaction in check. The schedules of incoming ships were carefully set and monitored by the Combine Port Authorities at each world in the net of trade among Kurita's suns. It was most irregular for supply ships to arrive so far ahead of schedule. By their very nature, privately registered freighters were much more likely to arrive late than early. The Procurement Department of the Combine Admiralty was not known for its efficiency, either.

Keeping her voice calm and professionally level, she made herself continue. ''My Lord, we ran a careful analysis of the DropShip's drive flare, course, and delta-V. The starship's transmission indicated the DropShip to be a *Union* Class, but there are discrepancies. A *Union* Class masses 3500 tons, and—''

''Don't you think I know the mass of a *Union* DropShip, Captain?'' Kodo's voice was silky now, and dangerous.

''Of course, my Lord. The . . . intruder masses 3200 tons. While this *could* be explained in terms of a light cargo load or low expendables, the discrepancies seemed important enough to warrant bringing them to your attention.''

''You have done so. Your analysis of the DropShip's mass discrepancy is masterful, a brilliant piece of routine deduction! The freighter has arrived on a purely routine resupply mission . . . a bit early, yes, but purely routine! Routine!'' His head shook again in the shocked silence, sour disapproval etching the corners of his mouth and eyes. ''Your file states that you have initiative, Captain. I can't say that my entry in your service record is going to support that contention. I suggest that, in future, you use that vaunted initiative and let me get on with my work!''

The bald head swivelled back to study the terminal screen at his desk. Recognizing the end of the interview, Captain Powell saluted, closed fist to breast. ''Thank you, Lord Admiral.''

Outside the Admiral's office suite, she put a hand against the corridor wall and let out a long sigh of relief. Lords of Space, but Old Baldy was in a bad mood today!

"Captain?"

"Eh?" A young Lieutenant from the Commo Department saluted as she looked up. "What is it?"

"Priority message from a courier, Captain. It just came through."

"I'll take it."

He handed her the sheet, saluted, and retreated. She read it, paused, then read it through again. *So.* Here was *proof* that the drive flare she'd watched through the telescopic scanners above the base hadn't belonged to a Combine resupply mission. It was a DropShip ferrying mercenary 'Mechs to support the rebellion on Verthandi. That was critical information. The question was . . . how best to use it?

If she gave it to Admiral Kodo, he might do nothing or else he might call an alert and take the credit for himself. In either case, it would be dangerous, personally dangerous, to directly contradict the man again when he was in such a mood. If she sidestepped Kodo and alerted Nagumo's headquarters directly, she would be court-martialed for bypassing the rigid Draconian chain of command. Well, the foggy old bastard wanted initiative, did he? She'd give him initiative.

Straightening, Powell turned and stalked toward her office. She couldn't put the base on alert without old Kodo's direct approval, but, by all the Black Hells of Space, she could intercept that DropShip with a routine patrol. Routine! Patrol One-Nine ought to be in a favorable position for a quick burn that would swing it close for a look-see. When the patrol was close enough to eyeball the intruder and bring it under its guns, and with other officers there as witnesses, *then* she would show the message to the Admiral.

Maybe then Baldy Kodo would recognize initiative when he saw it.

Verthandi was swelling in the *Phobos*'s after screens. It appeared as a globe of gold and tan mingled with dark green and blue patches at the pole, and painted with the swirls of gilt-edged storm clouds and weather fronts dwarfed by distance. The world's moon, an airless, ancient, and crater-pocked rock a scant 110,000 kilometers from its primary, moved in stately procession along its orbital path. It circled Verthandi about once every four-and-a-half standard days. World and moon filled one of the narrow bridge viewscreens, as stars and glory crowded through the others that revealed the encircling Deep to the instrument-crammed bridge.

Grayson stood on the command podium, just behind the horseshoe of screens and terminals of the captain's seat. He leaned across Martinez's shoulder and pointed at the nav console screen where a pair of blips marked targets tracked by the DropShip around the curve of the planet on an intercept course.

"I see them, Major," she said. There was neither scorn nor fear in her words, but he sensed the underlying tautness. "Escorts, I'd say. They're not shaping for an attack pass."

The ship's senior commtech looked up from his own console nearby. "Incoming message, Captain," he said. "Standard Combine protocol . . . but their IFF code is a new one."

"We expected that," Martinez said. "It's been a few s-years since the *Invidious* visited Kurita space and took those recordings. Open a channel, and pipe it up here. We'll play dumb."

Grayson looked across the bridge crowded with ship personnel and instrumentation to catch the eye of their Verthandian employer. He could see the sweat glistening on Erudin's forehead, and he found himself holding his breath. The plan for their approach to Verthandi had been worked out long before the boost from Galatea.

"Inbound DropShip, this is a fleet blockade patrol in the service of the Duke Hassid Ricol and the Grand Fleet of the Draconis Combine." The radio voice was sharp through the hiss of static. "You have entered interdicted territory. Identify yourself."

Grayson picked up the microphone. The encounter had been discussed and rehearsed, but his throat was tight with tension. "This is DropShip *Li Tao,* inbound to Verthandi with a consignment of military supplies from the freighter *Chi Lung.*" He paced his words carefully, overriding his nervousness. The eyes of everyone on the bridge were on him as he spoke to the unseen fighter pilot in the void beyond. A computer screen by Martinez's right elbow flickered, then rearranged patterns of green light and black into schematic outlines of the approaching fighters, flanked by the cold words of statistics and performance. They were *Shilones*, canted, twin-finned wing shapes massing 65 tons each, carrying missiles and a trio of lasers. No threat to a real *Union* Class, they could savage the lighter armor of the *Invidious*'s converted DropShips, and they promised the rapid approach of heavier warships against which the *Phobos* could not last long.

There was an awkward hesitation, a pause of a second or so as radio waves crawled between points a sizable fraction of a light second apart. The delay felt endless.

"*Li Tao*, your IFF codes obsolete. We will approach to make visual confirmation."

"Can't help that," Grayson replied in what he hoped sounded like a convincingly offhand manner. "We've been in the boonies for quite a while. But come on in and eyeball us, if you like. Hope you guys like what you see."

The approaching patrol ignored the attempt at banter. "Make no attempt to alter your present vector. We will give you precise instructions for additional delta-V and vectoring momentarily. You will proceed directly to the Combine base on Verthandi-Alpha. Under no circumstances are you to approach the planet or make any course or thrust corrections without our specific orders."

Martinez arched one eyebrow as Grayson returned the microphone to her console. "Touchy, aren't they?"

Time passed. The *Shilone* fighters narrowed the range, their thrusters burning furiously to match course and speed with the still-decelerating DropShip. Martinez watched the latest listing of computer predictions of vector and delta-V for the Combine fighters and shook her head. "If they keep burning fuel like that, they're not going to make it home."

"There's their ride home," Grayson replied, pointing to another blip rounding the curve of Verthandi's horizon. Fresh information spilled across the computer screen. The new target was a *Leopard* Class DropShip massing 1700 tons. Though lighter and less heavily armed and armored than a *Union*, it was still more than a match for the *Phobos*. "If that thing catches us, we've had it."

Having been trained for ground combat in a Battle-Mech, Grayson shared most MechWarriors' general dislike for all AeroSpace Fighters. The interservice rivalry between ground-hogs and air-heads was a long and venerable one, dating back to Terran times. In actual battle, that rivalry became an intense hatred for enemy fighter pilots who could cleave the air above a 'Mech battlefield, leaving a wake of shattered, burning war machines.

Friendly DropShips were, of course, the only way 'Mech armies had of moving from a JumpShip to a world and back again, and so members of a 'Mech unit and the crew of their transport could become quite close, despite the good-natured rivalry. When it came to enemy DropShips, however, MechWarriors both respected and feared them. On the ground, those heavily armed and armored giants could burn down approaching 'Mechs with almost practiced ease. Worse was the approach to the battlefields of a new world, when MechWarriors had to sit and watch the developing battle in space around them, unable to affect the course of events, unable to direct their weapons against approaching enemies, unable to do anything but curse or pray. For Grayson, it was somewhat easier being on the bridge, watching the approach of the enemy. For the rest of the men and women aboard the *Phobos*, locked in cramped cubicles and surrounded by gray metal and the worried faces of their comrades, the wait must crawl on, unendurably.

And this is what you've trained for so long, he told himself. *To lead men and women into battle. Victory or death . . . Glory and honor . . .* All Grayson felt, however, was an agony of fear that he might have made his last and biggest mistake.

Bridge computers unfolded new equations. The *Shilones* were almost within visual range now. Though much more distant, the *Leopard* was moving along a course that would block the *Phobos* if she attempted to bolt and run toward the planet.

Radio telemetry told of other developments. At least two more fighters were swinging in close orbit around Verthandi from the far side, and another DropShip was readying for boost at the base on Verthandi-Alpha. The

Dracos might not be certain that *Phobos* was other than what she claimed to be, but they certainly were taking no chances.

Moment by moment, the *Phobos* was being boxed in by forces she could not outrun and could never hope to overcome.

Governor General Masayoshi Nagumo scowled at the image of Admiral Kodo on the comscreen. The time delay between Verthandi and Verthandi-Alpha was less than four-tenths of a second, but twice that was needed to make the transmission and to receive the reply. The almost one-second delay acted as an unwelcome drag on extended conversations.

The worst part of it, Nagumo decided, was that he could not choose the moment at which to explosively interrupt a subordinate in mid-apology or explanation. Here was Kodo, for example, talking for almost a full second before Nagumo's acid, single-word commentary could cut off the Admiral's complaint about the low level of initiative and efficiency among the members of the Combine garrison stationed on Verthandi-Alpha. The delay was a short one, but enough to irritate an already-irritated Governor General.

"The situation is *not* routine," Nagumo said, once Kodo had fallen silent. Around him, the Techs and staff in the Regis Command Center also listened apprehensively. "I am gratified, at least, that you had enough daring and initiative to order a patrol to check out the intruder. That is, after all, the purpose of a blockade, *is it not?*" The last words were thrust at Kodo's bald image, like edged weapons.

"Yes, my Lord." Kodo was sweating heavily, the overhead fluoros in his office gleaming from his moist scalp. "I . . . I felt it my duty to position our patrol, with a heavy back-up, to check the intruder carefully, and to be in position to block him from Verthandi, just in case. He cannot possibly avoid us."

"Good. You will take precautions that the intruder not be allowed closer than 70,000 kilometers to Verthandi. When it lands at Verthandi-Alpha, I want your Techs to take that ship apart if necessary to search for contraband or hidden passengers. The cargo is to be reloaded and transhipped here on one of our DropShips. Understood?"

"Y-yes, my Lord."

Nagumo nodded, but his scowl deepened. Kodo had proved himself incompetent in having only a single patrol—a *Leopard* Class named *Xao,* and two fighters—in a position where they could approach the intruder. Two more fighters were in close orbit around Verthandi and could be deployed if the intruder broke free of the outer patrol and made a run for the planet. Other fighters and another DropShip were being readied now at Verthandi-Alpha's base in case the intruder's object was a sneak raid on the planet's moon.

Too many possibilities remained. The intruder should have been intercepted farther from Verthandi, hours ago when the blockading force had more options and more time to exercise them. At that point, the intruder would have been travelling at a higher speed, of course, and so more fuel would have been needed for an intercept, but certainly that was preferable to gambling all in the last handful of hours before the in-bound vessel hit Verthandi's atmosphere. The ships that were in place *ought* to be sufficient to handle the threat, but . . . *damn* Kodo!

Nagumo clenched his jaw. It was too late now for recriminations, nor could he choose a replacement for Kodo at the moment. "Very well," was all he said. "How long until visual contact is made?"

"Patrol One-Nine has the intruder in sight, Lord. It will be another few minutes before they close enough to make out details."

"I am putting all space defense forces on full alert. Maintain an open line to this office. I want to listen directly to the communications between your patrol and the intruder."

"Yes, my Lord."

Minutes crawled. The intruder was approaching Verthandi from the system's zenith point, to sunward, and was now some 200,000 kilometers out, somewhat above the plane of the ecliptic. Verthandi-Alpha was on the opposite side of Verthandi from the approaching DropShip. Was that deliberate? Nagumo wondered. In any case, the intruder would have to be escorted past Verthandi and to a safe grounding on the moon.

A voice half-smothered in static cut through the command center. "What the hell is that thing?"

The terminal screen of the Tech seated in front of Nagumo glowed with the traceries of voice patterns and stress analysis. Quick-flowing words of light identified the speaker as Lieutenant Kestrel Syrnan, pilot of the lead patrol fighter. Other data showed vector, range, and scan data. The target itself appeared on another screen, relayed by the *Shilone*'s on-board cameras to the DropShip *Xao*, and thence to receivers on Verthandi and Verthandi-Alpha.

"I'm reading a normal scan, Lieutenant. Radar profile and computer ID make her to be a *Union* Class, 3500 tons. She could be one of ours." That voice was Smetnov, the wingman. Stress patterns flared. Though his voice was unnaturally calm, the instruments measuring the stress in his tone betrayed his fear. This, Nagumo had learned, was Smetnov's first active patrol sighting.

"I know what the computer says, Pilot," Syrnan replied. His voice was showing stress too, though it was well-controlled. "But she just doesn't feel right, somehow."

Nagumo studied the TV image transmitted from Syrnan's ship. The screen showed a dully-reflective, metallic globe, rust-streaked and worn. On one flank was the black-on-scarlet circled dragon, emblem of the Combine. Chinese ideographs picked out the vessel's name—*Li Tao*—and the name of her parent vessel, *Chi Lung*.

A confusion of voices intruded on the radio link. Nagumo heard someone—a woman, he thought—speaking with rapid urgency, and then Kodo's bark, "Get her out of here!"

"Kodo! What's going on?"

The Admiral's voice came over the speaker. "Nothing, my Lord. One of my junior officers chose an inopportune moment to present a courier message."

Syrnan was right. That vessel didn't feel right. There was something missing . . . what? "What message?" Nagumo demanded.

"My Lord, it is nothing."

"Read it to me!"

"Uh . . ." There were muttered sounds and confused background noises as the image of the intruder grew larger.

What was odd about that vessel?

There! It was difficult to see in the orange-dim light of Norn, but the vessel was rotating slightly, and the play of shadow against the hull cried out to Nagumo's experienced eye. That DropShip was no *Union* class. The particle projection cannons normally mounted on bow and flanks were missing. Paint had been artfully applied to imitate the weapons' shadows, but now that the ship had rolled, the angle of light made the disguise less convincing. There should be autocannons, too, but the vessel had none.

"My Lord!" Kodo's voice was urgent. "It's from one of our agents on Galatea! 'Report mercenary unit probably in employ of rebels en route to Verthandi.' "

"It's a trick!" Nagumo shouted. "Relay command here, my authority! Attack! Attack the intruder!"

The fighter pilot had already arrived at the same conclusion. Long fractions of seconds before Nagumo's command could have reached him, his own order was heard at the command center. "Smetnov! Overthrust! Punch it!" The TV image was lost as the *Shilone* fighter wheeled and accelerated at a gruelling four Gs.

"Emergency! Emergency!" Syrnan's voice was frantic now. "Flight One-Niner to base ship! Intruder is hostile. Repeat, hostile! Intruder now changing course to zero-zero-three mark fiver, at two Gs!"

Nagumo glanced up as the static hiss from the overhead speakers chopped off. "What's happening, dammit?"

"Transmission interrupted," a Tech said. "Contact lost with both elements of One-Nine. *Xao* confirms the intruder's new course." The Tech glanced up at Nagumo, his face pale under the center's harsh lighting. "The intruder is accelerating toward Verthandi, Lord."

Nagumo paused, considering. "Get me Colonel Kevlavic."

Mayhap the intruder could be stopped before it entered atmosphere. If not, it would be up to Kevlavic to eliminate the danger as soon as the ship touched down on Verthandi's surface.

Mercenaries! he muttered inwardly. *Damnation!*

Grayson and the bridge crew of the *Phobos* had been listening in to the radio transmissions between the two *Shilone* fighters and their base ship. The transmissions were unintelligible without the computer codes that would unscramble an enemy's battlespeech, but the sudden surge of emotion in the Draco pilot's voice had been unmistakable.

The alarm had been sounded. Ilse Martinez glanced across at Grayson and with a raising of her eyebrows asked his permission to fire.

"You may fire, Captain," he said with studied formality, and a lance of coherent light from the *Phobos*'s single heavy laser gutted one of the *Shilones*.

"Stand by for high-G maneuvers," Martinez said, her voice sharp but calm. Grayson scarcely had time to lower himself into an empty bridge observer's chair before the *Phobos*'s drives throbbed to a full two Gs, and her captain gave the orders that swung her onto a new course.

The damaged *Shilone* was out of the fight. The other was boosting at a back-breaking 4 Gs, angling for maneuvering room.

Missiles blossomed from the *Phobos*'s missile bays in the next instant. Two struck the accelerating fighter, disintegrating one wing and sending the craft off, powerless and tumbling end over end. Either or both fighters might yet still be in the fight, but their radios and radars were silenced, their power plants momentarily stilled. At twenty meters per second squared, the *Phobos* sped toward the swelling golden globe of Verthandi.

Moments later, Martinez cut the ship's boost and the *Phobos* fell free, saving fuel against the maneuvers that would soon be necessary. Radar and imaging cameras showed the *Leopard* Class DropShip, with a pair of fighters flanking her, now balanced on dazzling drive flares in an attempt to cut the *Phobos* off from Verthandi. The *Leopard* was already cutting between *Phobos* and the planet, in a position to anticipate her maneuvers. All

Captain Martinez could do was to make those maneuvers unpredictable enough to keep that Combine DropShip guessing.

At a range of 90,000 kilometers, the *Leopard* Class vessel opened fire.

The endless Succession Wars that had engulfed humanity for centuries had claimed many victims. One of the first was the high-level of technology required to manufacture the sophisticated electronic gear necessary to keep both warships and BattleMechs in operation. Mankind had long ago lost the know-how to construct the comparatively simple computer chips needed to direct self-targeting and fire-and-forget homer missiles, for example. Space battles now resembled the maneuver and broadside exchanges of gunfire characteristic of the ancient Age of Sail more than they did battles of the 20th and 21st centuries. Missiles arced across intervening space along courses and at velocities set by heavier shipboard computers, aiming for predicted impact points. Would-be targets combined random bursts of powered flight or deceleration with free fall so that predicted impact points were always someplace other than where the missile actually exploded.

The first enemy volley missed. The enemy DropShip and its two tiny escorts, in close orbit now around Verthandi, passed around the curvature of the planet and out of sight. Verthandi's moon slowly settled behind the sweep of the planet's green-patched north pole as the *Phobos* dropped ever nearer.

Grayson swam to the captain's console, weightless now as the *Phobos* drifted in unpowered freefall, her drives silent. "We'll need our screen out, Captain," he said. Martinez nodded.

"Those fighters will try to close when they come around the planet's curve again," she said. "They'll try to pin us down to let the DropShip move in and work us over at leisure. We can't let any of them get too close."

Devic Erudin was clinging to a stanchion, looking deathly ill. Grayson did not particularly enjoy freefall, but he was not as badly affected by it as some. Combat, especially, could be rough on anyone not used to being shipboard during rough maneuvers. He swam across to Erudin's side.

"Do you want to go below?"

Erudin managed a greenish smile, and shook his head. "Strange to talk about *below,* when I seem to have lost my grip on up and down," he said. He belched once, heavily, and added, "I seem to have lost my grip on my stomach as well."

"If you feel sick," Grayson warned, "leave the bridge. These people can't take the time to clean up after you."

Erudin nodded and seemed to make an effort to collect himself. "What's happening now? What's the Captain doing?"

Grayson glanced across at Martinez, who was speaking with steady urgency into a microphone at her console.

"We're dropping our pups . . . the two *Chippewa* fighters we brought on board at Galatea. We'll need them to screen us from the Combine fighters. We're releasing them while the enemy blockading vessels are hidden on the other side of the planet, along with the planet's moon." He shrugged. "We're probably under observation from the ground, so what we're doing won't be much of a surprise. You never know, though. Every little bit, they say . . ."

"And . . . and the enemy DropShip I heard them talking about?"

Grayson shook his head. "We'll have to wait and see about that one. It's going to be a squeaker, though." He raised one eyebrow. "So much for the nonexistent blockade, Citizen."

"I . . . I don't understand. They haven't been this vigilant."

"You've been away for awhile. Or maybe it was just bad luck that we ran into their patrol."

"Will . . . will we get through?"

Grayson looked across the deck toward the bridge viewscreen, which showed the bulk of the planet whose golden light now flooded the crowded bridge.

"Well, Citizen, I guess we'll find out in a few minutes."

When the Combine ships emerged again from behind the planet, they would strike.

8

Sue Ellen Klein was wedged so tightly into the narrow cockpit of her *Chippewa* that she could scarcely move, but it was times like this when she felt most free and alive. The *Chippewa* was large for a fighter, massing 90 tons, yet most of that was in the broad, knife-lean wing-body of the craft. The cockpit was perched at the wing's center, between the aft-jutting, boom-joined double tail. From that vantage point, the pilot had an unobstructed view of Glory through the transplex cockpit bubble. The stars crowded close, and the golden light of Verthandi bathed Sue Ellen's face when she unsealed and raised the visor of her helmet.

The wing-body of Jeffric Sherman's *Chippewa* glittered sharp and bright against the stars a kilometer distant. She knew, too, that the *Phobos* was again balanced on white fire, decelerating at over two Gs aft and beneath the sweep of her own wing.

The two fighters had been launched while at a higher intrinsic velocity, which was carrying them now beyond the *Phobos* and deeper into Verthandi's gravitational field. Instruments strained to glean tidbits of data from random noise. Of the multitude of probabilities spilling across the computer screen, which would be the vector of the enemy ships when they reappeared on the *Chippewa*'s scanners?

Klein opened a ship-to-ship direct beam microwave channel. It allowed short-ranged communications for coordinating fighter maneuvers without letting the enemy listen in.

"Chip One to Chip Two," she said. It was cold in her cockpit. The life support systems were deliberately kept at a low setting to conserve power that would be needed later. Besides that, the *Chippewa*'s problem would soon be too much heat, not too little. Sue Ellen's breath puffed in wispy clouds before her face.

"Go ahead, One."

"In position. Keep alert, love."

"Right. Watch it, though. We're still pretty close to the *Phobos*. We may be monitored."

"The *hell* with them," she said. "If that bastard wants to eavesdrop, he's welcome." She said it loudly but deliberately, and when no third voice came across the com, she giggled. "I think we're safe, darling, but we're really going to *have* to stop meeting like this!"

"I'll go along with you there. I'd rather meet you in a nice warm bed, with a bottle of Chateau Davion '09. This gives us more privacy than we had on the *Phobos*, but I'm afraid it still leaves a little something to be desired."

"Well, I'll tell you. When we get back to the *Phobos*, we'll open up the watchstander's bunkroom on the fighter bay level and we'll—"

"Hold it, Sue! Bogies! Recorders on!" There was a breathless moment, then she heard, "Two enemy fighters, vectoring low across the planet. Jumping hell, they must be skimming atmosphere!"

Her own instruments showed the same story, close-paired Kurita fighters angling up from Verthandi's atmosphere. Her onboard computer cycled through scanner data and sketched out the ID schematics. They were SL-15 *Slayers*, delta-winged and sleek, each massing 80 tons and carrying six medium lasers and a heavy autocannon apiece. *Slayers* were deadly at close combat, fully capable of shredding her heavier *Chippewa* in a single pass.

A long-range com channel opened. "*Phobos* to pups," the voice said. "Bandit *Slayers* vectoring toward *Phobos*, bearing thu-ree-four-niner, mark two. Intercept and—"

Klein cut the voice off with a savage slap on the power switch, but kept her ship-to-ship microwave channel open. "Arming weapons," she said, then brought the visor down across her face and sealed it. A touch of a switch brought her fighter's heads-up display into glowing brightness an arm's length before her eyes.

"Arming weapons," Jeffric replied. "Luck, my love . . ."

"Luck . . ."

Blood sang in her ears with the racing of her pulse. She lived! That exhilaration was edged with fear that something might happen to Jeff. As always, she managed to dismiss the thought. Even then, the memory of her brother crowded to the fore. *Alec* . . . She shook her head, inwardly commanding herself, *No!* Instead, she gave in to the raw consuming passion of coming battle. Personal extinction, the memory of Alec, the possibility of the death of her lover, all were unthinkable with the surge of battle in heart and hands, with the senses so alive, so charged with excitement. Even the sweet thrill of sex paled by comparison.

Her instrument panel flashed red warning; the enemy had fired, but missed.

The *Chippewa* was not nearly as heavily armored as the *Slayer,* but the weapons mounted in its broad wings more than made up for it. A pair of light lasers guarded aft, six medium and heavy lasers aimed forward, and the space beneath the pilot's feet extending into the nose contained bundles of short and long-ranged missiles. At a range of 20,000 kilometers, Sue Ellen triggered a spread of SRMs, then punched her PlasmaStar 270 drive into throbbing life. Jeff's drives flared blue-white in almost the same instant. The miniature suns of missile drives intertwined into the distance against Verthandi's growing disk.

With her eyes locked on the readings of her HUD display, Klein counted off seconds, then flipped her *Chippewa* end for end. Five Gs crushed her into her seat, the roar of the drive hammering through her vessel's hull to pound and claw at her body through the padded seat. The maneuver was precisely timed. Her *Chippewa* fell tailfirst past the approaching *Slayers,* then accelerated after them with rapidly compounding speed. Missiles laced the sky with burning traceries; a hit flooded her cockpit with silent, white light that polarized her helmet visor black.

"Sue! I got one!" Jeff's voice over the microwave channel was ragged with excitement.

"He's still kicking," she replied. Her heads-up display

pinpointed the damaged *Slayer*, tumbling out of control but struggling to regain flight attitude with its control thrusters. She locked onto the target and triggered her fighter's heavy, wing-mounted lasers in rapid succession. Spectroscopic scanners told of metal vapor boiling into space. She fired her own thrusters again to align her craft for another shot.

"Sue! More company! Planetward, three-five-five, mark two!"

She cursed as she glanced from doppler radar to computer ID, then caught her lower lip between her teeth. There were two more SL-15s climbing out of Verthandi's atmosphere. They must have been waiting for just such an opportunity to catch the Legion's fighter screen between the two halves of their forces. It was a trap!

"They're boxing us, Jeff! We'll have to bull past the first two and close with the *Phobos!*"

"Affirmative! Punch it!"

The *Chippewa*s had drifted apart by several hundred kilometers in the brief fight. They swung now to align with the distance-dimmed flare of the *Phobos*'s drive just above the baleful orange eye of Norn, then boosted hard. One *Slayer* drew across Klein's HUD sights, lasers scoring hits along her starboard wing. Flakes of paint and metal glittered in the sunlight, streaming aft in a metallic cascade as she continued to accelerate.

She checked Jeff's position quickly. He was under drive, slipping past the dead hulk of the *Slayer* they'd already killed, angling for a deflection shot at the *Slayer* that was attacking her. She triggered another salvo of missiles and another burst of laser fire. The heat in the cockpit was already beginning to penetrate her suit, and she was slick with sweat. A fighter's biggest problem in combat was excess heat, and every thruster burn, every discharge of laser or missile, added to the problem. Sue Ellen ignored the growing discomfort, held stock-still as her *Chippewa* closed on the target with agonizing slowness, then shrieked victory as her lasers scored multiple hits on the enemy's charred and scored armor plate.

The *Slayer*'s thrusters fired frantically, knocking the damaged ship onto a new course. Seconds later, Sue's *Chippewa* plowed through the expanding cloud of paint chips and solidified droplets of recently vaporized metal from the enemy ship hit a moment before. Thousands of tiny, high-speed impacts sounded against her hull, like flung handsful of gravel. The target was aft now, boosting planetward at high-G.

Where was Jeff? She ignored the fireworks cascade across her HUD scanner display. Her instruments were temporarily blinded by the cloud of debris and would not be reliable for several seconds. Instead, she craned her neck, searching the black sky until she saw a moving glitter of light reflected from what might have been Jeff's wing surface.

If it weren't Jeff's *Chippewa*, then it was the first enemy *Slayer*, now dead and drifting in the sunlight.

That first *Slayer* was not dead, only damaged. Alive and cunning, its pilot watched Jeffric Sherman's *Chippewa* drift across his own HUD at point-blank range. The *Slayer*'s main drive was out, and his life support was failing. He still had a positive power feed to his lasers, and his autocannon was loaded and ready.

The pilot's name was Raoul da Silva, and he'd long dreamed of being a great AeroSpace Fighter ace among House Kurita's legions. The fact that he hadn't yet scored his first kill had never dimmed that dream. Now, though, the possibility that he might die over Verthandi without ever knowing victory in ship-to-ship combat filled him with an infinite sense of loss and loneliness. He had killed before, but somehow the helpless rebel vehicles, the village buildings, the streaming rabble fleeing from burning Verthandian towns had never seemed more than impersonal targets, like holographic shadows in a flight combat simulator. What Raoul had dreamed of was the glory of fighter pilot facing fighter pilot, two keen minds in deadly contest.

His ship was ruined and would not make atmosphere again, of that Raoul was certain. If the intruders could be destroyed, there was still a good chance his comrades could rescue him. Once the intruder DropShip was dead, the nearby *Xao* would mount a search for survivors. Unless Raoul could take the enemy out now, he would drift forever in a metal tomb, growing colder and colder. His last hours would become a contest between cold and suffocation for the privilege of ending Raoul's short life.

Providence had arranged that he could still strike back. If luck was with him, he might yet kill one of the intruder fighters, and might even survive to fight again another day. . . . If luck was not with him, he would die, but knowing he had scored at least one kill, man-to-man.

He made a minute adjustment. His *Slayer* rolled slightly, long shadows from torn metal falling across the curved armor of the ship's nose. The *Chippewa* was less than a kilometer away, large in his HUD crosshairs. Raoul's hand closed on the firing switch. All five forward-mounted lasers triggered in a salvo that sliced through the *Chippewa*'s armor like hot wires through butter. The Combine pilot added his autocannon to the barrage, a steady stream of explosive shells shredding the control and port wing surfaces of the stricken enemy craft.

Raoul's lips were drawn back from his teeth in a fierce, berserker's grin, his yell of triumph deafening inside the confines of the *Slayer*'s cockpit.

Sue Ellen Klein's victory shout became a wail of anguish. Her *Chippewa*'s hull creaked protest as she piled on Gs in an attempt to change course, to kill her own velocity and swing into a new intercept vector. Jeff was maneuvering, too, his drive flaring against the trailing cloud of debris from his ship's wounds. The target fell into the crosshairs, still firing, savaging Jeff's *Chippewa* with repeated hits.

Missiles lanced across space. One struck the *Slayer* squarely just behind its cockpit. Transplast melted in starsurface heat. The *Slayer* began tumbling, broken pieces of instrumentation and armor trailing from the gaping wound of the stricken ship's cockpit. Also tumbling was Jeff's *Chippewa*, moving outbound, away from Verthandi. It took Sue Ellen a few precious minutes to close with Jeff's ship, matching course and speed.

What she saw sickened her. The *Chippewa*'s cockpit appeared intact, but the portside wing was nearly torn away. The starboard wing was holed in five places, and most of Jeff's stabilizer had been torn away. A spaghetti tangle of conduit tubing and wiring, hydraulic piping, and shredded armor plate trailed after the fighter, creating a ghastly image of disembowelment. A ring of dust-fine debris, water vapor, and leaking atmosphere condensing and freezing in the vacuum of space expanded outward from the wreckage. She knew that ship would never make a controlled entry into atmosphere again.

Her maneuver had taken her out of the direct line between the *Phobos* and the *Slayers*. All three surviving SL-15s seemed to be ignoring her and were closing on the DropShip instead. Frantic now, but dulled by worry and the sudden dwindling of her battle fever, she tried to raise Jeff ship-to-ship.

"I'm here," he said. "I'm O.K . . . Some leakage, but I'm not hurt too badly. The controls are gone, though and so is the power. The old girl has had it, I'm afraid."

"No! No, Jeff! Blow your hatch! I'll make pick-up!" She began struggling with her harness. The cockpit of the *Chippewa* was crowded with one. With two, it would be claustrophobic, but at least the two of them would make it back to the *Phobos*.

There was a long silence before Sherman replied. "I . . . don't think so, hon. My legs, they're . . . hurt. Not bad, but . . . there's . . . there's no pain, but my pressure suit is pretty badly torn up down there." There was another pause, and then a sob came across her com channel. "Oh, God, Sue . . . it's starting to hurt . . ."

"Fire control!" Captain Martinez had to yell to be heard above the roar reverberating through the ship. Her nav screen showed twisted trails of light marking the incoming paths of the Kurita *Slayer*s. Autocannon shells hosed across the *Phobos*'s hull, their explosions cratering armor and opening savage gashes. "Fire control released to weapons stations! Fire at will!"

Missiles arced into blackness, seeking the glitter of the DropShip's minute attackers. Lasers burned briefly, invisibly, probing those spots where computers linked to the *Phobos*'s scanners predicted that the three SL-15s should be. Occasionally, those predictions might be correct.

The wing of one *Slayer* glowed white-hot when the *Phobos*'s heavy laser struck it. Droplets of molten armor streamed into space, a brief-lived contrail of dancing sparks. All three delta fighters streaked by the *Phobos* at high speed, lasers carving into the DropShip's hull as they passed. The *Phobos*'s weapons replied, tracking the fighters, scoring hits, but none were fatal. All three *Slayer*s end-overed, and their drives burned white hot as they decelerated, lining up for another pass.

Martinez turned on Grayson. "We're taking too much damage, Major." She gestured toward the main view-screen, where Verthandi loomed huge. "Another pass or two by those people and we might not survive re-entry. If we accelerate now, we could outdistance them, maybe loop around the planet and make it back to the zenith point."

Grayson allowed a half smile. "What for? The *Invidious* jumped out as soon as she recharged."

"But another starship might jump in . . ."

"Any ships coming insystem are going to be Combine vessels, Captain . . . or do you want to go ahead and surrender now?"

"I'm stating options, Major." Martinez dropped her voice so low that Grayson could scarcely hear. "At this point, surrender might not be such a bad idea."

Grayson shook his head. "Plot your course, Captain. Grounding in the Azure Sea, at the coordinates Citizen Erudin gave you. I prefer to take my chances with your piloting than the Combine's mercy."

"Yes, sir."

Martinez had not called him that before. The word sounded strange on her lips.

"Captain!" The com officer looked up from his console. "Captain Martinez! I've got a distress beacon from one of the *Chippewa*s!"

She turned from Grayson. "Damn! Where?"

"Planetward. Close in. I've got voice."

"Put it on speaker."

"*Phobos! Phobos!* This is Chip One!" Klein's voice was faint, distorted by the hash of static and distance. "Come in, *Phobos!*"

Martinez picked up a mike from her console. "*Phobos* here."

"*Phobos!* Jeff's been hit! Home on the beacon trans-mission and pick us up! If you can manage rendezvous, we can save him!"

Martinez looked at Grayson, eyebrows raised, the skin taut under the blue wing tatoos.

Grayson looked from her to the navscreen. The fighters

were outbound, but slowing. In hours, Verthandi's gravity would drag them to a halt, would drag them into the
long fall back. Pick-up would be possible, of course. It
would take long hours more for the crippled *Chippewa*
to fall into Verthandi's atmosphere.

But what would be happening in the meantime? The
Leopard DropShip was already emerging from behind
Verthandi's horizon, closer to the *Chippewa*s than the
*Chippewa*s were to *Phobos*. The *Phobos* might make it
past the enemy DropShip if she could maintain her present speed and course toward the planet, not decelerating
until the final plunge into Verthandi's atmosphere. But
the *Chippewa*s were on another vector, outbound. To
match course and speed with them . . .

Grayson balanced the life of one wounded fighter pilot
against the lives of all aboard the *Phobos*. No longer was
it a question of mission. This was sheer survival. He
gestured toward the microphone, and Martinez handed it
to him. He took a deep breath, held the device to his
lips, and spoke. "Chip One, this is Carlyle. *Phobos* cannot rendezvous, do you understand? We cannot make
pick-up on Chip Two."

"He's dying! You can't leave us!"

"Chip One, this is an order." Grayson had not be-
lieved the words would hurt so much. He scarcely knew
Klein and Sherman, but the pain was knife-sharp.
"Abandon Chip Two and return to *Phobos*. The enemy
DropShip is shaping an intercept orbit and we must meet
her. Do you copy?"

"Carlyle, damn you, you can't do this to us!"

"Lieutenant Klein! There's nothing you can do for
him! Return to *Phobos*, and take your station!"

"I'll *tell* you what you can do with your damn station!
I'll see you in hell, Grayson Carlyle! In *hell!*"

As if to underscore her words, the *Phobos*'s hull rang
anew with the impact and thundering bellow of autocannon rounds. Somewhere, far down the curve of the
DropShip's hull, a storage compartment had been
breached, its atmosphere erupting explosively into vacuum.

The deltaform SL-15s passed again. The *Phobos*'s lasers sought and found. The drive of one stuttered and
winked out at the touch of three beams sweeping across

its after hull. The craft began a slow tumble into Darkness.

Now it was the *Leopard* bearing down, driving toward the *Phobos* at three Gs. LRMs struck her lower hull, rupturing a 'Mech storage bay, smashing a starboard laser turret. The bay door blew out into space, winking off and on as it dwindled into the black. The *Phobos*'s missiles swarmed back along the same path. Laser beams, visible only on the bridge combat screens as lances of green and red, stabbed, probed, and struck. From somewhere, an alarm shrilled, but the sound was dull behind the babble of voices of the bridge crew. A computer voice announced pressure loss in Compartment Three.

Martinez looked up from her console. "Better take your seat, Major," she said. "We're committed, and here's where things get rough!"

Grayson strapped himself into his observer's chair. Events were beyond his control now, which gave him a moment to spare a thought for the two *Chippewa* pilots. Could he have done anything differently? If the *Phobos* had rendezvoused with Jeffric Sherman's fighter, all of them would have died . . . or they would have been forced to surrender. Computer imaging showed the *Leopard* huge on the main screen. A pair of now familiar delta shapes streaked past the larger form, those *Slayers* closing for another run. Somewhere a voice recited range figures for a fire control station. "Nine-zero-zero, eight zero-zero, seven-zero-zero . . ." Was the voice a computer, or was it the unnaturally calm voice of a trained professional rising above the surge of emotions, of pain, of fear?

Surrender was unthinkable. Possibly, *possibly,* in a declared war with established sides, the Gray Death Legion might have considered it in hopes of being exchanged or pledged. Mercenaries aiding a rebellion on a world already conquered by the Draconis Combine was a different matter altogether. The Dracos' simplest solution would be to arrange for the entire unit to quietly vanish. Besides, these Combine forces fought under the banner of Duke Hassid Ricol, the Red Duke, mastermind of the plot that had resulted in the death of Grayson's father. How could he ever quietly surrender, knowing there was a chance to strike at Ricol, to attack him, to hurt him . . .

Grayson's will to vengeance was not yet dead, but he'd abandoned Jeffric Sherman to die.

Where was right in all of this?

The *Phobos* bucked wildly. The noise of atmosphere rose outside, a distant susurration that built and surged, then built again into an overwhelming roar.

"Targets, incoming!" Someone's voice rose above the roar, sharp with new fear. "Bearing oh-five-oh, mark ten, high! *He's coming in!*"

As the DropShip plunged deeper into thickening atmosphere, it met this new attack with concentrated laser fire. The *Slayer*'s massive nose and belly armor absorbed most of the onslaught, as its own lasers sliced into the pocked and cratered target growing large in its pilot's sights.

One laser struck the *Slayer* full in the cockpit, at a range too short to allow polarization of the canopy to rob the beam of more than a fraction of its strength. The fighter's cockpit turned brilliant under the beam's megajoule caress. The canopy fragmented, giving the pilot no time to scream or even comprehend before his body transformed into superheated vapor. Though the *Slayer* pilot was dead, his fighter bore on at three kilometers per second, a gaping scar now glowing red across its upper hull.

The impact caught the *Phobos* a glancing blow, but it was enough to stagger the larger ship and to lay open its fuel tanks in a ragged gash across the ship's flank. The wreckage of the dead *Slayer* sprayed outward in a final blossoming of destructive brilliance that kicked the *Phobos* forward and down. The jolt sent the bridge crew reeling against consoles or lurching against the restraining straps of their harnesses as lights failed and damage alarms shrilled. The ionization shell of re-entry flickered wildly about the stricken, helpless DropShip as it plunged and rolled uncontrollably toward the planet below.

═══ 9 ═══

Sue Ellen Klein followed Jeff's crippled *Chippewa* into atmosphere. Re-entry friction had heated the wildly bucking craft to a cherry glow, and fragments from the damaged ship began flaking off in a glittering stream of fiery particles. Fifty kilometers behind, the larger fragments tapped against Klein's cockpit like the beginnings of a summer's shower. *Pit . . . pat . . . pit-pit . . . pitter-pat. . . .*

She could no longer use her radio. Her ship-to-ship frequency was jammed by Jeff's soul-searing shrieks as his ruptured cockpit began melting around him. There was one final duty she could perform for Jeffric, her friend . . . her lover. Tears wet her face and smeared the inside of her helmet visor as she brought the HUD targeting display up one last time. Crosshairs centered on the other *Chippewa,* now almost consumed in a billowing fireball, brilliant against Verthandi's cloud cover. Over the radio, the shrill screams continued, more desperate, chopped and broken now by the growing static from the ionization of superheated air.

"Goodbye, Jeff," she said softly, knowing that he could no longer hear her. "I love you . . ." Then her thumb came down on the firing button, sending paired Exostar short-range missiles across the gap between her ship and Jeffric's. The fireball erupted in flaming, hurtling fragments, then Jeff's screams ended with a suddenness that made her gasp.

Almost . . . she almost continued her own death plunge deeper into atmosphere, but her own well-trained pilot's mind took command and brought the ship's nose up. Like a stone skipped across calm water, the *Chippewa* skimmed across Verthandi's upper atmosphere, hurtling into space once more. In the planet's shadow and with her drive throttled down, Sue Ellen's ship cooled rapidly. She remained frozen in place, aware only that her thumb still pressed the bright red firing button that had released Jeffric from his agony. Nothing could release hers, though, as she moaned into the cooling silence, "I *had* to, Jeff . . . I had to . . ."

Sirens wailed across the wide, flat valley lined with broad-bladed stalks of deep blue vegetation. A mobile headquarters, a wheeled, multiple-trailered vehicle that dwarfed the men standing in its shadow, blared warning through its external speakers. Nearby, a *Marauder* hulked, motionless and waiting. Across the valley, one heavy *Orion* and a pair of *Stingers* also waited mutely while thunder boomed from a green-clouded sky.

The *Leopard* DropShip settled to the ground among billowing clouds of dust, whipping bluesward, and venting steam. Her hull armor was scored in several places by recent battle, but the ideographs above the black-on-scarlet circled dragon insignia still picked out the ship's name: *Xao*.

Colonel Kevlavic stepped down the ladder from the mobile HQ's cab and received a subordinate's salute. "Board the command as soon as its ramps are down, Lieutenant," he said. "I will lead the lance personally."

"Sir!"

His communicator chirruped at his belt, and he touched the switch to receive. "My Lord Colonel," a voice tinned in the speaker clipped to his ear. "Communication received from the *Subotai*. She has completed boarding of the company of Galleons, and is boosting now. Her ETA at Hunter's Cape is twenty minutes."

"Good."

"We've also got confirmation of close air support from Regisport, my Lord."

"Very well. Inform *Subotai*'s commander that we should ground at the rendezvous at the same time." He checked his wrist computer. "Make it 1240 hours, local." Kevlavic was not convinced that they would need the Galleon light tanks, but they would provide useful close support and covering fire if there were rebel forces in the vicinity. 'Mech operations in the Silvan Basin were always hazardous. Small rebel units were everywhere and anywhere. Though they posed no real threat to 'Mechs, a determined attack could threaten the defensive perimeter established around a DropShip landing zone.

Below him, the *Xao*'s 'Mech holds gaped wide. The Colonel brought the transceiver to his mouth. "Stand by, Com Central. We're moving." He clicked to battle frequency. "This is Kevlavic. Lance, form up for boarding."

As the three 'Mechs began lumbering across the valley toward the *Leopard* DropShip, Kevlavic climbed the ladder dangling by the leg of his *Marauder,* hauled himself through the narrow belly hatch, and slid behind the battle machine's controls. He swung the neurohelmet and its trailing tangle of cables down from its mount and secured it across his shoulders, then checked the adjustment of the feedback loop that would mesh his sense of balance to the great machine's electronic actuators and coordinators. The *Marauder* stirred and lifted one armored foot. The thud of its ponderous steps hammered through the 'Mech's open cockpit hatch as it began moving toward the valley.

The Governor General's instructions had been most explicit. Though the mission was a simple one, Nagumo's face and manner had showed his concern that it be successful. And when the Governor General was concerned, Colonel Kevlavic was concerned. It was a good way to retain rank, honor, and life.

The intruder ship had been badly damaged during the last moments of its approach to Verthandi, and probably was destroyed during its spectacular flaming re-entry. Planet-bound radar and the combat scanners aboard the *Xao* had tracked its trajectory across the northern hemisphere of the planet. They had lost the signal under the clouds, somewhere among the jungles, marshes, and salt dunes of Hunter's Cape, along the coast of the Azure Sea, six hundred kilometers north of Regis.

It was unlikely that either vessel or passengers had survived, but an immediate inspection was still vital. Rebel forces were strong along the Azure Sea coast, and further east, in the Vrieshaven District. Even if the blockade runner's crew was dead, the rebels might be able to salvage cargo and military supplies from the shattered wreckage. They might even find BattleMechs still cradled in their travel cocoons. Even more important, the wreckage might contain some clue to the intruder DropShip's origins and masters.

Nagumo's orders had also gone out to the two Kurita DropShips in the system. They were to ground, not at Regis, but to the north, at the edge of the Bluesward Plateau, where a company of light tanks attached to Kevlavic's command and one lance of his own 'Mech regiment awaited their Colonel's return. Though such a mission would normally be assigned to a company Commander or even to the Lieutenant in command of a single 'Mech lance, this was a special case. Colonel Kevlavic was not in the habit of delegating to junior officers when the mission was as important to the high command as was this one. He would personally search Hunter's Cape for the crash site of the downed intruder DropShip.

The operation's only possible weak point would be if there were any problem coordinating the *Xao*'s landing with the *Subotai*'s. A delay in either ship's arrival would leave the other ship's forces without support.

As he backed his *Marauder* into the harness supports in the *Xao*'s hold, the Colonel dismissed these thoughts. In twenty minutes, his 'Mechs would be on the ground. He had no doubt that they could handle anything they were likely to find at the crash site, be it survivors or the whole, damned rebel army. AeroSpace Fighters from Regisport would provide close air support.

Kevlavic was sure the *Subotai*'s tanks would not even be needed.

A hundred kilometers above the cloud-swirled ochers and greens of Verthandi's surface, the *Subotai* Captain had noted the automated distress beacon of a small craft. The ship was on a free-flight course close to her own vessel's, and so she altered course to intercept it. The Captain assumed that it was one of the Kurita fighters damaged in the short battle with the intruder DropShip.

It turned out that she was wrong. The damaged fighter was a *Chippewa*, a design not in use in Kurita space. The young woman that the *Subotai*'s Techs pulled from the cockpit seemed to be in shock, unseeing, unspeaking.

The Captain ordered a medic to care for the prisoner and that she be given food and a comfortable place to sleep. Though the war was over for this pilot, the *Subotai* Captain had heard enough rumors about Kurita interrogation units that she wondered if the young pilot might not have been better off in her metal coffin in space. That was not for her to decide, though, and she knew it. It was her duty to report to her superiors with the prisoner, not to tell them what to do with her. Besides, she might even get a commendation for the chance capture of one of the enemy pilots.

With silent bursts from her steering jets, the *Subotai* eased back into a re-entry approach vector that would take her and her cargo of *Galleon* tanks to the rendezvous at Hunter's Cape. She would be arriving late.

Tollen Brasednewic held up one hand, and the ragged line of soldiers behind him froze in place. Their guide slipped through the twilight created by the jungle foliage, while they waited, straining every sense against the background warble of unseen lifeforms. Chirimsims brayed and chirped in the distance.

They were a piratical-looking band, and none knew that better than Brasednewic himself. No two were dressed or armed the same, their uniforms a hodgepodge of civilian clothing and bits of uniforms and body armor taken from Kurita troops. Brasednewic carried a 5 mm Magna laser rifle taken from a Combine soldier, and Yolev cradled the massive squad machine gun he'd lifted from the body of a Verthandian militiaman. The rest carried a variety of hunting rifles, competition weapons, and handguns. Javed carried a single-shot flare pistol, with extra rounds for the ungainly, snub-nosed launcher stuffed into the pouch slung at his belt. From the brush behind them came the low rush of silenced swamp skimmer engines. That meant the pilots were keeping their vehicles ready for a fast getaway, if one was necessary.

Their guide was Li Chin, son of a local plantation owner named Li Wu. None of the rebels trusted the man entirely, not with so many Orientals serving in the ranks and in command of the hated Kurita legions. Li had often

helped the rebels before, however, warning them of
sweeps by Kurita patrols and of ambushes along the roads
at the jungle fringe. This time, Li's story of a spaceship
thundering across his plantation and into the sea to the
north had been too intriguing to ignore. If the man was
telling the truth, the vessel had crashed just a few hours
before, and it might yet be possible to salvage the wreckage before the hated Brownjackets arrived on the scene.

That Kurita troops would arrive was a foregone conclusion. The spacecraft was almost certainly one of
theirs, probably containing military supplies that they
would not want to fall into the hands of Brasednewic's
little rebel band. Radio transponders or emergency bea-
cons would bring other DropShips to rescue the first.
Maybe, though, with cunning and a bit of luck, they
could arrange a surprise for old Nagumo's troops when
they arrived. It would be nice to be the hunter rather than
the hunted for a change.

Li signaled them ahead. They moved forward cautiously, parting the vines and overhanging branches that
partly blocked the path. Beyond the jungle was the tidal
marsh, a barren wasteland of salt pools, sand bars, and
mudflats. Beyond that lay the sea.

The sound of the surf was a gentle, distant thunder,
intermittent behind the racketing of bright-winged ma-
rine ornithoids circling above the water's edge. The sea
was flat and azure-blue, tinged with green from the sky.
Not far from shore, the surface of the water was broken
by the hemispherical curve of a huge, metal shell lifting
and falling with the waves that broke against its steel-
grey flanks.

Brasednewic raised his Micheaux electronic 'nocs to
his eyes and touched the zoom adjustment. That hand
scanner was a battered souvenir of a raid on Port Gaspin,
and the carrying strap bore the stain of where it had bit-
ten into the throat of its former owner. At high magnification, he could make out streaks of rust across the
DropShip's hull and the vast, coal-black scars that spoke
of violent re-entry. High up along the flank, the re-entry
burns could not quite mask the black-on-red dragon circle of Kurita. Down at the waterline, waves broke and
surged through a gaping hole. Everywhere, there were
puckered craters and the slashed and partly melted gouges

of laser fire. The surf rumbled and roiled in white foam around the hulks of what appeared to be hull armor fragments or blocks of heavy machinery scattered about the wreck and sunken in the shallows along the shore. There could be no doubt that this DropShip had been brought down in combat.

The rebel leader dropped the scanner from his face, suddenly puzzled. What combat? If a Kurita ship had been knocked down, that meant friendly ships must be in the Norn System. But whose? The rebels had no ships of their own, no AeroSpace Fighters, no way at all of striking at Kurita DropShips from the sky. Who had? And why?

He raised the scanner again. Movement had attracted his eye, a disturbance along the beach. He could make out a party of men, apparently the wet and bedraggled survivors of the crash. There were too many to count. Many seemed to be . . . what? Digging, it looked like. They were digging in the sand. What were they doing . . . burying their dead? Scratching an SOS into the sand? Strange. As he watched, black smoke began boiling from the largest knot of people.

His jaw muscles clenched as he ground his teeth together, a nervous habit acquired long before the coming of Kurita's soldiers. Troops and vehicles from Regis would be along at any moment to rescue their own, and they would be drawn by the smoke. The rebels would have to strike fast if they hoped to capture some of those survivors for interrogation.

Brasednewic gave orders, hand signals understood and passed on by the men waiting silently behind him. Preparation was silent, save for the soft clicks of bolt-action and slide auto-weapons being cocked to fire rounds. The band split up into teams of four and five men apiece, each group slipping through the jungle and out onto the mudflats by a separate route. Messengers melted back into the swamp to alert the skimmer pilots.

The survivors numbered perhaps fifty or sixty, though small parties were scattered up and down the beach collecting boxes and crates of supplies that had drifted ashore from the wreck. None appeared to be posted as lookout, and none appeared to be armed. Brasednewic

smiled to himself. So much the better. This was going
to be too easy.

Grayson looked up as his communicator whispered in
his ear. "They're moving, Captain. Spread out along the
jungle line, range one hundred meters."

"I've got them, Lori," Grayson said. "Be ready."

He stood up, still a bit unsteady on his feet. The shock
of the fiery plummet through Verthandi's atmosphere, of
Martinez's last-second thruster maneuvers, and their
nearly successful landing at the edge of the Azure Sea
had left him weak and rubber-kneed.

It was Martinez's skill that had kept them from plunging too steeply into the atmosphere. After the grazing
collision with the plummeting fighter, she had recovered
control of the ship and braced them against the shuddering vibrations of re-entry, tail-first. They had not burned
on their descent, though the hull temperature had soared
so high that outer hull elements of the main drive had
slagged away entirely. Enough thrusters had survived the
heat to allow their semi-guided touchdown at the water's
edge.

Once down, the sea had poured in through the rents
and slashes in the DropShip's hull, of course, but the
wreck looked far worse than it actually was. Five of the
Phobos's crew had been injured in the descent, but no
one was killed. That they were all alive with much of
their gear still intact, Grayson was more than willing to
count as a miracle. There was even a chance that the
Phobos might even fly again, if they could find enough
time and a well-stocked repair facility. Repairing the
Phobos would require a second miracle.

Now, though, Grayson was willing to defer Miracle
Number Two if they could only secure a third miracle in
very short order. Forces that Devic Erudin had identified
as rebels were approaching rapidly, and Grayson knew
they had to establish friendly relations with them, fast.
If he failed, the firefight could end their mission before
it had properly begun.

Sergeant Ramage was on his knees nearby, using an
entrenching tool from the *Phobos*'s equipment locker to
scrape a hasty depression into the sand. "You look right
at home, Ram," Grayson said, "and that hole looks deep

enough. Why don't you pass that thing on to someone else?''

"Bloody funny," Ramage said, but he grinned as he handed the tool to Tomlinson, a young Tech kneeling nearby.

"You never looked better, Tom," Grayson said to the Tech. Tomlinson was another Trellwanese, a red-haired minor genius with things mechanical, and Grayson's own personal Tech. Tom had replaced his usual layer of grease with a smearing of wet sand and mud.

"I'll be ready to join Ramage's commandos after this," Tomlinson said, and Grayson laughed. Ramage had been boasting of late how he would put the Verthandian rebel recruits through a Trellwan-style commando training course. For reasons not entirely clear to Grayson, that included plenty of digging.

He walked on, pacing slowly across the beach past others of his command preparing their trenches or gathering crates washed up on the beach from the *Phobos* gashed-open hold. "Steady, everybody," he said, keeping his voice low but penetrating. "They're coming. Be ready . . . my command . . ."

He found Erudin squatting close by the fire that several troopers had coaxed from a pile of damp driftwood with a hand laser. "Your friends are on their way. Are you sure you don't have any kind of password or recognition signal we can use?"

Miserable, Erudin shook his head. "We're a good 200 kilometers from where we're supposed to be. The local commander *may* have heard I'd be bringing help back, but he wouldn't know when . . . and he wouldn't expect it here. There's a password I was to transmit on a certain radio frequency once we were grounded to let him know it was me. I doubt anyone patrolling out here would know about that." He gestured toward the wreck behind them. "That black dragon on your ship isn't going to help, either."

"Don't you have any way of maintaining communication throughout your . . . army?"

Erudin spat into the sand. "Army? Captain, the Resistance is made up of maybe eighty or a hundred 'armies' wandering all over Verthandi's northern latitudes. I think the biggest must number something like a thousand men and women, but they're scattered among towns and plantations throughout the Vrieshaven District. The smallest numbers exactly one—usually some lone scavenger who likes to slit the throats of drunken militiamen in Regis alleys. They—''

A signal keened in the speaker in Grayson's ear. ''Hold it,'' he said. ''Here they come.''

In a glimmering curtain of spray, a skimmerfoil burst from the cover of an arm of jungle reaching out onto the mudflats. At the same moment, bands of ragged men bearing awkward weapons rose from rocks and from behind low sand dunes. There was a stutter of automatic rifle fire.

''Now! Everybody down!'' Grayson yelled, and across the beach, men and women who had been waiting for just such an attack threw themselves flat into the shallow trenches they'd been scraping into the wet sand. Grayson alone remained standing. This was the riskiest part of the plan, for now he was the only target the attacking rebels had. At the same time, though, the rebels would know something unusual was happening if this lone survivor stood, empty-handed and defenseless, on the suddenly deserted beach. He was counting on surprise and curiosity to make them hold their fire.

Autorifle slugs chittered through the air a meter above his head, and the deeper-throated wham of a hunting rifle popped a geyser of sand near his feet. Just as Grayson was thinking that guerrilla soldiers might not have the luxury of indulging their curiosity, someone began bellowing an order to cease fire. The charging rebels dropped in their tracks, wary of a trap, weapons ready.

''Hold your fire!'' Grayson yelled. He remembered training sessions with Weapons Master Griffith in his father's regiment, and it all seemed so long ago. He shook himself. Was it only one standard year since those days? *Pitch your voice so it carries, but keep it sharp with authority, with control. If you're talking to your own troops, they have to know you're in control. If you're talking to strangers, you can't let them hear your fear.*

''We're friends,'' he continued, holding his arms out from his sides, showing that he was unarmed. ''We want to talk.''

''It's a trick, Colonel,'' a voice barked from behind a

sand dune. There was a crack and something hot plucked at Grayson's sleeve.

"Hold your fire, dammit!" another voice replied. "Dober, put that thing up!"

"I'm Captain Carlyle, Gray Death Mercenary Legion," Grayson continued. He had to stifle the tremor at the back of his throat, and his knees felt weaker now than they had after the crash. He wanted very much to drop to the sand, out of sight, but he knew that any sudden movement would unleash a storm of gunfire. "We were brought here to help you!"

There was an angry mutter from some unseen watcher, but Grayson couldn't catch the words. The second voice called back across the mudflats. "How do we know this ain't some kind of trick?"

"One of your people is here! Devic Erudin! He brought us here. Talk to him!"

There was no answer. With his boot, Grayson nudged Erudin, lying flat in his shallow trench. "Come on, Citizen Erudin. Stand up . . . very slowly. Keep your hands where they can see them."

The two stood for endless seconds. Grayson could almost hear the discussion that must be going on among the dunes behind the beach. *These strangers could be telling the truth. Or Erudin might be a plant, or a brain-channeled captive. It could be a trap, but if it's not, the real Dracos will be along any moment, and the beach will become a trap for all of us!*

Grayson knew that his own success now depended on the daring of the rebel commander. The man stood up. He wore denim work clothes and a sleeveless, olive drab Kurita jacket with the insignias torn off. A heavy commercial laser rifle was clenched in muddy hands, its power pack strapped to the man's thigh, its muzzle steady on Grayson's chest. On his head was a shapeless black beret. His shaggy red beard was streaked with mud.

"You want to talk," the man said. "Go ahead an' talk!"

The rebels were not easily convinced, but it turned out that Tollen Brasednewic, self-styled Colonel of the rebel militia, had indeed heard that someone had been smuggled offworld to attempt to hire mercenaries.

"But, damn it all," the rebel leader said as he watched

Grayson's men put out their smoky fire. "What if we'd been Dracos? You couldn't know we'd find you first!"

"I was given to understand that they don't come into the jungle that much."

Brasednewic spat into the sand. "And you say you came here to teach us? They'll know you crashed or landed somewhere along here, and they'll be looking for you! A DropShip, even a wrecked one, would be a real prize!"

"The idea was to land in the sea near a place where the ship could be camouflaged and easily hidden."

"It don't look like you're going to manage that now, unless you want to try to disguise that hulk as a rock!"

"No," Grayson admitted. "Still, we figured it would take them a while to get organized and to work out a search pattern."

"Maybe so. But damn it all! What if *we'd* a' been a Kurita patrol? First lesson you'd better learn about Verthandi, feller, is don't take *nothing* out here for granted!"

Grayson smiled and touched the communicator at his throat. "Lori, come on up and meet our hosts. Gently, now. Don't startle them."

One of the shapeless masses of metal lying in the surf between wreck and shore stirred, then rose, white water cascading from the flanks, joints, and the sleek, right-arm laser. Ten meters tall, the machine stood knee-deep in the surf, then strode forward, moving up onto the beach with a creak of interlocking metal parts and the dull thud of the 'Mech's 55-ton step. Brasednewic's jaw dropped as he looked up . . . up . . . and up. The *Shadow Hawk* was Grayson's own, with Lori Kalmar at the controls. On either side, a hundred meters up and down the beach, two more 'Mechs rose from their watery hiding places, Delmar Clay's *Wolverine* and Davis McCall's *Rifleman*.

"You see," Grayson said as Brasednewic continued to gape up at the armored monster towering over him. "We weren't *completely* trusting. Think we're crazy?"

Time was precious now. Brasednewic's band numbered fifty men and women and included five swift, flat-bottomed swamp skimmers that would be of help unloading cargo from the wreck of the *Phobos*. Grayson posted the *Wolverine* and the *Rifleman* inland, at the edge of the jungle. While their electronic senses strained for the first hint of approaching Combine forces, Lori set to work in the *Shadow Hawk*, using the 'Mech's powerful arms and hands to help with the unloading.

They'd only had time to unload the three heavies after they'd crashed. The other four 'Mechs, Lori's *Locust*, a *Stinger*, and two *Wasps*, all appeared to be intact in their shipboard cocoons, but were still sealed in storage bays. Besides these, there was a small mountain of weapons, gear, and supplies to be unloaded onto the beach. According to the rebels, a second clock was ticking away besides the one that would eventually bring Kurita forces to the crash site. Verthandi-Alpha, large and close, was the cause of Verthandi's extremely high, twice-daily tides. Those tides were not as severe here above 70 degrees north latitude as they would have been close to the equator, but they were bad enough to sweep hundreds of meters up the broad, flat beaches of the Azure coast. The *Phobos* would be nearly submerged by the time high tide arrived in only three hours more.

Rebels and mercenaries worked frantically. Once the *Stinger* and one *Wasp* were broken free of their bays, Hassan Khaled and Piter Debrowski saddled them up and brought them out into the light. Now they worked together to free Yorulis's *Wasp* from its cradle, as a steady line of rebels and mercenaries used swamp skimmers and rafts to haul ashore the last of the *Phobos*'s stored supplies. With Lori temporarily in command of the *Shadow Hawk* and with time short, it was decided to leave her *Locust* aboard the DropShip for now.

"Captain!" Lori's voice over the earpiece snapped Grayson to new awareness. "Incoming . . . by air!"

"What is it?"

"Looks like a DropShip on its way from Regis," Lori said, "and there's a pair of fighters flying escort."

"That's confirmed, Captain." The second voice was Martinez, from the bridge of the *Phobos* where she was supervising the first steps of damage-control for the craft. Whether or not the ship would ever fly again was an open question, but if they couldn't buy Martinez and her Techs some time, there was no chance at all. "We have them on the doppler radar up here. Range, eighty kilometers. ETA, two minutes.''

''Right. Now, abandon ship!'' The grounded hulk of the *Phobos* would be a prime target for aircraft.

''But Captain, we have auxiliary power up to three lasers! We could provide back-up.''

Grayson thought furiously. He weighed the value of three additional lasers in the coming fight with enemy air support against going back on his first order, then made his decision.

''O.K. Do it. Get your non-essential personnel under cover, and be ready to bail out if your armor starts coming apart.'' He doubted that the enemy would shoot the *Phobos* to pieces, for the DropShip was too valuable a prize. What they might do was to try to take out her lasers once they knew she was operational. ''One more thing, Ilse. You fire on my command. Got it? Hold your fire until I give you the nod!''

''You got it, Skipper!''

He shifted his communicator to the general combat frequency. ''Scramble, everyone! We've got two minutes to visitors!''

Crates of supplies were left lying on the beach while swamp skimmers laden with troops pulled out of the swirling surf and skidded on cushions of air across sand and mud into the jungle. BattleMechs lurched from the water and strode swiftly off the beach. They left great, crisscrossing trails of footprints, each as long as a man was high, but there wasn't anything that could be done about that. Grayson had hoped that the incoming tide would erase the prints, but they'd run out of time. The Dracos would have learned soon enough that 'Mechs had been aboard the downed DropShip and that they'd escaped. Now they'd learn about it slightly earlier than Grayson had originally hoped.

He turned and sprinted across the beach toward the jungle. ''Lori!'' He gasped as he ran. ''Pick me up!''

The *Shadow Hawk* appeared against the treeline, moving with a ponderous, deliberate lope that ate up the ground between 'Mech and running man. The *Hawk*'s visor canopy was open, a chain-link ladder dangling across its chest. Grayson caught hold of the ladder and swarmed up the battle machine's front as Lori turned the

Hawk gently to face the jungle and began moving back toward cover.

The *Shadow Hawk*'s cockpit was cramped even when only its pilot was squeezed into the control seat beneath the tangle of conduits and cable connecting the pilot's neurohelmet to the control receptors along the cockpit overhead. When the ladder was winched in and the visor canopy sealed shut, there was but a slim strip of space behind and to the left of the pilot seat. Grayson wedged himself into that crevice, his head ducked low to clear the coolant pipes, mounting lugs, and wiring bundles for the emergency escape charges. If things got rough, if the 'Mech was knocked down or was forced to run with him aboard, he would be in serious danger. The *Shadow Hawk*'s cramped cockpit was still preferable to the open beach. From here, he would also be better able to direct the battle.

Lori sat in the chair, her hands on the console controls, her head and cascade of blond hair completely covered by the grotesque, black-visored mask of the neurohelmet. It was already stuffily warm inside the close space, and Lori had stripped to boots, briefs, and T-shirt in preparation for the even greater heat to come. As the 'Mech lurched its way forward, Grayson clung to overhead struts with both hands, telling himself to ignore the pleasant sight of her bare legs and to concentrate instead on the instrumentation above them.

Shadow spilled across the 'Mech's armor-embraced canopy. They were among the trees at the jungle's edge.

"Just in time," Lori said, her voice muffled from inside the helmet.

He tried without success to read what emotion might be in her words. He was worried about how she might face this, her first combat since Thunder Rift, but that had not been the reason why he'd joined her. There'd not been time to free her *Locust*, and so he needed to be aboard a 'Mech himself to coordinate the battle.

"If we spotted them, it's likely they spotted us," he said, "but they'll have to work to find us."

"The ship's radar echo might've blended in with the trees and water," she said, "and the tide's coming in awfully fast. If we're lucky, they might not even see—"

"No such luck," he said, interrupting. Outside, thunder pealed, and a pair of sleek SL-15s banked low over jungle and beach, stooping to circle the wrecked DropShip.

"They've found us!"

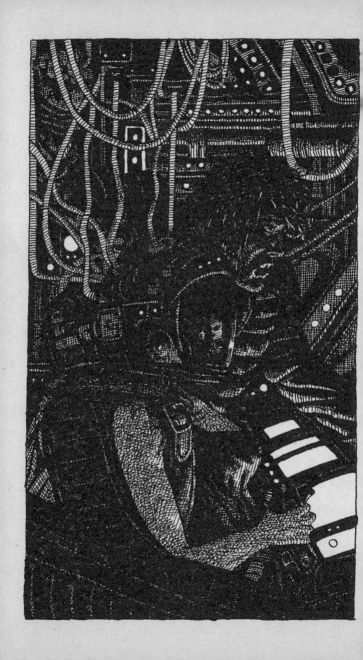

10

Grayson reached over Lori's shoulder, stabbing at the frequency settings on the com console. "McCall! This is Carlyle!" he said.

"McCall, aye," the Caledonian responded. "A'm trackenit tha' beasties, sair."

"Hold your fire until you've got your best shot. And concentrate on the aircraft, not on ground 'Mechs. We're counting on you for anti-aircraft cover."

"Aye, Captain. Ye've go' it."

The RFL-3N *Rifleman*, with its paired heavy lasers and autocannon mounted on each shoulder had been designed as a fire support 'Mech, but was well-equipped for its secondary role as an anti-aircraft tracing and weapons platform. The odd, propellor-like antennae of the 'Mech's D2j tracking system mounted above and behind the cockpit provided rapid target acquisition that was particularly useful against airborne threats.

Grayson spoke again. "All 'Mechs, this is Carlyle. Hold your fire! Ready . . . on my command . . ."

The pair of enemy *Slayer*s thundered overhead again, but did not fire. *They're searching*, he thought, *but they still don't know we're here!* He felt a small thrill of pride that none of the 'Mechs in his command had loosed a shot at the two fighters during their first pass.

He watched the traceries of the fighters' paths on the *Hawk*'s battlescreen. If they were scanning for active communications, they'd pick up the 'Mech band the next time he gave an order. If the fighters had IR or magnetometer gear, his men would be spotted almost at once. In any case, the 'Mechs would not remain unnoticed among the jungle growth for long.

"Now, McCall! Your best shot!"

The *Slayer*s banked sharply, arrowing toward . . . the *Wolverine!*

"Clay! Duck and roll!" Autocannon fire spat from the SL-15s, shredding treetop foliage in a whirlwind of leaf and branch fragments and splintering blasts. The jungle floor shuddered as the fighters whipped overhead at treetop level, spilling slender cylinders that glittered as they fell. The jungle erupted in flame and noise.

Davis McCall's *Rifleman* stepped from the jungle as the *Slayer*s raced side by side across the mudflats and out over the sea. His 'Mech's arms were already raised, the autocannons spitting fire as empty, smoking shell casings flipped onto the sand. The flash and flicker of explosions chewing along the starboard side of one of the fighters made it lurch heavily to one side.

"Now, *Phobos!* Fire!"

Lasers ignited streaks of tortured air. Chunks of smoking metal hurtled from the fighter already damaged. The other *Slayer* banked left, twisting to avoid the unexpected fire.

"Clay! Report!"

"I'm fine, Captain," Clay's voice replied. "The bombs came in close, but not quite close enough. Thanks for the alert."

"Any time. Give McCall a hand."

Martinez interrupted from her station aboard the *Phobos.* "Captain! The DropShip is coming in to the east! Range two thousand meters!"

"Right. All units . . . did you hear? Company's coming!" That would be 'Mechs . . . and groundsupport troops. What was the rebel leader's name? "Tollen! Are you listening in?"

"Here, Carlyle."

"Have your people faced 'Mechs before?"

A pause. "Men . . . against 'Mechs? What the hell do . . ."

"Listen . . . you'll have to trust me on this. I'm not asking you to face 'Mechs, but those out there are going to have support troops somewhere nearby."

"Listen, Captain . . . you're crazy if you think my people are going to face up to a whole, damned Kurita *army* . . ."

"Not an army. Probably no more than a platoon or two of mop-up troops. I need infantry to keep them off our backs, and my people aren't organized yet." The Gray Death's personal weapons lay still wrapped in their protective slickers, cased in the transport lockers littering the beach behind him. It had been important not to show weapons to the approaching rebels, but it might have been better if his people had dug fewer trenches and opened more crates. Some of the hundred-odd people in his command had guns by now, but not nearly enough.

He considered quickly, then decided to give their new allies an option. "It's up to you. Take off if you'd rather, but you know we need your help."

Tollen sounded grim. "We'll stay, but my people will deploy to *my* orders, not yours."

"Fair enough. Ramage?"

"Here, Captain."

"How many do you have armed?"

"Ten or fifteen, Captain. Not enough."

"Never mind. Have unarmed personnel rendezvous with the skimmers and stay out of trouble. Everyone with guns, join the rebel troops and obey Tollen's orders. Got that?"

"Sir!"

"Colonel? Do you mind taking a few new recruits?"

Brasednewic didn't speak for several seconds as he digested this unexpected trust on the part of the offworlder. "Very well!" There was another pause, and then, "And Captain! Good hunting!"

The *Wolverine* had emerged from the trees a hundred meters east of McCall and was firing its autocannon, the stream of shells crossing the double stream from the *Rifleman*. The *Phobos* added lancing beams of coherent light. The stricken aircraft staggered once again, billowing smoke. A flash and glitter of light marked the pilot's ejection, and then the *Slayer* began rolling wing over wing as it swooped and crashed into the jungle to the south. The explosion shivered the leaves on the trees.

The other *Slayer* pulled up abruptly, gaining altitude. The *Rifleman* tracked it, using laser fire now to save its on-board ammo.

"DropShip, *Leopard* Class," Martinez reported from

her observation point. "Setting down two klicks east. He's unbuttoning."

"Lori, let's see what the other fellows are up to."

"Right, boss." She seemed steady, even excited as the battle took shape. Deft motions of her hands at the 'Mech's twin control sticks set the *Shadow Hawk* in motion, while the 'Mech's metal hands parted branches and a heavy gray drapery of something remarkably akin to Terran spanish moss. From the jungle's edge, they could see four enemy 'Mechs moving down the DropShip's ramps and spreading out across the beach.

At two kilometers, it was difficult to make them out. Lori queried her computer for a scanner ID. Diagrams traced themselves across her screen, green light on black, and words flashed across the drawings.

"Not good," Grayson said. "A *Marauder* and an *Orion*—two heavies. A pair of *Stingers*. We can take the *Stingers*, no problem. But those two . . ."

Grayson had faced a *Marauder* before. He had, in fact, faced two of them, one after the other in the last struggle at Thunder Rift, on Trellwan. A heavy 'Mech weighing 75 tons, it moved with a menacing, crablike stride on rear-canted legs, and its oversized forearms mounted paired PPCs and medium lasers. The autocannon protruded from its exposed mount above the egg-shaped hull like a black spear.

The *Orion* was an old design. Grayson had never seen one up close, though he'd studied them during his training. It massed as much as the *Marauder* at its side, though its squat, angular chassis was vaguely humanoid. The blunt muzzle of an autocannon protruded from an armored bay on its right side. Like the *Marauder,* it was handless, with medium lasers set into the massive vambraces instead. The cockpit head was set low between the shoulders, the slit view-ports giving the appearance of eyes.

"Khaled!"

"Here, Captain."

"I think we're in luck. They're deploying a lance of 'Mechs, but no support troops. Gather the two *Wasps*. Stay in the jungle, but look for an opportunity to circle behind as we draw them in. They have a pair of heavies, but all together, we outweigh them. We can take them if we save you for a surprise!''

"Yes, *Kolarasi,*" the ex-Saurimat said, his voice taut with excitement. *"Allah akbar!''*

"Right. O.K., let's show ourselves, Lori," Grayson said. "I want them down here, out from under the guns of that *Leopard.''*

The *Shadow Hawk* stepped fully from the jungle, and the enemy 'Mechs hurried their pace. Missiles and beams lanced out from the DropShip, but flew either too high or else splashed close by the *Phobos,* searching for the range. In ground combat, DropShips depended on a high volume of fire rather than accuracy to protect themselves from advancing 'Mechs, and they suffered the same fire-control problems at long ranges that 'Mechs did. The *Leopard's* fire should not prove too dangerous unless they ventured nearer.

The *Phobos* returned the fire. BattleMechs on both sides began shooting, too, though neither unit expected to do much more than keep the other side cautious at this range of over a kilometer. With most 'Mech tracking units being centuries old and all cobbled together from other, even older units, they were not up to pinpoint accuracy across more than a few hundred meters.

The Gray Death's 'Mechs held their ground while the Kurita 'Mechs closed. By this time, the Draco scanners would have identified all three visible 'Mechs and tallied the odds in favor of the attackers, four 'Mechs to three, 190 tons to 170. The Kurita machines proceeded even closer.

At 500 meters, they were within effective range, and McCall's *Rifleman* began scoring hits on the *Marauder* with his autocannon. Each flash and bang of an impacting shell gouged heavy armor, sending bits and flakes of metal flying back over the *Marauder's* shell. Lori joined in, firing the *Hawk's* autocannon in a long, ragged volley that stitched shells across the *Marauder's* port side and arm. Delmar Clay, meanwhile, turned his *Wolverine's* SRMs and autocannon on the *Orion.*

The two Kurita light 'Mechs hung back, shielded by the bulk of their comrades.

Cannon fire thundered. The Dracos were probably surprised that they'd stood and fought, Grayson thought.

Rebel forces, or the mercenary units helping them, could not afford to stand up to a Kurita line unit and slug it out. The Combine had plenty of 'Mechs on Verthandi, plus an unending pipeline of tools and repair parts from offworld. Each of the Grey Death's 'Mechs was priceless, and spare parts would be tough to come by. Delmar Clay's *Wolverine* staggered back a step as autocannon fire opened craters in the big 'Mech's chest.

"Keep moving, everybody," Grayson ordered over the battle circuit. "It's a long way to the nearest friendly repair facility!"

"Cap'n! McCall here. It's gettin' a wee bit warmish in here. Ah'm goin' for a wee dip!"

"Right. We may join you."

As the exchange of heavy cannon and laser fire continued, the *Hawk*'s cockpit was rapidly becoming stiflingly hot. Grayson wiped at the perspiration beading his forehead and flicked it to the deck, then grabbed for a stanchion as Lori tilted the machine sharply in response to a laser burst that scorched the *Hawk*'s right side. He wished he could take off his uniform jacket, but there was no room. Anyway, the *Orion* was charging now, its lumbering gait heading straight toward the mercenary 'Mechs.

"Watch him," Grayson barked. "If he gets in the middle of us, we won't be able to fire at him without firing at each other!"

McCall, his *Rifleman* now waste-deep in the surging, incoming tide, swivelled his 'Mech's torso and hosed fire across the charging *Orion*, but it was Lori who thought to direct autocannon fire at the big 'Mech's feet. Craters gouged the sand, filling immediately with dirty water. One of the *Orion*'s broad feet came down into a shell hole with a splash, overbalancing the 'Mech and toppling it forward into the foam.

As McCall's lasers scorched low across the sand from the sea, wet sand by the fallen *Orion* sizzled and exploded in gouts of steam. Lori brought the *Hawk*'s right arm to the point, its medium laser fanning white hot-destruction across the *Orion*'s backpack electronics. Firing its jump-jets with a rushing hiss, an enemy *Stinger* leaped, balanced, and then descended in steam and smoke. Cradling its right hand laser like a pistol, it fired at the *Shadow Hawk*'s cockpit as it touched down.

Grayson had already averted his eyes. Without the shielded visor of the neurohelmet, the laser's monocolor pulse would have blinded him, even through the mirrored surface of the *Hawk*'s shielded vision slits. He felt heat, intense heat, wash through the cockpit, and then the thunder of the *Hawk*'s shoulder-mounted autocannon smacked into the lighter *Stinger* and sent it tumbling backward into the sand.

Shellfire streamed across the *Marauder*, which had halted at the fall of the *Orion*. The *Stinger* at its side exchanged laser fire with the *Rifleman*, which was now striding out of the sea, foam streaming from its legs. The *Hawk*'s battlecom circuits garbled strange, shouted words. *"Droch annailed sassanach! Oed an sluic!"*

"McCall!" The Caledonian was totally absorbed in his firefight with the Kurita 'Mechs. "McCall! Behind you!"

"Rach gus sluic!" The *Rifleman* continued its inexorable advance, autocannons stuttering, shell casings spilling into the water. Low, skimming the water behind McCall's 'Mech, the AeroSpace Fighter that had fled skyward earlier was returning, its nose lasers and autocannon twinkling in deadly synchronization.

Founts of water gushed and sprayed on either side of the *Rifleman*, and explosions blossomed along its back. The flat antennae of the D2j tracking system burst into fragments, and the 'Mech's right arm went suddenly limp, the autocannon barrels swinging down to point into the water.

The lasers aboard the *Phobos* swung heavily to track the new, unexpected target, but too slowly. Lori brought the *Shadow Hawk*'s laser into line and triggered a rippling pulse of coherent light flat across the beach, scant meters above the *Rifleman*'s head and into the onrushing fighter. Shellfire and laser bursts were tracking past the toppling *Rifleman* now, blasting sand, mud, and steam into the sky in an impenetrable curtain. Lori just kept firing at where she thought the target to be, tracking higher, then straight overhead as a shadow blackened the sky and thunder pealed. Then the *Phobos* fired, sending streaks of light burning through the sky.

Red lights winked on Lori's console. "Damn!" she said. "A shell took out our autocannon on that run!"

Grayson had not even felt the impact. He studied the battlescreen. The fighter was continuing its flight due south. "I think you hurt him, Lori . . . or Ilse did. He's not going to stop until he hits Regis!"

"Now, if we could just convince *them.*"

The *Rifleman* was down, partly submerged in the swift-rising tide, braced half-erect on knees and gun barrels. Its fall had signaled a general advance for the Kurita 'Mechs.

Clay's *Wolverine* laid down a blistering salvo of laser, autocannon, and SRM fire. Missiles wove between the Kurita 'Mechs, flashing with sudden, sharp impact, raining the enemy with mud, pocking their armor with shell-bursts and the charred, black slashes of laser strikes. Suddenly outnumbered four to two, the *Wolverine* and the *Shadow Hawk* stepped closer together, almost side by side, spraying their attackers with concentrated fire.

The *Stinger* was down again, not moving. Before Grayson could react to the sudden turn of events, three more 'Mechs had stepped onto the beach from the jungle two hundred meters beyond the attackers. Grayson almost pointed out the new targets to Lori, then shouted in pure joy as he realized that the newcomers were the Gray Death's own light 'Mechs. Hassan Khaled in his *Stinger* was snapping shots into the rear of the *Maurauder* with vicious abandon. Both *Wasps* had joined Clay's *Wolverine* in a wicked crossfire that trapped the *Orion* and had the heavy machine reeling.

The Kurita 'Mechs wavered. If they broke and ran, they would run right through the light 'Mechs closing in behind them.

"Khaled!" Grayson cried into the com circuit. "Scatter your force! Clay! You follow us!" He urged Lori forward with a hand on her shoulder as though he were propelling the *Hawk* itself. Lori's sweat-soaked T-shirt was wringing wet under his fingers. The *Shadow Hawk* fired its jump jets, causing Grayson to clutch again for the overhead stanchions. The machine crashed to earth on the far side of the fallen enemy *Stinger,* but then recovered its balance and continued its advance toward the foe.

The remaining *Stinger* turned and fled, crashing head-long into Khaled's *Stinger,* which was charging from the

other direction. Both 'Mechs went down, arms and legs
flailing. The *Orion* was limping heavily. The heavy, oily
green sheen of coolant was smeared along its left leg like
blood and also gushed from a shattered knee joint. Smoke
boiled from a scar in its left side.

The *Marauder* held its ground, buying time, perhaps,
for its fellows. Both the *Hawk* and the *Wolverine* concentrated their fire on the *Marauder.* For a full thirty seconds
of blazing, fire-licked hell, the three 'Mechs exchanged
laser fire at close quarters. The *Hawk*'s cockpit was an
oven, an inferno that brought Grayson to the point of
collapse. Heat overload alarms were shrilling as red lights
rippled across Lori's board. Four times he saw her slap
the override switch when the on-board computer threatened shutdown. After that, he lost count.

Lori guided the overheated machine through ankle-
deep water, working toward deeper water where the sea
would act as shield and coolant. The *Marauder* crabbed
sideways. Though still firing, it was retreating now toward its DropShip.

Grayson spared a glance for the grounded DropShip
and stifled a yelp of surprise. There were *two* Kurita
Leopards there now. The second must have grounded un-
heard and unseen during the battle. There was a stir of
movement below the second ship, but he couldn't make
out what it was.

"Let me have a magnification of the landing site," he
said, and Lori punched a combination of buttons. The
combat screen lit up with a magnified view of the base
of the newly grounded DropShip.

Galleons.

Grayson knew the GAL-100 from his ID lectures of
years before. The tank was a fast, light tracked vehicle
designed to support 'Mechs or infantry, or both. Instead
of a full turret, a medium laser on a universal platform
mount rotated on its broad, flat back, and a pair of light
lasers were set in vertical shell turret mounts on either
side just above the leader wheels. The Galleon was fast,
faster than any 'Mech, though the sand of the beach might
slow them some here. Its single disadvantage was its light
armor, but the tanks were small and relatively cheap to
produce. Most battlefield commanders could afford to
lose three or four Galleons to kill a single 'Mech.

This latest turn of the battle made Grayson curse bitterly under his breath. The enemy 'Mechs were beaten, broken, but he could count at least six Galleons moving down the beach. And there could be more behind, masked by their fellows. *Those* were the support forces he'd thought the enemy had neglected to throw in.

Grayson was gripped by a momentary indecision. His 'Mech force could not be pushed for much longer. One of his heavies was down, and both the *Wolverine* and the *Shadow Hawk* had been squandering ammunition in attempts to overwhelm their targets with raw firepower. Worse, the *Hawk* could not withstand its current heat load much longer, and each discharge of the laser made things worse. He was sure that things were just as bad aboard Clay's machine. It was time to retreat, *now,* while they could. Yet it was wrenching to think of abandoning the field like this, with victory so *close* . . .

The Galleons were racing across the beach now, their treads kicking up spray behind them. Lori began firing with her laser, snapping shots off slowly and with great deliberation. Her heat alarms were shrilling again. Grayson had another thought. Would they be able to escape? The Galleons were racing to cut them off on each side from jungle and sea. With their high speed, they were devilishly hard to hit.

A flash of light snapped across Khaled's *Stinger* as a laser struck home. Light flooded the *Hawk*'s cockpit and Grayson covered his eyes. When he looked up again, purple blotches danced before his eyes, almost totally obscuring his vision. Briefly, he knew sharp panic, but the fear subsided as his vision cleared. The beam that had caught the *Shadow Hawk*'s head had not struck the vision screens squarely. It had been partly reflected laser light that had so dazzled Grayson's eyes.

Lori stabbed off the last of the *Hawk*'s head-mounted SRMs. "I don't think we can hold them, Gray!"

Explosions echoed across the beach, cracks and hollow-sounding booms under flame-shot clouds. A tank died horribly, flame boiling from its engine vents and its turret. A crewman struggled to free himself from an escape hatch, looking tiny and pitiful against the consuming blaze.

The tanks slowed and stopped, their lasers tracking new targets.

At first, Grayson had thought the explosions were the *Hawk*'s missiles, but it was something else. Small containers, possibly glass, were being hurtled from the jungle's edge, breaking over the tanks' backs or on the surface of the water. When they broke, fire billowed skyward. Where the fire touched the water already lapping at the tanks' treads, it spread, burning furiously.

Skimmers burst from the jungle, just clearing the mud and shallow water. Men rode those skimmers. Some carried guns, but most were hurling containers at the Galleons, then ducking low to pick up and light another.

Grayson recognized the weapon. It was a glass bottle filled with a mixture of gasoline and oil, the neck stuffed shut with a strip of cloth soaked in the mixture. When the cloth was lit and the bottle hurled, it became an effective grenade. Such weapons had been used by resistance forces against tanks on Terra long before man ventured to the stars.

"Go, Lori! Go! This is our chance!"

Brasednewic's rebels splashed among the trees near the water's edge, firing steadily to keep the crewmen buttoned up tight inside their vehicles. The skimmers circled, hungry. Another tank was alight. The others were retreating, except two that had strayed into muddy ground already meter-deep in the incoming tide. One struggled, its engine racing. The other sat motionless with its deck already awash.

The *Shadow Hawk*'s last LRM sighed from its tube, the weapon status light for that tube flashing green to red. A Galleon exploded. Fragments of armor rained into the water in a widening circle around the tank. Smoke mushroomed from it, casting rippling shadows across sand and jungle.

Firing into the retreating enemy forces, Debrowski's *Wasp* and the *Wolverine* strode through smoky water that was knee-deep on the 'Mechs.

"All 'Mechs!" Grayson said, his voice unnaturally loud in the close, hot cabin of the *Hawk*. "All 'Mechs! Break off pursuit!"

Jaleg Yorulis protested from his *Wasp*. "But Captain! We've got 'em running!"

"They're running, all right, right back under the cover of those DropShips. Break off!"

Grayson fought down his own surge of battle lust. Their victory was complete, or as complete as they were likely to manage with a pair of heavily armed DropShips backing up the enemy. Missiles ratcheted overhead from the enemy landing zone, exploding in sand and fury behind them.

Grayson gave the order to withdraw.

11

Clay in his *Wolverine* was already helping McCall's *Rifleman* to its feet. Grayson winced when he saw the damage the *Rifleman* had sustained, and his mind began cycling furiously through what he would say to McCall. He had ordered the Caledonian to watch for aircraft, but the man must have been so absorbed by the ground battle that he'd completely missed the Kurita SL-15's strafing run from his rear. That mistake could have been fatal. It might well have ruined the unit's heaviest 'Mech.

A muted roar from the east warned of the Kurita force's departure. Both DropShips hovered on laboring thrusters, then turned and arced slowly off toward the south above the jungle. Explosions and a rising pall of smoke marked where supplies unloaded during the battle had been destroyed lest they fall into rebel hands or tempt a rebel attack during reloading. As the sound of the *Leopard*'s departure faded, a new sound began rising from the beach and surrounding jungle growth. It took Grayson a moment to recognize that it was the sound of men and women, cheering.

Grayson touched the *Shadow Hawk*'s canopy release panel, and swung it open. The outside air, tropically hot and damp, rushed into the *Hawk*'s cockpit like an autumn wind, dry and deliciously cool compared to the hothouse humidity inside. He hung against the overhead stanchions a moment, gulping the air, suddenly aware of how good fresh air smelled compared to the stench of his and Lori's sweat and fear. The sharp scent of scorched armor also flavored the fresh air. Pings, pops, and creakings of hot metal rose from the *Shadow Hawk*'s weapons tubes and from scarred and scorched patches of armor where, briefly, megajoules of laser energy had touched.

The cheers continued to sound around him, clearer now than when he'd heard them through the 'Mech's external pick-ups. Both rebels and mercenary troops were emerging from the jungle, splashing through the shallow, high-tide water, or standing in animated knots among the boles and roots of beach-edge trees and jungle plants. Some exchanged slaps on the back or vigorous handshakes, and many were engaged in animated discussion of the battle just past. Sergeant Ramage and Tollen Brasednewic were trotting side by side at the head of a mixed squad of troops in the direction of the nearest stranded Galleon. The tank's crew was already climbing out, moving clumsily with their hands in the air.

Lori locked the *Shadow Hawk* in place and cracked her helmet, letting Grayson help her swing it off her shoulders and into its rack above her seat. Her hair fell in lank, damp stands across her shoulders. She shook her head and wiped wet hair from her eyes.

"Pretty good for someone who was sure she would fail," he said gently. In truth, he'd completely forgotten his concern about Lori's fears once the battle had begun. She had acted coolly, professionally, without hesitation.

She replied with a smile, though her eyes were guarded. Lori, too, reveled a moment in the cool breeze moving through the open cockpit before fishing a towel out of an equipment locker under her seat to sop the sweat from her face and neck. When she had finished, Grayson used the towel himself. His own uniform was as soaked as her brief attire, and far less comfortable. It didn't cool as the air blew over it, but bunched, chafed, and sent sudden rivulets of sweat tickling down his spine and sides. The water below looked inviting, and he longed for a swim. For the moment, he was too weak to do anything more than hang on and breathe.

Nearby, Grayson saw McCall and Clay leaning from the opened hatches of their own machines. The light 'Mech pilots were still relatively fresh, not having sustained combat as long as the heavies. They now stood guard in the quickening tide as a Kurita pilot climbed out of one of the two captured *Stinger*s. The other *Stinger*, still flat on its back, had taken a round in the head. Smoke still wisped above the gore-shocked scar where the 'Mech's cockpit had been.

Lori smoothed wet hair back from her face. "Captain, if you'd excuse me, I'd like to get dressed."

Grayson smiled. "Pardon me for barging into your dressing room, and thanks for the ride." He reached up and punched the winch release that dropped the *Shadow Hawk*'s ladder, then lowered himself to the ground, careful to avoid hot spots on the 'Mech's armor.

The water under the *Hawk* was knee-deep on him and felt wonderful when he splashed it across his face.

"My Lord, there was no way we could have reached Hunter's Cape with more 'Mechs or tanks. There were only two DropShips available, and small ones at that." Stiffly at attention, Kevlavic stood in Nagumo's office at the University of Regis, his eyes focused at the greenish sky through the window behind the Governor General's shoulder. He swallowed once before adding, "We did not expect such fierce resistance, Lord. We thought to find only battered survivors of the DropShip's crash. We were met by accurate and concentrated fire from at least two enemy 'Mech lances—and possibly a full company. They were supported by a large and powerful guerrilla force with whom they must have established contact moments before our arrival."

Nagumo sat quietly, neither accusing nor condemning. "I see. Anything else?"

"There was one serious tactical and logistical flaw in the operation that contributed to our defeat."

"Yes?"

"The DropShip *Subotai* arrived at the LZ almost eight minutes after the *Xao* was down and unloaded. The light tanks were not on the field until my lance was already being forced to withdraw. Had we been able to operate together, things might have gone differently."

"Perhaps," said Nagumo, his face impassive, voice noncommital. Close support between 'Mechs and ground support units was always a touchy subject during analysis of BattleMech operations. Some commanders swore that close cooperation between troops in light, swift vehicles and the lumbering 'Mechs could vastly increase a 'Mech unit's combat effectiveness. Others argued just as vigorously that ground units got in the way, that they slowed the 'Mechs and hindered their freedom to fire, that accidents and misidentification too frequently caused troops armed with anti-'Mech weaponry to fire into friendly, valuable machines. Nagumo was a traditionalist who felt 'Mech operations should remain separate from conventional orders of battle, but he was open-minded enough to allow a subordinate such as Kevlavic to approach things in his own way. No matter now, for the blame would rest squarely on his own shoulders.

"Perhaps," Nagumo said again. "Then, too, a second lance of BattleMechs might have served better. What is the final tally of damage?"

Kevlavic noted his commander's use of the word "damage," rather than "casualties," but lost no time in pondering it. In BattleMech units, equipment was far more valuable than lives. Humans could be replaced, but in an increasingly lostech universe, it was becoming harder and harder to replace man's war machines.

"Lord, both light 'Mechs were lost, one with severe damage to the cockpit. We must assume the enemy will be able to field one against us, but it seems unlikely that their service facilities will be up to repairing the other. For the same reason, we can assume their *Rifleman* is permanently out of action."

"We can assume nothing of the sort," Nagumo replied, still quiet. His eyes sparked in the harsh office lighting. "There are industrial complexes in rebel-controlled regions, centers for servicing industrial or AgroMechs, especially among the plantations. We haven't found them all . . . yet."

"Y-yes, my Lord. The *Orion* was badly damaged, but retired from the field under its own power. My senior Tech estimates that seventy hours of work will put it back in service again and that all necessary parts and tools are available. My *Marauder* suffered considerable damage to its armor, and its left arm PPC was knocked out. Again, nothing that cannot be repaired in our facilities here. Of twelve Galleons, four were destroyed."

"Not to mention one aircraft shot down," Nagumo interjected impatiently, "and the second so badly damaged it may not fly again." He was particularly worried about the losses to his AeroSpace Fighter force. First the losses during the battle in space, and now this. . . .

"The enemy may be able to recover one or more of those tanks," he continued, almost to himself. "The report from the *Xao*'s Captain suggests that two of the Galleons were merely trapped in mud. When the tide recedes, the rebels may be able to free them with the help from their 'Mechs. Colonel, I fear this . . . this debacle will not look good on your record at all."

"No, my Lord."

"In fact, I wonder if we shouldn't be looking for someone more . . . adaptable to lead your regiment."

"As . . . as my Lord commands."

Nagumo appeared to consider, then smiled. The sight of the Governor General's teeth did not put Kevlavic at ease.

"No, Colonel. I believe that a man must learn from his mistakes. You will have another chance to demonstrate that you are capable of learning."

"Thank you, my Lord!"

"Not at all, not at all. In fact, I direct you to take as much of your regiment as you need to hunt these outsiders down. I want that 'Mech unit destroyed, Colonel, before they can offer effective help to the insurgents. You are not to make any more assumptions about the enemy's abilities or weaknesses or strengths. Mistaken assumptions will lead you to underestimate him, to your sorrow. Do you understand?"

"Yes, my Lord!"

"My patience will not extend to another disaster such as that at Hunter's Cape. You shall not fail me again. Clear?"

"Perfectly, my Lord!"

"Then go. I want a progress report from you daily and an operational plan by this time tomorrow. Dismissed."

Ilse Martinez leaned over the table that had been improvised from a strip of sheet metal laid across a pair of upright steel drums on the beach. A freshening breeze from the sea and a darkening sky tugged at her curls. Grayson held the map they were examining flat between both hands. She straightened up, shaking her head.

"Captain, do you know what you're asking me to do?"

Grayson's glance shifted across to Brasednewic, who fingered the grip on the laser rifle slung over his shoulder and looked away. His expression as much as said, *This is your argument, not mine.*

"Captain Martinez," Grayson began formally, "do you know what will happen if you don't?" Though not aboard her vessel, he used the title to remind her of the responsibility of her command. *Which she's already aware of or she wouldn't be so set against it,* he thought.

"The *Phobos* is a *space ship,* Captain," she said, "and, at the moment, not an especially good one. We've got the leaks fixed, but. . . ."

"If we leave the *Phobos* where she is, the Dracos will be back," Grayson said. "And, this time, more of them. We lucked out today, lucked out plain and simple, because their attack wasn't coordinated, because they weren't expecting us to be ready for them, and because we had some help from Tollen and his people. If we stay here and fight them again, we'll be wiped out. And if we take off inland with these people"—he stabbed at Brasednewic with a thumb—"how long do you think the *Phobos* will remain intact?"

"She's safe enough from storms."

"I'm not talking about storms! Look, a DropShip is a small mountain of Star League technology and spare parts! Computers! Weapons! A fusion power plant and enough power module relays to run an army of BattleMechs! Conduits, piping, tubing, and wiring; semiconductors, superconductors, circuit boards, function chips, neural flow circuitry, and God knows what else! The Kurita commanders know a DropShip crashed here, and they know she's relatively intact. Intact enough to shoot down their AeroSpace Fighters! They'll have every DropShip they can muster back here, and an army to boot, just as quick as they can manage to gather the forces and fuel the ships! They'll expect us to salvage what we can, of course, but how much do you think we could salvage, starting now? How long do you think we have?"

"Nagumo is not slow about recovering other bits of technology," Brasednewic added. "If one of our 'Mechs is abandoned or destroyed, he has Techs swarming over it within hours, even if we blow it with a self-destruct charge.''

"They'd dismantle the *Phobos* for the armor plate, if nothing else,'' Grayson said.

"I know, I know. I don't want old *Phobos* to fall into their hands any more than you do . . .''

"Then you have to see that this is the only way! At worst, we sink the *Phobos* to the bottom of the Azure Sea, someplace where Kurita recovery craft can't possibly get at her!''

"What about my crew? I can't do this alone, you know!''

"It'll be dangerous. But you have a skimmer ready to take you all off. You'll abandon ship if you have to, but we've got to try!''

She turned from the map and gazed across the line of breakers at the *Phobos*. The tide had gone out since the battle, leaving a broad stretch of beach between them and the foaming breakers. The DropShip seemed higher in the water now that the tide was lower. The crude repairs to the gash in her hull were visible, layers of sheet metal and armor tack welded across the hole. Streams of water spewed from vents in her sides, indicating where damage control parties were at work pumping out the sea water that had flooded her lower decks after the crash. Small, blue-black clouds scudded beneath the lowering overcast.

"I don't think anyone has ever tried something like this before.''

"That doesn't mean it can't be done!''

She turned again and looked at the map. It was laboriously hand-drawn, and Grayson wondered about its accuracy. Brasednewic had produced it when Grayson had asked him about the geography of the coastline.

"Okay, we're . . . where?''

With a grime-coated finger, Brasednewic indicated a strip of beach close by a hook of land jutting north into the sea. "Here. Hunter's Cape, it's called.''

"And you want me to sail the *Phobos*—by sea!—all the way across to . . . here!''

Grayson nodded. "To Ostafjord, yes. At the mouth of the Skraelingas River. The village of Westlee is here, across the bay.''

"Five hundred kilometers!''

"More, since you'll have to skirt south of this island here."

"And you want to tear apart my reactor to do it . . ."

"Not 'tear apart!' Look—" he reached for a compad and stylus, illuminated the smooth data screen, and began sketching in lines of light. "The *Phobos* uses a small fusion reactor to heat and compress hydrogen up to the fusion point, with powerful magnetic fields to contain and direct what amounts to a small, controlled, and ongoing fusion explosion, right?"

"Very small, and a lot cleaner. Yes."

"Well, the design would also let you simply heat hydrogen, turn it into a super-heated gas, and blast that aft through the tubes as reaction mass. That was the principle of the first nuclear spacecraft. You pitch reaction mass aft, and it shoves the spacecraft forward."

"It's also a lot cruder, and a lot less efficient than a thermonuclear field pulse."

"Right, but we don't need efficiency here."

"No, what we need is fuel! We ruptured our hydrogen tanks in the landing and lost what little was left of our fuel reserves. We're going to have to cook some more H if we're to move anywhere."

"That's just it. We don't need to use H if we convert the drive to a simple reaction mass engine." He sketched rapidly. "We jury-rig intake valves here . . . here . . . here . . . and pump in sea water. The pumps circulate the water through the fusion reactor, which burns the H you have left just to produce heat and keep your weapons powered up. Steam is vented out the tubes. We flood the ship—"

"Flood!"

"Just a little! Just enough to give it some balance and keep the jet tubes underwater, and to give her a bit of a list. Steam blasts out the tubes under water, and you travel in the direction of your list!"

She chewed at her lip, staring at Grayson's doodles. "There are a lot of practical problems."

Grayson waved stylus and pad. "I don't give a damn about practical problems," he said. "You know your ship, and you have a small army of engineering Techs and officers who can lick practical problems. If not, we'll give them guns and stick 'em in with the foot soldiers!"

Ilse tore her eyes from the pad and brought them up to meet Grayson's. "God damn," she said, and the words were almost reverent. "You want me to convert my DropShip to a steam-powered sailing ship!" She shook her head, then moved the compad aside so she could again study Brasednewic's chart. "I must be getting as crazy as you are, Captain. You've got me thinking about ways to . . ."

She stopped short. "Look, assuming we can do it, what about our Kurita friends? Something as big as a DropShip quietly cruising across their ocean. I don't think they're going to care for that!"

"They know the *Phobos* is here, at Hunter's Cape. You make the conversion as fast as you can. . . . Before tonight if possible."

"Tonight!" The word was a wail of protest and horror.

"That would be lovely, thank you! I'm not sure how much speed you'll get out of her, but you have unlimited fuel, and the fusion-heated steam is bound to give her quite a shove. Your speed may be limited by the ship's structural integrity, but I imagine you'll be moving at a pretty good clip. You'll travel at night. If you leave tonight, we can probably count on this cloud cover holding, and that will protect you from infrared detectors in orbit. I doubt that they have radar scanner satellites in orbit. That'd be impractical on a planet with this much jungle mixed with open terrain. By the time they get a ship here—tomorrow sometime, I imagine—you're well out of their way. Their first assumption will be that the *Phobos* broke up in the surf or in high winds. They're not going to believe that we'd actually try to sail her across 500 klicks of open sea."

"You've got *that* right."

"If the cloud cover breaks, there's a chance you'll be spotted, of course. With luck, you could make it all the way to this fjord without being spotted, and the enemy'll be left thinking the *Phobos* is at the bottom of the Azure Sea."

"It wouldn't take much for them to be right." She looked again at the wreck of the DropShip, rolling slightly with the swell now that most of the water had been pumped from her lower compartments.

"You're right," Martinez said at last. "It's worth a

try, though God help me, I don't know how we'll be able to sail tonight!''

"We can't wait for tomorrow," Grayson said. "It'll take them at least until then to collect an army to throw at us. But no longer. Not if they want to stop us from stripping the DropShip. They'll be here tomorrow, say, by local noon. You've got to be a good hundred kilometers out to sea by then if you don't want their air cover to spot you."

"You'll lend a hand with your people, and some 'Mechs for muscle?"

"Of course," Grayson said, thinking about the light 'Mechs now aboard the *Phobos,* unloading the *Locust.* "In fact, it would probably be a good idea if you took one of the 'Mechs along with you. We don't know what you'll run into, once you reach land."

"I wouldn't mind someone riding shotgun."

"Fine. Now, which one? I need the *Locust* with me." He trusted Lori's instincts as a scout, and her 'Mech's speed would be wasted aboard the *Phobos.* "And the *Wolverine* and the *Rifleman* are my heavies. You could have Debrowski, Yorulis, or Khaled. I'd suggest Khaled. I know he's had plenty of combat experience. I don't know how either of the other two would handle independent duty."

She chewed her lip, then said, "Khaled, then. The guy gives me the shivers, but you're right about his experience. It shows, even if he doesn't say much."

Grayson nodded. "Good. I'll tell him."

"Then we'd better get started. So help me, Captain Carlyle, if I get seasick on my deck, I'm going to see to it that you have the fun of cleaning it up!''

Grayson watched Martinez stride down the beach, waving for a skimmer to carry her across the water to the *Phobos.* The plan to save the DropShip was one born of desperation. So much could go wrong. . . .

Shaking his head, he rolled up the map and returned it to Brasednewic. "What's next for the rest of us, then?" he asked. "Devic Erudin had planned for us to meet with your Revolutionary Council."

"I could take you there, I suppose," the big man said, "but it's a long march through thick terrain. All jungle and swamp, like this''—he waved behind him toward the treeline—''and worse.''

''Impenetrable for 'Mechs?''

''No. At least, I don't think so. We've got some 'Mechs, you know, but no one who can pilot them in combat.''

''How's that?''

''Oh, we have lots of guys and gals that can operate 'Mechs because of the many plantations burned out from the jungle below the Basin Rim through here. Most of them use AgroMechs to plant and harvest their crops, and there's a big logging operation off to the east that uses big, four-legged 'Mechs to cut, strip, and drag trees. Piloting an AgroMech isn't all that different from running one of those things.'' He gestured toward Grayson's *Shadow Hawk*, standing empty on the beach nearby.

''We've got some BattleMechs, too, left over from the little planetary defense force from the days before Kurita took over. And some were brought in by government militia MechWarriors who got tired of doing Nagumo's garbage details. Those militiamen are not very well trained, especially not against other 'Mechs.''

That was understandable, Grayson thought, because the Kurita occupation forces would not wish to encourage an active BattleMech force with well-trained pilots within their puppet government's army. They would use Verthandian government 'Mech lances as oversized policemen on riot-control duty to scatter mobs and to awe disgruntled populations, rather than as actual combat units.

''Anyway, AgroMechs follow those trails all the time. Hell, most of 'em are old forest logging roads made by LoggerMechs in the first place, years ago. Our BattleMechs don't get out much, but when they do, they don't get into trouble if they stay on the main forest roads.

''Off the roads, it's different. There are places that'll suck a 'Mech down in the blink of an eye, mud pits that are as good as bottomless so far as a 20-ton piece of machinery's concerned. But you'll make it if you stick with us.''

''Well, that's it, then. Will you take us?''

Brasednewic rubbed at the stubble on his chin. ''Well . . .''

Grayson folded his arms. "If you're looking for payment, we don't have much to offer you."

"A proper share of the booty we took today would go right," the rebel said. "Like those tanks over there. We took 'em, your mercs and my boys together. Were you mercs figuring on drafting them into *your* army?"

Grayson laughed, raising his hands, palms out. "Right now, I've got all I can worry about looking after my own equipment! If that's the coin that will get us to where we're supposed to go, by all means, take them!"

The rebel brightened. "We'll take 'em off your hands, then . . ."

"And if you want, I'll loan you some of my Techs to get them up and running."

Brasednewic looked surprised. "You're generous, for a merc."

That again. "There's more to this than money, friend. At this point, I'm more concerned about turning our two armies into one."

The rebel looked thoughtful, and Grayson guessed he was thinking about problems that command of such a joint-effort army would create. The man's face cleared, as he no doubt reached the conclusion that such decisions were best left to the Revolutionary Council.

"Right. I'm sending some of my skimmers on back to Fox Island ahead of our main column," Tollen said. "They'll take my wounded and also the news that we've got these tanks on the way. You want to go with them?"

"I don't think so. I'll come in with my people and my 'Mech."

"Sounds good. Well, that Erudin fellow can go on ahead to let 'em know we're coming. They're a bit touchy about unannounced visits."

"Understandable. I have to see to the fitting of our DropShip first anyway. And . . ." He looked up past the rebel commander's shoulder and saw a stocky form standing alone further down the beach. "If you would excuse me, I have to talk to one of my people. I've been keeping him waiting deliberately, but I think he's been stewing long enough."

Brasednewic snapped off an informal salute by touching the rolled-up map to his brow. "Right you are, then.

But we're going to have to move fast. I'd like to be off this beach and moving by midnight."

"That'll depend on how fast we get that DropShip afloat," Grayson replied, "but we'll certainly do our best. If we're not ready by then, leave us a scout, and we'll follow."

Grayson had not been looking forward to his interview with Davis McCall. He liked the lanky Caledonian, liked his cheerful manner and carefree grin. But likeable or not, McCall had a dressing-down coming to him, and the responsibility to deliver it was Grayson's.

"McCall, there are unit commanders who would have you shot for what you pulled this morning."

"Aye, sair." There were shouts in the distance and the clank of heavy block and tackles being hauled up the flank of the damaged *Rifleman*. A dazzling pinpoint of light appeared and wavered at the 'Mech's twin-barreled arm where a Legion astech was at work with a cutting torch. Sparks danced and showered on the ground.

Since joining the Gray Death, McCall had shown an almost touching affection for his *Bannockburn*. Grayson could tell from the man's eyes that he longed to be across the beach with his beloved war machine as repair crews cobbled together repairs enough to keep her moving and fighting until she could reach a secure machine shop. McCall remained at attention, however, his eyes focused somewhere within the jungle canopy above the beach.

"I ordered you to ignore ground combat, if necessary, to concentrate on your detectors," Grayson continued. "If that *Slayer* had been carrying an inferno cluster, we wouldn't be standing here talking about it now, would we?"

"No, sair." The Caledonian flexed his hands, and rallied. "But sair, tha' micklin' wee fighter had gone when his wingman was dooned! Ah dinnae ken . . ."

"You didn't *think*, dammit! I can't have people in my unit who have to be told how to think!"

"Sair . . . ye're nae bootin' me oot a' th' Legion . . ."

"If you mean terminating your contract, no, I'm not." Grayson looked hard at McCall, his gray eyes cold. "The *Rifleman* is yours and we need your *Rifleman*. Nor would I turn you loose here with no place to go but the Governor General's camp! Mostly, though, I don't want to lose you. You're a good man, Davis, and good men are more precious than BattleMechs!''

New light rose in McCall's eyes. "Thank you, sair!''

"Don't thank me. Prove your gratitude by following orders next time, and by using that thick Caledonian head of yours! Forget it, now. What's the damage?''

"Och, mah puir, wee bairn wa' snickered good! Ma' *Bannockburn*'s left arm actuators were junked, an' both legs tookit a lo' a' damage.''

"Never mind the details. How long to fix it?''

"Well, sair, her port arm actuators are killit, and tha' D2j detector antennae needs replacin', too. Captain, tha' *Bannockburn* needs a refit a' . . .''

"We don't have a repair facility, dammit! We don't have anything but what we've brought off the *Phobos!* How much to get her underway again?''

"She'll move noo under her ai'n steam, Captain. Tae get her intae fightin' trim, oh . . . och, aye, another ten hours. But tha' puir lassie'll nae be usin' her port arm o' weapons until we gi'e her a new actuator group. An' tha's something we nae ha'e here. An' her fire control'll be by guess an' by gosh until we replace her D2j.''

"That 'poor lassie'll have to make do until we get her to a heavy machine shop. But you'll have your ten hours when we reach a rebel base. And maybe we can see about actuators when we're there. I understand there are a lot of AgroMechs produced on this world, and we might be able to adapt one to your needs.''

"Aye, there's tha'. Wi' tha' right tools, ah could tinker somethin' tae makit do.''

"Good. You're pretty good at . . . 'tinkering', aren't you?''

"Oh, aye, aye. It helps havin' Sco'ish ancestors, ye ken.''

"Well, I'm delighted to hear it. As of now, I'm pulling you off of *Bannockburn.*''

"Sair!'' Shock marked McCall's face, and he cast another worried, longing glance at his crippled 'Mech.

Grayson shook his head. "Those Techs over there can get her ready for the march to the rebel HQ. I'll put my own Tech, Tomlinson, on the crew. Right now, I want

you out on the *Phobos*, helping rig her to pump and heat
sea water.''

''Sea water, sair?''

''Sea water. You're going to help teach the *Phobos* to
swim. You can consider *that* your punishment for disobeying orders!''

Grayson returned the astonished MechWarrior's salute
and walked over to where Brasednewic was waiting in
the shade near the treeline at the far edge of the beach.
Everywhere, men and women struggled with heavy
equipment or wandered in seemingly aimless patterns
across a beach strewn with debris and the refuse of a
small army. From further up the beach came the grumbling of diesel motors as the Galleon tanks were fired up
and sent clanking down a trail that a rebel guide had
pointed out in the forest. The rebel army, uncertain what
to do in the midst of this purposeful chaos, lounged in
small groups in the shade of trees, dicing, playing cards,
talking, sleeping, or simply watching the frantic activities of their unexpected new allies.

Somehow, Grayson was going to have to transform this
chaos into a fighting army, or the Gray Death would never
leave Verthandi again.

═══ 12 ═══

It stormed during the night, but throughout the rest of the long, Verthandian day, Grayson's people had worked to refit the unit's BattleMechs, to unload necessary supplies and equipment from the *Phobos*, and to ready the DropShip herself for the sea voyage.

The conversion of a gut-torn DropShip into an unwieldy and practically unsteerable, steam-powered boat was risky enough that Grayson wanted to salvage all the equipment he could before consigning the vessel to the mercies of the Azure Sea. The actual refitting of the pumps and conduits that would gulp in sea water took only a bit more than five hours, speeded up with the help of 'Mechs able to lift massive sections of hull plate or machinery weighing nearly as much as they did. The longest part of the refit was the transferral of bulky 'Mech harnesses, booms, and repair rigs from the 'Mech bays to the shore.

It was two hours past dark when the *Phobos* was ready to set sail. It was already raining, with winds gusting in wave-flattening bursts that caused the lightened DropShip to shudder. The motion aboard was queasily uncomfortable as the DropShip moved with the slap and lurch of the waves. The tide was in now, and lightening the ship's holds had brought her up off the bottom. The motion was made worse by the fact that selected outboard holds along one side of the cargo deck had been pumped full of water, giving the ship a twenty-degree list. Movement along her decks was treacherous and accomplished by slowly and carefully planting feet and hands with each step.

Grayson picked his way across the *Phobos*'s bridge.

Martinez was in her control seat, strapped in against the increasingly violent efforts of wind and wave.

"A storm is up, Captain," he said

"It is, indeed, Major," she replied. Now that the *Phobos* was again a ship in the purest sense of the word, Grayson had his honorary, if temporary, promotion back. "That could be bit of good luck."

Grayson nodded. "It means the Dracos won't have recon aircraft up tonight, and you'll certainly be screened from enemy satellites. Their patrols won't be close enough to pick you up on infrared scan, either."

"Hell, it means they'll think we broke up and sank in the storm! Well, it's about time our luck changed!"

"I'm glad you feel that way, Captain, because you've got to sail this thing in weather I wouldn't care to face inside a *Marauder!*"

Martinez touched a panel on the armrest control block. One of her console monitors came on, displaying a computer-generated map. It was based on the Azure Sea charts they had been studying earlier in the day. She used a stylus to trace across an arm of the sea to a convoluted thrusting of water into the land. "The Skraelingas River. Any idea what's there?"

"None, beyond what Brasednewic was able to tell us," Grayson replied. "There are plantations nearby, and he says their owners support the revolution. You should be able to trade machine parts and such for food."

"Food doesn't bother me. It's hiding from the damned Dracos! This storm won't last forever, and a DropShip'll show up to a satellite like a big fat bug on a dinner plate!"

"Only if they catch you at sea, Captain, under clear skies. The cove Brasednewic told us about . . . here . . . you should be able to ground the *Phobos* there, where the tide won't move her. Though you might have to wait for high tide to do it. It's close in under the rocks of these cliffs, just inside the mouth of Ostafjord. You've got camouflage netting enough to hide the ship, as long as you douse your reactor to kill your infrared signature."

"I'm not doubting the analysis. We just don't know what it's *really* like there. Suppose those rock cliffs are too low or there are unmapped sand bars that keep me from getting close? Suppose I can't get the *Phobos* close enough under the cliffs? Suppose . . . oh, the hell with it. I'll worry about it when I get there.'' She looked at Grayson, her dark eyes somber under their tatooed wings. "I wish you well, Grayson," she said, the formalities of command forgotten for the time. "I hope to see you again . . . soon."

"You've got a skimmer ready in your number three hold. If you start to founder, let the old tub go, and abandon ship. We can join up later."

"It's not me I'm worried about, Major. It's you! I'm not sure I trust these Verthandians yet. And you folks have got a long way to go." She laughed. "I'd rather face five hundred kilometers of open ocean in a storm than that damned, Kurita-infested jungle!"

He smiled and extended his hand. Ilse took it gravely. "I'll get word to you somehow," he said, shaking her hand. "Just as soon as we're set up with a decent headquarters, supplies, repair facilities, and so forth. Then we can see about getting the *Phobos* spaceworthy again."

"For now, Major, I'll just be happy if she stays *seaworthy!*"

The rain was driving up the beach in sleeting walls, pelting at Grayson's face and hair with savage fury. He heard the DropShip's engines throb to life, a deep, rumbling sputter that carried above the pounding of the surf and the roar of wind and rain. Visibility was so low, however, that he couldn't make out the ship as she got underway. Good. That meant that other eyes in the jungle wouldn't see her departure, either.

Moments later, the combined column of rebels and mercenaries set off into the jungle on their own voyage. The rain offered advantages to the land party as well as to the seagoing *Phobos*. Rebel forces travelling through the jungle were always threatened by Kurita satellites or orbiting spacecraft spying down from two hundred kilometers overhead. Though Verthandi's skies were frequently cloudy and the jungle canopy provided nearly unbroken cover across most of the Silvan Basin, there were frequent clearings and stretches of open ground. Even a fragmentary patch of blue-green sky might be enough for a satellite to catch sunglint and the movement of a hovercraft column. BattleMechs pushing along the jungle paths were harder still to hide. The rebels had long ago learned to move through the jungle by night and to take advantage of the blessed natural invisibility offered by clouds and rainstorms. The secret rebel base and the Verthandian Revolutionary Council lay across almost four hundred kilometers of jungle, and it took all night to get there.

Verthandi, was, above all, an agricultural world. There was heavy industry centered near the principal cities, of course, and petroleum and various metal ores. Chromite, principally, and bauxite, were dug or pumped from the edge of the deserts to the south. It was the fertile land along the jungle basin slopes that was Verthandi's most important economic asset, however.

Paradoxically, the soil of the lush jungle floor was impoverished, leached beggar-poor of minerals by constant water erosion. In most places, the jungle canopy was so thick that not enough sunlight entered to support undergrowth, resulting in surprisingly little dead vegetation or humus. The swamps were another matter, bottomless layers of muck and ooze stinking with decay. Neither terrain was suited to farming.

Verthandi's fertility existed in the area known as the Silvan Basin, which had been formed in ages past when a massive asteroid had smashed out a depression in the planet's jungle belt. The land sloped down sharply from the encircling high ground plateaus and rugged mountains. At the northern base of the slope, in a narrow circle clear around the world's pole at roughly 60° north, was a fertile zone where erosion from the southern slopes combined with runoff from the spring floods on the high plateaus. The land here was wet, laced with swamps and stretches of tropical undergrowth far more impenetrable than any true jungle. Scattered here and there among the bogs were islands, solid ground where plantations raised kevla, blueleaf, and garlbean as well as bananas, sugarcane, cotton, and grovacas. Further into the swamps were clearings for rice, rubber, and jute. High along the basin slopes, the steep-sided jungle ridge called Basin Rim, there were plantations that grew coffee and cacao.

Despite the war, the Dracos had attempted to keep up the flow of the world's lifeblood of commerce. Verthandi's puppet government in Regis continued to collect taxes in the form of a percentage of each harvest, and Drop-

Ships loaded with jute, rubber, garlbean, cotton, or blue-leaf periodically roared skyward from the prairie north of Regis to freighters waiting at the system's jump points. The image of trade and a productive economy was largely show by this time, however. All across Verthandi, many abandoned plantations had fallen into rot and ruin, while villagers went to war against one another. Like all revolutions, the war on Verthandi was as much a civil war of neighbor against neighbor as it was a revolt against foreign masters.

Grayson had learned or guessed much of this from conversations with Erudin on the voyage from Galatea. He learned more in the night-long march through the jungle, speaking with Tollen Brasednewic on a short-range, directional microwave com circuit that allowed them to question one another without alerting possible eavesdroppers on the mountain ridges above. He was, therefore, somewhat prepared for it when the rebel hovercraft led the mercenary 'Mechs and hover transports across a shallow stream and into the village.

Fox Island was a large and fertile wedge of solid ground lying at the confluence of a pair of rivers flowing from the foot of the Bluesward Plateau. The Ericksson family had owned and operated the Fox Island Plantation since the world was first colonized by Terrans of Scandinavian descent, over six hundred years before. Gunnar Ericksson was clan head and owner now, and his land-hold was a fair-sized village tucked away in the verdant blue-green of the jungle-shrouded island.

Everywhere, knots of people busied themselves un-crating supplies or disassembling machinery. The knocking of hammers could be heard farther back among the trees where a new warehouse was being hastily constructed. High in a treetop, a pair of rebel troops stood on a narrow camouflaged platform, TK assault rifles cradled in their arms. Not that the rifle or the lookouts would be of much use in a sudden airstrike, but the discipline was necessary and the routine of military duties comforting. Indeed, the whole camp had a reassuringly professional but relaxed atmosphere. Erudin reminded Grayson that these rebels had been fighting Kurita soldiers and the troops of the Kurita puppet government on

Verthandi for nearly ten years, and those who had survived this long were very good at what they did.

They fought to keep their world from dying, for the Draconis Combine was systematically stripping the world bare. The government DropShips that ferried goods skyward were carrying them to freighters bound for Luthien and other worlds of the Combine. When the ships returned, they brought back, not machine parts or automated equipment, but Kurita soldiers and BattleMechs. Propaganda had it that the legitimate Verthandian government had "hired" these as protection from attack by the Lyran Commonwealth or the rebel bandits who skulked in the forests of the Silvan Basin.

The existence of the rebel base fascinated Grayson. According to Tollen, Kurita satellite photos of the area revealed only workers in the Fox Island fields, with no unusual activity among the countless clearings and inhabited areas that dotted the island. In fact, those workers were rebel soldiers. On those infrequent days when the skies were clear, however, most of the rebels went indoors or underground to avoid detection by the enemy's spy satellites. When officials from the puppet Verthandian government arrived to assess taxes or to investigate rumors of armed men or jungle-based smugglers, they saw nothing out of the ordinary. Or at least, so far they hadn't.

As Grayson brought his *Shadow Hawk* to a halt in the broad clearing in front of a long, low mansion with a sweeping, roofed veranda, rebel soldiers and technicians gathered to watch the arrival of the six mercenary BattleMechs. It was still raining, though the high winds and lightning of the night before had fallen off. Despite the weather, the rebels' work went on. They seemed to be raising a new building, with the help of a *Wasp* and a pair of civilian 'Mechs of unfamiliar design. Here, too, the rebels made the best use possible of chance clouds and rain. Judging by the progress on the building, the structure would be up and well-camouflaged by the time the sun shone into the village clearing again.

The members of the Verthandian Revolutionary Council met Grayson as he descended from the ladder of his 'Mech. Devic Erudin was there, looking far fresher than Grayson felt after his trek through the jungle. For the first

time since Grayson had known the man, Erudin was
smiling broadly as he introduced the other members of
Verthandi's Revolutionary Council.

Gunnar Ericksson seemed to be the group's leader.
Though there was no indication of relative rank, Grayson
sensed the others deferring to him. With his prematurely
white hair, he had the bearing of a man born to his world's
aristocracy. As the village, the plantation, and the island
were all his, Grayson gathered that he spent much of his
time playing the Loyalist landowner who paid his taxes
and who maintained a small, private army on his own
plantation to guarantee the loyalty of those who lived
there. In reality, his island had become the headquarters
for the largest rebel army in the region, for reasons geo-
logical as well as political. The grip of his handshake
was strong, and when Grayson admitted he'd heard much
about the man, Ericksson's laughter was hearty and gen-
uine.

James "Jungle Jim" Thorvald was another descendant
of Verthandi's Norse settlers. Tall, blond, and broad, his
politican's smile had won him a seat on the Council of
Academicians before the coming of Kurita's legions.
Outlawed for anti-Combine agitation after the New Order
was proclaimed, he had fled to the jungle plantation.
When Kurita forces levelled Thorvaldfast and poisoned
the water, he had became General Thorvald. He vanished
into the Silvan Basin, emerging only to raid Kurita camps
for food and supplies, and eventually gathering an army
in the lowland regions north of the Bluesward. Fox Island
became his alternate headquarters, the storehouses and
barracks on the northern fields his army's secret camp.

The tall and lovely Carlotta Helgameyer was scarcely
more than a girl, but one of those rare individuals able
to convey an air of aristocratic elegance while clad in
grease-stained Tech coveralls or camouflage fatigues. She
was, in fact, on the academic staff at Regis and still
maintained her teaching post there. She explained that
the Kurita masters commanded that life go on as it always
had to foster the illusion that life *was* normal now, that
the rebels were nothing but misguided bandits, and that
happier memories of self-government were the warped
maunderings of ungrateful malcontents. Academician
Helgameyer was the rebel alliance's link with rebel

groups within the city of Regis itself. There were, she assured Grayson, hundreds, perhaps thousands, of brave men and women within the walls of the University, only waiting for the chance to join the uprising that would drive the Kurita conqueror off Verthandi forever.

Doctor Karl Olssen was from a plantation village further to the east, in the Vrieshaven District, and represented one of the largest and best-organized of the rebel bands on the planet. He said little but admitted to Grayson that his own son was among those whom the mercenaries were expected to train.

Grayson already knew much about Devic Erudin. Born and raised in the city of Vyorness several hundred kilometers west of Regis, he had been elected by his fellow rebels to represent them when the Revolutionary Council was formed. Quiet and retiring to the point of timidity, he resembled nothing so much as an owlish university professor. Though he might not resemble a rebel leader, Grayson knew that Erudin was the one who had volunteered to board a DropShip under the guns of Kurita troops and then to take passage on a freighter to another world where he could find and hire mercenaries. It had been Erudin entrusted with vanadium stolen from Kurita convoys to buy supplies the rebellion needed, and Erudin who had found and hired the mercenaries needed to forge an army capable of fighting against Kurita 'Mechs. Grayson found himself admiring Devic Erudin more than any of the other Verthandians he had met so far.

Sitting with the five leaders, drinking the bitter local coffee and rich Verthandian tea in the library of the Ericksson mansion, he realized that this was a revolt of the world's aristocrats. With the possible exception of Erudin, every one of these rebel leaders were members of what Brasednewic referred to as the "Old Families," descendants of the Scandanavian settlers who had come to Verthandi six centuries before. Grayson had learned earlier that Brasednewic's family had arrived two centuries later, emigrants fleeing the devastations of the Succession Wars on planets deeper within the Inner Sphere. There was a subtle tension between the Old Families and the late-comers, the ones still referred to by people of Scandanavian heritage as "refugees". Private animosities and feuds had been set aside for the duration of the revolution, or so it was claimed. Grayson wondered how long this state of affairs could last.

"We certainly appreciate your coming here to Verthandi, Captain," Ericksson said to him by way of welcome. The others nodded agreement, but the atmosphere remained reserved, slightly formal. A copy of the contract between the Council and the Gray Death lay unmentioned on the elegant white cloth that covered the table where they sat. Grayson's eyes widened slightly when he saw that a small, flat plastic case lay beside the contract printout, a case with the lone, glowing red eye of a power indicator light at one end. It was a pocket transcriber, and it was recording their conversation.

So, he thought. *This is for the record, just in case there's a dispute later, and we must go before the bonding authority. These folks are cautious.*

Ericksson continued, smiling. "We have long recognized the need for . . . for outside help in our struggle against the Combine."

"We'll do what we can, sir," Grayson replied, then gestured at the printout on the table. "Our contract specifies that we are to form a training cadre and drill your people in the fine points of anti-Mech warfare. I gather, too, that you have a small nucleus of BattleMechs and want our help training pilots."

"Precisely," said Helgameyer. "We have a large army, weapons, and the support of most of the people. But without special training and equipment, soldiers are no use at all against BattleMechs."

"It's the training more than the equipment, ma'am," Grayson said. "We'll do what we can for you."

"There is one small point," Olssen said, but he seemed nervous, ill at ease. His eyes strayed to the recorder.

"Yes, sir?"

"Well, a couple of points, actually."

"Yes?"

"One is the matter of command. Another is your participation in combat here."

Ah! Grayson thought. *So that's it!*

"There should be no problem there," Grayson said, his voice mild. "The contract specifically places my unit under the direct command of your Council. In short, you give the orders, and we obey. At least so far as those orders don't put my own command unnecessarily at risk.''

"That's just it," Carlotta said. "Your actions upon landing at Hunter's Cape have already put your command at risk. Captain, we did not hire you to engage in battle with the enemy!''

"Eh?''

"Citizen Erudin has explained the terms of the contract he worked out with you," Ericksson said. "To be frank, we cannot afford to pay for your participation in combat.''

"I understand that, of course," Grayson said. "We also have an obligation to defend ourselves.''

"When the enemy ships landed," Olssen said, "you could have slipped away into the jungle. Kurita forces rarely track our people far under the forest canopy.''

"That's fine . . . for your people. We had certain equipment that had to be off-loaded, including the military supplies your agents purchased offworld. I also had to see to the safety of the DropShip.'' He did not add that the *Phobos* was by now well on its way to Ostafjord. He wondered if he should also caution Brasednewic not to mention the fact. The strain in Grayson's new relationship with these people was a tangible presence in the room, and that strain bred distrust. "We couldn't let all of that to fall into the enemy's hands.''

Thorvald spoke for the first time. "So long as you understand, merc. If your people get killed and your 'Mechs get shot up, we're not paying your bill. That's for the record!''

"'Understood," Grayson said, keeping his voice carefully neutral. "That's our responsibility. I do hope your . . . hospitality extends to your 'Mech maintenance facilities and repair shops. We took some damage at Hunter's Cape, and—''

"And you expect us to make it good?" Thorvald was openly hostile.

"The contract specifies 'routine resupply and maintenance'.''

"*Routine,* Captain, *routine.*'' Helgameyer looked from one face to another of those gathered around the table. "We are not unreasonable, Captain Carlyle, and certainly you are welcome to use our facilities. But we do want it clear from the start—'' her eyes indicated the recorder ''—for the record, Captain, that we have brought you here to train our people, not to fight for us.''

''That is clearly understood, Citizen Helgameyer.''

Thorvald appeared mollified, but was still gruff. ''We can't expect *offworlders* to understand our struggle. We fight for freedom, not money.''

That again. There was no point in arguing. ''I understand, General. But I must make it clear, *for the record,* that the Gray Death Legion will defend itself in any way that I, its commander, deem necessary. If that means we take on the whole Kurita army, we'll do it.'' He spread his hands. ''After all, it's not as if you hired yourself an army to fight your revolution for you. Half a dozen 'Mechs and less than a hundred men and women can do a splendid job training your cadre, but we would look pretty foolish taking on the entire Kurita garrison. I may be a mercenary . . . but I'm *not* crazy!''

Thorvald did not look convinced by that final statement, but the others smiled and seemed to relax a bit.

''Well, now that *that's* out of the way,'' Ericksson said, ''let me extend to you and your people the hospitality of my plantation. If there's anything we can do.''

''Thank you, Citizen. I have to see to my people, and you'd also better show us where to park our 'Mechs out of sight. I don't imagine you'd care to have a Kurita recon satellite scan show them sitting on your front porch!''

Ericksson nodded. ''Quite right. There's nothing to fear, however. I'll have some of my people lead you around to the Caves.''

''The Caves?''

He smiled. ''At the north end of Fox Island. You have to understand that the polar depression we call the Silvan Basin is the remnant of an ancient collision of a massive asteroid with our world perhaps ten, maybe hundreds of thousands of years ago. The Basin Rim cliffs are the rim of the crater.

''The impact gouged out the crater, and turned the floor molten. Later, as the molten rock cooled, cracks developed. Some of those cracks became the paths for streams and rivers running down from the cliffs. Vast cave systems were opened up, and one of the largest lies beneath this island. The first Scandanavian colonists to Verthandi found them, and discovered that they would provide a convenient source for all the heavy and industrial metals they could use. It seems that the asteroid had concentrated various metals up close to the surface, within easy reach.

"My grandfather founded Verthandi's largest Agro-Mech company, and he started it here in the Fox Island caves, where shelter was free and various metals easy to obtain and smelt. Most of the forges, casting equipment, and the big 'Mech rigs and cradles are still there, too big to move and too useful to junk. The main manufacturing center is in Regis now, but there is a sizable 'Mech facility still in operation on, or rather under, the island. Of course, we've seen to it that records of its existence 'vanished' in a tragic fire, just about the time the Combine moved in. This is the primary facility for all of the rebellion's 'Mechs and heavy machinery now. There are facilities there that your people can use as a barracks, and I assure you that your 'Mechs will be well hidden."

"Sounds ideal," Grayson said, fascinated by the description.

"I doubt that we could have kept our operation secret as long as we have without the Caves. The concentration of metal ores in the surrounding rocks helps screen us from enemy spy satellites and instrument probes."

"Well, that being the case, there's only one thing more I need."

"And that is?"

"About twenty hours of sleep. I've been on my feet . . . or on my 'Mech's feet, ever since I got to Verthandi, and that was about this time yesterday. I can't even remember how long it's been since we pushed past the Kurita blockade that I've had more than a catnap. If you'll have someone show us to those quarters, Citizens, I think my people and I are due for some down-time."

13

The Verthandi BattleMech training program began early the next morning.

Ericksson had not exaggerated the size and complexity of the Fox Island caverns. Their opening was a cathedral-sized gap in the face of a sheer, gray cliff. Grayson could see that the area at the bottom of the cliff had once been paved. Patches of ferrocrete still showed beneath a riot of moss, ferns, and exuberant jungle growth, and empty, overgrown stone buildings still squatted under mats of the omnipresent tropical vegetation. The cave opening itself was festooned with blue-green vines and hanging streamers. What's more, the entrance was so tall and narrow that even a long-angle satellite photo taken on a cloudless day would show the opening as no more than a shadowed fold in the face of the limestone bluff.

Once he was inside, the impression of a remote and untouched jungle cave was instantly dispelled. The ceiling rose from the smooth, sandy floor of the cave in a vault fifty meters high. Fluoros were strung across the empty space, casting harsh pools of light everywhere, and the far wall opened into numerous corridors that led to the bowels of the island. Everywhere were grim-faced men and women in combat fatigues repairing equipment, going through the motions of weapons firing and reloading drills, cleaning weapons, hauling crates and boxes of supplies, or walking sentry.

Stored about the outer cavern's walls was a treasure trove of tools and electronic equipment. The bulky apparatus for calibrating 'Mech actuators and feedback sensors was there, as was a Descartes MkXXI computer, ideal for programming 'Mech on-board systems. When

Grayson recognized the squat, gray shapes of a pair of 'Mech simulators against one wall, he felt a pang of nostalgia. It had been in such semiportable, computer-moderated 'Mech simulators that he had received his own BattleMech training.

Nearby, a rebel *Stinger* occupied a 'Mech repair cradle. Straddling it was a cross-braced mobile power crane that held a two-ton chunk of composite armor plate suspended above the 'Mech's exposed torso circuitry with effortless ease. Rebel Techs and astechs climbed the crude scaffolding and webwork that surrounded the 'Mech. The arc-glare of a welding torch danced at the *Stinger*'s head, showering white sparks. Tomlinson, Grayson's Tech, and Karellan, the Legion's senior Tech, had both already assured him that they would be able to repair the damage to his *Shadow Hawk*'s autocannon as well as the antennae on the *Rifleman*. Indeed, here was everything needed to service, repair, and maintain the unit's 'Mechs.

Much of the equipment was of commercial manufacture. Grayson, was not surprised to learn that the biggest industry on Verthandi was Ericksson-Agro, a respected manufacturer of AgroMechs for use on farms and plantations. The treasure cache under the Ericksson landhold had been where Olaf Ericksson, Ericksson's great-grandfather, had launched himself on the path to financial success at the head of the local AgroMech manufacturing empire. He could also see the ores Ericksson had described. Rock formations in walls and the distant ceiling threw back a metallic glint. It was easy to see how a cave system such as this could have fueled the creation of Ericksson-Agro.

There were AgroMechs within the caves, too, fourteen of them. Most were outfitted with jury-rigged machine guns and autocannons that would be next to useless against BattleMechs, but effective enough against troops and light vehicles. Eight of them were vast, four-legged machines that Ericksson called LoggerMechs, 60-ton, boxcar-shaped monsters designed to cut and drag timber in Verthandi's jungle logging camps.

And there were BattleMechs as well, two full lances of them. Besides the *Stinger* in the repair brace, there was a 55-ton *Dervish*, a pair of *Phoenix Hawk*s, a battle-worn, 70-ton *Warhammer,* two *Wasps,* and a *Locust.* They bore various numbers, emblems, and camouflage paint schemes. Ericksson had explained that a few were Kurita machines, brought in by former Loyalist MechWarriors who had had enough of their Kurita masters. The rest, including the *Warhammer,* had belonged to the handful of men and women of the planet's Defense Militia in the days before the Kurita forces came. General Thorvald himself had been a MechWarrior as well as a popular member of the Council of Academicians. The *Warhammer* was Thorvald's own personal 'Mech, an heirloom of Scandanavian warrior ancestors from the days of the Star League.

With six of the seven Gray Death BattleMechs now present, the great, silent metal machines dominated the cavern.

"Yes, we've been able to assemble and hide everything we need for quite a nice little army here," Ericksson said as he led Grayson into the cave. "The computers and electronics are left over from great-granddad's day, when he started building and repairing AgroMechs for the plantations around here. And there's room enough to hide these 'Mechs and the whole rebel army." He stopped and fixed Grayson with a penetrating, appraising look. "We've done well for ourselves without outside help," he said. "But we can't fight BattleMechs on our own. With the right training, we can take on Nagumo's whole army, and win! That's why we need you and your people."

The training itself was far more involved than Ericksson's statement made it sound. It was after that conversation in the caverns that Grayson met the Free Verthandi Rangers, the people his unit was supposed to train. Like most rebel armies, this one was a mixed lot. There were a few grizzled veterans from the rebel field army who had volunteered to learn how to fight 'Mechs. Most, however, were fresh-faced and idealistic young men and women, some no more than twelve or thirteen standard years of age. Harriman Olssen, son of the rebel Council's Olssen, was all of fifteen.

Grayson had been the son of the commander of an independent BattleMech mercenary company, and his earliest memories were of BattleMechs and the special men and women who piloted them. He had been only ten when he'd been formally inducted into Carlyle's Commandos from the household of family members, technicians, and specialists who formed the body behind the regiment's fighting head. For ten years after that he had studied, worked, fought, and sweated under the tutelage of Weapons Master Kai Griffith and others, honing mind, body, and reactions into the blend of skills a Mech-Warrior needed. He had trained his body hard, sharpened his mind. Mental disciplines akin to those of the ancient martial arts had taught him to become one with his weapons, whether they were bare hands, laser, or BattleMech, allowing him to bring mind and body into subtle union. He had still been a MechWarrior Apprentice when disaster fell. On Trellwan, his father had been killed, the Commandos scattered, and Grayson himself had been stranded on an enemy-garrisoned world because everyone thought he was dead.

Not every unit went to the same lengths to train their prospective MechWarriors. Many used some variant of a military academy, a series of courses lasting between three and six standard years. Yet it was true that the basic skills necessary for maneuvering a BattleMech in combat could be mastered in a few weeks of intensive training. Entire 'Mech armies had been fielded by young pilots who barely knew how to trigger their weapons. Needless to say, the battle records of such green armies were not impressive, save in the length of their casualty lists. Yet Verthandi's Revolutionary Council wanted the Gray Death to prepare just such an army, a small one, for slaughter.

Grayson was bound by the word of his contract. Here in the Caves, he was supposed to teach this gang of mostly boys and girls the art of BattleMech warfare. For the first time, he seriously regretted ever having signed that contract.

At sea, the storm continued, lashing at the jury-rigged *Phobos*. Winds and rain threatened to nudge her yawing, pitching, twenty-degree list into the final lurch to the bottom. Ilse Martinez sat at the controls, watching seasickness overtake one of her engineering Techs on the canted deck. She averted her eyes at the last moment to study the pressure gauges for the hot water boilers that the Caledonian had helped design and wire, all the while cursing unintelligibly. With the drunken stagger of the ship and the mingled stinks of fear and vomit assaulting her senses, her own stomach was none too steady at the moment.

Steam pressure was still holding as throbbing pumps gulped in sea water and funneled it past the *Phobos*'s drive reactor. Steam and hot water continued to thrust the DropShip unsteadily through the foaming sea. At times, they seemed to be barely making way, but they *were* moving. As long as the storm lasted, they were also safe from hostile, prying eyes.

She muttered something vicious.

"Ma'am?" The sick Tech looked up, his face pale and drawn, his arm wedged against a support beam to steady himself against the ship's motion.

"Nothing, Groton. Nothing. Remind me to order an all-hands evolution when we make port. This ship stinks, and we're going to have a scrub-down, fore and aft!"

Groton looked, if possible, more miserable than before. "Aye, Captain."

She checked the repeater screen, which showed a computer-generated map of the Azure Sea and the point of light plotted on it by the ship's inertial tracking system.

"God help me," she added, more to herself than to the Tech. "If we make it, I won't know whether to curse that bastard Carlyle for being a genius, or curse myself for following him into this mess!"

"I don't care what you've been told or taught, a BattleMech is not invincible!"

Sergeant Ramage paced a narrow track in front of the twenty-odd Ranger trainees gathered to hear his lecture. They were seated on the sandy floor of the cave entrance. At their backs, the sky was overcast, but showed signs of revealing the afternoon sun. The Order of the Day was that 'Mechs and large concentrations of people were to remain under cover. Looming behind Ramage was the bulk of a *Stinger,* and his lanky frame reached barely halfway up the *Stinger*'s armored leg to its knee.

Grayson leaned back against the slick wetness of a boulder at the cave entrance, folded his arms, and listened closely to Ramage's performance. Grayson himself had trained Ramage. The career infantry NCO had formerly been a sergeant in the planetary defense militia on Trellwan until Grayson had taught combat tactics to him and the other Trellwanese. Ramage was doing a good job, Grayson decided. He was a lively instructor, and his voice and gestures communicated that enthusiasm. He'd already established a rapport with his students.

Grayson could find no fault with the Verthandians' willingness, determination, or courage, either, which had been put to many a grueling test in the last three weeks. The students had been organized into lances, with one Gray Death veteran trooper from the combat platoon acting as lance corporal to three Verthandians. Company, platoon, and battalion command elements were formed of mixtures of mercenaries and natives, for the Verthandians would have to fight under their own officers when the time came, not under the offworlders. Recruit officers learned side by side with their enlisted counterparts.

The Gray Death's technical platoon was involved as well. Sergeant Karellan was in charge of organizing the Verthandian Techs into military technical squads. Fortunately, the Verthandians were well-trained in a wide range of mechanical and technical skills. The Legion would definitely not lack repair and maintenance personnel.

Grayson's big worry was the combat recruits. There were two separate groups of them. One consisted of those who knew how to pilot 'Mechs and now needed to learn how to do so in combat. That group was small and select; Grayson had met all of its members and given several lectures, as had all the Legion's MechWarriors. They were an eager group. Several among them, including tall, rangy Collin Dace and Rolf Montido, were experienced combat warriors. Others, like Vikki Traxen, Nadine Cheka, Olin Sonovarro, and Carlin Adams, had only recently learned how to pilot a 'Mech and had never been in combat at all.

Ramage had taken the second group in hand as his personal charges. They were to be the nucleus of the Verthandian ground forces, trained in anti-'Mech commando tactics and transformed into an elite force. Though far larger than the first group, many had already dropped out, choosing to remain instead in the regular rebel army. Enough remained that Ramage had subdivided them so that some were at practice while he gave demonstrations to others.

The class that Grayson was observing happened to be composed entirely of young people, with none older than nineteen standard years, and some as young as thirteen. That morning had seen them wading, crawling, swinging, and mostly running through the obstacle course Ramage had set up outside the cave, followed by several hours of the digging that Ramage had promised. After a hastily gobbled midday meal, now was the time for lessons of a more academic nature.

Ramage stopped in mid-pace and fixed a teenage girl with his fire-bright eyes. When he suddenly pointed at her, she gasped. "You!" he said intently. "You, by yourself, could bring down the biggest big game of all, ninety tons of fighting steel! If you keep your heads, *you* can be the masters of a battlefield, not . . ." He paused to jerk his thumb over his shoulder at the *Stinger* behind them. "Not these big lummoxes!"

He feigned surprise. "You don't believe me? O.K., watch this."

Ramage walked across the cave floor to a pile of supplies and crates close to where Grayson was standing. He picked up a canvas bag the size of a large travel case, winked gravely at Grayson, then returned to his lecture position in front of the *Stinger*. The bag itself was festooned with slender hooks of black wire, and had a length of cable capped by a plastic cylinder with a pull ring dangling from it.

"This," he said, "is a satchel charge. It contains four two-kilo blocks of C-90 plastique, four detonators, and a fuse igniter with a six-second delay. Now, pay attention, because I'm only going to do this once." He touched his throat mike. "Jaleg? Move out!"

The audience heard no reply because Ramage was wearing an ear speaker, but the *Stinger* looming behind him abruptly stirred, shifted, then spun to the right. The massive right foot came up off the ground, swinging forward.

Ramage shouted to be heard against the creak-rumble

of joint flanges and internal driver rods. "Imagine that I've been hiding in the bushes here!"

The *Stinger*'s right foot came down in minor chords of thunder. Its left foot shifted, swung forward.

Ramage was already moving, running toward the 'Mech's right foot with the satchel charge trailing by its strap. He planted one foot on the crevice between two joints in the 'Mech's ankle armor, swung his next foot onto the top of the 'Mech's foot. The 'Mech's right foot was moving again now, and Ramage used the assist from the mechanical foot's motion to propel him up the front of the 'Mech's leg. His feet and left hand found purchase on armor joints and the narrow throat of a heat sink orifice. His other hand was bringing the satchel charge up and around in a side arm swing. Catapulted by the strap, the charge hurtled at the *Stinger*'s knee joint just as a gap opened between the armor plates of knee and upper leg, where the machines thigh and lower leg protective flanges rode over the main knee bearing.

The gap was small, too small to admit so large an object as the satchel. Several of the satchel's wire hooks caught on the joint's moving parts, meshing with them as the joint closed with the 'Mech's forward motion. The rest of the bag snagged on the *Stinger*'s knee and hung there. Ramage grabbed the ring dangling from the cable and jumped. The ring came free in his hand, leaving a wisp of smoke trailing from the bag as the *Stinger* continued its stride. Ramage landed in the sand with an acrobatic roll and was up on his feet and running back toward the demonstration area without a pause. Behind him, there was a sharp crack, and white smoke gushed from the satchel on the BattleMech's leg.

The *Stinger* came to a halt. A moment later, the upper hatch on the 'Mech's head swung open, and Jaleg Yorulis squeezed his torso up out of the tiny cockpit. "I think I'm dead!" he called, and the trainees laughed and applauded.

"That," Ramage said, dusting sand from his khakis, "is called kneecapping. Unfortunately, my commanding officer won't let me use *real* C-90 on our own 'Mechs because he says it's too hard to clean up the mess." He rolled his eyes at Grayson and was rewarded by more laughter.

"If that had been real plastique on real 'Mech," he continued, "I guarantee you that that 'Mech would have been hurting bad when the explosives went off. At the least, it would have been limping. With luck, I could have torn its leg off at the knee and sent the whole critter toppling to the ground, crippled and useless. If I'd wanted to substitute a thermite detonator and a couple of plastic bags filled with CSC or just plain gasoline and oil, I could have engulfed the whole lower torso of the 'Mech in a fireball. Not as effective as an inferno round, of course, but I promise you that 'Mech's going to be having heat problems, right about then.

"Now don't think what I did is easy! Every 'Mech has its own individual weak points. What I just did wouldn't have any effect at all on a *Marauder*. Their legs are too well-armored. But for some 'Mechs with weak knees— *Stingers* and *Wasps*, for instance—this tactic can be deadly. *Commandos*, especially, are good targets for kneecapping. They've got a gap between thigh and knee where you could stuff the whole satchel, without using the hooks! Almost always, you can cripple 'em. Yes . . . question?"

The girl he'd pointed at earlier stood among the other trainees, her slim arms behind her back. "But how are you supposed to get that close, sir? You said you were hiding in a bush, but wouldn't the 'Mech see you?"

"You have no idea just how hard it is to see anything when you're buttoned up inside. Hell, it's hard enough seeing other 'Mechs, much less people! Yes, they have IR sensors and all-round vision scanners. Some also have motion sensors and computer scanner interlock, but usually a BattleMech is looking for other 'Mechs or something big enough to kill him, like fighters. He's probably too busy to watch for lone infantrymen. Even if he sees somebody crouching in the bushes, nine times out of ten, he's going to discount the guy as harmless. If he doesn't, the secret is to work in teams. If the 'Mech goes after you, you run and decoy the 'Mech while your buddy gets him from the rear. You just hope your buddy can run as fast as you do right about then!"

There was more laughter at that. "O.K., take ten," Ramage told them. He skirted the group as it started to break up and walked over to Grayson.

"Sounds like you're having a good time," Grayson told him.

Ramage looked grim. "Look, Captain, can I level with you?"

"Of course."

"This is all one malfin' big screw-up. You realize that, don't you?"

Grayson closed his eyes. He'd seen this coming for the past several days. "What do you mean, Sarge?"

"Dammit, Captain, we're grooming these . . . these kids for a slaughter! How can we possibly train them to hold their own in a fight against Kurita's 'Mechs in a few short weeks?"

"Now Sergeant . . ."

"Did you hear me back there? The whole point was to tell them how to do it . . . to let them know they *could* do it. But good God, if I told them the whole truth, they'd *know* better than to go chasing after enemy 'Mechs on the battlefield!"

"Some of them have been doing just that. They're in the middle of this war, too. And they volunteered."

"Of course, they volunteered . . . when their friends and older brothers and sisters did! God help me, they're swallowing everything I feed them. Take on a 'Mech with a satchel charge? Sure, it's been done. But they don't know how often some hotshot 'Mech pilot *does* see someone hiding in a bush and goes ahead and steps on the guy because he just might be carrying an inferno launcher, satchel charge, or a portable SRM—or just for the hell of it!"

"Sounded like you were giving them a pretty encouraging lecture, just the same."

"God help me. *God* help me! I'm giving them the same lecture you gave me back on Trellwan, and I'm sure you heard it from your instructors back when you were in training. Sure, an ordinary guy can take on a BattleMech with his bare hands and a few kilos of plastic explosive . . . but damn it all! The one guy that makes it is going to do it over the bodies of how many of his buddies? These kids don't know what war is like! We'll fill their heads with glorious notions of bringing down Battle-Mechs, and they'll try. But most of them are going to end up very dead!"

Grayson looked past Ramage toward the students, who had gathered around the *Stinger*'s foot to watch Jaleg pull the canvas bag free of the knee joint, laughing and shouting suggestions to the 'dead' MechWarrior miraculously come back to life.

Beyond the *Stinger* and its audience, under the glare of overhead fluoros, Grayson could make out Lori Kalmar's slender form, dwarfed by the dinosaur bulk of a green-painted LoggerMech. At this distance, he could not hear her over the dull roar of machinery echoing through the cave, but the animated movement of her arms suggested she was presenting the 'Mech's pilot with a royal dressing down. The 'Mech's right forefoot was locked behind its left forefoot, and the apprentice seemed to be having trouble untangling them. Still deeper into the cave, a boiler-room crash marked a 'Mech-to-'Mech practice confrontation as Debrowski sparred in his *Wasp* with one of the Verthandi Rangers' *Stinger*s. The *Stinger* was flat on its back, looking up at the mercenary 'Mech.

"You're right," Grayson said finally. "Of course you're right. I agree with you, but so help me, I don't know how to answer it yet. I'm working on it, but I don't know what we can do that'll keep us from murdering these kids . . . and satisfy the clients, too."

"*Damn* the clients!"

"Damn it *all*, Ramage, do *you* think I'm doing this for the money, too? It happens there's this small matter of our own survival, Sarge. Like whether we're ever going to get off this jungle rock!"

He looked away, beyond the mouth of the cave and into the jungle beyond. He was breathing hard, and felt his hands knotted at his sides. It nagged at him that he'd not yet heard from the *Phobos,* though the Revolutionary Council had assured him that their people would relay word as soon as anything was known. If the DropShip had made it to a safe harbor, it was going to take months of work—not to mention considerable stores of repair parts and a long stay in a drydock repair facility—before she would fly again. And the *Phobos* was still their only ticket off Verthandi, providing her repairs could be completed. It was a vicious circle, because *that* would not be possible until the war was won.

"If we don't find a way to help these people win their

war,'' Grayson added, ''Governor General Nagumo is going to find us, and it'll be our lives *and* theirs.''

''You're sayin' better them than us?''

''No! It's not them or us, it's them *and* us! If we don't figure something out, Nagumo is going to come for all of us pretty damn quick, even if he has to uproot this jungle tree by tree to do it. I just don't know what to do about it, yet.''

Ramage shook his head. ''I've read the contract, too, Captain, and I'll be damned if I can see a way out. Maybe we should turn the army on the rebel command! They might be able to take them!'' He raised his hands, as if fending Grayson off. ''All right, I'll keep feeding them the lessons. But you'd better find some way to keep them off the field for another three or four years, because as of now, any Kurita 'Mech would grind them up like so much raw meat.''

14

Governor General Nagumo hitched one thigh over the corner of his desk, leaned back with his arms folded across his unadorned black jacket, and smiled. The young woman seated before him cast glances nervously about the room, taking in the spartan furnishings, the azelwood desk piled high with hardcopy printouts, the floor-to-ceiling windows looking down onto the Regis University central campus. She had soft, short-cropped brown hair, and her eyes were cold and distant.

"So, Miss Klein," Nagumo said. "May I call you Sue Ellen? Good. How are you settling in at the barracks?"

"Fine, my Lord," she said. She brushed nervously at the sleeve of her Kurita-issue uniform tunic. "Everything is . . . fine."

"Good, very good." He waved toward a collection of bottles and glasses on a table along one wall. "Would you care for a drink?"

She shook her head. Puzzlement, a hint of worry showed on her face. "No, thank you, Lord."

"As you wish. Well, I suppose you're wondering why I wanted to see you."

She nodded, still refusing to return his gaze. "The Governor General cannot be in the habit of talking to every mercenary Aero-Space Fighter pilot in his command, Lord. Or every . . . prisoner."

"Well, girl, you are a very special case. You must realize that, yes?"

She nodded again.

He continued. "You signed on with this new mercenary unit. The Gray Death Legion, you called it? Yes,

and while running our blockade, you fought bravely but—
for some reason—your comrades abandoned you.''

She leaned back slightly in her chair, her knuckles
showing white against the chair's carved wooden arms.
''There's no mystery there, Lord. If my . . . my comrades had stopped to pick me up, they would have had to
fight the *Leopard* that was closing on them. They didn't
have the armor or firepower to win such an engagement.
They were forced to abandon me and . . . and my wingman, to escape into Verthandi's atmosphere.'' Pain and
a touch of fear crossed her face. ''Lord, I went over all
of this with your interrogators weeks ago!''

''Yes, well, I'm terribly sorry for what you've had to
go through. Poor girl! The commander of the *Subotai*
was quite right to pick you up when she found you in
Verthandi-orbit, but Admiral Kodo should have informed
me that he had you and not turned such a . . . prize over
to his interrogation teams. It was a week before I knew
that my people held you, and another week before the
whole story was known and I could order you released!
Certainly, you should have been offered the opportunity
to join us at once, rather than having to endure that blundering fool Kodo's doubtful hospitality on Verthandi-Alpha!
I promise you, Sue Ellen, that the officers responsible will
be disciplined!''

She raised her head, her chin firm. ''Thank you, Lord,
but I really am fine now. As far as your officers were
concerned, I was just another enemy prisoner. I'm not
complaining about my treatment.''

He looked at her thoughtfully. ''You are a remarkable
young lady, Sue Ellen. I wonder at the . . .'' He seemed
to grope momentarily for the word. ''I wonder at the
callousness of your commander in leaving you behind.''
He looked straight at her then, pursuing another line of
thought. ''And your comrade, the one who died. He was
dear to you, I gather.''

''Yes.'' Softly.

''You fired into the cockpit of his *Chippewa*. You followed his fighter into the atmosphere, firing into it until
it exploded.''

''Yes.'' Softer still. Her face twisted in pain. For a moment, she struggled to control it. ''He was . . . burning.
I heard him over my comlink. He couldn't eject, and he

was wounded . . . bad . . . and as he started re-entry, he was burning alive. I . . . couldn't . . . I . . . couldn't . . .''

She cried silently, barely suppressed heaves wracking her shoulders. Her face was contorted and wet, her grief an inner torture become naked. Nagumo slid off the desk and stepped alongside her, laying a hand protectively across her upper back.

Sue Ellen Klein did not realize that Nagumo had learned of her capture less than a day after the event. That, he thought with a smile, was something she need never know. The testimony of the officer who had made pick-up on her had made it clear that Klein was broken completely by the torment of having to blow her lover to oblivion. As she was already numb with grief and loss, normal interrogation techniques had not been necessary. In any case, her state of shock would probably have made interrogation useless.

Nagumo's orders to Kodo had been quite explicit: hold her, observe her, question her, but under no circumstances allow her to come to harm! Nagumo sensed that Lieutenant Sue Ellen Klein was a very special catch indeed, perhaps the key to destroying the mercenaries recently come to Verthandi.

Dr. Janson Vlade, one of the House Ricol's interrogation team psychiatric specialists, had been assigned to monitor Klein's progress in the weeks following her capture. It had been Vlade's recommendation that she was strong enough now for Nagumo to proceed with recruitment. He had briefed Nagumo carefully in what to say and do in this interview.

"That was a brave thing to do," he was saying to her now. "I know how tremendously difficult it must have been. But it shows your special strength. You could not abandon a comrade to such a horrible death. You acted as you did to spare him that fate, at such terrible cost to yourself."

"I . . . I didn't know what to do." She gulped hard a couple of times, fighting past the tears and the constriction of her throat. "There was no way to get Jeffric out. No way . . . Nothing I could do . . ."

"Your comrade fought bravely. I respect his memory."

"Th-thank you."

"I respect you as well, Lieutenant, for doing the honorable, the heroic, thing. You made a sacrifice more dear, I suspect, than giving up your own life."

"N-no. It was nothing like that, Lord." The tears threatened to return. "My Lord, I really . . . can't talk about it . . ." The tears threatened to return.

"I understand." He massaged her neck, rubbing gently. "But I wanted you to know I respect such courage. It is why we are offering you the chance to sign on with the Red Duke's household troops. Duke Hassid Ricol, my master, respects such bravery as well. We have a place for you here, Lieutenant. Laying your oath with Duke Ricol could take you far indeed. Promotion . . . Reward . . ."

"My Lord, please understand when I say . . . I don't want to go far. I just . . . I just want to forget."

"Of course. Well, you may go now. Take some time to become acquainted with your new comrades. Do you have enough money? Your quarters are adequate? Good. You'll find, I believe, that things are not as terrible within the service of House Kurita as enemy propaganda may have led you to believe. Take your time. Get to know us. I'll want to talk to you again in a week or so, after you've had time to settle in."

"My Lord, you are too kind."

"Not at all, my dear. I need people like you within my command."

"Thank you, my Lord."

He watched her leave the office and waited for some minutes after the door had closed behind her. Then he touched a key on his intercom. A man's face appeared on the comcircuit screen, a lean face, dry and sharp. The red piping of a House Ricol Spectech showed at his high-closed collar.

"Well, Vlade, your conclusions?"

"She will come over, Lord, but she is not ready yet."

"The readings?"

"We were picking up excellent readings through the chair's electrodes, yes. Let me see . . ." The man picked up a sheaf of printout paper and thumbed through it. "Your hints of promotion, of reward . . . she didn't react at all to those stimuli, Lord. I'm not even sure she heard them. Her grief is real. It is going to take her time to recover.''

"Go on."

"Ah, well . . .'' He looked at the printouts again. "There were markedly strong responses each time you brought the conversation around to her former commander, to his abandoning her and her comrade, the one she calls Jeffric, and to Jeffric's death. We can't know for certain, but I feel it very likely that this Jeffric was a lover. It is difficult to account for the depth and scope of her grief in any other way.''

"Go on."

"What particularly interested me was her response when you touched her. From what I knew of her profile, I expected her to react negatively, if at all. Instead it was positive. Quite positive.''

"Hmpf! And how do you interpret *that?*''

"She is lonely, afraid . . . a very vulnerable young woman, right now, Lord. She doesn't realize it herself, I'm sure, but she is hungry for companionship.''

Nagumo snorted. "Are you suggesting I make love to her to get the information I want? I'm getting rather old for such games, Vlade!''

"Of course, Lord, that is for you to decide, of course. I mean . . . you're certainly not too old—'' Vlade broke off, embarrassed or at least flustered.

"Never mind, Doctor. Get to the point.''

"Well, Lord, I must point out that the reaction to your touch was not necessarily a reaction to *your* touch, but only to the sense of closeness, the erotic stimulation itself. I point out that she has already opened a conversational relationship with one of the young men you assigned to her squadron.''

"Which one?''

"Captain Vincent Mills.''

"Ah, good.''

"He is one of yours, of course.''

Nagumo ignored the statement. "Is she ready to be approached yet, do you think?''

Vlade frowned. "She needs more time, Lord. Time to get her bearings, to establish a relationship with Mills or some other strong person whom she can trust. She needs to realize her loneliness after the death of her lover, and time to come to terms with what she may perceive as her own betrayal of his memory. At some point, though, her grief may become so great that she will need comfort, seek closeness with someone she perceives as a strong protector."

"How much longer?"

"A week? Two?" Vlade shrugged. "It's impossible to say. This is, after all, a young, grief-stricken woman, not a machine."

"Mmm. And if I order you to use more traditional interrogation methods?"

Vlade paused, licked his lips. "Lord, we *could* use more direct methods, certainly. But there is still considerable risk. In her present mental condition, the pain and terror of interrogation would heighten her sense of being betrayed *again*. She could be driven so deeply into shock that she would never recover. She might possibly go insane, become catatonic."

"And what I want to know might be lost forever. Or she could die before she reveals it. Very well, Doctor. I don't have *much* time, but I can wait. If we can get Klein to co-operate of her own free will, so much the better."

"Yes, Lord."

"Compile a report on the readings you took. I want this in her dossier."

"Yes, Lord."

"Dismissed."

Nagumo studied the blanked screen for a moment before turning to gaze out the window into the overcast sky above Regis. Psychiatrists were so quick to remind others that the bundles of hopes, dreams, fears, and griefs that they studied were people and not machines. *Well . . . perhaps.* But Nagumo was used to playing upon those tangled emotions in much the same way that a master MechWarrior like Kevlavic played upon the controls of his *Marauder.* It did not take Dr. Vlade and his hidden sensors and computer printouts to tell Nagumo that the Klein girl had responded to his touch. He had sensed her response, had felt her loneliness in the same instant that he'd guessed that she would not draw away from him.

Klein must know something of this Gray Death Legion that had come to Verthandi. Sometime within the next several weeks, he would learn it from her, learn how to use it against her former employer. In the meantime, he could afford to watch and wait for the rebel force's next move.

Governor General Nagumo was supremely confident of the outcome.

Hassan Khaled's *Stinger* rose dripping from the waves off the beach close by the mountain-hemmed fishing village of Westlee. It was still dark, though dawn was only moments away. It was a bad time for reconnaissance of a possibly hostile area, but there was no other choice.

The *Phobos* had made the crossing, was already within sight of this port. With the rising of Norn, the DropShip would be clearly visible from land. If there were unfriendly forces here, they would have to be neutralized first. Tollen Brasednewic's information indicated that Westlee was a haven for rebel sympathizers, and that the rare Loyalist force that came to the village never lingered, but still. . . .

He studied the screens arrayed across the tightly enclosed confines of the *Stinger*'s cockpit. The infrared scan showed a heat source, some distance off in *that* direction. Now what could that be? With rapid strides, he paced his *Stinger* up the beach, bringing it into the shelter of some ramshackle and weather-battered buildings above the tideline. The buildings would offer shelter as the day approached.

Khaled was Saurimat, an *ikwan* of the Quick Death, and that basic fact would never, could never change, though his brothers would kill him now if they met him face to face. The memory of their final parting was still dark, dark, indeed. As Saurimat, he had drilled relentlessly to understand what it meant to command, to make life and death decisions that put responsibility for the mission's success in his own hands. The Saurimat masters taught that such decisions were best made in the ice-blooded embrace of *farir kalb*, literally "empty heart". In that self-induced emotionless state, love and hate, fear and bravado receded to the point where they could not touch the warrior's mind, or his decisions.

He had been studying the young commander of the Gray Death ever since signing on with the Legion. Carlyle's passions, the turmoil of emotions he carried constantly within himself, were easy to see. And yet the idea of converting the stricken DropShip for traveling over the sea had been inspired! The gamble should have failed, and yet somehow the ship had made it. Even blinded by emotions, Carlyle possessed a gift for leadership that Khaled did not fully understand. There was much to be learned here.

Movement!

A 'Mech, a *Wasp* with Kurita markings, was approaching, only dimly seen in the half-light of the predawn. Its pilot had not yet seen him, but the machine was moving toward him with long strides. In another moment . . .

There was a crackling rattle of gunfire, sharp and crisp in the morning air. The spark of a ricochet winked against one massively armored shoulder. The *Wasp* paused, its squat turret-head rotating, seeking the source of the attack, the medium laser held rifle-like in massive, mechanical hands.

Someone was attacking the Kurita 'Mech with small arms! Though that fact told something about the political leanings of the town's population, it said little for the same people's intelligence. Or, had someone in the town seen Khaled's own emergence from the sea and known that he must be with the mercenary forces lately come to Verthandi? If so, the attack was a timely one, staged deliberately to provide him with opportunity.

Inshallah! He willed his mind and heart cold, repeating the phrase that swept him into the grip of *farir kalb.*

The heart is empty, the body a weapon, the mind and body are one.

He seized the opportunity. *The mind and body are one* . . .

The *Stinger* sprang forward, closing the range to the *Wasp* in twenty rapid strides. He dared not fire and risk slaughtering his new allies, nor could he risk alerting other Kurita forces that might be nearby. One of his *Stinger*'s arms descended in a lightning stroke that crumpled the *Wasp*'s laser from behind. His right leg swept around and up, smashing into the *Wasp*'s knee in a crushing blow that sent the enemy machine lurching to one side.

Inshallah! The mind and body are one! Allah Akbar!

Before the *Wasp* hit the ground, one of Khaled's armored fists had rocketed down, fingers knife-edged, penetrating the target 'Mech's cockpit at the weakest point. The enemy 'Mech went limp as Khaled straightened, withdrawing his *Stinger*'s hand from the shattered head. Only then did Khaled will himself to think again.

The townspeople emerged from their hiding places, weapons in hand, cheering wildly. In the harbor, the light of the early sun caught the *Phobos*'s hull in a wet and golden gleam.

====== **15** ======

Another week passed. Runners from the Azure Coast carried word to Grayson that the *Phobos* had arrived safely at Westlee. Storm and cloud cover had cloaked much of the sea passage. On the few clear nights, an ocean was a big place to hide something so small and unexpected as a DropShip. Now, Martinez had her command safely berthed, well under the sheltering lee of a massive cliff. Friendly rebel forces in the village had helped defeat the few Kurita and Loyalist troops in the area, actions that would probably be written off to random rebel activity rather than to the arrival of a damaged mercenary spaceship.

Ilse had included a scrawled message of her own for Grayson: *You were right. Damn you for being a genius. Repairs proceeding—Ilse.*

That single piece of news cheered Grayson more than he'd thought was possible. Though the legion's situation was still serious, there now existed at least a slight possibility that the DropShip could be repaired—given time, material, hard work, and decent facilities. One day, the Legion might yet escape this world. Despite the good news about the *Phobos*, other concerns were more critical than ever.

"General, in my estimation, four weeks is simply not enough time!"

"Captain, that's longer than I was at first willing to grant you. We cannot sit by doing nothing and watch the destruction of our world. The army—including the Free Verthandi Rangers—must be ready to move out in three days."

Grayson had been expecting and dreading this interview for weeks. His mission of turning a rabble of mostly youngsters into MechWarriors and support troops had become instead a bitter struggle—the struggle with himself as much as with the rebel army command. On one hand, his contract obliged him to transform these people into soldiers. That meant that the longer he had to work with them, the better their chances of survival. On the other hand, Grayson felt that it would take years to mold this motley group into soldiers ready to take on the dreaded Kurita 'Mech forces of Governor General Nagumo.

Almost since the day he had arrived at Fox Island, he had been pursuing a campaign of raising alternate possibilities but without notable success. His principal suggestion was that a campaign be begun among the citizens of Verthandi, urging them to rise en masse against their Kurita overlords. Thorvald and Ericksson assured him that the people would never move on their own without a demonstration of the rebel army's power and ability. And that 'army' was the band of youngsters the Gray Death was now attempting to train.

"Three days! General, some of those people are just kids!"

"They've got to be ready," Thorvald replied. He arched an eyebrow. "They are ready! I watched you putting the apprentices through their paces in the 'Mechs yesterday. They looked good."

"And so far they haven't fired a single shot, except in the simulators. God in heaven, General, you send those kids in against Kurita 'Mechs and you're not going to *have* an army!"

Thorvald's eyes met Grayson's disapprovingly. "Just what is it they lack?"

"Lack? Experience! Experience, and maybe five or six more years of training to learn the difference between a PPC and a hunting rifle."

"Some of the older ones have had plenty of experience, Captain."

"Sure, sniping at militia sentries and stealing cans of food! But most of them, the kids especially, have never been under fire. General, do you know what that *means?*"

"Many of these . . . these *kids* have been fighting the

Brownjackets for ten years now. Your people have been invaluable in organizing them, and now it is time to let them prove what they can do—on the field.''

"Shouldn't I be the one to judge when they're ready?"

"No, sir, you should not! I've seen what they can do. For this operation, they won't need fancy tactics like taking out enemy 'Mechs with satchel charges. What they need to know is combat organization, discipline, and confidence—all of which you've given them, Captain! I've *seen* it!"

Grayson shook his head violently. "Confidence isn't enough in the face of PPC and laser fire! They need experience!"

"What do you suggest as a means of giving them . . . experience?"

"When they're ready, I suppose we could try raiding a Government Militia depot, something lightly guarded."

Thorvald leaned back, picked up a stylus, and turned it between his fingers. After a moment, he seemed to reach a decision. "Captain, I can promise you they'll have their experience. In three days, we're opening our offensive against Nagumo. If it's successful, there will be no further need of raids or BattleMech training at all. One battle, and the campaign will be won!"

Grayson looked skeptical. "One campaign, General? And suppose the offensive *isn't* successful?"

"Captain, I wasn't going to give you details on the operation. There was no need for you to know, and always the danger that one of you might be captured and interrogated. Or even that the information could be . . . purchased, to put it bluntly."

Grayson silently clenched teeth and hands, but let the remark pass.

"I need your cooperation," Thorvald was saying. "Your forces will not be participating in the operation, of course, but we will need your help in preparing the assault, steadying the troops ahead of time, and readying the 'Mechs. I'm telling you so that I can elicit your active cooperation. Fair enough?"

"I'm listening, sir."

"Needless to say, this is classified High Secret."

"You have my word as well as my bond, General. What else can I give you?"

Thorvald sighed, opened a desk drawer, and removed a map, which he spread out before Grayson. "You've seen the topology of the area. The jungle basin. Fox Island, the Basin Rim, with the Bluesward Plateau south, and the planet's capital, Regis, here . . . about a hundred kilometers from here."

The general pulled out a second, larger map, this one a maze of streets and buildings. "This is Regis. The city sprawls out to the south from the University of Regis. You have to understand, Captain, that the University has always been the center of culture, government, even trade, here on Verthandi. A sizable population of students and teachers live in and around the Campus. These thick walls are relics of a civil war on our world four centuries ago, but they make the University a fortress in its own right.

"The Kurita invaders saw this immediately. The place is easily defended. What you must also know is that the tradition of free thought and free speech on Verthandi centers on the University. It's difficult to explain to someone from outside our culture, but suffice to say that every notable Verthandian in the arts or sciences, all our civic and religious leaders and speakers, every leading citizen of the planet was trained here. Our ruling body is called the Council of Academicians. Each has taken special graduate courses in government at the University.

"The Combine forces allowed the University to continue. To do otherwise would have been an open declaration of war. What they wanted was to absorb us quietly. With Verthandi's long-standing tradition of free thought, it wasn't that easy.

"Nagumo himself has his headquarters inside the University, somewhere in the Central Tower, and many of his troops are quartered there. Nagumo thinks to keep control of the population by maintaining his personal headquarters there.

"This is our plan. Nagumo's forces are supplemented, of course, by collaborators—calling themselves Loyalists—among the Verthandian population. They make up the militia forces. Then there're our own rebel armies, living out in the bush. The vast majority of people on Verthandi aren't Loyalists and they aren't rebels. They're just people who may not particularly like the Kurita presence on our planet but are too scared or disorganized to do anything about it.''

"That's the way it is in most wars, General.''

"True enough. We believe the University is the key to controlling the situation, Captain. If our army, including the Free Verthandi Rangers, can take and hold the University, even for just a few hours, we believe that the entire population will finally rise up against the Dracos. We'll have the entire city . . . and soon, an entire planetary population to back us. The Dracos can never manage to keep more than a handful of units on Verthandi. With the entire countryside hostile to them and supplies difficult to bring in on a long and roundabout logistical line, we believe they'll soon decide that it's just too much trouble trying to hold onto Verthandi.''

"So, you want the Rangers to take the University? Just like that?'' Grayson was picturing the walls depicted on the map as they must be in real life, meters thick, meters high, set with hardpoints armed with 'Mech-killing weapons. "They walk up and kick down the front gates?''

Thorvald smiled. "For that aspect of the operation, we will have the invaluable assistance of Citizen Ericksson. His family owns the large AgroMech industrial facility, here, next to the University. There are underground passageways between the plant and the University, some of them large enough for 'Mechs. The Ericksson family has always worked closely with University officials and provided the 'Mech electronics for various technical courses. The tunnels were built to facilitate the transfer of machines and equipment to and from the plant.

"The plan is this. At night, the entire rebel army will move by various Basin rim roads to the Bluesward and then make their way south to the city. Other rebel groups already in Regis will prepare to join us. The Verthandi Rangers will follow this route, here, masked from observers in the city by the walls of this gully. They'll move quickly across the savannah under the cover of darkness, and enter the AgroMech plant here. Ericksson and local rebels will meet them and guide them into the University.

"We have timed our approach so that we will be just about at this point—here—at 0100. At that time, a team of rebel soldiers will create a diversion within the city by setting fire to a warehouse on the south end of town. The fire should draw Draco attention away from the northern perimeter, and will also serve to dazzle the IR scanners of reconnaissance satellites if the weather happens to be clear. Code signals have been arranged so that we can alert the rebels in the city to any delay and so that they can transmit a code phrase when the fire has been set.

"The attack will strike simultaneously at militia and Combine targets throughout Regis at precisely 0145. The University garrison will be neutralized by our 'Mechs appearing suddenly behind their walls. After that, the University will become a rebel fortress, and Kurita units retreating to take cover there will be trapped and destroyed.

"The appearance of our forces will be the signal for a general rising among all Verthandians who have been afraid to join us so far. Carlotta Helgameyer has contacted each of the rebel leaders within the city and arranged it all. Nagumo, if he lives, will find himself facing an army, not of a thousand, but of a hundred thousand, even hundreds of thousands. No 'Mech regiment can hope to maintain control of an entire world against such numbers."

"That's the plan?" Grayson asked when the recitation finally ended. Thorvald nodded.

"Are you asking my opinion?"

The General nodded again.

"First off, how do you expect your Verthandi Rangers to find their way across the savannah in the dark?"

"Eh? What do you mean? You've been training them in night ops."

"Training them, yes, but training and experience are two entirely different things. And none of the mercenaries has been over that ground by day, much less at night! The Rangers'll take casualties just getting to Regis.

"Second, I've never yet known an operation that involved untrained troops to start out on time. Suppose your people are delayed and can't take advantage of the diversion in Regis? O.K., you've arranged for coded messages, but what if your people in the city get confused with their codes, or the enemy captures them and beats the codes out of them?

"Finally, General, it seems to me that you're counting too much on this supposed rising of the citizens of Regis."

Thorvald's palms came down on his desk, making a report like the crack of a gun. "That's enough, sir. This is our world and our people. I think we know our situation and capabilities better than any hireling outsider! I'll have you know that Gunnar Ericksson was a popular Academician before the Combine took over. The people love him, and his appearance at the head of a rebel army within the University walls will trigger an uprising unlike any seen in history!"

Grayson was unconvinced. "You need more than a popular leader, sir."

"And you, Carlyle, are becoming an obstructionist!"

"I beg your pardon, General. I'm trying to be a realist."

"Then be realistic by fulfilling your contractual obligations, Captain. The assault on Regis begins after sundown three days from today. The Free Verthandi Rangers have a crucial role to play in this operation. On their shoulders will ride the success of our revolution! See to it that they are informed and prepared. I might suggest, Captain," Thorvald added with a wry smile, "that you put them through some additional night maneuvers between now and then."

"And during the attack itself? Where do you want my people?"

"The Gray Death will remain in quarters here at Fox island. I see no reason to risk your men or equipment in this operation. You know already, Captain Carlyle, that we cannot afford to have you participate as combatants. The Regis assault will be strictly a Verthandian affair.

"Dismissed."

16

"**M**ove it, people, move it!" General Thorvald ground his teeth in frustration, and his fist came down on the arm of the control seat in his *Warhammer*'s cockpit.

A plaintive voice sounded in his earspeaker. "we can't move him, General!"

"Clear a way! 'I'm coming up there!"

The *Warhammer* shouldered past a *Stinger* and a *Phoenix Hawk,* moving rapidly up the gravel-paved road. They were still surrounded by jungle, but stars showed through gaps in the trees further up the hill. They had almost reached the crest of the rim basin when *this* had happened.

One of the cumbersome LoggerMechs was down on its front knees, the hindquarters of the four-legged machine protruding into the air in an ungainly and somewhat vulnerable position. The shoulder of the road had given way under a careless misstep. The 'Mech's right foreleg had gone off the road in a rattle of stones and dirt, leaving the 'Mech on its knees with no way to achieve the purchase necessary to right itself once more. The pilot's attempts to raise the machine on just its left leg had only sent a fresh avalanche of loose rock down the slope. The 'Mech now leaned heavily on its shoulder against the embankment to its left, unable to move and completely blocking the road.

Thorvald read the numeral on the stalled machine's flank. "Adams!"

"Yessir!" Adam's voice was tinny and quick with fear. "Should I punch out, sir?"

"No, no! Don't eject! Everything's going to be all right! Just sit tight."

"Yessir! You . . . you're not going to push me off the edge, are you, sir?"

"No, Adams, we're going to get you off of there. Stay calm. Don't touch anything."

"Yessir!"

Thorvald considered the problem for a moment. There was still plenty of time to reach Regis before their confederates in the city created the planned diversion, and he wanted to arrive with every 'Mech intact. To lose one here and now would be to admit that the merc commander was right, and Thorvald still harbored a simmering resentment against the man. The General had been opposed to seeking professional foreign help from the start, believing that a large enough rebel force could slip into the University and bring about the rising called for in the plan. It had been that fool Ericksson who had volunteered his AgroMechs and suggested the underground tunnels from the Ericksson-Agro plant.

He locked the *Warhammer*'s legs and disconnected from his helmet. After pulling on his tunic against the relatively cool night air, he opened the hatch and dropped down the chain ladder to the road. The LoggerMech loomed just ahead. He picked his way up the hill and walked under the Mech's belly, examining the ground where the leg had broken through the shoulder. Three other 'Mechs, another LoggerMech, the *Dervish*, and the *Locust*, had been ahead of Adams' machine in the line and were waiting just ahead.

He pulled out the hand comlink clipped to his tunic. "Adams? This is the General. Unlock your lead chain and let it drag, will you?"

"Yes, sir."

There was a sharp rattle from above, then a clank and a thud as the carballoy chain composed of fifty-kilo links trailed onto the road between the LoggerMech's forelegs. Thorvald signaled the lead LoggerMech. "Gunderson, back your machine down here. We'll use you to tow Adams out. Montido, we'll have to use your *Dervish* to lift the chain to Gunderson's tow ring."

There was a moment's blind shuffling in the darkness. "Uh, General? This is Montido. How do I get hold of that chain?"

"Good God, man, pick it up!"

"Uh, sir? My *Dervish* doesn't have hands."

Thorvald closed his eyes and sagged back against a tree. Around him, ground troops who had gathered to watch looked at one another with carefully masked expressions. Of the three lead 'Mechs, only the *Dervish* was remotely humanoid. Somehow, Thorvald had assumed that it was equipped with hands, forgetting that its forearms ended in paired laser projectors and SRM launchers. Why hadn't he put one of the *Phoenix Hawks* in the lead?

"O.K., Montido. Stand down." He thought furiously, rubbing his eyes with both hands. He needed a 'Mech with hands to lift the massive chain from the ground between the knees of Adam's LoggerMech and to connect it to the tow ring on the belly of Gunderson's Logger-Mech. All of his hand-equipped 'Mechs were further down the road and couldn't get past because of Adams' stalled machine.

The obvious alternative was for one of the *Phoenix Hawks, Wasps,* or the *Stinger* to fire its jump jets and vault over the blocking 'Mech to the far side. All were jump-capable, and all had hands. The problem was that jumping was a tricky maneuver, one that could get even experienced pilots into trouble on occasion. An inexperienced pilot could come down wrong and wreck his BattleMech, perhaps killing himself in the process.

A second alternative was to have one of those 'Mechs go around the LoggerMech True, the hill was steep and the jungle growth was fairly thick here, but *Wasps* and *Stingers* were designed to be maneuverable. One of them should be able to slip around downslope from Adams, climb the hill farther up, and get into position to connect the chain. Nadine Cheka was the *Stinger* pilot, a young woman who seemed to have a real knack for handling her 'Mech.

General Thorvald raised the comlink to his lips and began giving the necessary orders.

Grayson, Ramage, McCall, and Lori stepped out onto the lighted floor of the cave. Around them, the 'Mechs of the Gray Death loomed huge and shadowy. As they started toward the maintenance area, a wide-eyed young

rebel stepped out to block them. "Halt!" he said, cradling his hunting rifle awkwardly at port arms.

"Hello, son," Ramage said. "Stand easy."

"Oh . . . uh, good evening, Sergeant. Oh, Captain
Carlyle!" The boy snapped to an impression of attention.
"Good evening, sir!"

Grayson smiled at him, and nodded. "It's Willoch,
isn't it?"

"Yessir!"

"We're going through to inspect our BattleMechs,
Willoch."

Grayson started forward, but Willoch shifted the rifle
uncertainly in his hands. "Uh . . . Captain, I'm afraid I
can't let you."

"Eh?"

"Colonel Brasednewic gave me orders, sir. Said he'd
have my hide if *anyone* went to those 'Mechs."

"The Colonel couldn't have meant us . . ."

"Uh . . . he said *especially* you . . . uh . . . sir!"

Grayson frowned. Though he'd expected to encounter
sentries in the 'Mech maintenance area, he still wasn't
sure of the best way to deal with them. He still didn't
know.

"We've got to go through, Willoch. Your friends may
be in trouble. We're going to go help them."

"But my orders, sir . . ." Almost he stepped aside,
doubt vivid behind his eyes.

As Grayson was speaking with the boy, Ramage moved
to where he was almost alongside the sentry. The blade-
stiff edge of his hand descended, and McCall stepped
forward in time to help catch the sentry and lower him
to the ground.

"Better this way," Ramage said, answering Grayson's
unspoken question. "If he lets us through, some stuffed
uniform could order him shot for disobeying orders. He's
a good kid, and I don't want him hurt."

"So you slugged him. Good thinking."

A stir of movement made Grayson turn. Clay, Yorulis,
and Debrowski appeared from up the tunnel, breathing
hard. "We had to dodge some rebel sentries," Yorulis
said, "but we made it."

Grayson looked at each face in turn. "You are still
agreed on this?"

"Cap'n," McCall said. "We ha' nae much time."

The others nodded agreement. "Even if their plan goes off perfectly," Lori said quietly, "it could still end up a slaughter. If we're there, we might be able to steady them."

"At least we won't be feeling that we're sending them out to do what we won't," Clay added.

Grayson had been unable to persuade Thorvald or Ericksson of the folly of an attack on Regis. Nor could he persuade the rebel Council to allow the Gray Death to accompany the assault. They insisted that the mercenaries were too expensive to risk in open battle and must remain behind, safe, until Regis was secured. After that, the Legion's help would be welcome in restoring order in the city and in securing the Kurita prisoners.

Grayson had wrestled with the problem for most of the past three days. When the Legion had begun training the Free Verthandi Rangers, the students had been strangers. Grayson, Ramage, and all the rest had felt concern about seeing untrained youngsters thrown into battle, but it was the detached concern of professionals for inefficiency and waste.

Now, after six weeks, Grayson and his men knew those students as people. Realizing that the Legion's fate was inextricably bound up with the fate of the Free Verthandi Rangers, Grayson felt responsible for those students because he been responsible for their training. He could not simply stand aside and watch them led off to face a situation for which they were not yet fully prepared. These were issues of honor and of personal accountability that went beyond the letter of the Gray Death Legion's contract with the Verthandian rebels.

"Ram, we'll see you when we get back. Until then, you're in charge."

"Luck, Captain."

The six Warriors hurried toward the main caverns and their waiting BattleMechs.

It was 0210, and the BattleMech strike force of the Free Verthandi Rangers moved through the broad gully at maximum speed, which proved to be lamentably slow. Though the light BattleMechs could easily have covered the distance in half the time, the lumbering AgroMechs, especially the logging machines, were not designed for speed or maneuverability. This was especially true because the gully floor was not as smooth as Thorvald had expected. They were following one of the wide, winding flow paths carved by runoff water during the seasonal heavy rains. At those times, this and the hundreds of other arroyos carved through the Bluesward became filled with swift-running, muddy water that catapulted down to the swamps and rivers as thundering waterfalls. At other times, the gullies were dry. This one provided perfect cover for an approach to Regis, a sheltered canyon that would shield them from IR and other night vision devices mounted around the city.

Centuries of erosion had carved out a nightmarish tangle of exposed boulders and deep pits. Sometimes, like now, the watercourse broadened and became flat enough to easily traverse, but Thorvald and his men had to be continually on the lookout for sudden areas of broken ground. 'Mechs with IR vision devices could usually see well enough, though interpreting what they saw was sometimes another matter. Most of the AgroMechs, however, were literally in the dark. They were dependent on low-power microwave transmissions from their faster companions to warn them of approaching rugged ground where a 'Mech had to slow to a cautious crawl.

It was slow going, and time was running out. It had taken nearly an hour to free Adams' LoggerMech from its predicament on the basin rim road. Nadine Cheka's *Stinger* had gotten stuck in undergrowth and loose soil just below the stranded machine. Her efforts to move up and out of the trap had set off another round of rockslides that threatened to sweep her and Adams' LoggerMech completely off the face of the slope. The problem had been solved by having a number of 'Mech pilots climb out of their machines to pass a heavy cable down the slope to Nadine. With the other end secured to a towring on the *Dervish*, she had managed to pull her way hand-over-hand up the slope, until at last her *Stinger* was on the up-slope side of Adams' LoggerMech.

After that, the job was simply a matter of picking up the tow chain from Adams' 'Mech and attaching it to the D-ring on Gunderson's 'Mech. With the second LoggerMech taking the strain on the dragchain, Adams

had at last been able to get enough purchase on the roadbed to pull his 'Mech's right leg back up onto hard ground
and to get it walking on all fours once more. Moments
later, they'd emerged from the jungle and onto the rolling
grassland of the Bluesward.

At 0045, Thorvald had transmitted a coded message
toward the distant city. *Attack delayed. Hold diversion
until 0200. Attack will commence at 0245.*

He'd waited a minute or two for an acknowledgement,
but heard nothing. That caused a slight, nagging worry,
but Thorvald refused to let it bother him. It could be an
equipment failure, or perhaps the rebels were not in a
position to answer at the moment. He certainly could not
afford to stand there waiting for the reply, and he would
not be able to hear the beamed microwave transmission
while his 'Mech was down in the gully. He decided that
the best course was to proceed to the jump-off point outside the city. At 0200, he would listen for the code
phrase, which would indicate that the diversion had been
set off at the new time. If he did not hear the phrase then,
he would consider aborting the attack. Thorvald felt that
it would be foolish to abandon the mission over something as insignificant as a few minutes' delay in acknowl-
edging a message.

The trek had gone relatively smoothly after that, at
least until Vikki Traxen misunderstood what she saw on
her IR scan and put her *Locust*'s foot into a hole in the
dry streambed, pitching her machine forward with a
crash. Traxen was unhurt, but a driver cam in her *Locust*'s left ankle had bent, and a coolant seal just above
had ruptured. Her 'Mech could walk, but with a quarter-
speed limp, and she'd had to cut off coolant flow to the
Locust's entire left leg. That meant further malfunctions
for certain, as maneuvers with the straining leg drove the
unit's internal temperature up.

Thorvald had sent Traxen limping to the rear, but only
after losing another ten minutes trying to open an access
panel to see whether the damage could be repaired. The
fall had sprung the panel's lock mechanism, and they'd
been forced in the end to use Collin Dace's *Phoenix Hawk*
with a raiser bar to pry it open.

Thorvald glanced for the fiftieth time at the digital

chronometer set into his main console. Time was tight, but they could still put it off.

With hands clasped behind his back, Nagumo watched the dying glow in the sky to the southeast. The warehouse fire had been stubborn and fierce, an explosive blaze among the tanks of azelwax stored there. A lance of Third Strike Regiment 'Mechs had finally got it under control using SRMs tipped with foam bombs. Damage had been confined to the warehouse and the buildings immediately adjacent. The whole affair was unremarkable and he would not even have been called out of bed, except that . . .

Security forces closing off the block had caught sight of a pair of men fleeing the area. When the force commander had given pursuit, the pair had turned on their pursuers and opened fire with handguns. In the brief firelight, one of the fugitives had been killed, the other cornered and captured. Two security personnel had been wounded in the struggle.

So, the fire had been set deliberately. That was not so unusual, for anti-Combine violence had increased in Regis over the past year or two. What had piqued Nagumo's interest was the fact that his men had found a small, personal transceiver on their prisoner, and it was of a type manufactured and sold on another world. That might not have been so unusual, either. High-tech items such as transceivers and comlinks were favorite trade items for cargo because they were low-bulk and high-profit. What did interest Nagumo was the trademark on this particular radio. It showed that the transceiver had been manufactured on Galatea, the planet that some called Mercenary's Star.

This incident, coupled with the fact that rebel emissaries from Verthandi had recently hired mercenaries on Galatea, was disquieting. It meant that the rebels operating in Regis were in touch with the rebels in the jungle. It also meant that rebels had started the warehouse fire. Under whose orders? From where? Within the city? Or from out of the jungle?

The mystery had deepened after close inspection proved that the Galatean radio was not working. The microsoldering on the powerboard was shoddy, and a broken circuit blocked incoming transmissions. Perhaps the radio had been intended only to alert someone else that the job was done? Or had the rebels simply not bothered to test their equipment before setting out on their mission?

What was their mission? Why destroy a warehouse filled with highly flammable azelwax at the southeast corner of Regis? There was no military value in that oily wax, though it did burn brightly. The owners of the wax had no connection with the occupying forces, and so revenge or terrorism was an unlikely motive. Why, then? That question had brought a sleepless Nagumo to his office, had moved him to wake Dr. Vlade and the other members of his interrogation team so that they could begin getting the answers from the prisoner as quickly as possible.

His desktop communicator chirruped at him. When Nagumo touched the receiver switch, Vlade's features appeared on the screen. There were stray flecks of blood on the psychiatrist's face, and the sleeves of his white smock were heavily stained. The doctor, Nagumo decided, must have been personally involved in the interrogation.

"Well?"

"My Lord, it is as you thought. The subject was working under the direction of rebel forces based in the jungle. His orders came from a woman he knows only as 'Carlotta'."

"Where is this rebel base?"

"He didn't know, Lord."

"You're certain of that?"

"My Lord, the subject broke completely. He withheld nothing from us." Vlade's mouth worked in what could have been a smile. "What he *did* know was much more important, however. The fire was a diversion for a rebel attack. The attack was to take place tonight. Right now, in fact, shortly before 0200."

"Now?"

"He was certain of the time, my Lord. He was surprised that the rebel 'Mechs had not already struck. The diversion was to be at 0100, the attack at 0145."

"Rebel 'Mechs!"

"Yes, Lord. He did not know how many or where they

were to strike. He knew only that a number of Battle-Mechs organized into a unit called the 'Free Verthandi Rangers' were to move into position while the warehouse fire distracted our units in Regis and momentarily blinded our IR-scanning satellites.''

Nagumo's brows rose, questioning. ''There's been no sign of enemy activity.''

''Perhaps the rebels called off the attack, but the people charged with setting the fire didn't get the word.''

''Possibly,'' Nagumo said. ''The broken radio might indicate that. Certainly, it means they couldn't warn their comrades that they'd been captured.''

''There might have been other rebel agents watching.''

''Yes.'' Nagumo stroked his graying mustache with one finger, pondering.

''One thing more, my Lord. There was a code phrase he was to transmit once the job was done.''

''What was it?''

''The words 'false dawn'. He named a microwave frequency. Obviously, they were unable to transmit.''

Nagumo nodded, his eyes cold. ''Well done, Doctor. Finish up there and go back to bed.''

Vlade bowed. ''Thank you, my Lord.'' The Governor General broke the connection.

An attack called off or mis-timed by faulty communications? The possibility was intriguing. He opened another line on his communicator. ''Get me the DWO.''

Seconds later, a black-uniformed officer appeared on screen. ''Duty Watch Officer, Major Ralston. Yes, my Lord General?''

''I have reason to believe that an enemy 'Mech force is planning an assault on Regis tonight. They may already be moving into position. Double your perimeter security, and organize roving patrols to check out the Bluesward.''

''Enemy 'Mechs, my Lord? But . . . yes, my Lord. At once, sir!''

''Do we have recon satellite coverage of the Regis area tonight?''

''Partial coverage, Lord. The cloud cover is heavy, but intermittent.''

''Pay particular attention to satellite reconnaissance data . . . everything in the general area of Regis within the past two hours. Burn a satellite to bring it on a quicker pass if you have to, but get it done. It could be that the warehouse fire in Regis was set partly to dazzle our recon sats' infra-red imaging. I'd like to know what it is they don't want us to see.''

''At once, Lord General!''

Moments later, Nagumo heard the distance-muted rasp of an alarm sounding through the building as the Draconis forces were put on yellow alert. Smiling to himself, he sat down in his chair, put his booted feet up on his desk, and waited.

17

Thorvald scowled in growing anxiety at the *Warhammer*'s commo set. The verification signal had been transmitted: *false dawn*.

But why now? It was still ten minutes before two, and he'd not been expecting the verification for another ten or fifteen minutes at least. How had the people in Regis managed to get his orders so turned around?

The other 'Mechs were climbing up out of the gully, which was quite shallow this close to the outskirts of Regis. They gathered now alongside his *Warhammer*. The University towers were clearly visible from here, black against a lighter sky, with pinpoints of lights visible here and there. The wall loomed below. They could see no sign of the fire, but perhaps it would not be visible clear across the expanse of Regis.

Down below, silent shapes flitted through the shadows. Elements of the rebel army had been gathering for the past hours, waiting for the arrival of his 'Mechs, but no doubt wondering why they were so late. Thorvald cursed the need for radio silence. All that was possible were short, highly directional bursts.

Well, no matter that the timing was off. Things had worked out surprisingly well after all. They had arrived an hour late, but they could still successfully carry out the attack if the diversionary fire did its job of distracting the enemy.

Thorvald turned the *Warhammer*'s back on the city, then showed a signal light. He positioned it so that the army waiting in the darkness to the north would see it, but not any eyes watching from the city. The blue light flashed once . . . twice . . . then three more times in rapid succession.

The attack was on, the signal declared. *Move out now!*

Silently, the rebel army flowed toward Regis.

"My Lord, we have them!"

Nagumo leaned closer to the com screen on his desk, studying the satellite image displayed there. The image was damnably fuzzy, distorted by the high-altitude layer of ice crystal clouds that had been preventing a clear view all evening. The city was plain enough, including the ragged white scar to the southeast where the ruins of the burned warehouse still smoldered. And there, to the north, a pattern of heat sources, points of yellow against the background green.

"We're still analyzing the transmission, Lord General," the DWO's voice went on, "but we're certain that we're tracking the heat outputs of at least twelve 'Mechs, together with very large numbers of men and small ground or hover vehicles. These"—a flashing computer-graphic circle isolated a cluster of yellow-orange points—"read as Galleon emissions."

"Hah!"

"A moment ago, our orbital visual scanners detected a coded flash of blue light. We wouldn't have seen it if we hadn't been looking right at it. We think it was an order to advance. The contact has been dispersing since then, but definitely moving toward Regis."

"Range?"

"Five kilometers due north of the University, my Lord."

"Our forces are in position?"

"Yes, Lord. We have infantry and conventional armor in reserve at various points in the city, as well as two full companies of 'Mechs, watching for a possible rebel strike by forces already in Regis. Two more companies are behind the University's north wall, and another on the Mall inside the compound. We are deploying four additional companies—Third Battalion of the Third Strike Regiment—outside Regis to the east and west. If you approve, m'Lord, we plan to let them advance, then close in from either side to trap them all."

"Plan approved. But Major . . ."

"Yes, my Lord?"

"Bring me prisoners. This action may crush the rebel army once and for all, but I still want prisoners! There are too many unknowns with this mercenary unit loose in the jungle."

"Understood, Lord General. I will pass the order on to the company commanders."

"Excellent, Major. Keep me advised." A smile was spreading across Nagumo's face. This was the opportunity he had been waiting for! For years, he had been fighting shadows that struck at times and places of their own choosing, then vanished wraithlike into the jungles. Now, at last, the rebels had been goaded into coming out of the jungles and attacking the heart of the Combine's strength on Verthandi. Here the issue would be settled once and for all. With luck—though Nagumo did not count on that elusive goddess—perhaps they would also manage to catch the mercenary 'Mechs, too. That would break any threat to the Draconis Combine's hold on Norn II once and for all.

Duke Hassid Ricol would be pleased.

Kilometers to the north, the Gray Death Legion's six BattleMechs hurried through the dark, travelling along the uneven, boulder-strewn surface of a gully already torn by the tread of the larger 'Mech force that had passed through hours before. They had met Vikki Traxen's *Locust* limping along in the opposite direction and learned the reason for the assault force's delay. At the rate they had been travelling, Thorvald's unit must only now be drawing close to the walls of the university.

Lori relaxed in the embrace of her *Locust*'s command chair, letting the smooth, flowing strides of the swift machine cradle her thoughts. She remembered Grayson Carlyle's urgency as he'd called them together, his passion in urging that they follow the rebel column. They'd burst into the cavern area where their 'Mechs were kept, surprising and disarming the rebel guards posted there. Then the Gray Death Techs and support personnel had hastily armed and powered them up.

What was it about Grayson that drove him so? All of them shared his concern about the youngsters being thrown into battle, but he seemed like a man possessed.

Was he convinced that their first fight would break them, and he wanted to be there to pick up the pieces?

Perhaps it was a little of both. She remembered his concern for her as she'd tried to piece together the shards of her own warrior's soul after Thunder Rift. He'd helped her pick up *those* pieces, though he probably didn't realize it. The skirmish at Hunter's Cape had had been so sharp and quick that it was over before she'd even remembered to be afraid. The fact that she'd come through without once hesitating gave her confidence, convinced her that she could still function in combat. The horror that had nearly claimed her at Thunder Rift remained, as did her fears and secret nightmares. What Lori was learning was that she could live with them and be a warrior in spite of them.

Grayson's presence in the cramped cockpit of the *Shadow Hawk* at Hunter's Cape had helped, as did the knowledge that he did care for her. The thought of Grayson filled her with a pleasant warmth, but Lori forced her thoughts back to the present moment and to their mission.

There was little time left. Picking their way through the rubble with sure-footed, IR-guided steps, the Gray Death Legion raced toward Regis.

As Thorvald's army approached the walls of the University, all was dark except for pinpoints of light gleaming here and there among the University towers. Men, vehicles, and the ragged line of lumbering rebel BattleMechs picked their way across the field, their goal a low line of storage buildings less than a kilometer ahead. The whispering grass of the savannah gave way at last to a macadam groundcar road and the orderly fields of a local farmer's blueleaf crop.

One moment all was dark and still. The next moment the sky flashed with light so brilliant that it was as though night were suddenly transformed to noon. Rebel soldiers on the ground froze in place, squinting up into the light of multiple high-intensity flares. The BattleMechs hesitated, edged now in blazing radiance that left them standing in their own black shadows. A babble of voices flooded over Thorvald's command circuit as the AgroMech pilots, lacking military-type cutouts on their night vision devices, went blind in the flares' artificial day. Before Thorvald could issue an order, bolts of laser fire and shells began falling among the rebel troops and 'Mechs.

The fire came from three directions, from the top of the northern wall of the University and from out of the blackness on either side. Thorvald whirled his *Warhammer* to starboard, raking the darkness with ragged, blue-green bolts from his twin PPCs. His own night vision devices were almost useless against the pulsing bursts of gunfire and destruction. He triggered his radar, but the screen showed only the blizzard of a strong, jamming source that must be very close.

A piercing scream wailed into his earpiece from someone on the command commo circuit. Nearby, a four-legged LoggerMech collapsed onto its forward knees, its broad but lightly armored back shredded like tissue and ablaze with the flame of incendiary warheads. Internal explosions ripped through the big 'Mech's belly, scattering chunks of armor and broken driver mechanism into the night. The screams on the command circuit were chopped off as fresh flame and debris geysered from the machine's cockpit. With searchlight beams zigzagging through the chaos, the whole scene of fire, night, and smoke was Dantean in its horror. Machine gun fire from the walls spat at small parties of rebels huddled among the debris of wrecked vehicles and cratered ground, while the deadly red blossom of an exploding fireball rose from a rebel ammunition hover craft.

Within the first ten seconds, Thorvald knew there was no hope of winning through to the Rangers' objective, that the entire plan of slipping into the citadel of the University was dead. Within another five seconds, his only worry would be how to extract his command from the jaws of an ambush that was closing in from left and right. The overhead flares died away, leaving the battlefield lit eerily with fires sputtering among the hulks of shattered machines, and burning trees and patches of grass, the stabs of particle beams, and the crisscrossing patterns of tracers. Other 'Mechs could be seen in the strobe-flashes of cannon fire and explosions now. There was at least a full company on either flank, and they were moving now to surround the Rangers, the trap complete.

"All units!" Thorvald snapped into the command circuit. "All units, this is Ranger One! Disengage! Repeat, disengage! Fall back and regroup!"

Perhaps the most difficult of military maneuvers, an orderly retreat under fire was far beyond the capabilities of most of the Ranger MechWarriors. Pinned down by savage fire, disoriented, many in near-shock at the sudden violence unleashed around them, they could only crouch their 'Mechs against lightning-blasted ground or keep them moving toward the imagined shelter of the University's north wall. A second LoggerMech was in flames now. A third squatted back on useless, shell-torn hind legs, bracing its forelegs against the dirt as it raked the darkness mindlessly with its hastily rigged machineguns. Bullets sparked and sang from ferrocrete walls and the armor of advancing Kurita 'Mechs.

Thorvald sent PPC fire scorching into an enemy *Marauder* hulking in the shadows just beyond an overturned skimmer burning in its own fuel. It had to be an enemy 'Mech, for there were no *Marauders* among the rebel 'Mechs. He was certain that he had seen at least three of the 75-ton behemoths edging closer for the kill.

Thorvald had scored a hit. As explosions flashed across the *Marauder*'s flank, it halted in mid-stride, turned, and leveled a barrage of charged particles and laser bolts that staggered the *Warhammer*. In his earpiece, alarms signalled rising temperatures and overloaded circuits. For an eternity of seconds, the two war machines stood there, a scant hundred meters apart, pouring fire into one another. Then the *Marauder* sidestepped Thorvald's fire and opened a devastating barrage at a Ranger *HarvestMech*. With a dozen well-placed autocannon shots at the 'Mech's spindly legs and scantily armored hull, the *Marauder* crippled the light agricultural machine, then lurched off into darkness.

Thorvald cursed once, then slapped the switch that cut on his 'Mech's left shoulder spotlight. The light made him a better target, or course, but it tied directly into his machine's O/P 1500 ARB tracking system which transformed the *Warhammer* into a deadly nightfighter. The beam of white light transfixed the *Marauder* in the midst of pursuing scattering clots of infantry with sweeping bursts from its medium lasers. Thorvald bellowed triumph and triggered a salvo of SRMs at his target, then released paired bursts from his PPCs. The *Marauder* stumbled, seemed to hesitate, then fell, an already damaged leg crumpling under Thorvald's fire as he rumbled in his *Warhammer* toward the crippled enemy.

Just then, something struck him from behind, with a force so powerful that it picked up Thorvald's 'Mech and hurled it forward. The impact threw him against his harness, and the feedback from the *Warhammer*'s balance sensors had him reeling. On pure instinct, he rolled his 'Mech aside, searching for a target.

More fire was probing toward him from the University wall, autocannon shells exploding in gouts of smoke, flame, and whining fragments of metal that rattled across the *Warhammer*'s hull. He shifted weight to his 'Mech's left arm to lever himself up and found that the load-bearing joint that supported his left-arm PPC had taken a direct hit. The weapon was still attached, but dangled uselessly, the power feed and drive mechanisms spilling like black spaghetti from rents in the joint armor. His searchlight was gone, too, torn away in that first armor-shredding blast.

Somehow, he got the *Warhammer* to its feet. Red and flashing amber fault lights lit the system status indicators on his consoles. Temperature warnings shrieked in his earpiece and wrote themselves in fiery letters across his heads-up display. Coolant leaks were draining his machine of its life's blood, sending its internal temperatures soaring.

Thorvald's *Warhammer* could not take much more.

MERCENANY'S STAR 179

18

The Gray Death 'Mechs were still ten kilometers away, but Grayson could already see the battle before the University to the south. Above the walls of the dry riverbed, the sky was lit with a pearly silver light. Streaks of color punctuated by flaring smears of brilliance marked gun and rocket fire in front of the barely visible towers of Regis.

"We're late," Lori said in his earpiece as they drew to a halt and studied the sky. The battle was audible as only a muted rumble, like summer thunder in the distance. "They've started without us, boss."

Grayson checked his chronometer. "And they haven't had time to get in position inside the University. Something has gone very seriously wrong."

Clay's voice came across the command circuit. "An ambush, then."

"Judging from the volume of fire . . . yes. The rebels are in trouble."

"We've got to help them," Lori said.

"What do the rest of you say?" Grayson's own thoughts were in turmoil. He wanted to press forward, help the Rangers who must be now battling for their lives. To do so could also mean the destruction of his own unit.

"We can't leave them in there alone," Lori insisted.

"We'd best move oot, sair, if we're going tae save tha' haggus."

"I don't know what 'haggus' is, Captain," Clay said, "but I think McCall is speaking for us all."

"Move it, then," Grayson said, his face set as death behind his neurohelmet visor. He felt very cold. "Lori, take the point."

Lori's *Locust* surged ahead as she picked her way across the uneven terrain. The other five 'Mechs followed in a line, with Grayson's *Shadow Hawk* in the van. The clashing thunder of their multi-ton jogging rattled the stones of the embankments on either side, creating miniature rockslides.

"Set IFF receivers," Grayson called. "They'll be on band seven." The computer-generated graphic of Lori's machine gleamed with a bright green light on Grayson's forward scanner. The flashes of light, and the brief but day-bright whiteness of flares grew brighter and higher in the sky as their 'Mech strides gobbled up the kilometers.

Lori swung her 'Mech to one side, her laser swinging to cover a looming shadow against the light ahead. Grayson brought his own laser up to the point, but held his fire. The computer schematic that drew itself was that of a *Wasp*, and it showed a green light within the wireframe torso.

"Identify!" Grayson barked. The *Wasp*'s right arm came up, its laser flaring blue-white. The beam passed somewhere into the sky above Grayson's *Shadow Hawk*.

"Hold your fire! This is Grayson! Put up your gun!"

The *Wasp* paused, hesitating. "That's got to be Olin Sonovarro," Grayson said. He lashed with his voice. "Report! What's the situation?"

Sonovarro's voice was a wail over the com. "S-sir . . . it's all gone to pieces! Th-they were waiting for us! Waiting in the dark, and . . . and . . ."

"Get a grip on yourself, trooper. Is your *Wasp* damaged?"

"No. No . . . sir."

"O.K. Fall in with us."

"I've had enough . . ."

"We're going in there to get the Rangers out as a unit, and you're bloody well going in with us! Clay . . . McCall . . . flank him!"

The 'Mechs swung into line again, Sonovarro's *Wasp* unwillingly in their midst. As they trotted into the fringe of the battlefield, they encountered two more Verthandi Rangers. One was the big *LoggerMech* pocked with rocket craters in its flank armor. The other was a spry, angular *PickerMech* with long, jointed arms that sported jury-rigged machine guns. The appearance of the Gray Death company and Grayson's quiet orders also brought these 'Mechs around and moving south once more.

Grayson learned the tactical situation from their pilots. Large numbers of Kurita 'Mechs had apparently been in position outside the University walls, ready to spring the trap when Thorvald and his 'Mechs blundered in. The rebel infantry was trapped, too, though the Ranger pilots all reported seeing plenty of rebel troops fleeing on foot back toward the distant swamp. From the sound of it, the rebel action had turned into a complete rout, with most of the Ranger 'Mechs still caught in a shrinking pocket.

"O.K., boys and girls, we're going to flank the flankers. We'll shift to the east and come in behind the Dracos on Thorvald's left. If we can hold that flank open, maybe Thorvald can get his people out. Ready? Remember to watch for the target's IFF!"

Grayson's 'Mech force clambered from the shallow ravine and into the light of battle. Searchlights stabbed and probed from the University walls, and autocannon fire raked the ground and the junked ruin of smashed AgroMechs. The lumbering form of a *HarvestMech* blundered across Grayson's HUD. He signalled the machine and got its pilot turned around and heading south.

Another 'Mech now loomed huge among the shadows. There was no need to query the machine's IFF. Grayson recognized its shape as a *Marauder*, scarred and battered but still firing bursts of PPC fury with both arms. Grayson brought his laser up to point and mashed down on the firing button. White light speared the heavier 'Mech as armor boiled from an already glowing wound on its left torso close to the ball-and-socket joint of its left arm. From Grayson's right, another burst of laser fire joined his as Lori's smaller *Locust* tore into the *Marauder* with unexpected savagery.

The *Marauder* spun away, its left arm dragging now. Grayson tracked the target relentlessly, bringing the crosshairs of his autocannon reticule down on the enemy 'Mech's crippled arm and triggering the weapon into a rolling crescendo of raw sound. Autocannon shells struck. Trailing sparks, the *Marauder*'s left arm went spinning into the night. The snapping flashes of electrical short circuiting lit the green coolant fluid spraying from the red-hot wound.

Another target appeared to the right, attacking Lori. Grayson's computer named it a CN9-A *Centurion*, a 50-ton 'Mech with a heavy, right-arm autocannon as well as missiles and lasers. The *Centurion's* autocannon was firing steadily, its muzzle flash lighting up its own angular body armor. Grayson fired his own autocannon in reply, a long, rolling burst of shells across the enemy 'Mech's torso armor, hammering at the flip-aside panels protecting its left-chest LRM launch tubes.

Shells from the CN9 struck Grayson's *Shadow Hawk* in the left leg and arm, the impact smashing him backward a step and jerking him about. The movement pulled his autocannon off target, and so he swung his right arm laser up for a second volley. The bolt streaking from the 'Mech's extended arm engulfed the *Centurion's* flat head in white light. With the pilot momentarily dazzled, Grayson urged his *Shadow Hawk* forward in a lumbering run. Too late, the *Centurion's* autocannon shifted its aim. Grayson's *Hawk* swept past the upraised weapon and cannonballed into the lighter 'Mech with a clang of impacting armor that rang in Grayson's cockpit like the unbearable clangor of an enormous bell. Both 'Mechs went down in a tangle of arms and legs.

This close, Grayson's slightly heavier 'Mech was actually at a disadvantage against the *Centurion*. He could bring to bear none of his own weapons on the 'Mech struggling underneath him, but the CN9 had a pair of Photech 806c medium lasers built into its torso. As the combatants grappled, the enemy triggered Photechs at point-blank range into the *Hawk's* armor, rocketing its internal temperature up by 50 degrees.

The only way Grayson could strike back was hand-to-hand. He closed his *Hawk's* left hand into a steel fist that drove with explosive force into the right side of the *Centurion's* head. Armor that could absorb or refract millions of joules of laser power was hard-pressed to deflect the kinetic energy of such a blow. The *Centurion's* armor plate buckled, and its neck traverse bearings groaned. Grayson struck again and again.

Even if the CN9's pilot were still conscious, he would be in no position to operate his 'Mech. Grayson's armored fist descended once more, striking knife-edged into the cockpit. High-impact plastic shattered, and a trickle of oily smoke trailed from the 'Mech's shattered head as Grayson withdrew the *Hawk's* steel fingers from the ruin of man and metal. During Grayson's brief but deadly fight with the *Centurion*, his men had swept past in their 'Mechs and begun to engage the other enemy machines at close range.

The Gray Death's arrival on the battlefield had provided unexpected reinforcements from an unexpected quarter, catching the Combine forces completely by surprise. As Grayson strode into the general melee, the blaze of a crumpled Kurita *Orion* lit his way. It had been caught in a deadly crossfire between McCall's *Rifleman* and Clay's *Wolverine*. The solid fuel cores of the missile reloads stored in the big 'Mech's left torso must have been hit and ignited.

As Grayson scanned the battlefield rapidly, his *Hawk's* IR imaging system highlighted other 'Mechs in white and red colors that stood out starkly from the cool blue of the screen. BattleMechs produce enormous amounts of heat just standing in one spot, idling. In combat, a 'Mech's heat stands out like a magnesium-tipped flare. Grayson's computer overlaid the IFF signals, quickly separating friend from foe.

The relentless advance of the Kurita forces was crowding the Verthandi Rangers, who were still up but fighting into a smaller and smaller pocket. The Gray Death Legion was already mingling with the rearmost of the enemy attackers. Jaleg Yorulis caught an enemy *Wasp* from behind with laser fire from his own *Wasp*. The first shot penetrated the enemy 'Mech's armor and smashed through to its jump jets. A second shot resulted in a savage, fire-spewing explosion that hurled the Kurita *Wasp* forward and down, trailing flaming debris.

Debrowski's *Wasp* had joined Lori's *Locust* in a flame-versus-laser duel with an oddly hunchbacked *Vulcan*. The 40-ton *Vulcan*, normally an even match for the two smaller 'Mechs, was already damaged and down on one leg. Its two antagonists had drawn well clear of the *Vulcan's* forward-pointing laser and autocannon, with Lori concentrating highly accurate laser fire against the stored tanks of CSC fuel for the anti-infantry flamer in the enemy's right arm.

The *Vulcan* had already snapped off short bursts from the flamer, but two nimble *Wasps* had slipped aside each time. It raised its right arm for another shot at Lori's 'Mech, but a bolt from her *Locust* had caught a fuel tank and the arm exploded in orange flame that towered into the spark-shot sky. For an instant, the *Vulcan* knelt there, half engulfed in the pillar of flame. When its stores of autocannon rounds suddenly exploded, its torso burst into fiery fragments and rattling shrapnel against Grayson's cockpit screens.

The trapped Ranger 'Mechs now had a way out. The only problem was how to let them know that their rescuers were their friends. As Grayson's *Shadow Hawk* moved through the newly opened gap in the Kurita line of battle, laser fire from a Ranger 'Mech lanced into Lori's 'Mech, then snapped across the fire-scorched terrain at Grayson's *Hawk*.

Calmly, with careful deliberation, Grayson raised his right arm laser, swivelled his 'Mech's torso to sweep the weapon's muzzle away from the huddled survivors of the Rangers, and brought it to bear on a Kurita *Phoenix Hawk* lurching toward him. He fired three times in rapid succession, scoring hits on the *Phoenix Hawk*'s left and center torso, which left gaping craters in its armor. The enemy pilot triggered his jump jets on the third hit, and rose on thundering blasts up and out of Grayson's line of fire.

Grayson spoke on the general command frequency. "This is Carlyle! We're here to pull you out! Where's General Thorvald?"

"Here," a voice answered. Grayson punched out a combination of keys on his computer terminal, bringing a graphics display that pinpointed the speaker with a flashing red arrow on his HUD. Thorvald's *Warhammer* lay on its side a hundred meters beyond the rest of the Ranger 'Mechs. Craters on its armor still glowed red hot when Grayson magnified the view on one of his scanner screens. "Here," Thorvald said again. "Meet me on the private command channel."

Grayson opened the new channel. "General, this is Carlyle." He increased magnification on his long-range scanner again, studying Thorvald's 'Mech as he spoke. That *Warhammer* would not walk again, not with those shredded leg drivers and actuators. Enemy fire from the wall and from farther off in the darkness continued to strike the general's fallen war machine. "General, we thought you might need some help."

"You're a mutinous bastard, aren't you?" Thorvald said, but his tone was without anger. "I'm glad you're here."

"I suggest a withdrawal, sir. If we can hold it open a bit longer, we can pull your command out that way."

"Quite right. I . . . I relinquish command to you, Captain." There was a click and then a sizzle as Thorvald switched back to the general command frequency. "All Rangers, this is Ranger One! Captain Carlyle is now in operational command! Group with him for withdrawal. And . . . and don't blame yourselves, people." His voice broke, but he recovered. "All this was . . . was my fault."

Grayson swept the area with his IR. There were no enemy 'Mechs close by and no enemy troops that he could see. The arrival of the Legion seemed to have surprised the Dracos enough that they'd scattered or pulled back, though autocannon and light artillery fire continued to drop in from the direction of the University walls. "General, it's clear in your area. Punch out, and I'll make pick-up."

"Negative, Captain."

"But General . . ."

"I said negative!" A *Marauder* appeared at 500 meters' range, strutting across the ground under the unsteady light of multiple fires. Thorvald's shattered *Warhammer* levered itself higher on its crippled left arm, brought its right arm PPC into line, and opened fire. Swatches of blue lightning crackled across the field, striking the *Marauder*'s legs. The *Marauder* sent a twin PPC bolt in reply, then went down, either damaged or suddenly cautious. Artillery fire geysered dirt and shrapnel close by Thorvald's 'Mech.

"Pull out," Thorvald continued as if the brief exchange had not interrupted him. "You need someone to hold the corridor open, and I'm it!"

"We can get you out, General. Don't—"

"Fulfill your contract and do what I say!" There was pain in the words, and Grayson realized Thorvald must be wounded. It was hard to see how the man could still be alive, so savaged was his 'Mech. "You can't help me . . . but I'll try to buy you some time. Now move!"

"Right," Grayson said quietly. Then, louder, "All units! Attention to orders!"

Speaking swiftly and with rapid-fire delivery, he laid out the orders that had been forming in his mind. The core of Ranger 'Mechs would begin moving northeast immediately, staying together, moving close behind Lori, who would act as guide. The light BattleMechs would follow, hosing the darkness to either side with beam fire to make enemy snipers rush their shots and to keep the Dracos from organizing a sudden offensive. To provide cover for the rest, Delmar Clay, Davis McCall, and Grayson would close in behind the retreating column. Backing slowly, they would lay down a covering barrage of short- and long-range missile fire and carefully spotted bolts from their lasers and PPCs.

Thorvald's fallen *Warhammer* continued to blaze away with lasers, SRMs, and his one remaining PPC as enemy 'Mechs again advanced out of the darkness. More important than Thorvald's fire was the fact that the enemy, not immediately aware of the retreat, would concentrate on his 'Mech like wolves on the downed member of an enemy pack. The longer they concentrated on the *Warhammer*, the more time Grayson had to get the Rangers and the Legion formed up and moving north.

It took nearly fifteen minutes for the Rangers to get moving. Some simply refused, finding the dubious shelter of a wrecked *LoggerMech* or a gouged-out shell hole preferable to the uncertainties of the fire-swept savannah to the north. Several 'Mechs were badly damaged and had to be carried by their mates. One of these, a crippled, gut-torn *PickerMech*, had to be literally peeled open by Clay's *Wolverine* because the hatch had jammed and AgroMechs were not equipped with an ejection system. The rebel foot soldiers were another problem. Most had already scattered toward the distant jungle when the BattleMech slugfest had begun. Here and there, isolated bands huddled in the darkness or waved frantically for help from the giants around them. There was no way to carry them. Grayson could only wave them off toward the north. To those officers and NCOs who still had radios, Grayson bellowed orders that their men should save what equipment and weapons they could as they withdrew.

They would need those weapons soon enough.

The retreat column was just forming up when the final enemy rush began. Shells fell among the straggling BattleMechs, whanging armored hulls with shrapnel fragments and gouging angry scars in unyielding metal as they struck glancing blows. A pair of medium Kurita 'Mechs, a *Hermes II* and a stubby-armed ASN-21 *Assassin*, broke out of the darkness to the west, firing blindly into the infantry vehicles and light 'Mechs as the confused rebel forces milled vaguely northward.

The *Assassin*'s LRMs struck a Galleon light tank, one of those captured from the enemy on the day the Gray Death had landed on Verthandi. The tank exploded in orange flame, hurtling metal chunks as the *Assassin*'s fire rocketed into its hull and detonated. Grayson saw Lori's 'Mech step between the rebel machines and the attackers, firing long, steady bursts of laser into the heavier *Assassin*. The ASN-21 broke stride, hurt by Lori's highly accurate fire.

While the *Hermes* closed on the *Locust*, its chest-mounted autocannon blazing wildly, Grayson opened fire on it with his laser. He knew that the *Hermes* carried a laser and a flamer besides its autocannon, and it was the flamer that had him worried.

He crouched lower in his 'Mech's control seat, hands clenched on the controls. Though Lori had proven herself in combat here on Verthandi, and on Trellwan before that, she did have one serious weakness in battle—her fear of death by fire. If the *Hermes* turned its flamer on her . . .

Grayson flexed his 'Mech's legs, triggered his jump jets, and leaped. The thrust from his backpack sent him soaring in a low and utterly graceless leap across 90 meters of open ground. He landed with a jarring crash, flexed the 'Mech's knees, and jumped again. This time, he landed within 300 meters of the *Hermes*, almost directly behind the smaller 'Mech.

Five LRMs lanced out of the tubes in the *Hawk*'s right

torso. Grayson triggered the reload cycle, then fired five more. Missiles drew trails of fire into the *Hermes'* back. Multiple explosions hurled the *Hermes* forward, knocking it flat. Seconds later, more missiles struck the prone form. There was no way to tell how bad the damage was. For the moment at least, one Kurita Mech Warrior was out of the fight. The *Hermes* lay still, making no attempt to move or stand.

The *Assassin,* meanwhile, had taken heavy fire from the *Locust* and from several of the retreating AgroMechs. There was visible damage to its left arm and to the armor on its torso. Machine gun fire hammered at the 'Mech from rebel troops and vehicles in the area, from the *Locust,* and from the AgroMechs clustered nearby. With enough time and enough hits, even machine gun fire can penetrate 'Mech armor. The sparks of high-velocity rounds pinging against the 40-ton 'Mech's head and torso armor must have scored some damage or at least made the pilot more cautious. The *Assassin* withdrew hurriedly, leaving its companion face down in the dirt.

"Get them moved out, Lori!" Grayson ordered. "We'll hold them here!"

Lori acknowledged, her voice calm and professional over the command circuit. She began moving along the line of rebel 'Mechs, snapping orders. Grayson returned to where the *Rifleman* and the *Wolverine* stood together, pouring fire into the night. He shouldered the *Hawk* between them, marked an already damaged *Marauder* as his target, and added his fire to theirs. Side by side, the three of them laid down a thundering barrage. The muzzle of Grayson's autocannon was white hot as the last round cranked through it. Then the weapon fell silent as he continued to blaze away with his laser and LRMs. His head-mounted SRM tubes had burned empty long minutes before.

Sweat drenched his face, arms, and body. His light mesh shirt was sodden and dripping, and his control seat was just as wet and slick. Autocannon shells shrilled and thundered among the three 'Mechs. Lasers stabbed and clung, tenaciously gnawing at armor already pitted and torn. Missiles lobbed in on dwindling trails of fire, most burying themselves in the churned-over ground and exploding with thumps that sprayed dirt and hot metal harmlessly against the 'Mechs' armored hulls. Only a few struck home, but with telling results. The *Wolverine*'s autocannon had been knocked out by an incoming LRM, but Clay continued firing with the ball turret laser mounted high on the big 'Mech's chest. The air above his *Wolverine* wavered and shimmered as torrents of heat poured from the machine's overworked heat sinks.

The Kurita 'Mechs gathered in the darkness, dimly visible as firelight caught and reflected from weapons, cockpit panels, and angles of joints and armor. They were massing for their final charge.

Weaker now, Thorvald's voice sounded in Grayson's ears. "Run for it, Carlyle! Take care of my people! Get them out!"

The *Warhammer*'s PPC spat lightning. An enemy *Orion* lumbered in from his blind side, the autocannon tucked under its right arm hammering furiously at the stricken rebel 'Mech. Grayson shifted his aim to the *Orion*, sending bolt after blue-tinged bolt of laser fire into the 'Mech's side. The volume of fire striking his *Shadow Hawk* from the wall and from Kurita 'Mechs was so great now that his computer was threatening total shutdown as his 'Mech's internal heat continued to rise.

Grayson knew there was nothing more he could do for Thorvald. His responsibility was now to his unit—which included both the Legion and the Rangers.

"Pull back," he ordered McCall and Clay. "Flank the column, and keep your eyes open."

His *Shadow Hawk* stood a moment more, firing away at the *Orion* half-a-kilometer distant. The machine was limping now, with heavy damage to its left side, leg, and arm. It nevertheless continued its advance on the downed *Warhammer*, now only a few tens of meters in front of it. Grayson saw with horror that the flames had engulfed the *Warhammer*'s head and torso after a direct hit from a *Vulcan* flamer. Yet, it continued firing its PPC again . . . and again . . . and again . . .

An enemy *Marauder* stepped between Grayson and the *Orion* he was targeting, slamming shell after exploding autocannon shell into Grayson's 'Mech. Grayson triggered the *Hawk*'s jump jets then, sending the 55-ton machine vaulting into the air on the rumbling twin jolts of fusion-heated steam from its backpack thrusters. The cabin temperature soared twenty degrees more, and red warnings flashed and shrieked of power shutdown and overload. He slapped an emergency override and cut a failed actuator out of the directed power circuits in the *Hawk's* right leg. The 'Mech fell to earth with a shuddering crunch that Grayson took with flexed metal knees and a reeling sense of vertigo as he fought to maintain his 'Mech's balance through his neurohelmet link. Then he was running through the night as long-ranged missiles continued to drop to the left and right.

Behind him, the final detonation of Thorvald's *Warhammer* lit up the night sky.

Book II

19

Nagumo travelled from the hardcopy in his hand to Colonel Kevlavic, then back again, his look of astonishment only slightly exaggerated for effect. "Six 'Mechs lost," he said, with mingled wonder and sarcasm. "A *Centurion*, a *Vulcan*, a *Wasp*, a *Hermes,* and two *Orions* . . . destroyed! Or so badly shot up they're useless for anything but scrap parts! Ten more 'Mechs badly damaged, including two of our *Marauders!* And for the rest . . . my senior Tech tells me his crew has maybe a thousand hours' worth of work scheduled now, just to repair the battle damage caused by *your* incompetence!"

Kevlavic remained at attention, his eyes riveted to the green sky beyond Nagumo's back. Nagumo regarded him belligerently, the fingers of his free hand drumming restlessly on the desk. Finally he shook the papers at Kevlavic. "You have nothing to say for yourself?"

"No, my Lord."

"You are a coward."

The Colonel's face went pale above the high-fastened collar of his black dress tunic. "No, my Lord!"

"You had that rabble in your hand . . . in your hand! Your failure has cost us four full BattleMech lances, destroyed or put out of action for weeks! You could have pursued that rabble, and you didn't! They were trapped, but then you let them get away!"

"I am not a coward, Lord! Nor are my men!"

Nagumo's eyes narrowed, but he smiled to himself. *Good. Get him angry, get him to say what he feels.*

"Then defend yourself! What happened?"

"We . . . I did not expect the second line of rebel 'Mechs, Lord. They attacked my right flank from the rear after we were already engaged with the first rebel group.''

''You did not expect it.'' Nagumo's voice dripped sarcasm. ''Since when does an enemy do what is *expected* of him! Surely you learned that at Hunter's Cape?''

''My . . . my Lord, I hold myself fully responsible.'' Kevlavic's face was death white now.

''So do I, Colonel.'' Nagumo dropped his voice to a purr, smooth and dangerous. ''So do I. Ah, but you needn't look so grim. I am not going to have you shot, though I confess that pleasant thought had occurred to me. I, too, underestimated the rebels. In that I must share the blame with you.'' He did not add that Duke Ricol would hold the Governor General completely responsible for this debacle, no matter who was to blame.

''The rebels showed unexpected tactical brilliance,'' Nagumo said. ''They sent in one force consisting mostly of agricultural machines bearing jury-rigged weaponry to spring our trap, then they trapped the trappers with a surprise assault from the rear. With *real* 'Mechs.''

''Yes, my Lord.''

''Still, it was costly for them and not as successful as it might have been if they'd thrown more 'Mechs into the fray. What were their losses?''

''Four of those quad-legged machines the indigs call *LoggerMechs*, Lord. Three other lighter AgroMechs. At least seven medium hovercraft. Supply and troop carriers, assault guns, and the like. And one heavy Battle-Mech . . . a *Warhammer*.''

''Seven AgroMechs and one BattleMech destroyed. Against our losses of two heavies, three mediums, and a light 'Mech. Not a very good showing, was it?''

''No, my Lord.''

''I'm more impressed by the losses sustained by their infantry. Tell me about that.''

''Besides the seven hovercraft, Lord, the rebel body count stands at thirty-eight confirmed kills. And we took prisoner a number of their wounded. Twelve, I believe.''

''They're being interrogated, of course.''

''Of course, my Lord.''

''Mmm. Your report mentions substantial damage to several enemy 'Mechs?''

''Yes, Lord. One heavy and two medium enemy

'Mechs covered the retreat of the others. They certainly sustained considerable damage. Considering their supply and maintenance problems, that's damage the rebels can ill afford. It is certain that other rebel 'Mechs also sustained severe hits.''

"I am delighted, Colonel, that you are so certain of the damage inflicted on the enemy. It makes your next assignment that much easier.''

Nagumo smiled as he watched Kevlavic's eyes blink shut, his jaw tense. *Let him sweat!*

"I am giving you this assignment because I do still have faith in your abilities, Colonel. You are an experienced leader, a skilled warrior. But you failed me at Hunter's Cape, and you have failed me now, outside the very walls of this city! Will you fail me a third time, Colonel?''

"No, my Lord! Whatever you want, I'll . . . What are your orders, my Lord?''

"Your orders are to track down and to destroy this rebel army, Colonel. As simple as that. If the rebel 'Mechs are as badly damaged as you claim in this report''—Nagumo slapped the printout with his hand—"then finding and eliminating them should be no problem at all.''

Kevlavic's eyes opened, his face still pale. "Yes, my Lord.''

"One more . . . detail. You have two local tenths—that's four standard weeks—to find and destroy the rebels. We are expecting visitors, and I want this matter completed by then.''

"Sir?''

"Duke Hassid Ricol will arrive soon to inspect his holdings. I intend to report to him personally that the largest coalition of rebel forces on this planet has been eliminated.''

"Duke Ricol . . .''

"Yes, Colonel. And if you have not satisfactorily carried out your mission by that time, if the rebels have not been eliminated, then you will be eliminated. Do I make myself clear, Colonel?''

"P-perfectly, my Lord.''

"Good. Just so we understand each other. Your failure could well mean my disgrace, even the forfeit of my life.

But before anything happens to me, I'll see to it that, well . . . I will not fall alone.''

"I understand, my Lord. We will find and eliminate the rebels to a man!"

"You have twenty-eight days, my man. Dismissed."

Nagumo waited until Kevlavic had saluted and hurried from the office before crumpling the printout into a disposal chute. Then he went over to the window, where he stood watching with hands clasped behind his back. Kevlavic was a military man, and he would use those means to carry out his orders. Nagumo was thinking now, though, of the other methods at his command. He was not about to entrust his own life and future to the actions of any subordinate.

He touched the panel on his desktop intercom. "Get me Company A of my personal Guards. I want to talk to Captain Mills." This time, nothing would be left to chance.

The rebel forces returned to Fox Island as dawn was breaking across the jungle. Grayson gave hurried orders to the 'Mechs to hide themselves within the cave. Two 'Mechs had quit on their cursing, battle-fagged pilots while still moving along the jungle trail down from the Basin Rim. Those machines, a *Stinger* and Montido's *Dervish,* had been carefully hidden under tarps and cut branches, well back under the forest canopy. They might eventually be able to repair the damaged machines where they stood. Enough, at least, to get them moving and back to the base.

Grayson's *Shadow Hawk* entered the cavern mouth, followed by a tight cluster of the tracked and hover vehicles that had fallen in with him during the descent down the Basin Rim. All around him, battle-grimed men and women were carrying or tending to the wounded, meeting comrades, or gathering in small clusters to talk about the battle. The MechWarriors, meanwhile, were descending from their machines. Techs and astechs swarmed around each BattleMech as it entered the shelter of the cave. More casualties were coming in, too, carried by comrades or smoke-stained hover transports. The Gray Death's support company included five medics, and the rebel forces also included a handful of men and women with medical training. Almost immediately, they were swamped by the wounded.

For Grayson, the hardest part of a battle was this aftermath—the casualty lists and repair estimates, the tactical assessment, and the endless worry about what the enemy would do next. That, and facing the rebel leaders. They would surely want to know what *he* planned to do next, but Grayson hadn't the faintest idea.

Indeed, the Rebel Council members stood waiting for him as he swung down the chain ladder dangling from his *Shadow Hawk*. Also with them was Colonel Brasednewic. The grim expressions on all their faces told Grayson that the Colonel had already filled them in on the battle before the walls of Regis.

"We got them out," he said cautiously.

Carlotta brushed a strand of blonde hair from her face with the back of her hand. From the weariness of her expression, she must have been lacking sleep. Indeed, the whole group looked as worn as Grayson felt.

"Tollen told us what happened," she said, "how you showed up and broke the enemy trap." Grayson noticed the glance that she and Brasednewic exchanged. There was warmth there and . . . something more?

Ericksson gestured toward the casualties being carried into the cave. "I told Thorvald this plan of his wouldn't work. Our army is . . . shattered!"

"*You* told him?" Olssen said. "You? As I recall, it was your suggestion to use the tunnel from your AgroMech plant."

"Only because that fool wanted to storm the main gate!"

"Citizens!" Carlotta interrupted. "Enough is enough!"

Brasednewic looked pointedly at Grayson. "What next?"

Grayson relaxed, letting his eyes close. After combat, he always felt weak as the tension finally released. He was as weary as if he'd just run ten kilometers on foot, but this day had a long way to go before he'd be able to sleep.

"I don't know, Colonel. We're still bound by our contract, of course, but I'm not sure how much good more training will do now. Your army has been beaten in the field. It'll take some doing just to repair the . . . the *psychological* damage.''

Tollen let his eyes stray toward the jungle. Shafts of orange sunlight were beginning to cut through gaps in the blue-green canopy. ''Some are wondering whether you plan to take your . . . services elsewhere. To the Dracos, perhaps.''

''Hardly,'' Grayson said, shaking his head wearily.

''The way I understand it, you were brought in to help train our people, our army, in how to fight 'Mechs. But right now, there's not much of an army left. Lots of our people have scattered and headed home by now. It'll be some time before they come back.''

''Let's talk straight,'' said Ericksson. ''Some of my people are wondering if we can trust you mercs. Your money's safe offplanet. *We* don't have anything more to offer you, that's certain! What's to keep your people from just . . . buying out of their contracts with you? Buying out and then hiring on elsewhere!''

Brasednewic smiled bitterly. ''The Revolutionary Council must have gambled everything they had to hire you and to buy the supplies we needed. Your people just might have a chance if you sell out to the Brownjackets.''

''Maybe we would,'' Grayson said, pausing as though to consider the suggestion. Why did they assume that mercenaries were loyal only to the highest offer? ''We might have a chance . . . a small one, *if* the Dracos were feeling merciful. But what do you think our chances would be next time we went looking for an employer?'' He shook his head. ''People have the idea that mercenaries just get up and switch sides for a better offer, but it doesn't work like that. If we broke our contract with you, we'd not only lose our bond on Galatea, but ComStar would see to it that we never got work again.''

''Well, I *know* that, but . . .'' Ericksson stopped and looked hard at Grayson. ''Maybe what we're wondering is just how much of a stake you have in our war here . . . besides the money.''

''You have no reason no hate the Combine,'' Tollen added. ''Not like we do.''

A sensation of ice spread through Grayson's stomach. No reason? He remembered his father, dead in the ruin of his *Phoenix Hawk* on the spaceport tarmac on Trellwan. He remembered the sight of the Draconis Combine *Marauder* that had killed him. That memory had driven him on Trellwan, and probably drove him even more now. More than he wanted to admit.

His hand closed into a fist, which he slowly made to relax. "Even mercenaries can have reasons to fight besides . . . money. Believe me."

"Maybe." Brasednewic was not looking at him, but toward the jungle outside. "But you'll have to prove it."

"You give us the support we need, and you'll have your proof." He saw Ramage waiting to talk to him. "Excuse me . . . gentlemen? Ma'am?"

"How'd it go?" Ramage asked. He wore a worried expression and his eyes strayed continually to the rebel leaders. As they argued some point, they also cast occasional glances back at Grayson and his NCO.

"What . . . with them? They're worried that we'll sell out. Can't say I blame them."

"What about the battle? We didn't pick up much through the comlink, other than the fact that you'd made it in and out."

"We got to them, but only just. Have you been talking to the rebel staff? What's the butcher's bill?"

Ramage shook his head. "I was with them in the comshack listening in, but I didn't learn much. Unit commanders are still reporting in, but it might take a week to hear from all of them. Figuring that maybe half have reported in who are going to, the rebs lost forty, maybe fifty, either dead or captured. Maybe twice that wounded. What about Thorvald? I heard he bought it."

"Dead." Grayson sagged back against the foot of his *Hawk,* vastly weary. "He was a brave man."

"Begging the Captain's pardon," Ramage said stiffly, "the man was a fool."

Grayson looked sharply at the Sergeant, but was too tired to do more than shake his head sadly. There was no point in discussing Thorvald's mistakes.

"You got 'em out, sir. *You* did."

"Maybe. But now we have to decide what to do with them. At this point, there's not a whole lot left of the Verthandian rebel army."

His eyes caught the movement of two young men crossing the sandy cave floor toward him, the lights overhead scattering faint, contrasting shadows as they walked. It was Felgard, the senior rebel Tech, and Sergeant Karellan, the Gray Death's senior Tech. They were in deep conversation, and Grayson knew what was troubling them without needing to be told. Every BattleMech in the little rebel group had sustained damage. To repair them, to even get them running at minimum efficiency again, was going to require a small mountain of spare parts and supplies, which the Verthandian rebels simply did not have.

"We're going to have to start over," Grayson continued, as he turned to greet the two Techs. "From the beginning."

It wasn't until late that evening that he was able to assemble his command personnel around a fire just beyond the cave. The site had been carefully chosen for the overhang of rocky cliff that sheltered it from detection by either orbiting spy satellite or patrol along the Basin Rim. The surrounding jungle was pitch black, though light spilled from the nearby cavern mouth. The continuing sounds of repair work on the rebel vehicles and 'Mechs mingled with the whistles, chirps, and squawks of the forest. Each of the Gray Death's MechWarriors was there, as well as Sergeant Ramage representing the non-'Mech military personnel, and Sergeant Karellan, head of the unit's technical staff.

Grayson stood outside the circle of firelight, hands on hips. The ten of them were a dirty and ragged-looking group. Each had been up all night during the march to Regis and then been through the battle there, and again up all day working to get the Legion's 'Mechs fully operational. Except for catnaps snatched here and there, some had had no sleep at all for thirty hours or more. The strain was showing.

"Thank you all for coming," Grayson said, stepping closer to the firelight. The faces looking up at him were dulled by fatigue and showed little emotion. "Before anything else happens, I thought we'd better decide what we're doing, where we're going."

Lori laughed, a bitter sound. "What choice is there?"

"You still think we should keep helping these malfing pongoes?" Clay asked. He twisted a short stick nervously between his fingers. "Their general, so-called, is dead . . . and good riddance."

Grayson stooped beside the fire, reached down, and thrust a half-burned brand deeper into the flames. Red sparks spiralled into the night. "The way I see it," he said finally, "is that we haven't got any choice. At the very least, we're stuck here until Captain Tor jumps back in-system. And what do you think his chances are of slipping in another DropShip past the Kurita blockade?"

There were murmurs from some. As Lori stared into the flames, a tiny muscle twitched near one eye. Grayson studied her face carefully, and decided that what he saw there was defeat. It was the same sense of futility he felt in himself. To behave otherwise took a strenuous effort. "All we can do is fight," he said. "Fight, and win."

"Win?" Clay snapped the twig he'd been playing with and tossed half into the fire. "The Dracos have four 'Mech regiments on this drekwater planet, and God knows how many troops! We have . . . what? Our few 'Mechs and a handful of farm machines!"

"It's a start, Delmar." Grayson attempted a smile. He was faced with a sudden, ludicrous vision. If everyone in the Gray Death resigned, he would have to fulfill the unit's contract obligations himself, a literal one-man army. Well, he could give classes in anti-'Mech warfare.

No, Lori would stay with him. And Ramage, and the others who had been with him on Trellwan. Though he'd not known McCall as long, he felt fairly sure that he would stay, too, no matter what. "All we need is a start. But I didn't say it would be easy."

Clay tossed the second piece of wood into the fire with a sharp, backhanded flip of the wrist. His expression showed disapproval.

"We *can* win," Grayson insisted. "They have the regiments, but they're scattered all over the planet. A planet, *any* planet, is one hell of a big place." He spread his hands. "The argument hasn't changed since we signed the contract. Not really. With our 'Mechs, and the people we have with us, we could turn things around for the rebels' campaign."

"How?"

"By hitting the Dracos where they're weak, when they're weak. By fighting a strictly guerrilla war. By refusing to fight on their terms. Keeping good relations with the civilians and the rebels, and using them as our source of food and non-military supplies." Grayson's answer had come out like rapid-fire.

"And what will we fight this war with?" said Clay. "We need military supplies, too."

"Wha', laddie," McCall said. "If tha' Dracos hae got the ammo an' weapons to fight wi', then we just go an' takit wha' we need frae' the source!"

Clay snorted, but Grayson nodded. "Exactly right. Our rebel friends will be able to pinpoint enemy supply dumps and depots for us, or put us in touch with Verthandian civilians who can. After that, it's just a matter of picking our time and method of approach very, very carefully."

Jaleg Yorulis stirred uneasily on his mossy log perch. "There is another choice," he said. "We could go over to Kurita."

The only sound was the crackling of the fire. Yorulis looked at the others, defiance quirking at the corners of his mouth and eyes. "Well? Why not? What chance do we have *fighting* them?"

"Plenty of chance," Lori replied slowly. She, too, seemed to be winning her inner struggle against despair. "They're big, clumsy, and slow," she said. "We're not. We'll have the help of the Verthandians. They won't."

"They'll catch us and . . ."

"Jaleg," Grayson interrupted. "Do you want out of your contract with the Legion?"

"Huh? No! I just . . ."

Grayson probed the fire again with his stick. Sparks showered and swirled. "This unit will *not* work for the Draconis Combine. Not while I'm in command." He raised his eyes from the fire until they met Yorulis', challenging the younger pilot. "Do you want to contest my command of this unit?"

"Of course not, Captain! But, I mean, it's ridiculous to think that we can take them, one on one! It seems to me that our contract with the Verthandi rebels is ended now. They have nothing left to fight with."

"They have us," Grayson said. "That's why they hired us. That's why we're here. To train them and to organize their army into an effective force. You, sir, may help us, or you may buy out of your contract."

''You know my bond's on Galatea.''

''So is mine. We'll trust you for it. But I'm telling you, if you buy out, you'll have to stay here. We won't have passage out until we control a port facility and Captain Tor can get a ship through the blockade to us. That's going to take some doing. Unless we can figure a way to get you out on a Kurita freighter. Even then, the chance of you getting picked up by their security is plenty high. The choice is yours, Pilot. Fight with us, or stay here out of the way until we can figure out what to do with you.''

Yorulis muttered something.

''Eh? Speak up.''

''I said I didn't sign a suicide pact! This whole thing is crazy!''

Grayson sighed. He switched on his wrist computer, then flicked a tab that flashed the word *RECORD* on and off in green letters on the small screen. He extended his wrist toward Yorulis. ''MechWarrior Jaleg Yorulis, do you hereby renounce the legal contract between yourself and the mercenary company known as the Gray Death Legion?''

''Huh? I didn't . . .''

Grayson switched the recorder off. ''Son, I can't have you a part of this unit if you are not wholeheartedly committed to it . . . to us! If we get into a scrap and you're standing on our flank, we *have* to know we can count on you! The people who hired us have to know that we're not going to switch over to the other side first chance we get. *That* means we had damn well better do everything legal, in the open, and strictly by the book, or they'll have our hides and ComStar will take what's left.

''So, if you want out, just say so! No penalty or bond forfeiture, and no hard feelings. If things go against us, you lie low for a month or two, then work your way on a Kurita freighter to someplace where you can get passage to Galatea. Or you sign on with a merc company working for the Combine. We won't be in a position to stop you . . . then. So? What'll it be? Are you in or out?''

''What about my 'Mech?''

Grayson's gray eyes were cold as ice. ''It's not *your* 'Mech until you've earned it. You can take with you what you brought into this agreement, your personal gear and the bond on Galatea. The *Stinger* belongs to the unit.''

Yorulis stared into the fire. ''I'll stick it,'' he said.

But can we depend on you? Grayson wondered. *It may be best—for you and for the rest of us—if you remain behind for the next few missions. We can't chance having you break during combat.*

He shifted his eyes to the others of the group. ''How about the rest of you? If you have any doubts, if you want out, now's the time to say it. Davis?'' Davis McCall grinned and gave a thumbs up gesture. Grayson turned to catch Clay's eye. ''How about it, Delmar?''

Clay nodded too, and added, ''It may be suicide, but I don't see any option.''

Grayson looked at Piter Debrowski. Debrowski and Yorulis were the biggest unknowns in the situation. Their only combat experience so far had been at Hunter's Cape and in the fracas outside Regis. They'd handled themselves well so far, but . . .

''Piter?''

''I'm with you, Captain. We can't go back now.''

''You're right about that,'' he said, looking into the dark beyond their little fire. ''God help us, we can't.''

20

Tollen Brasednewic shifted the 5 mm laser rifle nervously in his arms. He was crouched at Grayson's side in the dense underbrush of the slope above the road across the Basin Rim. "They're coming," he said, eyes fixed on the lower ground.

"I hear them," Grayson said, cradling a TK assault rifle salvaged from the *Phobos* after the landing. He checked the 100-round magazine cassette fitted into the weapon's stock, but did not look in the direction of the sound that was beginning to penetrate the rustle of wind and the shrieks of aviforms in the jungle canopy. "You'd better give the signal."

The merging of rebels with mercenaries into a single combat unit was a touchy business. Technically, Brasednewic held the militia rank of Colonel, outranking Grayson's rank of Captain. In actuality, the two shared command, but Grayson was well aware that the redbearded rebel resented having to take some orders from an offworlder. After all, the rebels had been fighting their Kurita occupier for ten years. What could offworld mercenaries teach them about war?

Brasednewic pulled out a palm-sized transceiver, flicked it on, and pressed a sender switch three times in quick succession. Kurita commo operators might hear the brief burst of carrier-wave static or the three rapid clicks, but it would carry no information for them, might not even be noticed. To the rebel and mercenary troops hiding in the jungle, the signal carried message aplenty. *They're coming. Be ready!*

The dull creak and clank of an approaching heavy 'Mech was louder now, mingled with the shrill keening of hovercraft. Grayson moved the TK around to the side of his body on its web sling and brought the electronic binoculars hanging from his neck up to his eyes. The road a hundred meters further up the slope was empty, but he had the scanner turned on a patch of ground farther down, not far from where he and Tollen were hiding. Nothing showed. No sign of digging revealed what they had done to the road.

When the lead vehicle came into view, it proved to be not a 'Mech, but a two-man scout hovercraft fitted with the antennae loops and magnetic gear of a mine detector. As it skimmed centimeters above the road, the craft's electronic sensors could probe the ground surface for metal, could probe the air itself for the lingering effluvium of various chemical explosives. From a safe distance, its sensors could detect mines buried on the road. These could be marked, disarmed, or exploded ahead of the advancing column of BattleMechs.

A hundred meters behind the hovercraft came the 'Mechs. In the lead were a *Stinger* and the odd, forward-jutting shape of a 35-ton JR7-D *Jenner*. Behind them were more hovercraft, open-topped and crowded with brown-garbed Kurita soldiers. Behind them were two more 'Mechs, a TBT-5N *Trebuchet* and a *Centurion*, both 50 tonners.

The mine detector slowed as it came almost opposite Grayson's and Brasednewic's position. Had its sniffers detected explosives? Or perhaps it caught the scent of the rebel troops who had passed that way only moments before. Or perhaps they were using an IR scanner to spot footprints visible as still-glowing patches of fading heat on the road.

Grayson hoped that the precautions they'd taken were enough. He'd had a small army of rebels walk down the hill past that spot, creating the effect of a large number of troops marching into the jungle. There should be nothing particularly ominous about that, especially because the stranded *Dervish* Grayson was using as bait was hidden only a kilometer farther down slope.

Montido's *Dervish* had provided the perfect bait. Tarpaulins and branches of jungle foliage had kept it shielded from orbiting Kurita spysats until the clear, cloudless morning that Grayson had ordered the camouflage be removed for a few hours. Though the rebels did not know at precisely what time the satellites would pass overhead, it was certain that the Combine forces would be watching the forest between the Basin Rim and the sea with great care. The crippled *Dervish* and the flares of the welding torches wielded by a small army of Techs and astechs working to get it operational again, would be clearly visible to the senses of any satellite or spacecraft passing a few hundred kilometers above.

Within two hours, rebel scouts at the edge of the Bluesward had reported enemy 'Mechs and hovercraft moving rapidly toward the Basin Rim. The ambushers, their weapons and special equipment chosen and readied ahead of time, rushed to their hiding places.

Now the Kurita force was moving down the road toward the crippled *Dervish*. Grayson had cautioned the ambushers beforehand that the enemy would be coming slowly and cautiously. They would realize that the appearance of the *Dervish* in their path could be bait for a trap, but they would try to arrive with enough force to thwart such a possibility.

The hovercraft with the mine detection gear hummed and skreeled on laboring fans just below Grayson's position, kicking up clouds of dust. Moving slowly, Grayson brought up his electronic binoculars again and studied carefully the ground beneath the hovercraft's plenum chamber. He could see nothing suspicious there, but had the enemy detected something? When the hovercraft tilted forward slightly and continue down the slope, Grayson breathed again. At his side, he felt Brasednewic breathe a sigh of relief, too.

The real targets of the ambush approached. Both men tensed again as the *Jenner* and the *Stinger* lumbered closer, low-hanging branches and vines scratching and catching at their hulls, then snapping free as they passed. Grayson froze into immobility. The 'Mechs' cockpits were level with his own position on the hill, and the pilots would be alert for an ambush. The greatest danger, however, lay with the rebel forces in the surrounding jungle. It would take only one man to panic or to discharge his weapon accidentally and early or to misunderstand orders that had been repeated and discussed again and again. Sometimes it seemed that there was always at least one guy who didn't get the word.

The two lead 'Mechs continued past without incident, and then a trio of troop carriers drifted down the slope on dust-boiling cushions of air. The soldiers aboard the open-decked hovercraft were Kurita regulars in uniforms of dull orange-brown under sleeveless protective jackets of darker brown armor cloth. Some carried flamers, while others cradled portable lasers or rapid-fire assault rifles. On each vehicle, one man stood behind a pintel-mounted weapon just aft of the covered, armored driver's cab. One swivelled a medium laser back and forth, as though fearful that the surrounding trees were going to suddenly bend down and attack. The other two rode shotgun, with heavy machine guns trailing long and glittering belts of linked ammo.

The troop carriers whining past at the speed of a slow walk were tempting, vulnerable targets. *Don't fire, anyone,* Grayson willed. *Don't move. Don't fire . . .*

The troop carriers passed, moving down the steep road, and none of the rebel forces had given away the ambush. As he watched the next pair of 'Mechs approach, excitement surged in his chest and set his heart to hammering. A *Centurion,* followed by a *Trebuchet.* Slowly, moving only centimeters at a time to keep from registering on the motion sensors that could be mounted on those 'Mechs, Grayson carried the transceiver to his lips. As he fixed his eyes on the spot on the road directly below, his heart beat harder. He could see where the passage of three more hovercraft had uncovered a bit of nylon rope carefully buried hours before. So far, however, the enemy had not noticed that telltale clue.

When the *Centurion* stepped across the exposed bit of rope, Grayson hissed *"Now!"*

Some twenty meters down the hill from the 'Mechs, the rebel and mercenary troops heard the command in their helmet coms. Each of six men yanked hard on the slender but cable-strong lengths of nylon rope they held, then scrambled for shelter farther down the slope. Those ropes, secured at intervals along their length by carefully fashioned pulleys of wood and plastic, went suddenly taut and broke from under the loosely packed dirt of the road. On the hill above, each line was attached to canvas satchels filled with explosives. These, in turn, were mounted to the far sides of heavy tree trunks by thin pull-ring igniters crimped to fuses cut to three-second lengths. Tugging the ropes yanked the satchels free from the trees, but the pull rings stayed firmly wired to the trunks. One satchel remained fixed to its tree because the right foot of the *Centurion* happened at that moment to be firmly planted on the rope in the road. The other five packets of high explosive whipped out onto the road, fuses burning.

Chemical sniffers or magnetic detectors would have detected conventional mines, even those made of non-ferrous materials. Tow mines, however, could be rigged far enough off the expected path of the targets that conventional detectors would not pick them up. If the tow ropes buried under several centimeters of earth had been accidentally uncovered and noticed, the prey would have been warned. That didn't happen and Grayson blessed his luck.

The *Trebuchet* stepped into one line, which had snapped up to the height of the 'Mech's knee and directly in front of it. The satchel charge whirled like a bolo on a shortening lead, wrapping around and around the BattleMech's leg until it snapped up against the armor just below the joint. An instant later, the three-second fuse burned into the chemical detonator cap.

The explosion of five kilos of TNT sheared away the surrounding foliage like an invisible scythe, leaving finger-sized chunks of armor buried in tree trunks twenty meters off. Four other explosions went off along the road at almost the same moment, each five meters apart. With that, the road rose in a wall of dirt and smoke, of flame and mangling fury. Only that first charge had actually entangled the leg of one of the 'Mechs, but the concussion of the other charges hurled both machines aside like dolls as most of that twenty-meter stretch of ground blew up. The roadbed itself crumbled out and spilled down the slope in an avalanche of debris. The *Centurion* lurched hard to its right, smashing into the wall of rock and vegetation that rose above the road. The *Trebuchet* teetered wildly, smoke and green coolant fluid gushing from its savaged right leg, then plunged feet-first down the collapsing slope.

Grayson peered into the smoke, then spoke into his transceiver again. "All units, watch the leaders. 'Mechs, move in! Ramage, see if you can keep those tail-end Charlies entertained!"

On the slope below him, but still above the road, a score of green-camouflaged commandos rose from their hiding places in brush-covered trenches to descend on the pair of temporarily helpless 'Mechs. Along with their motley collection of regular weapons, each commando also carried a satchel charge. As they closed on the downed Draco 'Mechs, they swung those satchels over their heads and let fly, then dropped flat to the ground to avoid the blast.

"We may be in luck down there," Grayson told Brasednewic. "Neither of those 'Mechs is designed for close-in scraps with infantry. No machine guns or flamers."

"Those hovercraft had machine guns," Tollen said, peering with his own binoculars through boiling smoke in the direction the hovercraft had travelled. "They'll be back any second, unless your trick decides to work."

Before Grayson could answer, a series of sharp, ringing cracks sounded from the misty north, followed by the drawn-out, popping creaks of falling trees. From their position, Grayson and Brasednewic could see one treetop shiver, then sweep across the sky to vanish in the smoke across the road.

Grayson's earcoms chirped a call signal, then came with Lori's voice. "The trees are down, and we have 'em boxed!"

"Go get them," Grayson replied. "Watch for the point 'Mechs."

Grayson could not see through the smoke to the new battle site a hundred meters up the road, but he could hear the staccato snaps of autorifle fire and the harsh bark of grenades and improvised explosives. Hovercraft ride on a cushion of air trapped within their plenum chambers, but their flight is no more than a few centimeters above the ground. Highly effective on water, in swampland, or on flat ground, hovercraft were at a severe disadvantage wherever surrounding vegetation and steep slopes made maneuver impossible. When TNT charges dropped a half-dozen trees across the road ahead of and behind the troop carrier column, the hovercraft were forced to stop. Autorifle fire from the heights above the road seared down into the open cargo compartments, aiming first for the mounted weapons gunners, then chewing through packed soldiers scrambling desperately to get clear of the slaughter.

As expected, the two lead 'Mechs turned at the first sounds of explosions and gunfire. The ambush was less than a minute old, but already the rest of the Kurita column was paralyzed, trapped and under attack from the surrounding jungle. The *Stinger* began using its hands to move fallen trees out of the road between it and the troop carriers. The handless *Jenner* could only stand by and blaze away at the trees with its lasers and SRMs. Shoulder-fired anti-armor missiles arced out of the forest, but the 'Mechs had very few clear targets. By the time the *Stinger* won through to the first hovercraft, the vehicle was a burning, grenade-shattered wreck, its passengers sprawled dead on the road or scattered into the jungle.

Lori's voice came through on Grayson's ear receiver again. "I think we made 'em mad, boss. The point 'Mechs are climbing off the road and coming after us."

"O.K. You know what to do. Execute."

"On our way."

For Grayson, the maddening part of the battle was being forced to remain where he was, in a position to see very little of what was going on around him. The sounds of gunfire and grenade blasts had died away to the north, though he could hear shrill screams from wounded men and the deep, ponderous thrum and crash of 'Mechs moving through the underbrush along the slope. Lori's command would be retreating ahead of the lead enemy 'Mechs now, drawing them deeper into the trees. Whatever happened there was out of his hands now. It was up to Lori to handle things.

Meanwhile, Sergeant Ramage's commandos had finished hurling their satchel charges and were dispersing into the jungle downslope from the road. Though both 50-ton 'Mechs had taken damage, neither was out of the fight. The *Trebuchet* was unable to move, its right leg nearly severed at the knee and the hull half-buried in the avalanche of the collapsing roadbed. The *Centurion*, however, was regaining its feet, but huge slabs of aligned-crystal steel armor had been peeled from the framework along its head and shoulder. The flip-top protective covers over the LRM tube array high on its right torso had also been smashed and crumpled.

The pilot must have been rattled by his rough handling. No sooner was the *Centurion* unsteadily on its feet when it began to blaze wildly into the jungle in all directions with its right arm autocannon. Spent casings clinked and glittered on the broken ground by its feet, and the snapping blasts of 30 mm autocannon projectiles splintered tree branches and stripped leaves in a wide circle around the wildly firing 'Mech. Several chance shots landed close to Grayson's and Brasednewic's position, but they exploded harmlessly in fountains of dirt and shredded vegetation.

Grayson crouched low in his trench until the firing stopped. His TK assault rifle was useless against the enemy 'Mech, and so all he could do was wait out the MechWarrior's rage. That *Centurion*'s pilot would have other things to think about very shortly.

There was a crashing in the brush to Grayson's right. He tapped Brasednewic's shoulder and pointed at the many brown-clad forms moving toward their position in a disordered rush. They were Kurita troops, survivors of the attack on the personnel carriers.

Grayson's TK was set for four-round burst fire, a measure that saved ammunition and avoided the muzzle climb associated with the weapon's 1200 rpm rate of fire. As his first target, he picked a Draco whose blue collar and shoulder tabs marked him as an officer. Because the man wore the sleeveless, armor-quilted jacket favored by House Kurita troops, Grayson drew careful aim on his head.

He stroked the trigger, and the TK sighed. Four caseless rounds made a barely discernible hiss as they cleaved the air to the Kurita officer thirty meters away. At least one round hit, snapping the man's head up and back and smashing him into the tree behind him. His blood was brutally red against the blue-green leaves it splattered.

Brasednewic's 5 mm laser rifle hummed, and an invisible bolt of coherent light struck another Kurita soldier full in the chest. The armor vest absorbed the bolt, but the man yelped as he slapped at the smoke puffing from the damaged garment. The laser rifle hummed again, and the soldier vanished into the underbrush—whether dead, wounded, or suddenly cautious, there was no way to tell.

The other Kurita troops suddenly vanished, too, but sent a handful of shots clipping the leaves above Grayson's head. One round buried itself into the trunk of a nearby tree. The situation could have become an uneasy stalemate, with Grayson and Brasednewic pitted against a large and desperate band of Kurita soldiers, but the *Centurion* stepped in and tipped the balance.

The 'Mech's sound or motion detectors must have picked up the volley of small arms fire from among the trees on the hill above him. It pivoted sharply to face the battle and opened fire blindly with laser bolts and a thundering burst from its autocannon. The MechWarrior had targeted the heaviest area of fire, and his shots tore into the underbrush where the Kurita troops were hiding.

Grayson grabbed Brasednewic's elbow. "Let's move out! Before it's our turn" The two of them crawled out of their trench and worked their way upslope, away from the drumroll of high explosives and the shrieks of dying Kurita troops.

During the initial attack, McCall's *Rifleman* and Clay's *Wolverine* had remained hidden above the road. Lying prone, covered by jungle vegetation, they were well-concealed from recon air or spacecraft by the jungle canopy. Paths down the slope to the ambush site had been carefully scouted earlier. Now, the two armored behemoths slashed aside light trees and vines and crashed into the open, lasers and autocannons belching fire. Fresh torrents of heavy weapons fire from the north marked the arrival of two more Gray Death *Stinger*s and the *Wasp*, who engaged the light 'Mechs of the Kurita patrol's van.

The *Centurion* halted in mid-stride, then spun toward and lurched into a shambling run back up the road toward the Basin Rim. McCall levelled paired lasers and autocannon at the fleeing 'Mech, pouring shot after shot into its back. If the CN9 took any damage, however, it was not immediately visible.

In the ruin of the road below Grayson's position, the *Trebuchet* stiffened into immobility and, second's later, its head split. The pilot emerged, streaming sweat, his hands raised. Orange- and brown-uniformed soldiers began straggling in from the brush in small clumps, weaponless, their hands also raised in surrender. Moments later, Lori reported that one of the enemy's *Stinger*s had surrendered, while the swifter *Jenner* had managed to slash an escape through the jungle.

Grayson set his autorifle's safety and stood up, suddenly tired. Brasednewic stood up, too, laser rifle canted across his shoulder. "Congratulations, Captain," he said. "Looks like maybe we *can* learn some things from you folks after all."

"That's what we came for, Colonel. But let's not underestimate these people."

"Who? The Dracos?"

"No . . . our people . . . yours and mine. It was their doing, this raid. They did it . . . together."

And as Grayson stepped down from the hill, his men—rebels and mercs together—began cheering wildly.

21

This far north, Verthandi's large moon never rose much above the southern horizon. Late in its third quarter, it hung like a ragged-edged orange sickle in an unusually cloudless sky just hours before dawn. The light of Verthandi-Alpha carried only faintly through the window where the man and woman lay in the dark. The man's fingers trailed across the woman's belly, tracing a delicate line from navel to sternum to throat, then circled down again to capture one smooth breast in a lingering caress. In the darkness, Sue Ellen Klein let out a soft moan.

"Hold me, Vincent," she whispered. "Just hold me, please . . ."

He drew her closer into his embrace. "What is it, Sue Ellen?"

"N-nothing." Her face was wet, the tears glistening by the light of the moon. "You've . . . all of you . . . have been so good to me."

"And why not? We're scarcely the monsters the Lyran Commonwealth makes us out to be."

"Oh, I know all that. It's just . . . oh, Vincent! I *killed* him!"

He held her tight, his hands exploring the hollows of her back, whispering into her ear until her sobs subsided. When at last she quieted, he said, "Darling, it wasn't you! You *know* that. But you've got to let go! Jeffric was killed by that bastard Carlyle . . . abandoned in a shot-up fighter and left to fry on re-entry. Sue Ellen, you saved him! You kept him from dying a horrible death! Tell me, what if it had been you in the crippled fighter, with your ship melting around you? Wouldn't he have done the same for you?''

''But it's all so confusing. I keep having dreams . . .''

''About Jeffric?''

''Some. Mostly, though, I *am* in the fighter, and Carlyle is outside, watching me burn. And Jeffric is with him, pleading with him, but Carlyle just crosses his arms and laughs. Or I'm all alone, hanging from a rock ledge, and there's this vast, empty blackness beneath and all around me, and I'm losing my grip . . .''

She shivered in his arms. ''That's the way it feels when I'm awake, like I'm just clinging to the edge, hanging on . . . and my fingers are giving way and I'm falling into the dark . . . and now I'm getting it in my dreams, too.''

''I've heard you moaning in your sleep.''

She drew back far enough to place her hand against his chest, to stroke at the mat of black hair there. ''Vincent, if it wasn't for you, I think I'd have gone insane. I mean it. I . . .. I couldn't live with myself for . . . for a while there. I'm grateful.''

He kissed her lingeringly. ''And I love you,'' he said, when their lips parted. ''You know, I'm glad to just . . . listen. If there's anything you want to get off your chest.'' He dropped his eyes, and smiled. ''Such a lovely chest.''

In reply, she snuggled closer. ''I wish I knew some deep, dark military secret I *could* get off my chest,'' she said after a time. ''Something I could give to you to help bring Carlyle down for good!''

He stroked her short hair. ''I wouldn't mind that myself. Maybe if we could trap him—you and I—it would lay to rest some of those ghosts for you. Got anything in mind?''

She shook her head. ''Nothing. I sat in on planning meetings, of course, but they didn't talk about anything really important. I knew . . . oh . . . where they were going to land, but that's not of any use now.''

''Military secrets become dated real fast,'' he agreed. ''Still, there might be something else.''

''I've told Governor Nagumo's people what I knew about the Gray Death's strength, what 'Mechs it had, and all of that, but they already knew.''

''What would really help would be some clue to where Carlyle might be hiding.''

"How could I give that? He knew this planet better than I did . . . and that's not saying much. All I know is that he was to make contact with members of the Revolutionary Council. That odd little man with glasses—Erudin—was supposed to bring them together."

"Maybe the name Erudin will help. The Governor has extensive files on the names and backgrounds of a number of Verthandi's citizens."

"Well, I already told him."

"Were there any other names mentioned?"

"Huh? Oh, I guess so, but I don't really remember. The names of people isn't going to help locate Carlyle now, is it?"

"I don't know, darling, but who knows what might help? Anything you remember—a name, a meeting place—*anything* might help."

She sighed. "Well, I know we were to meet the Revolutionary Council out in the jungle someplace. That seemed strange to me at the time. I had this picture of us all standing around knee-deep in mud. Erudin laughed when I asked how we were supposed to move 'Mechs through the mud. He said Ericksson's place was all dry land and full of sur . . . What's the matter?"

Mills was staring at her with nearly savage intensity. "Ericksson? Who is this Ericksson?"

"Someone we were supposed to meet. Why? Do you know the name? Is it important?"

"I don't know, Sue Ellen, but a lot of the Old Families on Verthandi are Scandinavian, with Scandinavian names. If Carlyle was supposed to meet with one of the Old Family people, it's possible . . . just possible . . ."

"Wait! Where are you going?"

Vincent Mills threw back the covers and groped for the trousers he had flung over a chair earlier. "Darling, you may have just given us the one bit of information we need to burn that bastard Carlyle once and for all."

"But . . ."

"You go back to sleep, my love. I've got to talk to someone about it, fast!"

Governor-General Nagumo knew about the name Ericksson even before Captain Mills had finished putting on his uniform. They had not told Mills about the micro-

phone installed in the bedroom because Dr. Vlade and
others feared that it might make the young captain self-
conscious during his sessions with the young prisoner.
The technician monitoring their love-making that night
had a call into Nagumo's office almost at once. Normally,
the major on duty would have had to decide whether this
bit of information was important enough to warrant wak-
ing Nagumo in his quarters, but this night Nagumo was
still in his office, going over the reports of that afternoon's fiasco in the jungle.

By the time Mills had crossed the central compound
of Regis University and asked to see Nagumo on urgent
business, Nagumo's computer Techs had pulled Gunnar
Erickkson's dossier from their files on prominent Verthandian citizens.

Nagumo began issuing orders, assembling his forces.
His final order dispatched two men from his personal
guard to Captain Mills' quarters. The Klein girl had
served her purpose, and she could not be trusted. Better
to bury her below the Tower for the time being.

Nagumo forgot about Sue Ellen Klein almost as soon
as he gave the order to pick her up. He was already en-
grossed in the display map on the wall of his office. Yes,
there it was, right where the computer had located it.

Fox Island . . .

There was another romantic rendezvous that night, this
one deep in the shadows that edged the perimeter of the
Fox Island plantation. Here, too, the orange sickle of
Verthandi-Alpha illuminated sky and trees with ruddy
light, though the moon's sweep was bisected by the black
shadow of the forest and the bulk of the Basin Rim cliffs.

These lovers' conversation also turned to the subject
of Grayson Carlyle.

"Is it that you don't trust him?" the woman asked as
she snuggled closer within the curve of the man's arm.
They lay together on a mossy hummock well away from
the plantation clearing, under the spreading blackness of
the forest canopy. Moonlight edged her profile and the
leaves overhead.

Carlotta Helgameyer often met her lover in this spot,
because there were reasons—political reasons—why they
could not openly admit their love.

"I supposed it's that I don't understand the man," Tollen said. He paused for a moment, his teeth grinding in unconscious habit while he thought. "I trust him, I think . . . but I don't understand him."

"What is there to understand?"

"He's . . . He doesn't act like a mercenary."

"You mean, he doesn't act like you think a mercenary *ought* to act."

"Well, yes. I suppose. But he's thrown himself into his mission here with such . . . such energy. As though there's more to it for him than the money."

"I would have thought that was obvious."

"What do you mean?"

"Well, it's obvious he cares for his people."

"I think there's more. He shares our hatred of the Dracos."

"And that's wrong?"

"I didn't say that. Of course it's not wrong . . . not from where *we* are! But we probably should have tried to find out more about the man before we hired him."

"Most of us on the Council were against the idea, you'll remember."

Tollen laughed. "It *was* Erudin's idea, wasn't it, Carlotta?"

"Thorvald thought he was trying to arrange some sort of power play against the Old Families. Old Gunnar Ericksson was the one who finally decided to bring them in, and told Devic to go ahead and try out his plan. That shook Thorvald. He thought Gunnar would go along with the rest of us. He wanted to kick Devic off the Council anyway."

He squeezed her tighter. "Yeah, well, you Old Families had better watch yourself now that us latecomers have the Gray Death on our side!"

"It's not funny, Tol."

"I know. I'm sorry. But this hiding what we feel for one another. It . . . gets to me."

"Me, too. Maybe things will change after the war's over."

"That'll be the day."

She remained quiet for a bit, then decided to change the subject. "Our people and the mercenaries did pretty well in the battle yesterday, didn't they?"

"Yes." He thought about it, teeth grinding once more. By any standards, the ambush had been a splendid success. They'd captured two of the four enemy 'Mechs, the *Stinger* and the cripple-legged *Trebuchet,* killed twenty-two Kurita soldiers and taken another thirty-six. Their own losses were only two killed and five wounded, and three of those wounded had been injured by their own explosives rather than by enemy fire.

They'd sent the *Stinger* and the prisoners back to Fox Island, while a band of rebel and mercenary Techs descended on the *Trebuchet* and on the hulks of the three bombed-out troop transports. With a few hours' grace, it was possible that the *Trebuchet* would be moving under its own power again. It had taken the Techs only minutes to strip the hovercraft of circuit boards, wiring, weapons, instrument fittings, engine housing, and an endless stream of useful items that might be handy later, in unlikely places or vehicles.

"They did very well, indeed," Tollen said, "and I have to admit that that youngster knows more about combat than I ever will. I don't know if it's just that he knows all the tricks or if he's some kind of tactical genius."

"Then it's good he's here. We haven't had such successes in the whole ten years of the war."

"Yeah, but it's become *his* war, somehow. Is that right, that we should step aside, and let him win the war for us? And what about afterward? Are we going to be able to get rid of him?"

"I thought you trusted him?"

"I don't know what to think anymore. This idea of his, to carry the war to the villages . . ." The teeth-grinding noises came again. Carlyle had said that the enemy had to be hit again and again, he had to be kept off-balance, kept inside his containments and garrison camps. More important, he insisted that the people must be enlisted in the fight against the invaders. Tollen knew that meant more towns like Mountain Vista would be reduced to rubble before this was over. More of his people would die in fire and horror. What was right?

"We're leaving tomorrow," he said at last.

"I heard."

"We're heading west. A raid in force, Carlyle calls it. To Scandiahelm. There's a Kurita garrison there."

Carlotta ran her hand along his chest. He could sense her compassion for his own pain, his uncertainty. "You'll come back to me?" she said.

"Carlotta mine," he whispered, sweeping her close, inhaling the scent of her, enfolding her warmth. "Nagumo's whole army couldn't keep me away, beloved . . ."

Lori, too, was thinking about Grayson that night, but the thoughts were not pleasant. She came awake in her quarters in the rebel compound, her skin glistening with sweat, the paralyzing fear of the nightmare still close. In the moon-spilled darkness, she sat breathing hard, trying to collect herself.

Rather than face sleep and the terror of more dreams, she decided to get dressed and give her *Locust* another check-through. As she pulled on her clothes, Lori's movements were sluggish. She'd thought the nightmares had gone for good. It was depressing to know that her fears and self-doubts were rising, hydra-headed, once more.

Grayson had the guerrilla-mercenary force in motion an hour before the sun came up. Their 'Mechs re-armed and re-equipped, the worst of the battle damage repaired by Techs who had worked furiously through the night, the raiding party set out along forest trails and logging roads toward the west. The group consisted of sixteen rebel 'Mechs led by Montido in his fully repaired *Dervish,* as well as all six of the mercenary 'Mechs.

Those rebel 'Mechs too badly damaged or too uncertain in their jury-rigged repairs or weaponry to survive a long, hard march would remain at the Fox Island cave. The rest started off after Grayson's mercenaries, moving swiftly by jungle trails and backwoods roads in the same westerly direction. Riding in hovercraft and swamp skimmers, Brasednewic's infantry accompanied the column, a force of perhaps 500 men and women in all. Because they were slower, the rebel Galleon tanks and other wheeled or tracked vehicles would remain behind.

With them was Jaleg Yorulis, his *Stinger* assigned to one of the Verthandian 'Mech trainees. Grayson had decided it wiser not risk him in combat.

22

As Grayson and his forces moved westward, the land rose steadily, tree cover growing thinner until the forest gave way to scattered patches of woodland among blue-green meadows and cultivated fields. Their destination was on Perres Point, a Kurita watch station at the very edge of the jungle and above the village of Scandiahelm. Here, the Basin Rim was a relatively gentle, forested ridge. The region above the ridge was part of the Blue-sward Plateau, tucked in between the Silvan forest and the Uppsala Mountains. Villages dotted the rolling countryside, interspersed with blueleaf plantations and gavel farms.

The Dracos had built watchstations on Verthandi wherever there was a sizable local population to control or an important resource to guard. At Perres Point, it was the inhabitants of the nearby villages who were held hostage. Several hamlets and farms had been burned already in retaliation for attacks on Kurita personnel in the area. The station itself consisted of a small supply depot and maintenance facility, a platoon of sixty soldiers, and one lance of BattleMechs of the Third Strike Regiment's Second Battalion, Company C.

The combined mercenary-rebel force hit the watch-station at dawn, catching the Kurita 'Mechs unmanned, the soldiers at breakfast. Less than two minutes after Grayson's *Shadow Hawk* crashed through the perimeter fence, the Kurita troops were throwing down their weapons. Four 'Mechs—a *Wolverine*, a *Phoenix Hawk*, a *Panther*, and a *Wasp*—had fallen into rebel hands. As had tons of supplies, rations, ammunition, and spare parts, a literal treasure for the ragged little army, purchased without a single death.

Grayson wished his next task would be as easy as ambushing the Kurita watchstation garrison. The rebel forces were still rounding up prisoners and loading captured spare parts and stores from the base and the nearby supply dump when a delegation of townspeople arrived from Scandiahelm. He received them inside the watchstation complex, in a bombproof chamber that had served as a mess hall. The delegation consisted of Scandiahelm's chief proctor, a graying, worried-eyed man in his fifties, and two companions. Grayson stood behind the mess table, flanked by Lori and Brasednewic. He smiled and extended a hand, but the proctor ignored it.

Instead, the man dropped a packet onto the messhall table in front of the mercenary commander. Grayson opened it, pulling out a sheaf of flat holos. He held up each in turn, letting the light from the overhead fluoros catch them. Each detailed some horror of war. Rubble spilled across a street. Bodies, sprawled and crazily twisted, lay in black pools. A forest of orange flames silhouetted a skyline. The unmistakable form of a *Marauder* rose against flame and blackness, its heavy forearms leveled above the crumbling ruin of what might have been a church. A tiny human figure clung to one arm, legs wildly flailing.

Grayson looked up from the holos, eyebrows arched. "What's all this?"

The proctor's mouth tightened. His face was pale above the high-collared black and scarlet jacket he wore. "That is . . . *was* the town of Mountain Vista. We thought you should see these."

"Yes?" Grayson remained impassive, but he knew what was coming next.

"Mountain Vista lies on the other side of Regis from us," one of the other Verthandians said. He had a bushy mustache and shared the proctor's look of fear and disapproval. "But it's not so far from Scandiahelm. Some misguided youths shot and killed a Kurita guardsman there. One BattleMech—only *one*, this *Marauder*—did all this to the town."

"I don't think I understand," Grayson carefully lied.

How was he supposed to handle this? "Whose side are you on?"

The proctor's frown deepened. "We're not *on* anyone's 'side', as you put it! By attacking this base, you have put Scandiahelm and every other nearby town in grave danger! Do you know what the Governor will *do* to us when he learns of this raid of yours?"

Grayson glanced at Brasednewic. The rebel leader stood, arms crossed, his face carefully neutral.

"I'd say there is a very good chance that they'll come and destroy your town," Grayson replied. "The question is, what are *you* going to do about it?"

The third Verthandian looked at his leader. "Kalev was right, Proctor Jorgenson. We should throw in with the Dracos."

"And beg for their mercy?" Grayson tapped the holos with the back of his hand. "Is this the Kurita mercy you seek? Or their justice?"

"You have left us little choice, offworlder," the proctor said. "You didn't even bother to consult with us before your attack . . ." Grayson considered the implications of consulting with the local civilians each time he contemplated an attack. "I apologize, gentlemen, for not consulting with you," was all he said, "but there simply was no time before the attack. And I fear we have little time to lose now before the Kurita forces gather in response to our action here." He turned to Lori. "Check and see how the loading is coming along. We move in one hour, ready or not."

That shook the three of them. "What? Wait! You can't mean to leave us!"

Grayson feigned surprise. "Why, I thought you planned to cooperate with Nagumo, to ask for his mercy. You can't expect us to remain while you and Nagumo dicker for our heads!"

"You misunderstand us, sir," Proctor Jorgenson said. "We dislike the Combine as much as you do. More, I daresay. This is *our* world they have taken, not yours! But what chance do we have against a regiment of BattleMechs? At least stay and protect us, now that you've stirred them up against us! To abandon us now would be . . . criminal!"

"Gentlemen, I would like to stay and help you, but

that is simply impossible. My army is outnumbered. To be trapped here, in the open, by Nagumo's superior forces would be an invitation to complete disaster. We must keep moving.''

''But what are we to do?'' The proctor's complaint was a thin wail. ''We'll be killed!''

''Do? Why . . . you could stay and make peace with Nagumo's Colonel, when he comes.''

Jorgenson's finger stabbed angrily at the holo of the *Marauder*. ''That is Nagumo's Colonel!'' he said. ''A moment after that young man in the holo surrendered, that monster dropped him to the street and stepped on him like an insect!''

''Then you had better run . . .''

''There are children in the town . . . women . . . old people . . .''

'' . . . or you can *fight!*''

''Fight? With what?''

Grayson turned to Tollen. ''Colonel, we captured more weapons in that supply dump than we can possibly carry with us. Go find Sergeant Ramage. The two of you organize a detail to pass out weapons and ammo to anyone from Scandiahelm who wants them. Show them how to use them. But quickly! We don't have much time!''

''Yes, *sir!*''

''And send a detail into Scandiahelm. We're going to need cargo transports to carry the loot. Hovercraft, if they have them.''

''You can't!'' the moustached Verthandian said. ''How will we get away . . .''

''On foot, or in the vehicles we'll leave you,'' Grayson replied. ''We won't take everything, and we're leaving you more than enough guns and supplies. That ought to pay for a few hover transports.''

''Give us *guns* . . . is that *it?*'' Jorgenson waved his arms, incredulous. ''What good are guns against Nagumo's BattleMechs?''

''Why, no good at all,'' Grayson said cheerfully, ''but they'll be quite useful against the Governor's men. You'll find that Nagumo doesn't have 'Mechs enough to garrison every village and hamlet on Verthandi. Why, he's going to be hard-pressed just trying to keep track of us.''

''But we're one village . . .''

"Then dammit, man, talk to your neighbors! Get the other villages to help! East of here the entire Vrieshaven district is in open revolt! Join them! Get others to join you! You've got—my God—what? A hundred thousand? Two hundred thousand people on this planet? Against maybe a hundred 'Mechs and a few thousand soldiers! There's no *way* they can hold this world if enough of you refuse to let them do it!"

Jorgenson looked dazed. "You . . . you'll help us?"

Grayson nodded. "I'll be back . . . or some of my people will. We'll help to train you, get your organized. We'll teach you what we know about fighting Battle-Mechs, what their weak points are. Believe me, you're not helpless! And you're not alone!"

"You bastard," the third Verthandian muttered, bitterness in his voice. "You bastard! You've just been maneuvering us into your war!"

"It's *your* war," Grayson said. "I'm just the hired help. But if you want the Dracos out, you'd better start fighting them yourselves!"

The proctor gathered up the holos and slipped them back into the packet. "How long before Nagumo attacks us?"

"I don't know. It may depend on whether or not this watchstation was able to get off a warning. Judging by their condition of . . . readiness, I'd say there's a good chance that it'll be days before anyone wonders why this place hasn't reported in. On the other hand, enemy fighters could be overhead in the next fifteen minutes."

"Then I must alert the town . . . and the other towns in the region. And I have to talk to the people, see who will . . . who will follow me. The rest, we'll have to see about moving them to caves we know of, in the mountains."

Grayson looked up sharply. The proctor still looked afraid, but there was a new light in the man's eyes. He was not as old as Grayson had first thought.

"I'll let you use one of my skimmers," Grayson said.

He led the civilian delegation back into the sunshine. Brasednewic was nearby, directing the loading of cases of rifles and ammunition on the cargo rack of a mercenary skimmer.

"Tollen, I want to see you for a moment."

When they were apart from the bustle of soldiers, Grayson spoke rapidly. "They're going to fight."

Brasednewic cast a skeptical glance across Grayson's shoulder to where the three civilians waited in the shadow of Grayson's inert *Shadow Hawk*. "Yes?"

"I want you to tell off a detail of your men, however many you think you'll need. Stay here with these people, get them organized and armed. Nagumo's going to hit this place in the next few days to make an example of them, and the village will need a cadre of veterans to stiffen them or they'll be done for."

"You think of that now, after dragging them into this?"

For one stark instant, Grayson's anguish showed in his eyes and face. "Dammit, Tollen, what would you have me do?"

"I . . . I'm sorry . . . Captain." He looked back at Jorgenson and the others. "It's hard. These are my people . . ."

"I know, I know, and I'm a damned outlander who can't understand. But if you people don't start fighting your own wars, I'm not going to be able to fight them for you!"

Brasednewic's gaze strayed back to Grayson, then to the ground beneath his boots. "You don't understand," he said. "These *are* my people. I was born down there, in Scandiahelm. I lived here for most of my life. Some of us *have* been fighting our own war . . . as best as we know how."

"I'm . . . sorry. I didn't know . . ."

"What difference does it make? Anyway, you're right. But you have to understand that . . . not all Verthandians think that what we . . . the rebels . . . are doing is right. My own family, for instance."

"Your family?"

"My mother was killed in a rebel attack, oh . . . maybe a year after the Dracos came. I . . . I was already with the rebels by then. I didn't hear about it for another couple of years. But my father and brother, they joined the Loyalists.

"You have to understand, a lot of people see the war as a chance to win out against the Old Families, as they're called. The Scandinavian families who hold most of the land and power on Verthandi."

Grayson didn't know what to say. He'd never been this close to the true horror of civil war.

Brasednewic shrugged. "It doesn't really matter any-more. My father was reported dead . . . lynched by a rebel mob . . . a year ago. I guess my brother is a Blue by now. He'd be old enough. I don't know where he is." He seemed to shake himself, to draw himself back to awareness of his surroundings. "As you say, Captain, a couple hundred of my people should be enough. We'll set up here, but with an HQ post back in the hills. I doubt that we'll be able to hold this place for long if Nagumo makes a determined push. But maybe I can keep these people together, get them fighting with some kind of organization."

Grayson nodded, then placed a hand on the rebel leader's shoulder. "I'm counting on you for that. Jorgenson mentioned caves in the mountains. Send a scout party up there and check them out. That could be the sort of reserve base we need. Oh, and I'll leave that *Wolverine* we captured."

"We'll need a pilot for it."

"I'll have Sergeant Ramage tell off some of his pilot trainees. Tell you what. We'll take the *Panther* and the *Phoenix Hawk* we captured, and leave you the *Wasp* and the *Wolverine*. But get them out of the area and hidden up in the hills as fast as you can. You won't be able to stand up to Nagumo with two 'Mechs and a couple of half-trained recruit pilots!"

Brasednewic was watching the three civilians and smiling as though to himself. "Not yet, maybe. But for the first time, I'm almost beginning to feel like we might have half a chance!"

The *Union* Class DropShip *Xao* entered Verthandi's atmosphere balanced atop a pillar of pulsing white fire. In recent days, the *Xao* had been engaged in orbital reconnaissance, a landing and retrieval operation to shuffle two platoons of infantry from their outpost at the edge of Vrieshaven back to the capital of Regis, and a supply run to Verthandi-Alpha and back. The ship had made the flight back with a unit detached from Admiral Kodo's command and assigned to special detached duty under Colonel Kevlavic's personal command.

Draconis Elite Strike Team 4 was typical of DEST forces used extensively throughout the Draconis Combine and was similar in concept to the elite commando units of other major Houses of the Successor States. Hand-picked from veteran units, put through rigorous physical and mental training courses that passed less than 5 percent of those selected, DEST unit personnel learned to use weapons ranging from Mk XXI blazers and poison-coated throwing stars to the plastic tip of a disposable stylus or their bare hands. They could make high altitude-low opening parachute drops from twenty kilometers up, swim for kilometers underwater using oxygen rebreather apparatus, scale sheer cliffs using special climbing gear, and penetrate the most closely guarded security zone with a bewildering array of miniaturized electronic lockpicks and scanners. Most could also pilot BattleMechs and had the codebreaking and electronic skills to penetrate a locked 'Mech's security systems.

DEST 4 had been assigned to Nagumo's command as a support element, but so far had spent the campaign in their barracks on Verthandi-Alpha. DEST special forces were too valuable to risk on anything other than important, easily identified tactical targets, and there are few of those in any guerrilla war. Now, however, DEST 4 had a target.

The *Xao* burned through Verthandi's stratosphere at a flat angle, shedding speed and heat in the roiling wake of its passage. For precisely thirty seconds, the ship's drives cut off and the spherical craft arrowed powerlessly through thin air. Two by two, silvery bubbles dropped from it, punching through the turbulence of the craft's shockwaves and toward the cloud-mottled green and blue of Verthandi's polar basin, 15,000 meters below. After falling another kilometer, the bubbles split like ripe melons. They disgorged heavily armed and armored men who uncurled from the fetal positions they'd held inside their aluminum prisons and spread black-clad arms and legs to the stiffening wind of their fall. Above and behind them, the *Xao*'s drive throbbed to life again, her passage marked by her white contrail of heated air against the icy blue.

In free fall, the commando team used computer-linked visor displays to lock onto a pinpoint target that was hidden by clouds but calculated by triangulation from three navigational satellites in space above them. Those satellites painted the clouds above the target with laser beams invisible to the naked eye, but made visible by the electronics of the helmet visors. Steering with arched backs and outstretched limbs, the commando team assembled in rough aerial formation and drifted in the direction of the target.

At 500 meters, black nylon drogue chutes silently deployed and steadied each man, checking his fall. At 200 meters, the main chutes deployed with a succession of barely audible pops, night-black flying wings that each commando steered with deadly purpose through the lower cloud deck and out into the clear, sultry air above Fox Island. The clearing of the Ericksson Plantation was plainly outlined in the infra-red optics of their helmet visors, as were the pinpoints of green light marking sentries, technicians working under the overcast night sky, rebels out for a late-night stroll, or a romantic rendezvous at the clearing edge.

The first commandos touched down in eerie silence, flipped their harness releases, and marked their targets. A sentry standing in the shadow of jungle growth gasped in surprise and collapsed as a black-clad knife reached from behind and slit his throat. A technician walking from the warehouse that hid one of the island's 'Mech maintenance sheds felt something hard and metallic thud against his ribs, then looked down in numb surprise at the four-armed throwing star protruding from his side. The blade's neurotoxin transformed the acetylcholine of his neural sheaths into something horribly else, something that spread with lightning speed from synapse to synapse throughout his suddenly dying body. The technician crumpled, unable to speak, to whimper, even to think.

Garn Dober, Brasednewic's second-in-command, stepped out onto the veranda of the plantation house, blinking into the darkness. He thought he'd heard something—the whisper of running footsteps, perhaps. His eyes were adjusted to the light inside the house, and so he could make out nothing in the clearing except the gray-black sky and the darker jungle. A shadow rose from beside the veranda steps and vaulted the railing. Dober cried out in surprise, but a black-gloved hand stifled the sound while black steel slashed and stabbed. Dober was left weaving on his knees, hands clenched uselessly across the gash low in his throat, from which blood welled in an unstoppable, strangling flood.

The shadow that stepped past him ignored the thud as Dober's body collapsed on its face. The veranda door was open. The DEST commando removed a small, metallic packet from a thigh pouch, twisted a control, and tossed the packet into the light. Instants later, the light through the door was replaced by a far brighter flash. Then a bang rocked the building and sent glass splintering out from a dozen windows into the night. There were screams as a dozen men and women in various stages of casual dress or undress stumbled through the smoke onto the veranda, their blinded eyes seeing neither Dober's body nor the shadows crouched and silent in the darkness beyond. Laser beams lanced through the night and unprotected flesh with equal ease. Screams and shouted questions changed to the piercing shrieks of the dying and horribly burned. Somewhere in the darkness, a subgun yammered a harsh challenge that was answered by an exploding bomb.

With every moment, more DEST troopers were landing on black and silent wings. At a sign from their leader, the black shadows scattered into the night, weapons at high port and ready. Several troopers rushed the mansion's door, then paused on each side of the rectangle now illuminated by the fire burning inside. On a silently communicated count, the black shapes swung around and through the doorway. A moment later, there were shots from inside, and another scream, then more shots and an urgent voice jabbering from an upstairs window, pleading.

The leader bent his head, shutting out the sounds around him in order to better hear the reports filtering through the commo gear in his helmet. One of his scouts reported that they'd found the cave mouth indicated by the planetological reports, that the rebel 'Mechs were there, unmanned, defenseless. A second report announced that the base radio shack was secure, the comtech on duty dead, the equipment fused into useless junk. A third informed him that a number of prisoners had been taken in the house, among them members of the so-called Rebel Council.

"The one called Ericksson," the leader said. "Has he been identified?"

"He was, sir." There was a pause. "He was shot trying to escape."

The leader smiled behind his visor. Gunnar Ericksson was a popular leader, and detaining him could have led to unfortunate political consequences. Regis Central had ordered that he be quietly eliminated. The other rebel leaders would know as much as Ericksson had known, and could doubtless be persuaded to talk.

He punched out a combination of buttons on the transceiver unit he wore on his arm. The carrier wave hiss of an open frequency sounded in his earphones. "Strike One to Strike Two," he said softly. His words were picked up by his throat mike and relayed through a listening satellite to a BattleMech com receiver, which by now should be only a few kilometers away.

"Strike One, this is Two," a voice answered. "Strike Two in position. Situation report."

The leader's grin broadened.

"Assault Phase One affirmative, repeat, affirmative. We have complete surprise."

"Excellent, Strike One! Is there resistance?"

The leader looked down at a sprawled form on the ground and nudged it with his boot. It was a young woman, scantily clad and very dead.

"Negative, Colonel. No resistance."

"And their 'Mechs?"

"I have a report that our scouts have found the caves. The 'Mechs are unmanned and in our hands. We'll have the area secured soon. All other targets have been secured and neutralized."

"Understood. We are on the road, on schedule. We'll be there in three hours."

"Confirmed, three hours. Strike One out."

Three hours. That meant the BattleMech company led by Colonel Kevlavic himself was on its way down the main road from Basin Rim and already past the area ravaged in the battle only two days before.

Someone screamed as the silent twin swords of blazer fire struck him down. Farther off, the dull thump of a fuel depot igniting startled the night-calling wildlife into silence.

Three hours? He looked down again at the rebel's body by his feet. By that time, things at the rebel base would be well in hand.

23

The rebel column had stopped for the night. Even along the broadest and firmest plantation trails and roads that crisscrossed beneath the trees, travel in the jungle was difficult, at best. The dark added little to their chances of concealing something as big, hot, and loud as a small army of BattleMechs when the enemy arsenal included infrared scanners and sonic trackers. Grayson and the other MechWarriors had stayed in their 'Mechs, taking turns standing watch, sleeping, or relaxing. Outside, the rebel troops stretched canvas and tarps from the sides of grounded vehicles and slept in makeshift tents, while others strolled the dark camp perimeter, watching shadows.

Restless, unable to sleep, Grayson heated water for coffee in a small brass pot over one of the power plant coolant ducts in the narrow engineering access space high in the *Shadow Hawk*'s thorax. He spent much of the night watching the *Hawk*'s scanners, but there was no sign of enemy movement. Once his radio band scanners picked up a burst of static that might have been anything—a meteor ionizing the upper atmosphere, a ship re-entry, or random radio noise generated by the Norn system's sun in Verthandi's magnetic field. A short time later, he thought he detected the warbling garble of scrambled radio transmissions, but very far away. His own base was under radio silence, of course, a necessary precaution to keep the enemy from triangulating their transmissions and getting a fix on the rebel HQ. That transmission *had* to be something of the enemy's.

What was Nagumo doing? What was he planning? Grayson knew with a cold lump of certainty in his gullet that his success against Verthandi's conquerors during the past two days owed much to luck and to the fact that he'd been able to gain a momentary initiative over Nagumo's forces. That initiative was a fragile, illusory state, however. Nagumo had only to make one move, strike one village, make one attack that forced Grayson to respond, and the initiative was lost, possibly forever. The enemy had so many forces, so many troops spread across a planet that was, after all, far larger than any one man could grasp. Grayson's forces were so few. Even if he could find a way to win this unequal struggle, how could he do it before Governor-General Nagumo scorched the surface of Verthandi to a cinder in a vicious war of retaliation and counterretaliation?

Once during his vigil, Grayson thought he detected a brief faint glow, a dim, false dawn in the cloud bellies above the treetops to the east. When the light quickly faded, he decided that it had been a figment of his own exhaustion.

Before it was fully light, the rebel band had breakfasted on canned rations and survival concentrates, saddled up their vehicles, and were on their way once more. He hoped to reach Fox Island well before 0900 local time, give his men time to resupply, and push on to the next target, another watchstation at the edge of the Vrieshaven district, 180 kilometers further east. After that, perhaps they could rest awhile.

Only a short while, though. Success depended on the rebel 'Mech force moving quickly and far afield, striking the Kurita garrisons wherever they were weak and lax in their watchfulness. To stop meant that the enemy could close in on them with fingers of steel, trapping them, crushing them.

He urged tired men and worn machines to a faster pace through an unforgiving jungle. Lori was in the lead in the light and swiftfooted *Locust*. They were still five kilometers from camp when her voice came across the command circuit. "Boss! I've got a reading ahead! Mansized, heading this way!"

Grayson's brow furrowed in puzzlement. There should be no sentries so far to the west of Fox Island. He acknowledged and steered the *Hawk* up the trail until it stood alongside the *Locust*. His own scanners detected

the motion—a man, following an erratic and uneven
course through the brush. Less than ten meters ahead of
the two 'Mechs, that man burst out onto the trail, where
he stood weaving unsteadily. Through a mask of blood,
he took in the apparition of two BattleMechs towering in
front of him, then fell face down into the soft ground.
Lori and Grayson reached him first. One of the Legion
medtechs joined them moments later, kit in hand. It
wasn't until the medic had wiped some of the blood and
dirt from the man's face that Grayson recognized him as
Jaleg Yorulis.

Yorulis' eyes fluttered open. "Don't . . . go back,"
he said, his voice a hoarse croak. *"They're* there . . ."

"Who? Who's there?"

"Dracos . . ."

Grayson went cold inside. "Jaleg! What happened?
Tell us!"

"Drac . . . commandos. Parachutes. They landed right
on top of us. Never knew . . . never knew they were
here. The . . . 'Mechs, they came through later."

" 'Mechs? Kurita BattleMechs?"

He nodded, the effort costing him blood and strength.
"They're still there . . . waiting . . . for you. . . ."

The medic ran his hands across Yorulis' body.
"Where'd they hit you, MechWarrior?"

Yorulis laughed, a ragged, gagging sound, and tried to
mop at the blood spilling from the corner of his mouth.
"Where didn't they get me?"

Grayson pursed his lips. He was no medic, but he knew
that Yorulis didn't have a chance outside a well-stocked
hospital, which they weren't likely to find out here. As
blood welled from holes high in the man's chest, the
medtech began slapping them with small plastic patches.
Those holes sucked and bubbled with each breath Yorulis
took.

"How many 'Mechs?" Grayson asked gently. The
medic looked up at Grayson as though about to protest,
but Grayson silenced him with a shake of his head and
repeated the question. "How many 'Mechs, Jaleg?"

"Don't . . . know. Comp'ny maybe. Maybe more."
He tossed his head back and forth. "Don't go back there.
They're . . . laying for you. Must've waited to get word
that you were out raiding their outposts . . . then moved

. . . fast. They got all the 'Mechs you left there. And the Techs. Herded them off south . . . somewhere . . .''

The full scope of the disaster was only now becoming clear to Grayson. Without their base, without Techs . . .

"Couldn't get to 'Mech," the wounded 'MechWarrior continued. "Never had a chance. They got the Council too, Captain. Rounded 'em up and marched 'em off. Don't know what happened to them."

"Ericksson?"

"Don't know. Don't . . . know. Didn't see him. I . . . snuck out, but a *Phoenix Hawk* spotted me, opened up with its machine guns. I guess they figured they killed me, because they stopped shooting after the third time I fell down." He started coughing then, and the blood flowed faster, soaking the medtech's patches. "I . . . guess maybe they were right."

"You take it easy," Grayson said, aware of how false the words sounded. "We'll get you patched up and . . ."

But Yorulis kept coughing, a wet, strangling gargle. His breaths were coming in short, quick, wet gasps. His eyes closed. "Never knew they were . . ."

And then he was dead.

Grayson stood up, his head swimming. There was a great deal of blood on his thin pullover shirt, and it had now soaked through to his skin. It felt hot and sticky. The medtech clenched his fists once, then silently repacked his kit without looking at Grayson. *He thinks I killed him*, Grayson thought. *Maybe he's right. But I had to know.*

Lori looked up at him, at the blood on his shirt and hands. "What now, boss?" she asked. "Do we take them at Fox Island?"

He looked at the body for a moment, his lips compressed into a thin, white line. Then he shook his head. "No. If they're waiting for us, they'll know what we have and be ready for us. We wouldn't stand a chance."

"Where'll we go, then?"

"We don't have much choice, do we?" He nodded toward the north. "The deep jungle looks like our only chance. We'll find a place to set up a new base with what we took from the watchstation, then see about making contact with some of the plantation owners around here." He closed his eyes, visualizing a map. "Westlee and Ostafjord are possibilities. The Dracos haven't found the *Phobos* yet. Maybe we can set up an HQ there. First, though, we've got to get clear of here!''

Even before that, Grayson had to explain to his people what had happened. Strapped again into his *Shadow Hawk,* he tersely described the situation, that the enemy had taken Fox Island and that the column would be turning north.

''But sir!'' A voice came over the circuit when he'd finished. ''What about . . . what about the Council! Did they get away?''

Grayson recognized the voice. It was Harriman Olssen, pilot of one of the *LoggerMechs* and son of Karl Olssen, the doctor on the Revolutionary Council.

''I'm sorry, Harriman. There's nothing we can do for them now.''

''We could go get them!''

''Not when they're waiting for us, at night, with God knows how many 'Mechs against the few of us.''

''No!''

''Pull back into line, Olssen!'' Grayson made the command sharp and short. The green-painted *LoggerMech* that had stepped from its place in line swayed, halted in place by the edge in Grayson's voice. ''The worst thing we could do would be to go charging in there, guns blazing . . . and wipe out what's left of the Free Verthandi Rangers!''

Many of the others felt much as Olssen did. Several among the MechWarrior apprentices and rebel soldiers had family, friends, or lovers among the Techs and astechs who had remained at Fox Island. Grayson himself felt the loss of the Gray Death Techs who had been left behind as a personal blow. What had happened to Tomlinson, the homely, carrot-haired boy who had been serving as his own personal Tech?

Harriman Olssen herded his four-legged 'Mech into line again, but Grayson felt accusation heavy in the air around him.

There was no choice but to go on. They carried Yorulis' body with them in the back of a hover transport. Li Chin, one of the rebels from Brasednewic's command, knew the area well enough to describe a trail running through the forest that would lead them northwest to the

Azure Coast above Ostafjord and away from the worst of
the swamps near Fox Island. Li claimed that the trail lay
off the main east-west path no more than a kilometer
ahead, but that meant going closer to the trap at their old
base before they could get farther away. Grayson considered, and agreed. Following the trail was their only option in the midst of jungle so thick and treacherously
unknown. He cautioned everyone in the column to strict
silence and ordered them to move out.

They found the northbound trail minutes later and
made the turn. It was not a clear branching of the trail,
and so Grayson posted his *Shadow Hawk* at the fork to
direct the column past him to the north. The jungle was
strangely silent except for the keening of hover vehicles
and the slogging step of marching BattleMechs. The
cloud layer had lifted, and the day was clear and bright,
with gold-orange sunlight slanting through the treetops.
Grayson fretted about the possibility that Kurita satellites
would spot the glint of sun on metal through the gaps in
the forest canopy.

Once the northward turn had been made, Grayson harassed his command relentlessly, urging them faster along
the trail. When a battered *PickerMech* broke down completely, Grayson had the pilot transfer to one of the infantry vehicles and left the derelict 'Mech at the side of
the trail. When some rebel troops complained about the
pace, Grayson offered to let them volunteer as a rear
guard. They could sit in the trail and rest, he told them,
if they would deal with the enemy 'Mechs that were certain to be on their trail. The Kurita 'Mechs waiting to
trap the rebel column at Fox Island would never let so
tempting a target as Grayson's little band escape when
they realized the rebels were not playing according to the
Draco script.

It was well past local noon when the enemy 'Mechs
found them.

Grayson had dropped back to the tail of the column to
urge a pair of straggling AgroMechs to pick up the pace.
They were *LoggerMechs*, clumsy on the narrow path and
difficult to maneuver among low trees and heavy hanging
vines and beard moss. They had fallen nearly a hundred
meters behind the rest of the rebel column, and Grayson
was afraid they would become lost. The trail branched

repeatedly along its winding, northward course, and it was possible that stragglers would become separated from the main force and never be able to link up again. One of the laggards was piloted by Harriman Olssen, the other by a young woman named Jenni Vikna.

"You wouldn't be trying to leave us now, would you?" Grayson said, but his voice was mild. "We have a long way to go. Close it up."

For a moment, he thought he was going to get an argument from Olssen, but the young man held his silence. Grayson remembered that the Vikna girl, too, had had someone at Fox Island. He'd often seen her walking with a young local astech.

"We've got to find *another* way to help them," he said gently.

Grayson used his *Hawk*'s arms to help clear a difficult spot through overhanging vines and guided them through. He could see their fatigue by the unsteadiness of their four-legged walkers as he urged them on.

"We need another twenty klicks," he said, "and then we can camp for the night. Come on! You can do twenty kilometers in your sleep."

At that moment, the enemy 'Mechs attacked.

24

The sudden appearance of the Kurita 'Mechs caught Grayson like a blow to the stomach. In the lead was a *Marauder* painted in green and brown jungle camouflage. Bright against its upper torso was the black-on-scarlet Kurita dragon insignia. Grayson immediately recognized the markings of the *Marauder* from the holos the proctor of Scandiahelm had shown him. And piloting that well-named 'Mech was the colonel in command of the Kurita 'Mech regiment on Verthandi.

A 35-ton *Panther* and a sleek, black-and-white *Phoenix Hawk* flanked the *Marauder*. Then came a loud, thrashing sound from the jungle behind them as another heavy machine moved swiftly through the brush.

Grayson's hand came down on his firing controls almost without conscious thought. His autocannon opened up with a hammering roar that sent shivers through the *Shadow Hawk* cockpit. Explosions flashed and sparked against the unyielding armor of the *Marauder*. The enemy 'Mech was at almost point-blank range, however, and one step forward took it out of Grayson's line-of-fire too quickly for him to adjust the autocannon's track. Instead, he palmed the *Hawk*'s laser control and brought his 'Mech's right arm slashing up to aim. As he squeezed the trigger, a point of intolerable brilliance flickered against the *Marauder*'s hull close by the heavily shielded cockpit. Bolts of laser and PPC fury from the *Phoenix Hawk* and the *Panther* were already shredding through the barn-sized and paper-thin hulls of the pair of *LoggerMechs*.

"Bandits!" Grayson yelled into the command circuit. "Bandits at the tail of the column! Watch for flankers!"

He cut loose with his missiles then, which lanced on hissing white contrails into the tangle of jungle and 'Mechs. The blasts shredded foliage and splintered trees. Struck full in the chest, the *Panther* lurched backward a step before its right arm PPC swung up to answer.

Grayson triggered his 'Mech's jump jets and vaulted into the sky. Branches and leaves smashed at his machine as it twisted in the air, threatening to send the 55-ton machine over on its side. He managed to stabilize and bring the *Shadow Hawk* down for an unsteady landing further up the path. One of the *LoggerMechs* stood to the side of the trail, pumping machine gun fire into the advancing *Marauder*.

Grayson checked the number painted on the side of the AgroMech. "Olssen! Machine guns are no good against heavies! Back off!"

"I can hold 'em until you get clear!" Olssen's voice shot back.

The *Marauder* seemed to shake off the fury sleeting against its broad hull. As the egg-shaped torso pivoted on its support track, the 'Mech's two massive, twin-barrelled arms dropped into line with the thin-skinned AgroMech. The *Marauder*'s PPCs spat man-made lightning, and the hull of the four-legged AgroMech seemed to crumple in the double blast. Forked blue bolts stabbed and flickered between the 'Mech and the ground as the built-up charge spent itself. The *Marauder*'s lasers added their fury to the destruction, as fire and smoke billowed from the *LoggerMech*'s savaged interior.

Jenni Vikna's *LoggerMech* came alongside the *Shadow Hawk* and seemed about to charge the enemy, but Grayson brought up one of his 'Mech's hands. "Fall back, Jenni. That's an order!"

"But Harriman's in trouble . . . ."

"Move out! Dammit, we can't help him!" he shouted, putting his *Hawk* between her *LoggerMech* and the battle. Keeping up a constant, sniping fire with his laser and missiles, he struck first at one 'Mech, then another, and another. There was smoke boiling from the *Panther*'s torso now, and an ugly gash where armor had peeled back and exposed the 35-ton 'Mech's missile firing circuitry.

An *Archer* joined the other three Kurita BattleMechs.

With the covers already rolled back from the bulky LRM pods on each shoulder, its low-built, forward-thrusting cockpit section was menacing and somehow insect-like. With the *Marauder* in the lead and the *Phoenix Hawk* close behind, the four Kurita 'Mechs crowded past Olssen's burning 'Mech and started toward Grayson.

He'd thought Harriman Olssen was out of the fight, but the crippled *LoggerMech* seemed to pull itself together where it squatted in a half-crouch at the side of the trail. Turning, Olssen lunged into the *Archer* as the Kurita 'Mech stepped past. The pair of 'Mechs went down in a tangle of legs, the *Archer* hammering at the AgroMech with flailing, ineffectual hands. The *Archer* pilot must have screamed something over his radio, for the *Marauder* and the *Phoenix Hawk,* both further along the trail, stopped their advance and whirled to face the struggling 'Mechs. The *Panther* sprang forward from the rear of the line, hammering at the thrashing tangle of metal.

In turning away from Grayson's 'Mech, the Kurita *Phoenix Hawk* had made a serious error, for its rear torso armor was extremely thin. Grayson slapped his *Shadow Hawk*'s targeting selector and swung his laser into line with the enemy 'Mech's back. Laser light pulsed, struck, and a point of arc-light intensity appeared directly between the folded wing shapes of the 'Mech's twin jump jet thrusters. His external sound pick-ups caught the rattling chatter of heavy machine guns close beside him as Jenni Vikkna added her 'Mech's lighter firepower to his.

Armor spat from the *Phoenix Hawk*'s back in jagged pieces, exposing tangled wiring and the smooth, silvery polish of an internal fuel tank. Sparks from machine gun ricochets spattered and stung, smashing at the exposed wound. Grayson fired again, saw wiring melt and splatter. There was a blue-white flash of short-circuiting connections as the enemy pilot mistakenly tried to fire his thrusters. Grayson knew at once what had happened, and instinctively flinched.

A ball of flame engulfed the *Phoenix Hawk* in an inferno that towered up through the trees, shrivelling blue-green leaves and scorching the bark of tree trunks on either side. The roar of the explosion quickly died, subsumed by the crackle of fast-burning jump fuel.

The fire cut off Grayson's view of the struggle over

Olssen's 'Mech, but it also cut the *Marauder* off from the rest of the Kurita column. He shifted his arm to the *Marauder*'s back, aiming for the tender joint where the hull joined the leg train assembly, just below the twin power booster jet turbines on the back of the machine's hull. He snapped off three shots with his laser, scoring close-range hits each time. Metal fragments scattered through the air, and the *Marauder* seemed to sag on its left leg as it turned to face him. One PPC flared . . . and missed. Grayson fired his laser and struck the heavier enemy 'Mech in one arm. The other *Marauder* PPC fired, and Grayson's *Hawk* rocked as the bolt of high-energy particles smashed its leg and melted armor. Red warning lights flared. Grayson's 'Mech was overheating from the combination of enemy hits and his free use of his own 'Mech's laser.

He fired once more, sending his last pair of SRMs arrowing into the *Marauder*'s hull, and following with a bolt of coherent light snapping into the gash they left. The *Marauder* seemed to hesitate, then spun and plunged into the dying flames alongside the charred and twisted wreckage of the *Phoenix Hawk*. The other two 'Mechs had already retreated up the path, and their leader lumbered after them.

Grayson barked orders. "Everybody! All units! Keep moving, double time! I don't know if they've had enough or are just regrouping. But we're not going to hang around here to find out!"

The rebel column pressed on deeper into the jungle, heading north. On the trail behind them, they left two monuments to their close brush with the Kurita trap, the burned-out hulk of the *Phoenix Hawk* and the smashed and gutted corpse of Harriman Olssen's *LoggerMech*.

The skirmish could not really be called a victory, but it could become one if they could escape. Yet the cost of victory would be dear. Harriman Olssen had been only 15 standard years old and Grayson's personal responsibility. Worse, Grayson had liked him.

Governor-Nagumo studied the reports, his scowl darker than ever. Colonel Kevlavic stood at attention, grease acquired from some minor but urgent repairs to his *Marauder* still fouling his usually immaculate uniform.

"Kevlavic, this is getting to be a habit with you. A very dangerous habit. They got away from you again!"

"Yes, sir." Kevlavic made no attempt to shift the blame. "Sir, I formally request replacement . . . and court-martial."

The request surprised Nagumo, but he held his reaction to a quick glance up from the printouts he was holding. "Court-martial? Why?"

"I . . . General, I don't know what else I could have done. I had limited intelligence . . . no clear idea of how many 'Mechs the enemy had close at hand. I had only four 'Mechs, with the rest deployed to guard the other approaches to Fox Island. We were set to trap the enemy when the satellite reconnaissance photos indicated that they weren't approaching the Island, but were turning off toward the north, into the deep jungle. I decided to reconnoiter in force with my lance. We blundered into a strong rear guard that was totally unexpected.

"Or maybe . . ." He shrugged, breaking his military demeanor with a gesture of shoulders and hands. "Maybe I only ran into stragglers, but I'm quite sure that the 'Mech I faced was that of the mercenary leader himself, the one the prisoners identified as Grayson Carlyle. It was a *Shadow Hawk* certainly, and we know of only one 'Mech of that type with the rebel forces.

"General, I had no way of knowing whether I faced one *Shadow Hawk* and a couple of stragglers, or the entire rebel column, turned to ambush their pursuers. After we destroyed one of the AgroMechs, I thought we might at least capture the rebel leader, but the enemy defense was unexpectedly determined. When one of my lance's 'Mechs was destroyed, and other of my 'Mechs had taken severe damage, I realized the entire lance was in danger, especially if there were more 'Mechs that I hadn't seen coming around my flanks. I ordered the retreat.

"I take full responsibility for the defeat and for my actions, General. But I swear . . . by heaven, by hell, by all the black holes of space . . . that I made the best command decisions I could. If I were faced again with the same situation, I couldn't make any of those decisions any differently."

Nagumo leaned forward over his desk, his fingers steepled before him. "Actually, Colonel, I tend to agree with you."

"S-sir?"

"If you had blundered ahead, not knowing what was waiting for you in the jungle, and lost your entire lance . . . yes, I probably would have had you shot . . . and *without* the benefit of a court-martial! As it was, we'll have to make the best of it. Your request for court-martial is denied. Don't worry. My report of this action will fully support your own."

"Thank you, General."

"Don't thank me yet! We still have to find some way of salvaging this . . . this debacle, before our Duke arrives."

"We haven't much time."

"We have no time! Not if we have to comb the jungle for these ragtag rebels and their mercenary friends!"

"We might determine where they are going and make a DropShip strike."

Nagumo's eyes strayed to the full-color map that filled the wall of his office opposite the window. It was a composite map assembled from dozens of satellite photos of the Azure Sea and jungle areas taken at different times to create a cloud-free mosaic. It showed considerable detail, but could not penetrate the blue-green opacity of the jungle vegetation.

Laid over the map was a network of dotted lines that marked the locations of known and probable jungle trails learned from documents seized at the Fox Island complex. His people were still sifting through the mounds of papers and computer files taken in the raid. With equal diligence, Dr. Vlade and his assistants were still sifting through the minds of prisoners taken on Fox Island. More trails, caches, or hidden bases might yet emerge in days or weeks to come. There was no way to predict what future intelligence discoveries would emerge. For now, though, the jungle remained impenetrable and closed.

"There are thousands of hectares of jungle out there, and an army of BattleMechs could be swallowed up without a trace." Nagumo's eyes narrowed. "The mercenaries are our biggest threat."

"Their training has obviously stiffened the main rebel army."

"More, it's given them a rallying point. I wonder . . ."

"My Lord?"

"I was wondering about their ship, the one that ran the blockade and brought the mercenaries to Verthandi in the first place."

"It was destroyed in a storm."

"Was it? Our air patrols reported debris on the beach at Hunter's Cape, but not enough to indicate the wreckage of something as massive as a DropShip."

"Our orbital stations would have detected a spacecraft lifting off, even in a storm. Certainly nothing lifted above atmosphere."

"I know." Nagumo closed his eyes, sighed. He was so tired. "Our strike at Fox Island should have finished them . . . rebels *and* mercenaries. No BattleMech unit can exist without its support units . . . Techs, 'Mech repair cradles, heavy machinery, cranes, spare parts . . . Without all that, those 'Mechs will begin to fall apart within days. They'll run out of ammunition after the first skirmish. They'll overheat and shut down with the first long, hard march. That is why your failure to close with the enemy column in the jungle is not so serious as it might have been. Without their precious Fox Island, the enemy is dead! But I wonder. If the DropShip survived . . ."

"But how, my Lord? They didn't lift off and it no longer sits at Hunter's Cape."

"Never mind, Colonel. Never mind. If their DropShip survives, it will have much equipment to replace what they've lost at Fox Island. But they can never replace the Techs and other trained personnel we took there, or the supplies. What's more, by capturing the members of the Revolutionary Council, we have broken the back of the rebellion. All that remains are bands of ragged bandits cowering in the jungle."

"Your orders then, my Lord?"

"We'll search for them and for that ship, just in case. If the ship survives, that's where the mercs will be, tied to it by lines of supply and the need for maintenance and repair. If the ship was destroyed, they must come to us . . . eventually. Our best hope is to wait until they decide to hit us again somewhere . . . and catch them then."

"Would they be stupid enough to attack us after losing their base?"

"They could have other bases out there," Nagumo said sharply. "I would. Most important, though, they *have* to attack us, or they don't have a rebellion. A ragged band of half-starved, half-armed rabble squatting out in the jungle is not a rebellion! Not when we control the cities, the spaceports, the farms, the factories—everything, in fact, of any importance at all on Verthandi!

"No, we keep vigilant. We should increase our air patrols over the sea, I think, and maintain an especially close satellite watch on the jungle between Regis and the Azure Coast. By the time Duke Ricol gets here, we'll either be able to report Verthandi secure, except for these bandits out in the wilderness . . . or we'll have met them on *our* ground . . . and beaten them!"

25

Lying between the jungle and the endless sea, Westlee was a fishing village of centuries-old stucco huts and houses jumbled together along winding streets. From the heights above the town, the sea was a spectacular sight, haze-shrouded beneath an overcast sky, but struck to fire by Norn's red-gold rays slanting through the clouds. Rock cliffs dominated the far side of the bay, sheer walls cloven by the gash that was the opening to Ostafjord. Farther out, half-hidden in grey mist and fiery gold was an island of black rock. It heaved skyward through the fog, its bulk casting sharp-edged shadows through the low-lying mists to the west.

Tiny beneath the mass of the fjord headland, unnoticed in skyfire and fog, the *Phobos* rested in the shadow of rock, grounded on a shallow beach and draped with unkempt tatters of canvas and camouflaged netting. Above the village, a solitary *Stinger* stood watch. After coded electronic passwords were challenged and exchanged, Grayson's *Shadow Hawk* stepped from a jungle logging trail into the morning sunlight.

The long march was over. The rebel column had travelled on the day after the skirmish near Fox Island, stopped briefly to rest and to jury-rig repairs on several of the nearly disintegrated AgroMechs, then pressed on into the night. The night march was necessary because Grayson knew their only hope was to put more distance between the rebel column and the enemy than the enemy believed possible.

The distance from Fox Island to Westlee was perhaps six hundred kilometers, but by way of the twisting roads and jungle paths, the distance actually travelled was more like a thousand. Limited by the lurching pace of the heavier AgroMechs, the column's top speed was something less than 60 kph. There were also frequent stops to repair minor failures in overheated circuits and stress-worn actuators or to give overheated cooling systems a chance to recycle.

The flesh-and-blood elements of the column were proving to be even weaker and more vulnerable to the strain than were the machines. Four apprentice pilots had passed out when the insufficient cooling systems of their AgroMechs failed, and it had taken time to revive them. Two *PickerMechs* had failed to complete the journey at all, and three hover transports had to be abandoned when their overworked turbofans simply gave out, with no way to repair them in the jungle. The remaining transports had been claustrophobically crowded after that. Even then, the fourteen-hour-long Verthandian night had not been enough to complete the march in darkness. They arrived at Westlee four hours past dawn, dirty and exhausted, their morale utterly crushed.

"Well, what the hell do we do now?" Ilse Martinez said at the staff meeting Grayson had called upon arrival. It was the question on all their minds, of course, and Grayson was glad that someone else had spoken it aloud. They were seated in the lounge of the *Phobos* to discuss that very matter.

Save for Jaleg Yorulis, all his 'Mech pilots were there. Earlier that day, they had buried the young Lyran MechWarrior in an unmarked grave up the beach. Sergeant Ramage was present as well, representing both the mercenary support troops and the rebel infantry, and Grayson had invited two of the oldest Verthandi Ranger MechWarriors, Rolf Montido and Collin Dace, as representatives of their people.

"We go on," Grayson said in response to Martinez. "We organize what we have left . . . and go on."

What we have left. The only thing that kept the destruction of the Fox Island camp from being a total disaster was that the 'Mechs and most of the rebel army had escaped. So much *had* been lost, though. All their support facilities and equipment, except for what the *Phobos* carried aboard. Fifteen of the Legion's Techs were lost, dead or marched off to captivity. That included both Tomlinson and Karellan, two of their best. All of the Verthandian astechs were dead or captured, as well as the rebel army's own Techs. And, of course, they had all lost friends, comrades with whom they had grown close in the past weeks.

The Revolutionary Council was gone as well, whether killed or captured. The Council was the whole reason for the Gray Death's presence on Verthandi in the first place. It was their paymaster, patron, and client.

Grayson leaned far back in his chair, with hands pressed flat over his eyes. He had changed into a uniform, but only because Yorulis' blood had so soaked the shorts and light mesh shirt he'd been wearing. Though he'd managed a fast shower before the meeting, he still felt coated with sweat, stench, and jungle mud.

"What's the condition of the ship?" he asked Ilse.

Clay was immaculate in his trim green and brown Roughriders uniform, but most of the others looked as dirty as Grayson still felt. Lori wore the same shorts and top that she'd made the march in, though she had taken a quick splash in the ocean surf to cool off. The rigors of the previous night showed, too, in the haggardness of their expressions and their dark-circled eyes. Each had had a meal and a couple of hours' sleep, but it would take more than that to erase the strain of the night's long march. Khaled, Martinez, and the others who had remained with *Phobos* looked fresh and well-rested by comparison.

"The ship," Martinez said patiently, "is not going anywhere until she gets a refit. Her number three tube is cracked and her primary heat exchangers are shot. The fusion pile needs flushing and relining, and the magnetic superconductors in the plasma bottle charge directors need replacement. But that stuff is hot . . . and I mean *hot* . . . and I'm not about to try any of *that* this side of a space dock! We barely made it here as a steamboat. We're not going to be a spacecraft again for a long time yet."

"You've checked the foundries or machine shops or whatever is available in Westlee." It was a statement, not a question. Grayson knew that the resourceful DropShip pilot would have tracked down all possible sources of spare parts and repair materials.

Ilse answered with a sour expression and a downturned thumb. "We could manage temporary repairs—enough to get us back to the jump point—with a lot of work and the facilities of the Regisport ship bays. Maybe."

"Then we're stuck here," Debrowksi said. Regisport, ten kilometers north of Regis itself, was heavily garrisoned, for it was the groundside link with the Kurita forces' own space supply lines. "We won't be able to make our rendezvous with Captain Tor."

"We knew that right along," Grayson said. His mind raced. He'd been considering their options all during the trek through the jungle. If they were to run for it, simply give up their Verthandian commitment and make a run for it, there was one chance . . .

"The *Invidious* is due back in-system in another 120 hours . . . make it four local days," he said. "Our only hope if we wanted to leave with her would be to capture a Kurita DropShip and run the blockade."

Clay's eyes narrowed. "Could we do that?"

The silence in the conference room thickened perceptibly as Grayson considered his answer. "Yes," he said at last. "Nagumo doesn't know when our starship is due back in system. He doesn't know it *is* due back. We could plan a raid, capture a DropShip at Regisport, and hightail it to the jump point before he could get organized. Yes, I believe we could pull it off."

McCall smiled through the grease on his face. "Aye, there's tha', but we ca' nae leavit tha' indigs in tha' lurch, noo, can we?"

Grayson glanced at Montido and Dace. "Indig" was generally received as a condescending or even hostile word on most worlds, but both Verthandians seemed inclined to let it pass. Perhaps they reasoned that McCall was as tired as the rest of them and not thinking clearly. Or perhaps they hadn't been able to follow his accented speech.

"I'd like to know what our contract says about all this," Lori said. "Our agreement was with the Revolutionary Council. Looks to me like we don't have any employers now."

Montido stirred. "May I speak, Captain?"

"Of course. It's why we asked you here."

He glanced at Dace, then looked down at the table. "I

think I speak for . . . for what's left of the Verthandi
Rangers when I say that we need you. More than ever,
we need you.''

"God knows how we could pay you, though,'' Dace
added.

"Right. If . . . if you want to go, get offplanet . . .
we'll help you capture the ship, but that will be the end
of us. There's no way we can keep fighting on our own.
Not now.''

Grayson shook his head slowly. "There are other things
at stake besides money,'' he said. It was surprising how
his own thoughts were falling into line as he discussed
the matter with the others. *How can we abandon them
now?* "The thought of stealing a Kurita DropShip is
tempting, but I'd have to live with myself as well.''

Debrowski stirred, frowning. "Sir . . . we can't still
hope to beat them . . .''

"Why not?''

"Captain, look! It's still just us . . . well, us and the
rebels, sir . . . against a regiment of 'Mechs and God
knows how many troops! We can't *hope* to win against
an army like that!''

Grayson looked in turn at each of the others. "A military unit cannot be run as a democracy . . . but all must
at least have some voice in this decision.'' He looked at
Montido and Dace. "Would you gentlemen excuse us for
a moment?''

When the Verthandians had left the room, Grayson
continued. "I think a show of hands is sufficient. Who
wants to stay and help these folks?''

Hands went up around the table: Lori and McCall together, Khaled an instant later. Clay looked at those
three, shrugged, and put up his own hand. Sergeant Ramage looked worried. "Captain, I can't speak for all my
people, you know that. A lot of the Legion people would
be delighted to get off this dirtball.''

"I daresay we all would, Sergeant.''

"I also know a lot of them have gotten close to the
rebels these past few weeks, I don't think anyone wants
to see them slaughtered by Nagumo's bastards.'' He
raised his hand.

Martinez put up her hand, too. "I still don't care for
the indigs,'' she said, "but I don't want to scuttle poor

old *Phobos*, especially after all the work and heartache
I've put into her!''

Debrowski was the only one left. He looked thoughtful, then added his hand to the rest. ''I'll vote with the
rest of you. Jaleg was my friend. Somehow, I don't want
to just leave him here, as though it had all been for nothing.''

''So we know what we *want* to do,'' Martinez said,
''but we still don't know how. I mean, we go out and
win the war, right? How?''

Grayson folded his hands together, steepled his fore-
fingers, and studied them. Despite his shower, they were
black with ground-in grime. He wondered if he'd even
gotten off all the blood.

''In one way, Piter is right,'' he said at last. ''We're
not going to win, not in the long run. We could spend
years in this jungle, knocking off Kurita supply depots
and patrols. But the Combine is going to keep right on
funneling men, 'Mechs, and supplies into Regis, and Nagumo's 'Mechs are going to keep right on hunting for us.
Sooner or later, they'll get lucky.''

Clay scowled. ''So what'll we do?''

''We start by doing what we've been doing, only a lot
more of it. We hit the Dracos every chance we get to
remind them there's a rebellion on. We build training
camps in the jungle, organize training cadres, do everything possible to arm, equip, and train local forces wherever we can find people who want to fight. We've got an
army big enough to fight the Dracos . . . if we can just
mobilize it.''

''A lot of them are Loyalists,'' Martinez pointed out.

''The majority are in the middle, uncommitted. It's
that way with any fight, of course . . . but we're going
to have to find ways to reach them. I think a lot of the
Loyalists will come over, too, if they're given the chance.

''But the *first* thing we do is put together the message
that we're going to beam at the *Invidious* when Captain
Tor pops back in-system.'' He looked at each of the others. ''We'll have him fetch us some help.''

''Who?'' Lori asked. ''Another bunch of merc
'Mechs?''

"No . . . something Free Verthandi needs more right now than a whole BattleMech army."

"What's that?"

"Recognition."

26

Sergeant Ramage gritted his teeth, took another turn of the nylon line about his gloved hands, and set his feet to the ferrocrete wall. His boots scraped faintly as he hauled himself hand over hand up the face of the three-story building.

From the valley on the far side of the building came the sound of gunfire. A moment before, he'd been crouched among the boulders on the crest of the ridge, watching the first moves of the Verthandi Rangers as they swarmed up over the Basin Rim, but he could see nothing now. The attack was going well so far, he knew. Rebel laser and autocannon fire had slashed into the scattered force of light enemy 'Mechs gathered on the edge of the plateau, catching them by surprise.

One hand found the top of the wall close beside the grapnel, which had lodged behind it. He eased his head up, took in the expanse of the flat, open rooftop. Against the far wall, he saw a pair of sentries whose backs were to him and whose eyes were glued to the viewpieces of their electronic binoculars. Sentries . . . or perhaps Techs from inside the building. They wore heavy automatic pistols in low-slung belt holsters, but neither carried a rifle or subgun.

That made sense. The base was supposed to be part of the Verthandian government's chain of military outposts along the Basin Rim. The flag wavering just below the spidery struts and braces of the station's massive deep space antennae was the green, red, and gold banner of Verthandi . . . Loyalist Verthandi, the Verthandi that danced to the tune of far Luthien. Yet, the two men observing the battle wore the severe black of Draconis Combine officers.

Advisors, then. Or watchdogs. Ramage wondered how much Nagumo trusted the native forces under his command. The two were intent on the panorama of the battle spread out below them. Neither noticed as he carefully drew the sonic stunner from its holster under his arm, switched off the safety, and drew down on the pair of them.

His weapon gave a sharp, warbling hum once . . . twice. The two Kurita officers crumpled onto the roof without a sound, and Ramage hoisted himself up and rolled across the rim of the parapet. He saw a wooden trap door and stairs leading into a lighted room below, but there was no sign of other officers, sentries, or soldiers. Turning toward the anxious rebels waiting in the shadows at the base of the building, he gave a thumbs up sign.

As the hand-picked team of ten commandos climbed the rope after him, Ramage stepped over to check the bodies of the two officers. Both were unconscious and would be so for hours. Chancing a peek over the wall, he saw the head and shoulders of an immobile *Panther* directly below him, the reason he'd chosen to enter the building up the back wall and down from the roof. That Kurita BattleMech sentry was there to prevent a direct assault on this deep-space transmitter station, an attractive rebel target. Its destruction could interfere with Kurita space fleet operations and communications, and it would be expensive to replace.

He spared a second to look down at the battle. With the sun so low on the southwestern horizon behind him, the battlefield was already in the shadow of the com station's ridge. Flashes of autocannon fire stabbed repeatedly through the gathering gloom, and the funeral pyre of a loyalist *Wasp* glowed like a flare. There were perhaps a dozen Loyalist 'Mechs on the field, more than the rebel scouts had reported, and many support units as well. Yet, the rebel assault was going well anyway. Five rebel 'Mechs were sweeping forward onto the field, plowing through the Loyalists' center. Ramage easily recognized Montido's big *Dervish* among them. Meanwhile, the three heaviest Legion 'Mechs—the *Shadow*

Hawk, Rifleman, and *Wolverine*—stayed on the edge of the Basin Rim, pouring round after high-explosive round into the scattering defenders.

At a soft noise behind him, Ramage whirled, stunner up. It was only Gundberg and Willoch slipping over the wall, followed by Chapley, Sorenson, and six more commandos clambering up the rope close behind. Their faces showed relief that the *Panther* had not come around the corner of the building on a check-and-see.

The ten Verthandians hauled up the grapnel rope and began unshouldering their assault rifles. Willoch handed Ramage his. Not knowing what waited on that third-floor roof, the sergeant had not wanted to make the climb encumbered by a rifle.

Tight-lipped and silent, Ramage deployed his men with nods and hand gestures. The next step was to get inside the building. He reholstered his stunner, clicked back the bolt on his TK to bring the first round into the chamber, flicked off the safety, and advanced toward the open trap door, rifle probing ahead.

Ramage got there just as a third Kurita officer was coming up the steps. Painfully young, he wore the collar pips of a junior lieutenant and carried three brimming cups of coffee in two hands.

Ramage stopped his finger before it could complete the trigger squeeze, swinging the butt of the rifle up instead. Planting the stock against the boy's sternum, he gave a firm shove that sent officer, cups, and coffee clattering backward down the stairs. Ramage followed feet-first, not bothering to use the steps. He landed with a knee-jarring crash close beside the shrieking heap of the Kurita Lieutenant.

Three other Kurita officers were in the room, just turning from the communications consoles that ringed the ferrocrete-walled room. His TK bucked three times with carefully placed four-round bursts that picked up the black-uniformed figures and flung them against the consoles in one-two-three order. The Lieutenant's wailing ceased abruptly as the smoking muzzle of the TK swung down level with his nose.

"You!" Ramage barked. "Any more?"

"D-down . . . downstairs . . ."

Five of his men descended the steps, rifles ready. Ra-

mage gestured them toward the door leading to the first
floor, but that door flew open before they could reach it.
The narrow confines of the building's upper story rang
with the chatter of automatic weapon bursts and small
arms fire. Two Kurita soldiers pitched back from a
wooden door suddenly pocked and splintered by bullets,
and Chapley went down, arms clasped across his belly.
Three other commandos slammed the door shut and
dragged a table across to brace it while the fifth guarded
the prisoner. Ramage slung his rifle and hurried to the
com station.

The console was similar to those he'd used aboard the
Invidious and the *Phobos*. For that matter, it was like
those he'd used on his homeworld of Trellwan. The main
panel was already warmed up and tracking, the antennae
trained on the Norn system's zenith jump point.

He'd thought it would be. If Captain Tor had kept to
his timetable and his promise to return in 900 hours, he
should have jumped in-system sometime earlier that afternoon, certainly within the past three hours. The arrival
of the *Invidious* would have sent an electromagnetic pulse
racing out from the jump point at the speed of light. A
little over eleven minutes later, that signal would have
raced through near-Verthandi space, triggering computer-
guarded alarms on planetary bases and ships. It had been
Grayson's guess that every deep-space tracking antenna
on Verthandi would have immediately been trained on
the newcomer, beaming challenges and listening for a
reply.

He was right. A computer screen at Ramage's right
hand showed what little was known about the newcomer.
It was a freighter, its IFF transponder code that of an
independent trader. Mass was estimated at 80,000 tons.
Its solar collector sail was already unfurled, but thus far,
no communications had been received.

Ramage smiled. It could only be the *Invidious*, right
on schedule.

He found another com channel and adjusted a setting.
Holding a microphone to his mouth, he pressed a trans-
mit key. "Skytalker, Skytalker, this is Climber One . . .
Do you read me?"

The voice that came back almost immediately was Lori
Kalmar's. "Climber here, Skytalker. I read."

"Jackpot! I say again . . . Jackpot! Ready to feed on kilo hotel seven seven niner thuh-ree."

"Got it, Climber. Channel open. Here she comes."

Grayson had appointed Lori to the task of carrying the precious recording tape once it had been cut in the *Phobos*'s communications center. Grayson's *Shadow Hawk* was needed for the battle with the Loyalist defenders, for a stray hit could put a key antenna out of commission at a vital moment. Ramage was not able to carry the tape himself in something as risky as a ranger assault. Besides, no one in the rebel forces could have known what sort of equipment they might find in a communications center supposedly belonging to the Loyalist government, but more likely staffed by Kurita ComTechs. To carry the transmitter gear needed to play the tape into the Kurita equipment would have seriously encumbered the commandos.

Though Grayson was certainly listening in, it was Lori in her *Locust* who had carried the tape and listened for Ramage's signal. She had followed the battle line but remained hull-down below the crest of Basin Rim, with only her transmitter antenna protruding above the ridge. On Ramage's signal, she had transmitted the signal to the captured Kurita com gear, where Ramage fed it into the station's recorders. Having compressed the message to a fiftieth of a second's zipsqueal, he then brought his finger down on the button that sent the signal flashing out toward the zenith point at the speed of light.

He looked up from the console. There was a thudding at the door, which shivered, raining flecks of splintered wood. Four pale faces looked across at Ramage.

He shrugged. "I don't think we're going back the way we came, boys." As if to back him up, there came a blast of light and sound from overhead, then a cascade of dust and smoke down the steps into the room. Three of the five commandos that Ramage had left above dropped into the room, their faces ashen, their knuckles white on the grips of their weapons.

The *Panther* outside had been alerted to their presence.

Ramage had cycled the recorded message as a zipsqueal loop going over and over, and he kept it playing now, sending burst after burst of computer-coded data into the sky. It would be eleven minutes before the first signal reached the *Invidious*, and eleven minutes more before any possible reply could make the return trip. He doubted that they could last over twenty-two minutes to hear it.

The north wall thundered, a sledgehammer of sound that rang in his ears and jarred dust from the bare ferrocrete blocks. The hammering blasted again, and the commandos looked wildly at one another. Would the *Panther* actually tear down the com station it was supposed to protect in order to get at the raiders inside? The thunderclap of sound exploded a third time, and the meter-thick walls visibly trembled. Apparently it would.

"Climber, this is Skytalker Leader." Grayson's voice was barely audible over the ringing in Ramage's ears, but he was very glad to hear it.

"Climber here! Message away!"

"I copy, Climber. What's your situation?"

The room thundered again. "Not good. The neighbors want to come in and play. We're trapped on the third floor . . . no way out."

"Try to hold on, Climber. We're in the thick of it out here and can't win through."

"Acknowledged, Skytalker. "We'll . . . hold." There was nothing else to say. The raiders had known that once they were discovered, their chances of rescue were not good. In endless planning sessions, Grayson and the others had argued insistently that Ramage not sacrifice himself. Ramage was equally insistent that he was the logical one—the *only* logical one—to lead it. He couldn't be budged, and Grayson had finally given in.

To transmit their coded message to the *Invidious*, they needed a deep-space transmitter. The *Phobos* had one, but they didn't dare use it. That could have given the enemy positive proof that the ship still existed, as well as a means to triangulate her position. The only alternative had been to—"borrow" was Grayson's word—a Kurita transmitter.

For a long minute, the Ranger commandos looked at one another silently, wondering what was next. Splinters spat and flew as submachine gun fire chewed at the door, then bullets shrieked through the room. Gundberg kicked backward, blood pumping, dead before he hit the floor.

Ramage cursed and levelled his TK at the closed door. The assault rifle bucked and thuttered on full auto, breaching the door in a dozen places and filling the air with more spinning chips and splinters of wood. Someone started screaming on the far side of the door, as more bullets began chewing through the wood from the other side. This blind firefight carried on for another ten seconds, then died away. There were several head-sized holes in the door's wood now. What would be next, Ramage wondered, a grenade or gas? Keeping low, he darted across to a position just beside the barricaded door. Perhaps from there, he could see the approach of someone with a grenade, and do something about it.

There was a noise outside, like the roar of a DropShip launch, and then the lights went dead. As the room became pitch-black, chunks of sound-proofing sprayed down from the ceiling on the defenders, a fifty-centimeter-thick support beam groaned and cracked, and ferrocrete blocks rained down from above. A twenty-kilo chunk landed squarely in the middle of the communications console, shattering glass and plastic and briefly lighting up the dark with a shower of sparks. There'd be no more broadcasting for the raiders, but that worry was behind them now. Looking up in horror, they saw that the *Panther* had fired its jump jets and was standing now on the roof overhead!

Another explosion of dust and broken stone, and an armored fist one meter across plunged down the stairway, fingers spreading wide like the legs of some monstrous beast. The gigantic metal fingers closed on a shrieking, kicking flurry of motion that jerked once and went limp in its crushing grasp. Ramage and the others looked away as the mangled body of the Kurita prisoner plopped wetly back to the rubble-strewn floor. The gigantic metal fingers opened again, nighmarish in the dust-choked gloom, searching, groping.

The hand jerked away, shattering more of the ceiling as it withdrew. From outside came the deep-throated stutter of an autocannon, and the blasts and shrieks of rapid-fire, high-explosive mayhem from overhead. The crash of a BattleMech falling to the ground close beside the building was unmistakable, louder than Armaggedon and heavy enough to shiver the com station's walls yet again. After that, it was very quiet.

The stairs were shattered, and the only way out now was through the door. When they'd heard nothing for several seconds, Ramage and the others pulled the up-ended table aside and kicked away the ruin of the door. There were three bodies on the platform at the top of the stairs outside and smoke wafting up from below. Rifles ready, the raiders ventured down the steps, two of them supporting their gutshot comrade.

The second floor was deserted, and another stairway invited. Another floor down, and late afternoon light poured through a partly missing and rubble-choked front wall. Grayson's *Shadow Hawk* stood outside, not far from the vast metal corpse of the Kurita *Panther,* now minus its head.

A transport skimmer whined to a stop close by the shattered wall. "Hop in," Grayson's voice said through his 'mech's external speaker. "Let's go home!"

On the battle plain below, the rebel 'Mechs were already withdrawing, leaving columns of smoke and guttering fires where three enemy 'Mechs and a half-dozen support vehicles lay in heaps of charred wreckage. Another Loyalist 'Mech, a *Griffin,* stood frozen in place, the top of its head blasted open where its pilot had decided to leave the fight with precipitous haste.

Ramage grinned and signalled his troops. "You heard the man! Let's make dust!"

Chapley died during the trip back through the jungle.

27

The elevator door opened on the lowest sub-basement floor, and Nagumo stepped out, light from the overhead fluoros catching the intertwining loops and circled dragons of gold at cuff and collar. Two stiff-faced troopers in full dress flanked him, their hands never far from their holstered automatics.

This level had once been part of the Regis University archives, but when the Kurita-backed new order had come to power, most of the records had been removed to a warehouse just outside the campus walls. A number of the basement rooms had become offices and facilities for what was euphemistically referred to as the ''Special Branch''. With its walls of ferrocrete and quarried stone block, meters thick in places, the place was perfect for the purpose. The screams of the guests of the Special Branch never penetrated to the upper levels of the building.

Nagumo was tired and harassed by growing worries. Rebel activity had been increasing during the past week, culminating with the raid on the deep-space transmitter just the day before. Instead of being broken after the raid on Fox Island, the damnable rebel movement seemed to be spreading like a cancer, infecting districts, villages, and whole regions that had until now been pacified.

Reports were on his desk of rebel attacks on Loyalist and Kurita outposts throughout the Bluesward and Vrieshaven, and even as far west as Scandiahelm. The toll in just this week since Fox Island had been ten 'Mechs destroyed or put out of commission indefinitely. At this rate, it would be the skeleton of an army that met Duke Ricol in six more days. *Six days!*

The raid on the transmitter was a particularly harrowing climax. The deep-space tracking system on Verthandi-Alpha had marked the arrival of a JumpShip at the Norn zenith jump point shortly before the raid on the transmitter, had monitored a coded burst-pulsed radio message (which had not yet yielded to Kodo's naval cryptoanalysis department) and had then vanished back into hyperspace. To Nagumo's mind, it could only mean a plea for more mercenary reinforcements.

The mercenaries could not know that he'd been informed of their arrival by his spy network on Galatea. He had immediately dispatched a courier to alert his Galatean network that the jump freighter *Invidious* might be returning to Galatea. Where else close by could they go to recruit more mercs? The Galatean network had Nagumo's personal sanction to do what was necessary to block that ship's mission.

Nagumo could not count on success there. In fact, he had to assume that reinforcements would be arriving. Meanwhile, his grip on Verthandi was slipping. Rebel raids all across the inhabited portion of the planet had forced Kurita troops and 'Mechs and Loyalist militia to keep to their garrison posts, to travel in convoys, to avoid travelling alone in rural areas. And now, a riot in the streets of the Regis Oldtown district. A riot! It had started as a demonstration—with students chanting "Death to the Dracos". Someone had fired a shot that killed a government militiaman, and then a platoon of Combine infantry had fired into the crowd. There were six dead before the lance of recon 'Mechs had broken up the mob. Sine then, the city had been simmering in sullen resentment.

What was he going to tell the Duke?

The guards outside the door to Room 6 saluted crisply, fists to chests, which Nagumo acknowledged with a curt nod. He gestured for his escort to remain there, in the passageway, then stepped through the massive door as one of the guards swung it open for him.

Dr. Vlade and two assistants were inside, their backs to him as they bent over a stainless steel table oddly out of place in the faintly dank and septic gloom. At the sound of the door, Vlade turned and smiled broadly. "My Lord, thank you for coming."

"What do you want, Vlade?"

He didn't have the time to watch Vlade play in his subbasement funhouse. The place stank of blood, sweat, and stark terror. Filth crusted the floor under Nagumo's immaculate boots.

"My Lord . . ."

"Make it fast, Vlade," he said. "I've got work to do."

"Of course, my Lord. I wouldn't have called you down at all. This interrogation was purely routine, you see . . . but I've stumbled across some fascinating information I thought you would want to hear for yourself, right away . . . rather than waiting for my report."

"Well?"

His chief interrogator gestured to the table, which was nearly as wide as it was long. Vlade's current guest was there, lying spread eagled by rope restraints at wrists and ankles.

"Well, my dear," Vlade said in a kindly, almost fatherly manner. He tilted the table top up and locked it in place, bringing its prisoner upright to face Nagumo. "Won't you tell the Governor General what you told me?"

The woman's head tossed from side to side, her eyes shut tight in a face glistening with sweat and tears. She spoke between deep and desperate gasps for air, the words coming with a tumbling urgency. "Please don't hurt me please don't hurt me please . . ."

Vlade looked across her at Nagumo. "This is Carlotta Helgameyer, my Lord. She is one of the members of that self-styled Revolutionary Council you captured at Fox Island."

"I know, Vlade. I've seen her dossier."

"Then you know that she is also a respected professor on the faculty of this university. And she's been giving me names. Haven't you, Carlotta?"

"Please, don't hurt . . . yes . . . yes . . . anything . . . Please don't hurt me . . ."

Nagumo's eyes widened in surprise. "You've broken her so easily? I don't see a mark on her."

"Well, we've had her for a week now, my Lord. We first had to assemble a psychological profile based on her physiological reactions during the first interviews. That told us that Carlotta doesn't like . . . pain. Do you, Carlotta?''

Nagumo crossed his arms. "Who does?"

"Ah, but this is special." Vlade reached down to a small instrument stand and picked up what looked like a fencing foil with a heavy, complex grip—a neural whip. He fiddled with controls at the handle, and at the tiny clicking sound, the woman's eyes opened wide and her pleading rose in pitch and volume. "Please . . . no . . . no . . . no . . . !"

He flicked the tip of the neural whip lightly across the woman's thigh, the touch wrenching a long shuddering scream from her. Vlade looked up at Nagumo, touched the blade to his own bare hand, and shrugged. "When I can get that . . . sincere a reaction with the power off, it's fairly safe to assume that the subject has been completely conditioned. You see . . ." He brought the blade down again, touching her stomach and eliciting another scream. "Carlotta has a problem in that she never knows whether the blade is going to be charged . . . so . . . or dead . . . or where it is going to touch her. When it gets to where the anticipation is as bad as any pain, well . . . she'll answer any question. And she'll answer it as truthfully as she can. Isn't that right my dear? We've been having a lovely conversation.''

"And what have you learned?" Nagumo felt a mild revulsion for Vlade and his light-hearted patter. The man got results, but with what struck Nagumo as unprofessional familiarity.

"We've learned that there is considerable pro-rebel sentiment among the students and faculty right here in the University. Students have been distributing anti-Combine literature and rather sensationalist accounts of recent rebel actions throughout Regis. They've been openly recruiting for the rebel forces, talking about training an army under these mercenaries off in the jungle. The riot yesterday started with a student demonstration, you know, but that sort of 'spontaneous' gesture has to be carefully planned and organized.''

"This woman was an organizer of the disturbance?"

"Oh, Carlotta has been very busy here in the capital when she hasn't been running around in the jungle with her rebel friends, haven't you, Carlotta? But she's had

lots of help. Members of the University faculty, even
some respected people on the Council of Academicians
itself have been organizing meetings, spreading sedi-
tion.''

"She's giving you names?''

"Oh, yes. She's been most cooperative. There is quite
a sizable number in this cabal, isn't there, Carlotta?
Prominent men in trusted positions in the local government.''

"This is new?'' Nagumo barked, but then paused to
think. He knew that the relationship between Regis University and the Verthandian government was an odd one.
The Verthandians took pride in the fact that their government leaders were trained for the job, that government
itself was a logical and disciplined science, administered
by trained professionals. The riots of the previous day
showed that the citizens of Regis did not always approach
politics with logic. Nagumo had thought that his enemy
was the rebel army and the mercenaries they'd brought
in to help them. Now the flames of rebellion were spreading, heedless of military defeat or the might of the Draconis Combine. Perhaps what they needed at this point
was not a military victory, but a blow against some
visible symbol of the revolution to demonstrate the occupation army's power.

If treasonous elements of the University and government could be turned into a public example, right now,
this week . . . a purge to demonstrate the firmness of his
will, then things might be quiet when Duke Ricol arrived. Certainly, it was better than hurrying blindly across
the face of Verthandi, reacting to the moves and threats
of a slippery, invisible opponent.

He turned to pick up a chair and brought it close to
the silver table. Drawing a handkerchief from his pocket,
he wiped dust and a stray splatter of something dry and
brown from the seat, then sat down.

"Very well. Let's hear what she has to say.''

The dream began as it always did.
Lori sat in the cramped cockpit of her *Locust*, her
hands on the controls, her body swaying with the rolling
of her machine. Urgency drove her, though she didn't
know what it was that had her heart racing, her pulse

roaring in her ears. The landscape that flowed past the *Locust*'s window was familiar . . . . a wasteland stark and bleak, spires of ice and mounds of snow under a sky of midnight blue. It was Sigurd, a world of frozen seas and towering glaciers. The world of her birth.

Sigurd would forever be associated in her mind with cold, but as she pressed her *Locust* forward, she felt not cold, but heat. She could feel the sweat on her face and chest, could feel it trickling down her spine to pool in the small of her back. This was more than the usual heat of a BattleMech in operation, more even than the heat of an overload in battle. Through her 'Mech's cockpit windows, she could see the reflected dazzle of flames close behind her.

Fire!

Her hands twisted the controls and the *Locust* spun. A low, thick-walled house of logs, clay, and handmade bricks dissolved in flames like sugar in hot tea. It was her own home burning.

In the night, the soldiers had come. Now the village was afire and her home was burning. She could hear her parents and brothers as they screamed, could feel the hands of the neighbor who had snatched her back as she'd tried to run back into that hell of flame and pain. No . . . not hands. The straps of her harness were digging at her shoulders like the remembered grip of that neighbor.

Daddy!

She struggled, thrashing. Daddy was in the flames somewhere. She had to reach him, but there was someone in the way. It was a tall, lean man whose back was to her. He stood between her and the burning house, and something rested across his shoulder, something short, stocky and horrifying.

When he turned, she saw it was Grayson Carlyle. He stood below her just as she'd seen him that first day, in a city street on Trellwan. They'd been on opposite sides, then, she unknowingly fighting for a Kurita warlord, he leading the local militia in a desperate defense.

He set his eye to the crude sight of the inferno launcher and brought the weapon into line with her cockpit. His mouth twisted into its familiar, lopsided grin as he squeezed the trigger . . .

She sat bolt upright in bed, wide awake. The bed sheets

were wringing wet, her hair plastered in damp tangles across her face and bare shoulders. She sat there a moment, breathing hard, taking in the dimly seen but familiar outlines of objects in her darkened cabin—the small terminal at her desk, her uniform locker, the nightstand by her bed. She crossed her arms across her breasts and sat there, trembling for a moment. It was only a dream. Only a dream.

He *hadn't* fired . . . he hadn't! She made herself remember what had really happened, fighting the terror. He had trapped her and her *Locust* in a blind alley, had captured her. He had *not* pulled the trigger as he so easily could have. Why did she keep dreaming that he had?

One hand groped in the darkness across her nightstand and touched the lighting panel. The overhead fluoros came up gradually, and she rubbed the sleep and hair from her eyes. The programmable clock at her bedside showed her the time in Verthandi reckoning . . . 0210. She knew by now that she would not get to sleep again soon.

Lori got up, slipped into the closet-sized washroom, and splashed water over her face until the clammy feeling was gone. After pulling on shorts, shirt, and low-topped boots, she left her cabin.

The *Phobos* did not shut down during the night. Unless the 'Mechs were out on a raid, however, the nightwatch stayed at their posts in engineering and on the bridge. She met no one as she followed the curve of C-Deck's outboard corridor clockwise to the crew's galley, then took the elevator up a level to B deck. With most of the crew asleep, the passageways were eerily silent, the only noise coming from the gentle hiss of air conditioning ducts and the shuffle of her own boots on the metal deck.

Lori stopped outside the lounge. Seated at the table was Grayson, a compad and a stack of printouts in front of him.

"Gray?" When he started to rise, she shook her head. "No, don't get up. Can I join you?"

"Of course." He stood up anyway as she entered the room. He was, she decided, a complex man. During a conference or on the battlefield, he seemed incapable of thinking of her as a woman, seemed to see in her only his Executive Officer. When they were alone, though, he often showed this maddeningly formal gallantry. Such manners were old-fashioned, faintly anachronistic outside of the courts and capitals of the Successor States. She wondered if he'd spent much time on one of the Inner Worlds to have acquired them. He smiled, offering her a chair, and she shivered. It was the same gentle, lopsided smile from her dream.

"Am I interrupting?"

"No, no. Just reports." That smile again. "I couldn't sleep," he said, "and somehow there's never time to go over these things during the day."

"I couldn't sleep, either."

"Can I get you something? Coffee?"

She shook her head, crossing her arms on the table before her. Grayson went back to reading the dispatch printouts. Lori watched him, searching for a way to open the conversation. "Well?" she said at last. "Good news or bad?"

He frowned, distracted. "Confused, mostly. This rebellion has gone way beyond our little bit of this planet and I can't keep up."

"Well, they've been fighting their war without our help for ten years now."

"Yeah, but it looks like a lot of folks are coming out of hiding now. Now that they've heard about us, heard that we're winning battles. They hear that Kurita can be beaten . . . and they come tumbling out to join the fun."

"That's to be expected, isn't it?"

His frown deepened. "I suppose so. But how are we supposed to coordinate everything that's happening? How can we . . . well. . . . Here, look at this." He slid several comroom printouts across the table. "A band of farmers attacked a Loyalist convoy at a place called Junction three days ago. They relayed word to us that Kurita 'Mechs retaliated by burning their town, and they're asking us for support. I can't even find Junction on the map! And here . . . there was a riot in the streets of Regis last night. Several hundred students and teachers demonstrating against the Kurita-backed government. They had to bring in 'Mechs to break up the crowd."

"That ought to stir things up."

"I'll say, because Regis University *is* the government! There were government militiamen in the mob! If Nagumo doesn't do something about that, he might as well pack up and leave. And if he *does* respond, there's not a damned thing we can do about it! I think half of Nagumo's 'Mechs are inside Regis . . . most of them in that university complex.'' His fist closed, a sharp, compulsive motion. Lori was surprised to see the pain behind his eyes. ''These people are looking to us for help. They're assuming we're *here* to help them, and a lot of them are going to be dead because of it.''

Lori felt a pang as she watched him. She almost reached out to touch him, but her inner turmoil stopped her. She liked Grayson. He was kind and gentle. She admired his quick intelligence and the way he could inspire respect, obedience, and admiration in the people he commanded. She had watched him come through the bloody campaign on Trellwan. Beginning with nothing, he had ended with a hodge-podge unit that had outmaneuvered the cunning Lord Hassid Ricol and forced him to give up the world he had stolen. Now he was facing Ricol again, or at least facing forces that answered to him. In only a month, he had begun to transform the rebel army into a fighting force that could meet the Red Duke's BattleMechs and win.

But why did she always see Grayson in her dreams as a destroyer, wreathed in fire, aiming that inferno launcher at her face? It frightened her, and the fact that she was afraid angered her, too.

The first time she had seen Grayson Carlyle, Lori had been piloting her *Locust* in battle on a world she'd never heard of before, fighting for masters she did not know. He had stood before her, alone, unarmored, an inferno launcher on his shoulder. He had commanded her to come out of her 'Mech and surrender, but he had not fired . . . had admitted to her later that he'd never intended to fire.

Later, at Thunder Rift, her *Locust* had burned and she had called to him and he had not come, not for long, long minutes. He'd been kilometers away at the time, fighting for his own life, but the horror of that engulfing fire, the feeling that Grayson had abandoned her, had left a deep and angry scar. She was only now coming to realize just how deep.

Lori's fear of fire was something she had grappled with

endlessly, fighting it when she went into battle, fighting it in the nightmares that plagued her sleep. When she was awake, she trusted Grayson as her commanding officer. But on some deeper level that was revealed only in dreams, she associated him with the blind panic and lack of control she'd felt while crouched behind the controls of her *Locust*. Grayson had nothing to do with the death of her parents, had nothing to do with her dread of burning and death by fire. By day, she could admire him, even want to be with him, but at night came the dreams of fire and death, and the image of a smiling Grayson, bracing the inferno launcher on his shoulder.

She *loved* him—*admit it!*—but how could that be possible when she found it so hard to trust him completely?

Lori wanted to talk to him about it. Her fears were twisted and unreasoning, but it seemed that she was beginning to understand them. She looked at Grayson and felt a sudden surge of longing that took her completely by surprise. "Gray . . ."

He looked up, the fatigue on his face startling her.

"I . . ." She stopped, flustered and confused. "How can I help?" she asked lamely.

"You can help, Lieutenant, by going back to bed and getting some sleep. We've got a little hike in the morning, remember, all the way back to Fox Island. I want you rested and fresh."

She dropped her eyes to hide her disappointment. Lieutenant! Perhaps, then, he no longer thought of her as anything more than his Executive Officer!

"Perhaps I'd better." Lori stood and turned to go. She stopped in the doorway, caught suddenly by the thought, the hope that he might call to her, ask her what was wrong, offer to talk. Or . . . he might follow her back to her cabin. The thought sent a shiver of fear through her— what would she say?—but the thought warmed her, too, and she found herself willing him to come after her.

Grayson remained at the table, one hand to his forehead as he read another dispatch, then used a stylus to enter a notation on his compad. He appeared to have forgotten her completely.

Lieutenant, indeed! She whirled and strode from the room.

* * *

The city of Regis was in flames.

From where Nagumo stood at his office window, the fire seemed to engulf the entire city. He clasped his hands behind his back, lifted his chin, pursed his lips. The rebel Helgameyer had named many of her colleagues, professors here at the University, staff members, even Academicians on the government council. Altogether, there had been 117 names on the list she had helped compile. Troopers had arrested every person on the list that very night, and the executions had begun at dawn in the University courtyard. Chief Academician Haraldssen had been the first to die. Nagumo ruled the planet directly now, in the name of his Duke.

The depth, the vehemence of the response of the citizens of Regis had caught Nagumo completely by surprise—and he was a man who did not like surprises. Instead of eliminating a handful of dissidents in a city already cowed by ten years of Combine occupation, the first volleys of the firing squads had been like the signal to open rebellion. It had started with the students. Armed with placards and banners, they had poured into the courtyard, chanting slogans and demanding freedom for those who had been taken during the night. The riot that had tumbled through the streets of Old Regis two days before was nothing compared to this.

The firing squads had turned their weapons on the crowd, and now twenty students lay dead in the courtyard. In response, the mob had produced its own weapons, rocks and bottles at first, and then a scattering of handguns and sidearms. Though these might have been stolen, they were more likely provided by Verthandian militiamen in the crowd.

After that, the entire city had seemed to rise like some angered giant roused from sleep. Nagumo had sent in the 2nd and 3rd Battalions of the Light Dragon Infantry, holding back the 1st Battalion to keep an eye on the Regis Blues. The Dragons had driven the mob out of the courtyard and into Prescott Square outside the University's front gates. And then Nagumo had ordered in the BattleMechs.

As they had two nights before, the mob had scattered, but Nagumo's warriors were under orders not to hold back. Like demons, BattleMechs had swept down on scattering bands of rioters, spraying death and destruction in a random and bloody orgy. The gates of the University had been shattered when rioters had attempted to flee back into the University and the 'Mechs had pursued them. To the twenty dead were added another two hundred more, as the 'Mechs pumped missiles, machine gun fire, auto-cannon rounds, and laser bolts into the panicking mob.

Elsewhere within the University walls, Nagumo's men had moved swiftly to exert full control over those government Academicians who had not already been arrested—"protective custody", he was calling it. They were in one of the conference rooms in this very building. Besides the Council of Academicians, 212 professors and teachers on the University Faculty had been "escorted to safety" and were under guard in the courtyard below. At the same time, the Regis Blues had been disarmed without incident, but only because their officers had been summoned to an urgent meeting and not been allowed to return to their men. Men and officers waited together now in a warehouse close beside the University. Nagumo still hadn't decided what to do about them.

Things seemed well in control, but Nagumo was not happy. He had seriously underestimated the public feeling of the Verthandians against their Combine guardians. It had been Duke Ricol's specific order that the University remain untouched, as evidence that Verthandian life, culture, and government continued unchanged under Kurita rule.

In one night, Nagumo had swept away everything that remained of Verthandi's government, and the campus courtyard was choked with bodies and prisoners pinned in the merciless beams of the searchlights turned on them.

Well, so be it. His Duke would remove him from command or else praise him for taking positive action. Nagumo was a fatalist about such matters. Events had slipped beyond his control, and now he could only attempt to ride them out as best he knew how. A planet-wide rebellion was too much for one man to deal with. But when Duke Ricol arrived, there *would* be peace in this city!

Light years away, the spy waited in the shelter of a Galaport blast pit, this time searching the sky. This time, he wore the flowing robe and dress cloak of a moderately successful local trader, attire chosen to attract no more notice than had his earlier disguise as a Lieutenant of the Port Authority.

Days before, a Draco courier had dropped out of hyperspace and beamed a coded message. It had impinged on the sensitive receiver hidden amid the clutter of satellite receiver antennae on the roofs of a middle-class residential area of Galaport. That message, when decoded, had brought the spy here.

Something glittered in the deep blue of the cloudless sky, and the spy brought his electronic binoculars to his eyes. In moments, the glitter had steadied to a pulsing jet of white flame supporting the globular mass of a freighter DropShip. He read off the lettering visible along the craft's flank. *Deimos,* DropShip One of the freighter *Invidious.*

He smiled to himself as the *Deimos* settled into a waiting cradle in clouds of dust and smoke. The target had arrived on schedule.

28

Renfred Tor matched his pace to the long-legged stride of the man who walked beside him. Salvor Steiner-Reese made Tor feel grubby and out of place, even on the streets of so egalitarian a town as Galaport. The Lyran Ambassador-at-Large was, as always, resplendent in scarlet trimmed with black. His elbow-length shoulder cloak was surely an inconvenience in Galatea's desert climate, but crisply immaculate nonetheless. The man was tall, powerfully built, autocratically handsome. His double-barrelled name openly proclaimed a much-publicized, if distant, relationship to the Archon of the Lyran Commonwealth.

For his part, Tor looked the part of a tramp freighter captain, his shipboard coveralls greasy and bare of either rank insignia or a ship ID patch. He carried a battered trade samples case in one hand.

"I'm afraid you don't understand, Captain Tor," the ambassador was saying. "There is simply no way the Commonwealth can involve itself in this matter!"

"You're right, Your Excellency, I *don't* understand. Jeri told me you'd at least be willing to listen!"

"And listen I have, sir! For the past hour! What would you have me do . . . involve House Steiner in interstellar war with the Draconis Combine . . . and for what? A handful of starving rebels on a planet *given* to the Combine by treaty a decade ago? Good lord, man, what do you take me for?"

Tor was not certain how to answer that one.

He had a friend at the Lyran Government building in the capital, a girl named Jeri whom he always looked up when in the Galatean system. She was pretty and fun.

More important, she knew most of the important people in the stellar crossroads that was Galatea. She had put him in touch with "an old friend" at the Government embassy. Galatea, as a member of the Lyran Commonwealth, did not rate the exchange of diplomatic personnel usual between separate governments, but an Ambassador-at-Large such as Steiner-Reese helped tie distant, planetary governments to the Royal Court on Tharkad. If Tor were to have any hope at all of winning support for Grayson and the Legion, Steiner-Reese was the man to see.

It looked as though the man was not willing to help.

"Look, Your Excellency," Tor said. He hefted the briefcase he carried in his right hand. "Doesn't this interest you at all?"

Tor had taken the precaution of withdrawing his own share of the metal deposited with the ComStar factor on Galatea. He believed the sight of all that lustrous gray metal might stir the imagination of the ambassador, and make Verthandi something more than an unfamiliar name.

"Frankly, Captain, no. Vanadium is a common enough element. Not here on Galatea, perhaps, but common enough elsewhere. There are hundreds of worlds within the Commonwealth, and most, sir, have adequate reserves of that metal."

"According to my man on Verthandi, Your Excellency, the Dracos have been mining like crazy in the southern desert. The planet was an agricultural backwater . . . until they came. Now they enslave the people and send them to work in the mines. Why?"

"Not for vanadium, certainly."

"No, sir. Not for vanadium. But possibly . . . for something else?"

"Like what?"

"I don't know."

"Oh, come now, Captain . . ."

"Please, sir, listen! In his message to me, Captain Carlyle described some of what he learned about Verthandi's history. The world was shaped thousands of years ago by a collision with an asteroid, an asteroid that struck near Verthandi's north pole. The impact created a vast basin that is now filled with jungle and sea. It must have hurled molten chunks of dense matter for thousands of kilometers into secondary impacts in the southern desert.''

"So?"

"Your Excellency, vanadium is common there. If vanadium, why not other metals, too? Chromium. Titanium. Niobium. Tungsten. Osmium. Perhaps in abundance. Perhaps in dense masses close to the surface, where MinerMechs can dig them out. Elements needed by industries on worlds clear across the Commonwealth.''

"You're asking me to believe that the natives of this world were just sitting on all this . . . this wealth, and were farming instead?''

"Oh, they were making use of the stuff. Grayson's message told about a local AgroMech plant that was started in a fracture cavern in the floor of that old impact crater. By and large, though, the original colonists were farmers fleeing persecution. They founded industry enough to support their own needs, but never bothered developing the mineral reserves further. They didn't need to.''

"An interesting possibility, Captain, but not one that would lead me to support an attack on the Kurita forces there!''

"I'm not saying you need an attack! But fleet maneuvers, possibly. You could arrange it with the Galatean Military Chargé d'Affaires.''

"You don't know what you're talking about, sir.'' Steiner-Reese was becoming progressively more undiplomatic by the moment, and Renfred Tor knew that he'd failed in his mission.

The three men following Tor and the Lyran Ambassador were neither close enough to hear the conversation nor to see the despair in Tor's face. They knew only that Arvid would pay them 5,000 CBs apiece to murder the freighter captain, Renfred Tor. The presence of the ambassador was a plus. His death would make the double murder look like the work of political terrorists.

The leader of the three nodded to the others, and each drew a lean, black Calaveri 10 mm automatic pistol from beneath the folds of his cloak. There were three sharp snicks as the assassins chambered their rounds, then they quickened their pace and closed on their unsuspecting targets.

"I guess I've wasted your time, then," Tor said.

"Not at all, not at all," the ambassador said. "I appreciate your problem, and I'm sorry I could not be of help. But don't hesitate to call on me some—"

He was interrupted by the sound of running feet close behind them. Tor and Steiner-Reese spun around, and saw three others rushing them from across the street. Their pursuers were bringing their pistols up into line with Tor's chest.

"No!" the ambassador shouted, but the first pair of gunshots drowned out the sound. Tor was holding his briefcase in front of him like a shield, but the twin, 10 mm slugs tore easily through the fragile plastic, hurling the freighter captain backward into a whitewashed wall. Three more shots followed as Tor lurched down onto the pavement, the face of his briefcase fragmenting with each ruthless impact.

"What are you doing?" the Ambassador shouted. By that time, three pistols were swinging around and up to point at him. As five shots roared out in rapid succession. Steiner-Reese instinctively felt for his chest, expecting to encounter blood. Instead, he clutched at a body still miraculously whole.

At the same moment, one of the thugs was flailing backwards into the street in a spray of blood. A second slumped to the pavement, his pistol a meter away from stiff fingers, which continued to spasm against the ferrocrete. The third clutched his suddenly bloody arm and shrieked agony. A sixth shot cracked, and his shriek changed to a harsh gargle as the man flopped onto the street between his two comrades.

Captain Tor stood up slowly, still clutching the shattered briefcase, the smoking barrel of a 9 mm automatic pistol protruding from underneath. He had drawn the weapon from some concealed spot in the case.

"Captain Tor! But how . . . ?"

Tor snapped the safety on his pistol and then tucked the weapon away. Picking apart some of the fragments of his briefcase, he exposed the dull gray lining of vanadium. Steiner-Reese could see the deep pits in the soft metal where the attackers' slugs had expended their energy.

"Vanadium's not all that dense," Tor explained, "but it was heavy enough to stop those bullets. Knocked me silly, though. I almost couldn't get my gun clear."

For Steiner-Reese, it had all happened so fast that his heart was still racing. "Good lord, man, they were trying to kill us! I must apologize. They must be terrorists, out to get me . . ."

Tor looked thoughtful. "I don't think so, sir." He shifted the case under one arm, took the ambassador's arm with his free hand and began steering the man down the street. "If they'd been terrorists, they'd have gone after you first, sir. No way the could mistake me for you. No, Your Excellency, they were gunning for me. I guess you were a bonus for them."

"But why?"

"Why do you think? It could be someone's afraid the Commonwealth will discover just how valuable Verthandi is. They were afraid I would get help from you." The words had come to Tor unbidden, an inspiration.

The ambassador nodded. "I'm beginning to believe you, Renfred. Will you come back with me to the embassy?"

"Certainly, sir." They began hurrying down the street. Galatea's constabulary would be along eventually to investigate the gunshots, though such attacks were relatively common in the less civilized parts of Galaport. Tor had no wish to be detained for questioning. "I am going to need a new samples case, though," he said.

Grayson studied the screen of the palm-sized electronic instrument in his hand. "No listening devices that I can see," he said. "The 'TronicsTechs can take care of the mines."

Sergeant Ramage nodded and pointed northward. "I've got a small army checking out the caves. Funny. They took all the equipment, of course, but they didn't blow the place afterward."

"Maybe they figure to use it themselves sometime."

The Gray Death, with its entourage of rebel soldiers and 'Mechs, had returned to Fox Island. Most waited at an encampment a few kilometers away in the jungle, but

Grayson had detailed Techs and the sharpest of the rebel trainees to check out the old camp. In the meantime, Lori and McCall had taken their 'Mechs up the Basin Rim Road to search for listening devices or booby traps.

It was beginning to look like Nagumo's people had done a half-hearted job here, once they'd finished with the assault itself. They'd burned the Ericksson mansion to the ground, of course, and leveled most of the barns, warehouses, and other structures as well. They'd taken all the electronics equipment, machine tools, electronics parts, computers, the pair of 'Mech simulators—anything that could be moved—and the rest they'd destroyed. Nagumo's forces had stripped the island of everything. Everything, that is, except the one thing the Gray Death needed the most.

A secret and unexpected site for an advance base camp.

The surprising thing was that the enemy forces had not been more thorough. Grayson had expected the electronics and machinery to be gone, but he'd also expected to find the cave dynamited, the island stripped bare of trees, the ground scorched. They had probably been in a hurry, he decided. From the reports he'd been getting, Nagumo's forces were being stretched tighter and tighter. The units that had staged this raid must have had to return to Regis as soon as they knew that the rebel column was beyond their reach to the south.

The place *had* been mined. The Dracos had sown both anti-personnel mines and anti-'Mech mines throughout the area, but the hand scanners his search team held were giving plenty of warning of the devices.

Khaled approached from the direction of the mansion. "We found them," he said, eyes dark and grave.

"In the house?"

The MechWarrior nodded. "Identification will be a problem."

Grayson turned and stared at the jungle, working to keep his feelings from showing. According to the muster books, eighteen of his own people had been at Fox Island when the raiders struck. Some might have been taken prisoner. Yorulis had been shot. The rest the Dracos had left in the burning house. Sixty-five rebels had been here as well. How many of them were still alive? Just counting the bodies left in the mansion would be a harrowing chore.

"We'll bury them in the jungle," he said quietly. "If we can't identify them then, well . . . that will be another we owe Nagumo for."

Khaled nodded.

Grayson turned to Ramage. "O.K., orders. When your people have gone over the area thoroughly—and I mean thoroughly—call them together. First off, deactivate all the anti-personnel traps and mines you can identify. We don't want our people forgetting where they are and blundering into them when they're out for a stroll. Next, I want . . . let's say two-thirds of the anti-'Mech mines left in place, including all those off toward the south perimeter, and on the approaches to the island."

Khaled's eyes lighted. "You want their patrols to assume we have not returned," he said.

"Right. And if they do, the remaining mines will have been moved."

Ramage grinned. "That ought to surprise them . . . unless they have their own detectors out."

"I'm hoping they'll be too busy for that. Next, I want to set up a camp, a small one, just a few tents and lean-tos." He pointed north, past the ruin of the machine shop. "Let's put it over there. Detail a watch to keep the place looking lived in. No fires yet . . . not until they're sure we're here. But have the stuff ready to make one. And plant a bunch of the mines you move in that area."

"Ah! So when Nagumo's 'Mechs come to check on someone living here again . . ."

"They walk into their own surprise. Correct. Make sure you get good people for that detail, though. They'll have to be ready to move quick. They'll be volunteers, of course."

Ramage nodded.

"O.K. I don't see any reason to stay here. If the caves check out, we'll use that as a place to keep our 'Mechs out of sight, and it'll be a good place for ammo trucks and supplies to rendezvous with us."

"Are you putting 'Mech facilities in down there?"

"Some." He scowled. "We're short on Techs."

"Most of them were here when the Dracos came."

"Two of the rebel MechWarriors are pretty fair Techs,

though. Olin Sonovarro and Vikki Traxen both worked with machinery and electronics before they opted for the outdoor life. Davis McCall may be an even better Tech than he is a MechWarrior. It's a wonder he didn't choose it in the first place. The money's certainly better.''

''Unless you were crazy enough to sign on with a mercenary unit fighting a rebellion on a jungle planet.''

''Yeah, well . . . Anyway, I may transfer them to the Tech department until we can scare up some more.''

Ramage rocked back on his heels, his thumbs hooked into his belt. He paused, looking as though he were smelling the air, before he answered. ''We're going to need all our Warriors pretty damn soon, Captain.''

''I'm well aware of it, Ram. But first we're going to need *Techs*. McCall told me the other night that it wouldn't take too long to rig a couple of repair cradles down in those caves. Some of the bracing and mounting brackets for blocks and tackle are still in place.''

''So? That's good news.''

''Right, because it means we'll be able to re-arm our 'Mechs right here, and not have to traipse clear back to Westlee to do it. McCall thinks we may be able to do some minor repair work here, too. Armor plate patches, circuit replacement, that sort of thing.''

''Won't be too difficult,'' Ramage agreed, ''if we can get the parts.''

''Oh, we'll get the parts,'' Grayson said. ''Governor General Nagumo will provide us with all the parts we need. I'm counting on him to provide us with some new BattleMechs, too.''

Ramage lifted an eyebrow. ''Getting cocky in your old age?''

''Nope. Getting tired of being shoved around by Nagumo, though. With this place back in operation as a base, we'll be able to shove *him* around for a change.''

Sergeant Rodney Pallonby tilted his *Phoenix Hawk*'s head, scanning the horizon through the cockpit screen. The land northeast of Regis was a terrain of low and rolling hills capped by patches of light woods. Visibility here wasn't as bad as over the Rim in the jungle, but there were places that were ideal for ambushes. Not that an ambush was likely with *this* convoy, but the Verthandian rebels had done some crazy things in recent weeks. An attack certainly wasn't out of the question.

He canted the *Phoenix Hawk*'s head down to check the column of prisoners. There were fifty of them, all women, ragged and dirty and held in single file by lengths of rope draped from neck to neck for the column's length. Draco soldiers, some in the black of officers, others in the dull orange and brown of a line regiment, walked in columns to either side.

Showing little emotion, the women plodded forward in line, heads bowed, wrists bound behind their backs. Pallonby decided that the events of the past twenty hours had probably short-circuited whatever emotions they might have felt. The battle at Regis University had left hundreds dead and many hundreds more prisoner in the rubble-choked University courtyard. For most of the day following the battle, the Governor General's personal Guard had been identifying ringleaders of the conspiracy that had infested the Loyalist Verthandian government. The shootings had gone on all day and through much of the night, leaving the corpses piled high in the streets outside the University.

All of the men who were left, and most of the women, had been chained together and marched off toward the south earlier that morning. The men would be employed in the mines at the desert's edge, mines run under Kurita supervision. Nagumo himself had picked out women, saying that they would be lifted offworld in a Kurita freighter, transported to another Combine world as hostages for the behavior of the rest. Pallonby wondered if it wasn't more likely that they were bound for joyhouses on Luthien or elsewhere across Kurita's domain. Women such as these would bring good prices from the right buyers, and someone like Nagumo would be certain to have those connections . . .

Pallonby brought the *Phoenix Hawk*'s head around sharply. A warning had gone off on his Magnetic Anomaly Detector. A MAD reading of that strength could mean a BattleMech, moving swiftly.

"Denik," he said into his command circuit. "Phillips, Hochstater! Did you guys get a flash on your MADs? Oh-seven-five degrees or so . . ."

The other three 'Mechs in the column paused in their

march, scanners searching. Pallonby nervously fingered his *Hawk*'s controls. If there were rebel 'Mechs out there, it could be a nasty fight. His force consisted of two *Phoenix Hawks*, a *Wasp*, and a *Stinger*. That was plenty of firepower to manage a column of prisoners and to keep rebel ground troops from making a try at a rescue, but not much good if it came to a knock-down, drag-out brawl with rebel 'Mechs.

His orders had suggested that he be alert for rebel ambushes, though they also expressed the official opinion that the rebels would not chance it. After all, if rebel 'Mechs attacked the column, fifty helpless women—the object of the rescue—would be trapped square in the middle of the firefight. The ropes and halters would assure that the women would not be able to scatter and hide. No rebel 'Mech commander would risk slaughtering them.

"I've got movement at one-oh-three," Phillips reported. A newcomer to the unit, Phillips was the brash, young *Wasp* pilot at the point. He was turning now, his laser held high toward the trees to the right. Pallonby turned, too. The low, scraggly growth cloaked a hillside half a kilometer away.

"Denik," Pallonby snapped. "Check it out."

"Acknowledged." The other *Phoenix Hawk* moved toward the slope, its Harmon heavy laser at the ready.

The *Shadow Hawk* seemed to rise out of nowhere, materializing from the trees a few meters to one side of Denik's machine. Pallonby shouted warning, but Denik was already pivoting his machine, his laser coming into line. The rebel 'Mech bounded forward, stepping inside the *Phoenix Hawk*'s reach. The armor shield mounted high on the *Shadow Hawk*'s left shoulder smashed into the lighter machine, and its left arm snapped across and clamped onto the *Phoenix Hawk*'s heavy laser.

Pallonby brought his own heavy laser up for a shot, but Denik's 'Mech and the attacking rebel's machine were too closely intertwined now. He set his *Phoenix Hawk* in motion, sprinting forward, watching for an opening.

The laser bolt caught him unaware, striking his 'Mech in the back, low on the right side of the torso. That single shot penetrated the relatively thin armor there, savaging power cable bundles and lighting his control panel with baleful red eyes. A second shot caught him an instant later in the right leg, scattering armor fragments in smoking arcs. He spun, seeking his attacker. A *Stinger* and a *Locust* were there, fifty meters away. The *Stinger* fired and the bolt caught Pallonby's 'Mech in the front torso, scorching metal and blistering paint. The *Locust* crouched slightly and spat a bolt of coherent light from the medium laser slung underneath its flat cockpit. It took Pallonby a moment to realize that the bolt was not aimed at him but had been directed a Hochstater's *Stinger*.

For a few rapid heartbeats, he stood paralyzed, wondering at which target to direct his own fire, but the initiative was lost when another laser bolt struck his *Phoenix Hawk* squarely in the back, enlarging the hole already burned through its thin armor. More red lights flashed. His jump jet circuits were gone, or so the warning indicators claimed. He elected not to test the matter, but threw his machine into a lurching roll across the ground, seeking cover.

"Regis Command!" he bawled into his radio transmitter. "This is Escort Two-Four! We are five kilometers north of Regis and under attack! Do you hear me, Regis? We are . . ."

The second rebel *Stinger* had been hiding on the other side of the column, waiting for its chance. It advanced now. With it came half a dozen hovercraft, lightly armored affairs mounting lasers and autocannons. A score of shells slewed from one chattering gun into the back of Phillips' *Wasp*, and the light BattleMech staggered and went down, arms flailing.

Pallonby switched back to his combat frequency. Whether or not Regis had heard him, he couldn't know. He had more immediate concerns at the moment.

"Hochstater! Watch behind you! Phillips is down!"

Hochstater's *Stinger* spun, firing wildly, hitting nothing. Pallonby glanced back toward the prisoner column. Where it should have been he saw nothing but tall weeds. The women must have thrown themselves flat as soon as the firing started. Pallonby realized now that the appearance of the *Shadow Hawk* had drawn his own 'Mechs far enough away from the column that the prisoners had not been in the line of fire.

When laser bolts seared the air close by his 'Mech's

head, he rolled to one side and then came up firing. The hovercraft were closer now, their weapons concentrating on his *Phoenix Hawk* and on Hochstater's *Stinger*. He could see rebel soldiers, too, advancing on foot to lead away small groups of his former prisoners. As he watched, several Kurita foot soldiers broke and ran from the line of advancing rebels. Machine gun fire from the rebel *Stinger* and the swift-moving hovercraft cut them down.

On the hillside, Denik's *Phoenix Hawk* had been crushed by its heavier opponent. With one large laser and a pair of Harmon medium lasers, a *Phoenix Hawk* should have outgunned the heavier *Shadow Hawk* at close-ranged because the *Shadow Hawk's* autocannons and LRM launchers were only effective at relatively long range. As close-up weapons, it had only a single medium laser and a pair of SRM tubes. This particular *Shadow Hawk* had managed to overcome its disadvantage by grappling with the *Phoenix Hawk* so closely that it couldn't use its arm-mounted lasers. After it had bashed in the 'Mech's head with one steal fist, that same *Shadow Hawk* now turned its autocannon and LRM tubes on Pallonby's own *Phoenix Hawk*.

=== 29 ===

Grayson's *Shadow Hawk* stepped across the broken body of his opponent and strode down the slope toward where the second enemy *Phoenix Hawk* stood with its arms raised in ungainly surrender. Smoke wreathed its torso from the pair of jagged wounds Lori and Nadine Cheka had planted in its back. Khaled's *Stinger* closed in from the far side of the shallow valley as hovercraft grounded to pick up the liberated prisoners.

"Looks like they're all safe," Ramage was saying through Grayson's command circuit. "No casualties among the women!"

"Great," Grayson said, relieved. They had planned the assault to draw the Kurita BattleMech escorts away from their prisoners, but stray rounds—or a vengeful Kurita soldier—could have had nightmarish consequences. The keys to making the attack a success were doing it with speed and decisiveness. "What about our people?"

"A couple wounded in the firefight with the foot soldiers. We were lucky."

"I won't argue that." Grayson turned his attention back to the enemy 'Mechs. The *Wasp* was out of the fight for the moment, but didn't seem badly damaged. The Kurita *Stinger* had halted and put up its own hands when the *Phoenix Hawk* had called it quits. Ramage's anti-Mech commandos were now dropping from their hovercraft alongside the pair of Kurita 20-tonners. Grayson saw the *Stinger*'s head split apart and the Kurita pilot wiggle out of the tight cockpit under the threat of Ramage's guns and satchel charges.

He opened a combat frequency. "Strike Two, this is Strike Leader. Operation complete."

A reply sounded in his earpiece. "Strike Leader, this is Two. Your target yelled for help, like you thought. It's leaving the city at a trot."

Grayson turned his 'Mech and looked south. Regis was a low sprawl across the horizon, with the University Towers stabbing up into an overcast gray-green sky. Two-and-a-half kilometers was ninety seconds for a trotting 'Mech. His infantry was still spread out across the valley, leading former prisoners and captured Kurita soldiers to empty hovercraft waiting among the trees. There were also the captured 'Mechs to think about.

"I copy, Two. What are they? Can you take them?"

Clay's voice replied with expressionless calm. "Two lances, Captain. I make it a *Phoenix Hawk* and a couple of *Shadow Hawks*, two *Wasps*, an *Archer*, what I think is a *Centurion*, and a *Warhammer*."

That was not good. The Strike Two ambush force consisted of both of Grayson's heavies—the *Rifleman* and the *Wolverine*—plus the main body of the rebel 'Mechs. Montido's 55-ton *Dervish* stiffened the unit, but most of the force consisted of *Wasps* and *Stingers*. Grayson had insisted that the AgroMechs be left out of it this time. The enemy lances were on the light side, but the *Archer* and the *Warhammer* were both 70-tonners and out of the ambushers' league. There was also the danger that 'Mechs would strike from the Kurita DropShip, a few kilometers to the northeast.

McCall's voice broke in. "Captain, if we can nae tak-eit *these* Sassenach, we'd best all look for a new callin'."

"We can take them, Lieutenant. We're in position, and they haven't spotted us yet."

Unless they'd picked up the radio chatter, of course. Strike Two was using directional microwave antennae locked into a receiver set up on Basin Rim, which then shunted their transmissions to Grayson's *Hawk* by a short-ranged relay. It was very possible that the enemy might tap in, however.

"We'll stay put, Two" he said. "Take them."

The ambush force lost two rebel *Stingers*, one shot to pieces by the combined fire of the enemy *Warhammer* and *Archer* when it tried to change position, and the other smashed by the enemy *Centurion*. Neither rebel pilot was able to eject before his 'Mech was destroyed. Relatively little damage was scored on the Kurita relief column: Clay's *Wolverine* claimed a *Wasp*, McCall's *Rifleman* chopped the *Phoenix Hawk* into scrap, and one of the Kurita *Shadow Hawks* was limping heavily as it retreated back into Regis.

The battle had an importance that far outweighed the casualties on either side. The relief column fought with its outgunned ambushers for the better part of twenty minutes before deciding that Escort Two-Four was beyond help from them—and who knew what other surprises those wooded hills north of Regis held? The Kurita forces could have summoned more 'Mechs from Regis. At what risk, though, when the scope of the ambush was not known? The Kurita lances elected to play it safe by withdrawing back to the shelter of Regis. The wreckage of the two rebel *Stingers* and the two Kurita 'Mechs was left where it was. There was too much danger that a sudden sortie would trap any Techs or warriors working to salvage the BattleMech hulks.

In exchange, Grayson's forces had captured a *Stinger* and a *Phoenix Hawk* intact and were able to haul off the wrecked *Wasp* and *Phoenix Hawk* as well. The *Wasp* was a real prize. A lucky shot had severed a primary driver link in the 'Mech's lightly armored spine and cut its power supply to its legs and arms, but the damage would be easy to repair. The *Phoenix Hawk* needed a new head. If they couldn't find one, its carcass would still provide spare parts for dozens of light rebel 'Mechs.

All in all, it was a highly successful raid, not to mention the fifty Verthandians rescued before they could be led aboard the grounded Kurita DropShip awaiting them.

Shortly after they reached their Fox Island camp, Lori brought Grayson the startling news that one of the rescued women was Sue Ellen Klein.

Rescued and rescuers had rendezvoused back at the Fox Island caves after the battle, pausing only to let a band of rebel AgroMechs race north with the Kurita prisoners in tow, a diversion that might keep the Dracos away from Fox Island for awhile. Grayson knew that they would be visiting Fox Island again, and soon. The longer he could put that visit off, the better prepared they would be to receive it.

As for Sue Ellen, Grayson barely recognized her. She was gaunt, with a haggard expression and a dullness in her eyes that twisted at Grayson's soul. He found her sitting on a log before a smoldering campfire, staring into the flames.

"Sue Ellen? It's me, Captain Carlyle. Are you O.K.?"

She refused to meet his eyes.

He extended a hand to her. "Can I get you anything? Coffee? No? Are you hurt? Sick?"

It took some minutes before she could speak. When she did, her voice was detached, so soft that Grayson had to lean forward to hear. "How did you escape?" she said.

"What do you mean?" he murmured.

"I . . . I wanted you dead. And apparently I told them something they could use. Something . . . something about a man named . . . Ericksson."

"You told them about Ericksson?"

She nodded. "I betrayed you."

Could he blame her? Grayson remembered her last words to him as the *Phobos* had plunged from the sky toward the Verthandian jungle. "Maybe you had reason to," he said gently. Somehow, he was not angry, knowing what she must have been through since last they'd met.

Her story, at least, explained the raid on Fox Island, the ambush in the jungle. It had been sheer good fortune that the Legion and the main body of the rebel army had been out of the camp at the time. Or perhaps the enemy had tracked them to their hideout, then waited for the main body to leave so that the base would be more defenseless.

"They used me," she continued, as if she hadn't heard him. "They flattered me and made me one of them and . . . and *used* me! A tool, a . . . a *thing!* And when they got what they wanted . . ."

She began to cry. Grayson reached out tentatively, took her shoulder, drew her close. They sat together by the fire for a long time. Sue Ellen, Grayson learned, had been literally dragged from the bed of the man who'd been questioning her, and thrown into one of the prison cells beneath the tallest tower of the University of Regis. There seemed to be no reason for her captivity beyond the fact that the Dracos had never really trusted her. They had promised her security and revenge and even love to get the information they wanted. Even after that, they had continued to question her from time to time, she said, showing him the scars on her arms and hands.

He held her for a long time after that, the two of them saying nothing.

Lori emerged from the darkness. "Captain?"

He looked up, nodded. Sue Ellen was asleep, her face tear stained and smudged where she leaned against his shoulder. Lori's face worked with some unnamed emotion at the sight of those two together.

"I've been talking to some of the other people we rescued," she said, her voice low. "There's another you should meet." With Lori's help, Grayson slipped out from the cradle he'd provided Sue Ellen. Leaving Lori with her, he went to meet the other freed captive.

Lori watched him go with mingled thoughts. Her own jealousy just now surprised her. *Why should I be surprised if he . . . he finds someone else? I haven't exactly been encouraging his attentions . . .*

Holding the worn, sleeping woman as Grayson had done, Lori suppressed a laugh. *Does being jealous mean I love the guy?*

Whatever the answer, she did know that Sue Ellen Klein was going to need friends. And in her heart, Lori was happy for anyone who might have Grayson for a friend.

Her name was Janice Taylor, and she was waiting for him by another fire not far off. He handed her a cup of coffee made with water boiled over an open fire and a packet of instant-mix crystals of uncertain vintage. "I'm not sure it'll taste like your Verthandian coffee . . ." he said.

She accepted it with both hands and a smile. "At least it's hot," she said, sipping at the mug, "and I'm not going to question its pedigree. Just so long as it takes care of my caffeine addiction."

Grayson sat down beside her. Jungle noises surrounded them, louder than the muted clank and drill-whine of the BattleMech repairs proceeding in the cave behind them.

"So you were a teacher at the University," he prompted.

"That's right. The history department."

"Then maybe you can tell us what's happening in Regis."

"I don't know what I could tell you, Captain. Like I said, I'm an historian, and I was never much interested in politics. I know there was some sort of a shake-up—maybe a plot against the Draco commander—inside the Council of Academicians. And there were riots that started out as a demonstration by the students and some faculty and staff. I guess things got out of hand, because the first thing I knew about it, there were BattleMechs rampaging through the streets of Regis, and soldiers arresting people in the University Quarters Wing."

"Got out of hand? I'd say so if people were demonstrating against Nagumo. Did they think he would quietly pack up and leave?"

"Verthandi has a long history of free expression," she said. "That's been stifled ever since the Kurita forces arrived, but that doesn't mean it's dead." She smiled. "To keep Verthandians from speaking their minds, well . . . you might as well command Norn not to shine."

"*That* I believe is beyond the capability of Kurita's legions," Grayson said, "but there's plenty else he could do to try to bring you into line."

"And he tried it." The smile was gone. "My brother and mother and father . . . they must be working in one of the mines in the desert by now . . . if they're still alive at all. They were rounded up, too, and I heard a soldier saying what was going to happen to them."

"Would you be able to locate these mines on a map?"

She nodded, and there was a dawning light in her eyes. "You . . . you might be able to get them out? My family, I mean?"

"No promises," Grayson said, trying to make the words gentle. "But I can't think of a better way to prove we're friendly to the people of Verthandi."

"There's hardly a need for that. Since you've started raiding Nagumo's outposts and camps, the rebels have become some kind of popular heroes. And you mercenaries are something of a legend. In the last ten years, the rebel army has only managed to raid a few camps and knock out maybe five or six Kurita 'Mechs. Since you offworlders arrived, it seems like Nagumo spends most of his time looking for a place to hide.''

''It would be nice if that were true. I don't think he'll make it that easy for us, though. Seriously . . . are the people in Regis ready to fight Nagumo? Or did what happened the other night knock the fight out of them?''

''I wish I could say.'' She shook her head. ''It started when some of the senior Academicians were arrested and shot. It surprised me, the way students and teachers and . . . and people not even connected with the University or the government came pouring out into the streets. A lot of them were killed, and most of the rest must have been rounded up and marched south. The ones that are left . . . well, they're scared. They might just join you, if they had half a chance. A lot of them seem to have hope now, knowing that Nagumo's thugs can be stopped. I know for sure that the ones in the mines would join you. They've already fought Nagumo . . . and we've been hearing stories about what goes on in those mines . . .'' She shuddered, clutching her empty mug.

''You'd like us to try to rescue those folks.''

''Can you blame me?''

''Of course not. But do you realize the risk?''

''I think so. We were in danger today, weren't we?''

Grayson nodded slowly. ''I tried to shave things to keep you folks out of the line of fire, and we had to move fast. But there was danger, yes. We knew they were taking you offworld. Once they got you away, there was no way we'd ever have gotten you back. It was do something and be damned if something went wrong . . . or do nothing and be damned for sure. I had to make the choice.''

She laid a hand on his arm. ''You chose right, Captain. When the first blasts went off, and I looked up to see those metal mountains crashing down on top of me, I thought the world was ending, right there. I fell on my face, and I couldn't do much because my hands were tied . . . but I think I must have been trying to dig a hole with my head. I've never been so terrified in my life, but then one of your soldiers was helping me up and cutting the ropes. It took a couple of minutes for it to sink in that I was really free. Free!

"The soldiers . . . the Kurita soldiers, I mean . . . they'd been talking about what was going to happen to us. Where they were taking us, you know? They were enjoying it . . . laughing at us . . . Captain, if you personally had shot me dead out there today, it would have been a favor. One way or the other, I'd have been free."

"But can you choose that for your parents . . . your brother?"

"I don't want them to die, Captain, but if half of what I've heard is true, they'll be dead soon anyway if no help comes."

"I won't even be able to promise we'd hit the right mine. The ones at Skovde are the largest, but there are others, and we don't have the numbers to hit them all."

"If you don't free my parents, you'll free someone else's parents . . . or husbands, or children. And I promise you that you'll be raising an army to help you free the rest of Verthandi."

Grayson nodded as he stared into the embers of the fire. "That, Miss Taylor, is what I'm counting on."

BOOK III

30

"To be blunt, General Nagumo," said Duke Hassid Ricol, "I am undecided as to whether or not to keep you in command. I ordered you to pacify this world, but the situation seems rather to have deteriorated in recent months, does it not?"

Nagumo had long since decided that a straightforward approach was his best hope. "It has, your Grace."

"You have an explanation? An excuse?"

"No excuses, your Grace."

"Ah, well. That is refreshing, at least. Failure seems inevitably to breed excuses, and I loathe them. An officer does what he is commanded, or he fails. Correct?" Ricol was tall and heavily built, his swarthy features partly masked by a square-cut black beard. As if that were not impressive enough, he wore an ornate, one-piece red suit trimmed in black, gold, and silver. He also wore the dramatic, stiff-collared cloak with braided silver aiguillettes in the fashion of the Inner Sphere.

"C-correct, your Grace."

"Your information on rebel whereabouts leaves much to be desired. Admiral Kodo stated in his report that a prisoner he captured gave the location of the rebel base. You raided and destroyed it, he says, but have not followed up the victory."

"That is true, your Grace. It's . . . you must understand, your Grace. It's the jungle."

The Red Duke's eyes narrowed. "What about it?"

"The rebels control the jungle completely. We have lost several patrols to date and a number of BattleMechs. It is becoming difficult to get the MechWarriors to take their machines into the jungle. And ineffective as well."

"How so?"

"We can only find the rebels when it suits them, your Grace. Their people can move in small groups throughout the Silvan lowlands, spotting our 'Mechs, trailing them. Sometimes they move their own 'Mechs to avoid a battle; other times, they might mass in one place to ambush us as we come through. And this mercenary regiment—the Gray Death, it's called. There don't seem to be many of them, but they're devilishly effective in jungle warfare. They seem to have convinced my senior regimental officer that the jungle is no place to fight 'Mechs."

Ricol's eyes flashed in anger. "Then perhaps you should find a more aggressive regimental commander!"

"Colonel Kevlavic is my best, your Grace. He commands the 3rd Strike Regiment . . . a good unit."

"Wait . . . the Gray Death, you said?"

Nagumo nodded. "We have good information on that, your Grace. From the prisoner Kobo mentioned. Actually, it was a young lady who served with him, and was . . . was induced to change sides."

"I see. Their leader's name, then, is Carlyle."

Nagumo's eyes widened. "Grayson Carlyle. Yes, your Grace. How did you know?"

"We've met before, he and I." Ricol raised a hand, flicked his fingers carelessly. "It doesn't matter. What plans have you made for crushing him?"

"Your Grace . . . I've had all I could manage just holding what we already control." He indicated the Verthandi map on the wall, stabbing at places with his forefinger. "Look! A deep space relay, here. The Skovde mines, four hundred kilometers south. Patrols here and here. There have been raids by rebels trained in highly unorthodox warfare techniques as far west as Bluesward. And they're spreading, like a disease."

"Grayson Carlyle is one man," the Duke said. "Those with him cannot number more than a few hundred at most. But he's turned rabble into a fighting unit before. I suspect that if you crush him, you'll crush this whole rebellion. Pursue the rebels into their home ground, into the jungle. If your Colonel won't do it, have him shot, and get someone else who *will* obey orders!"

Nagumo shook his head sadly as he looked at the blotch of deep green marking Verthandi's jungle basin. "That

Carlyle is a damned ghost. . . . If the odds are not to his liking, he just seems to vanish into thin air.''

"Confound it, man! He must have bases! Supply sources!''

"He steals a lot of his supplies from us, and the rest must come from sympathetic farmers and plantation owners. We destroyed the rebels' main repair and refitting center here, on Fox Island, but we didn't remain there afterward. Instead of waiting around for an attack from all sides in a hostile environment, I felt it wiser to lay mines and then withdraw to the safety of Regis. We have been unable to locate another base site.''

"Bah! Have you checked Fox Island again?''

"Your Grace? No . . . but that base was destroyed and mined, as I said.''

"Grayson Carlyle is . . . resourceful. The one thing a BattleMech force must have, however, is a place to rebuild and rearm their 'Mechs. If you've ruled out a possible hiding place for these mercenaries because you've already been there once, then I suggest to you that *that* is where you will find them!''

"Possibly . . .'' Nagumo's eyes widened. "Possibly! There were caves there. Colonel Kevlavic did report the existence of caves on Fox Island. Caves that functioned as the rebels' maintenance bays and machine shops. But we *destroyed* all their heavy equipment, except for what we carted away!''

"General, I submit that they are getting it from someplace, or you would already have stopped the rebellion cold. Good gods, man! How do you think he is repairing and re-arming his BattleMechs? Perhaps he salvaged the Dropship that Kodo reported as destroyed.''

"I . . . that is . . . your Grace, the wrecked DropShip was washed away in a storm! I had assumed . . .''

"I loathe assumptions, General, even more than I loathe excuses!''

"Yes, your Grace!''

"I will be here in Verthandi for several days at least. I must return to Luthien within two months, but time remains to see that matters here are . . . progressing satisfactorily. I will evaluate the effectiveness and the efficiency of all military factors here. Those that do not measure up will be . . . replaced. Am I understood?''

"Perfectly, your Grace."

"Good. Now, has anyone thought to wonder what Carlyle is doing here? When last I saw him, he was a goodly number of light years away, off toward the Periphery."

"Yes, your Grace. My intelligence sources indicate that the rebels brought the mercenaries here to train their soldiers. This Carlyle seems to have some skill in unorthodox tactics. Taking 'Mechs with satchel charges, man-portable rocket launchers, that sort of thing."

"He is a . . . a gifted warrior."

"He is also threatening the accepted order of battle. BattleMechs rule the battlefield and always have! It is unthinkable that foot soldiers could bring them down!"

"There were foot soldiers in war long before there were BattleMechs, Governor. You would do well to remember that," said the Duke. "We will simply have to find a way to crush Grayson, and through him, to strike down your rebels."

"But how?"

"No man is infallible. Each of us has his weakness, a blind spot. You will find Carlyle's, and you will exploit it."

"I, your Grace?"

"You will remain in command, at least for now. Meet with your staff, and then present me with a plan for moving against Fox Island in a surprise attack by this time tomorrow."

"Y-yes, your Grace."

"Don't fail me again, Nagumo." Ricol held out his hand, palm up, and slowly closed his fingers into a fist. "I mean to have Grayson Carlyle. More than I want this planet for the Draconis Combine, I want Carlyle. And you, General, are going to deliver him to me."

31

Grayson held his hand to the side of his neurohelmet, pressing the comspeaker tight against his ear. Ramage's voice was faint, routed through five separate relay stations, but his words were clear.

"It's at least a full company, Captain," he was saying. "They deployed down the Rim Road in tight order, covered by infantry, and with low-level fighter cover."

"Are the fighters giving you any trouble?"

"Not so far. They've been low over the clearing where the plantation used to be, but they haven't been able to spot us yet."

"How long until the column reaches you?"

"Half an hour. Maybe less."

"Right. Play it according to plan. We'll let you know how it goes."

"Yeah, do that. Ramage out."

Grayson switched to the general combat frequency. Through the cockpit viewport of his *Shadow Hawk*, he could see other 'Mechs of the hastily assembled strike force strung out along the ravine ahead of him. The Gray Death BattleMechs stood motionless close by the walls of the ravine. In the shadows beneath the trees, Verthandian rebels moved in small groups or lounged beside their camouflaged hover transports. Lori's *Locust* stood on the crest above the valley, its spindly form silhouetted against the orange sun of Norn. The sky was clear, which made for hazardous movement in the open. On the plus side, though, if the enemy was moving against Fox Island, Kurita air surveillance would be turned toward the jungle, not here, well into the Bluesward Plateau.

The Li Plantation lay several kilometers behind them,

for Grayson did not want the rebel 'Mechs too close to Li Wu's buildings. Instead, he had located this sheltered gully where the strike force could assemble without risking detection by satellite or Aero-Space Fighter.

He hoped this maneuver would not bring the Dracos down on the Li family. Both the elder Li Wu and his son Li Chin had already rendered invaluable service to the rebellion. It was Chin who had guided them through the jungle to Westlee after the capture of Fox Island, and Wu had brought word that the Dracos seemed to be mustering for a surprise attack. And that was exactly what Grayson had been waiting for. A surprise attack meant the Dracos would be using their three remaining AeroSpace Fighters for air cover, which gave Grayson a precious opportunity. As soon as word came that the Kurita forces were on the march, he'd mustered the rebel forces at the Li farm.

He pressed the transmit panel. "All units. Saddle up. It's time to move!"

The rebel column moved up an earth embankment to the crest of the ravine. From there, Regis lay like a distant gray forest.

"How long do we have?" Tollen asked, his voice harsh.

Grayson remembered the rebel's outburst on his return from Scandiahelm, and shuddered. Tollen Brasednewic now seemed to be a man whose emotions were held tightly in check, but only just barely. The trust between them had vanished, as if it had never been.

"Half an hour until things get hot on Fox Island," Grayson replied. "Figure ten, maybe fifteen minutes after that until it's our turn."

Racing across the Bluesward, six BattleMechs, fifteen hover transports, and two dozen skimmers carried a total of nearly two hundred troops. The 'Mechs maintained a steady, ground-eating pace. Though moving at less than full speed to keep heat build-up to a minimum, the machines devoured the ground in five-meter strides. Grayson knew that, off to the west, the newly-arrived Kurita DropShips squatted in the Regis spaceport, but he spared no time looking at them. The plan required that they cover the forty kilometers between the Li Plantation and Regis as quickly as possible.

The chances were good that the Dracos would not observe their approach. House-sized boulders and patches of forest broke up much of this section of the plateau, offering abundant cover. What's more, the chance of a spy satellite searching their small part of the plain at that moment was relatively slim.

Hearing a rush of distant sound over his external pickups, Grayson swiveled his *Shadow Hawk*'s head in the direction indicated by his instruments—a hair south of west. "Here they come, boys and girls," he said. "Freeze! McCall! Be ready!"

The column came to a halt, remaining motionless among the boulders and a scattering of trees. McCall's *Rifleman* assumed a combat-ready stance, its quad weapon barrels searching the western sky.

A trio of black dots raced northward across the sky, almost touching the horizon. They moved rapidly, slipping behind the spherical shadows of the DropShips at the spaceport. In the space of three heartbeats, they'd crossed the distance from Regis to the low, gray-black line of forest marking the Basin Rim and the Silvan jungle beyond. Only McCall's 'Mech moved, its torso swivelling slowly as its weapons tracked.

"Tha' laddies missed us, sair," the Caledonian said.

"Right you are." The dots had vanished below the Basin Rim. Grayson thought about Ramage and the others waiting out the Kurita assault beneath the jungle canopy. "Step it up, everyone! We have to get in place, fast!" The remaining kilometers dwindled, and a view of Regis began to fill the 'Mech's cockpit screens ahead.

The airfield was right where Li Chin had said it was, beneath the northeast walls of the University itself. The Kurita AeroSpace Fighters were gone, flying combat cover for the raid on Fox Island. Through telescopic imaging, Grayson could make out the ground crew and Techs moving among the buildings and stacks of supplies. The field itself was a crude affair, little more than a leveled stretch of bulldozed ground. The heavy construction 'Mechs that had plowed the strip were still sitting in the shadow of the University wall. A *Crusader* walked sentry go. There were also human guards pacing narrow strips in front of the stockpiled caches of fuel and ammunition. Behind the airfield, a gate under the main

University tower stood open. Small hover vehicles moved between the gate and the newly erected military barracks along the airstrip, and a platoon of Regis Blue militia marched in precision-step out of the city.

It still looked as though the merc-and-rebel force had not been seen.

Grayson used BattleMech hand gestures rather than risk having his orders picked up by nearby receivers that might happen to be tuned to their combat channel. 'Mechs and transports dispersed through the bluegrass. While the 'Mechs lowered themselves clumsily to their hands and knees in the concealing vegetation, the troops alighted from the vehicles. They were now less than two kilometers from Regis, with the walls and towers of the University rising above them against the sky. Grayson knew they couldn't hope to remain undiscovered for long, of course. It would take only one Blue Militia sentry idly looking down from a parapet to notice the heavy gray forms of BattleMechs lying in the brush a kilometer away.

They wouldn't have long to wait, however. As Grayson lowered his *Shadow Hawk* into a prone position, he switched his communicator to the relay channel. He didn't transmit, of course, not this close to the enemy's stronghold. What he could do was listen for a signal.

It came less than five minutes later.

"Strikeforce! Strikeforce! Clear sky and green!" The message repeated three times and would be repeated again at intervals. As Grayson switched back to the combat channel, battle thrill was already charging his heart and mind. At once familiar and disturbing, the fearful thumping of his heart was tinged with excitement.

"Ready!"

Three dots appeared in the northern sky, vectoring almost directly toward the 'Mech strike force. The first of the dots grew into the shape of an SL-17 *Shilone,* its landing gear down as it dropped toward the runway. Its two companions, delta-shaped *Slayer*'s, arrowed across the field and off over the city, breaking left and right to begin their own landing passes. Grayson watched carefully. There was no telling how much fuel or ammo those three fighters still carried. The assault could not begin until all three craft were on the ground.

As the *Shilone* rolled to a stop, Techs and astechs were

already gathering around, checking for damage. Someone braced a ladder against the side of the cockpit. The whine of the *Slayer*s descending to the runway grew in the distance.

Grayson kept his attention focused on the runway. Then . . .

"Go!" he said sharply.

Six BattleMechs rose as one from the brush and bluegrass, and sprinted toward the airstrip. The distance to the field seemed suddenly far greater than it had a moment before, when every meter nearer the University walls had seemed to offer more chance of discovery. Now the remaining ground seemed endless.

Ground crews continued to work with the fighters. The *Crusader* pilot had turned his 'Mech to watch the bustle of activity. Even the sentries on the walls above were momentarily diverted.

When someone looked up and saw the advancing BattleMechs, there was a shout, a warning. Grayson saw Techs gesturing wildly, saw the 65-ton *Crusader* turning ponderously, its left and right arms bringing laser and LRM batteries to bear. Grayson checked his instrumentation. The *Crusader* was 300 meters distant, well within range, while the nearest of the fighters were to one side and beyond, too far to be good targets.

"Keep going, everyone!" he shouted into the command circuit. "I'll hold the sentry!"

Grayson changed course slightly, swerving his *Shadow Hawk* to run directly toward the larger *Crusader*. The Kurita 'Mech outweighed Grayson's *Hawk* by ten tons, but Grayson did not expect to stand and slug it out for long.

Five long-range missiles arced on twisting contrails of white smoke from the tubes set in the *Hawk*'s right torso. He saw one impact, then another, and another, solid hits high up on the *Crusader*'s chest. An alarm shrieked of incoming missiles and he sidestepped to the left, fast. Explosions rattled gravel from his 'Mech's hull as he followed the missile salvo with a rapid-fire volley of laser bolts, then broke into an all-out, lumbering run that hurled his 'Mech across the remaining meters.

Something slammed into the *Hawk*'s torso, low and to the right. The explosion staggered him, but he kept the

'Mech on its feet and moving. Other explosions bracketed the ground around him, and laser fire glanced from his left arm. He triggered the twin SRM tubes mounted on the *Hawk*'s head, the roar of the departing rockets thundering in the narrow cockpit. Smoke swirled in battle fog, momentarily so thick that he lost sight of the enemy. Changing direction, he lurched to the left. He considered triggering his combat radar, but quickly abandoned the idea. Using radar would give away his own position as readily as it would locate the enemy. The smoke thinned, and he stepped into the clear.

Grayson was close beside the end of the runway, the University walls above him. Flashes along the parapets showed where troops were hosing the attackers with machine gun and recoilless rifle fire, and bullets whanging off his hull armor reverberated through Grayson's 'Mech.

McCall's *Rifleman* had stepped all the way out onto the runway, twin autocannons and twin lasers flashing destruction and thunder into the hull of the *Shilone* only 250 meters away. Grayson saw part of the cockpit splinter in the flash of an autocannon shell, saw fragments of armor vaulting into the sky. A hundred meters further on, one of the *Slayer*'s burned as Clay's *Wolverine* plied it with bolt after deadly bolt. Techs and astechs scattered wildly before the onslaught. A few, braver or more foolhardy than the rest, had stopped and were blazing away at the BattleMechs along the field with rifles and hand lasers, but to no effect.

"Ain brred'ach! Sassenach!" Grayson heard the words over his battle circuit rather than through his external pick-ups, but the Caledonian's intent was plain enough. His *Rifleman* advanced, weapons blazing, and the ragtag defenders threw down their weapons and fled in abject panic.

A blur of motion near the barracks on the far side of the field caught Grayson's eye. Lasers flashed, and one of the barracks took fire, throwing black smoke into the clear sky. The farthest *Slayer* came under a fusillade of fire that riddled wings and control surfaces, smashed at the cockpit, and pocked the hull with heat-charred streaks and craters.

Three for three. If the Kurita fighters weren't destroyed, they would be out of commission for a long, long time to come.

"Round up!" Grayson called. "Let's move out!"

Khaled's *Stinger* stood side by side with Lori's *Locust*, spraying the parapets with laser fire. The defenders on the walls had scattered, but those two continued to lay down covering fire to protect the rebel hovercraft. Debrowski's *Wasp* moved northward, watching for foot soldier assault teams waiting to ambush the 'Mechs as they withdrew.

"Way's clear, Captain," Debrowski reported. Grayson acknowledged and signaled the others. With their weapons still covering the city walls, they began to fall back to the north.

Explosions sent gouts of dirt and rock into the sky. Clay yelled a warning. "Watch the *Crusader*, on the right!"

The *Crusader* was 200 meters away to the east and closing, but there was nothing to block the Gray Death's retreat back toward the jungle and safety.

Grayson checked his forces, suddenly worried. All the other 'Mechs were accounted for, but where were the rebel troops? After their sweep through the far side of the airfield, they should have been well to the north by now. Yet they were nowhere to be seen. He swung his *Hawk* around, searching, and went cold inside. A pitched battle had developed close by the gate, where Brasednewic's troops had dismounted from their hovercraft and were forcing their way into the University gate. The carefully orchestrated plan was threatening to unravel before Grayson's eyes as the Verthandian rebels stormed the University tower.

Autocannon shells smashed into the *Shadow Hawk*'s left side. In the east, the *Crusader* was advancing. Through the smoke and rising dust, Grayson could make out at least two more full lances of Kurita 'Mechs in close formation less than a kilometer away. A churning dust cloud behind the 'Mechs marked a small fleet of racing hovercraft, each loaded with Kurita line troops and Regis Blues.

The plan had definitely gone wrong.

32

"**B**rasednewic! What in the hell do you think you're doing?''

"The way's open, Captain!'' the rebel commander replied. "We can push through to the University grounds!''

"And be trapped in a bottle . . . or can't you see that army approaching from the east?'' Grayson didn't wait for an answer. "McCall! Clay! Help me hold off the Kurita 'Mechs! Lori, Debrowski! See if you can help Brasednewic!''

Grayson's autocannon was delivering its rapid-fire thunder as he spoke, the shells smashing into the *Crusader*'s head and torso in a steady stream. McCall joined him, catching the enemy 'Mech in a deadly autocannon crossfire. The range was too great for precisely aimed head shots, however, and the enemy 'Mech too large to be felled quickly by a few lucky hits. The *Crusader* stopped its advance, took a few steps backward under the withering fire, then straightened as though in a heavy wind and began to advance once more.

Grayson saw that the enemy 'Mechs alongside were lighter machines, a scattering of *Wasps*, *Stingers*, and *Commando*s, probably members of the Kurita Light Recon lance they'd encountered in the raid to free the Verthandian prisoners. They did not seem anxious to advance into the sleeting fire the three Gray Death 'Mechs were laying down, even though most of it was concentrated on the larger *Crusader*.

"We're pulling out, Chief!'' That was Lori's voice, and a quick glance at the gateway under the University towers showed the last of the hover vehicles pulling off on sharply tilted fans, sending rooster tails of dust high into the air behind them. The ferrocrete under the gateway arch was littered with bodies, blue Loyalist uniforms mingled with the greens, browns, and grays of the rebel troops. More blue uniforms were spilling through the gate as he watched. Lori's *Locust* backed away, her machine guns raking the advancing mob until it wavered, broke, and tumbled back in disorder.

Grayson turned back to face the BattleMechs. The *Crusader* was much closer now, less than two hundred meters. This was going to be tricky.

"McCall! Clay! Fall back, but be ready to give me cover!"

The *Rifleman* and the *Wolverine* turned and lumbered north behind the *Shadow Hawk*. Laser bolts flashed and burned to Grayson's left. The recon 'Mechs had spread out in a rough semicircle, and some of them were working their way to the north in an attempt to cut off the Gray Death's retreat.

Missiles smashed into the *Shadow Hawk*'s right arm as red lights flashed across Grayson's control panel. He brought the right arm laser into line, punched the firing control, and bit back a savage curse as the weapon refused to fire. He triggered his SRM tubes instead, and watched his last two missiles arc across the narrowing range and into the *Crusader*'s chest.

He looked to the north. Lori was in a close-range duel with a *Stinger,* and Clay and McCall were exchanging shots with enemy 'Mechs hidden by a patch of woods. Where was Debrowski?

SRMs from the *Crusader* smashed close beside him and sent his *Shadow Hawk* into a lumbering run. Grayson knew the slower *Crusader* wouldn't be able to catch him from behind. That left only the light scout 'Mechs ahead to worry about.

Where was Debrowski? "Strike Force Five, this is Strike Force Leader! Where the hell are you, Debrowski?"

There was no answer. He brought the *Shadow Hawk* alongside Lori's 'Mech and joined her in blasting at the enemy *Stinger* until the scout 'Mech turned, fired its jump jets, and broke free.

"Has anyone seen Debrowski's 'Mech?" Grayson asked on the open band. "Did he get clear?"

"Captain!" Lori said. "Look south!"

Grayson spun his *Hawk*. The smoke from the burning AeroSpace Fighter was lying low and heavy between the Gray Death 'Mechs and the University, but Grayson could see a giant figure emerge from it, reaching forward and down. The Kurita *Crusader* had not followed Grayson after all, but had sought out another target.

Debrowski's *Stinger* lay full-length on the ground some distance to the east of where Grayson had held the line with Clay and McCall. Perhaps the *Stinger* had gotten lost in the smoke and strayed in the wrong direction. Perhaps Debrowski had been navigating through the smoke by a compass whose reading had been jarred by weapons fire. Whatever the cause, his *Stinger* had taken hits that left his 'Mech's left leg in tatters and smashed the laser mounted on its right arm. Now Debrowski was trying to drag his helpless machine clear of the looming *Crusader*. Even from a range of six hundred meters, Grayson could see that the *Stinger*'s radio antennae had been sheared away from its head. That explained Debrowski's silence.

The *Crusader* outweighed the *Stinger* three to one. One massive fist rose, paused, and descended. Lori gave a soft cry as the *Stinger*'s head splintered like a crystal egg.

Numb, barely able to speak, Grayson somehow managed to give the order. The surviving Grey Death 'Mechs withdrew from the field after their hovercraft, which had long since fled north.

The Kurita 'Mechs made no attempt to follow.

The two men faced one another, eye level with eye. Rebels and Legion members alike surrounded them. "We barely escaped with our lives," Grayson said. "Piter Debrowski didn't make it at all. And it's your fault!"

After a long and grueling trek over little-used jungle trails, the Strike Force had returned to Fox Island to find that the commando forces remaining behind had been victorious. Two full companies of BattleMechs, twenty-four machines, had raided the island, zeroing in on the small encampment that Grayson had ordered manned by a handful of volunteers. The lead Kurita 'Mechs had blundered into the booby traps reset by Ramage's Techs, and the ordered battle formation had dissolved in chaos.

Ramage's commandos had struck from the surrounding jungle, bringing down a *Phoenix Hawk* and a *Centurion* and badly damaging three more light and medium 'Mechs. The Kurita pilots, already nervous about operations this far into the jungle, had withdrawn. Overhead, the *Slayer* and *Shilone* had circled helplessly above the jungle canopy.

Montido's rebel Warrior recruits had ambushed the withdrawing enemy 'Mechs along the Rim Road as they were withdrawing from the island. They managed to claim a damaged *Stinger* and a pair of *Commando*s. Grayson's plan to destroy or cripple the fighters as they landed at their base below the University walls had succeeded as well, though at the cost of Debrowski and his *Stinger*. All in all, the day had gone heavily in favor of the rebel forces.

Crowding near their leaders, no one could understand what had set off the confrontation.

Tollen Brasednewic scowled back at Grayson, his dark eyes locked with the younger man's gray ones. "And it seems to me you're going too far telling us how to run our war! The council that hired you isn't around any more. Why don't you people go back where you came from, and leave us to settle our own affairs!"

Collin Dace stepped between the two men. "Tollen, no! We'd never have made it this far without Captain Carlyle, and you know it!"

"Do I?" He laughed, derisively. "Do I, indeed? We were doing all right on our own. Then he comes along, and what have we lost? The whole rebel council, wiped out. And the dead . . . how many dead have we lost? Damn it, when the Blues scattered at the airfield today, they left that gate wide open! With our two hundred boys, we could have walked right in and taken the citadel, only *he* says to pull out! Pull out, with victory right in front of us!"

Grayson crossed his arms. "Whether you like the idea or not, Colonel, we're in your war now. We've lost too many dead of our own to turn our backs on Verthandi, even if we could. But if we're going to fight together, we're going to have to pull together . . . with one leader."

"So it's come to that, eh? You think you're man enough

to take me . . . *merc?*'' Tollen spat out the final word as
though it were an obscenity.

"It doesn't make any sense for the two of us to fight,"
Grayson said carefully. He and Brasednewic were about
the same height, but the rebel leader easily outweighed
him by at least ten kilos. "I suggest we use common
sense instead."

"Enough talk!" Brasednewic had his fingers curled
into massive fists now, his scowl transformed to a snarl.
"I had a chance to rescue Carlotta, and you botched it
for me!"

Grayson's eyes widened. So he'd been right about Brasednewic and Carlotta. They were lovers.

Montido looked confused. "But she was Old Family . . ."

"Damn you, don't talk about her as if she's dead!"
Then, more quietly, "So, she's Old Family? You think
that mattered . . . to us?"

Grayson watched something akin to embarrassment
flick across the faces of some rebels. As for himself, he
felt painfully out of place, as though witness to a very
private family argument. The rift between the descendants of the planet's first settlers and the refugees who'd
come later was old and deep. Feelings about men and
women who crossed that line seemed to run high on both
sides.

"Damm it!" Brasednewic shouted, "Carlotta and I
loved each other!" His head swiveled from side to side
as though he were daring anyone to make an issue of the
statement. "And we still love each another! Nagumo's
bastards won't have killed her yet, not if they think she
might be useful to them, for propaganda, or whatever. I
would have had her out of there today . . . only . . .
only . . ."

Tears choked him. Grayson put a hand on the rebel
chief's shoulder. "I think I know how you feel," he said.

"How the *hell* can you know that?" This time there
was no anger in the words, only pain and loss.

"You aren't the only one who's lost someone he
loves." Grayson spoke softly, remembering his father.
"But you can't use your people for your own personal
vendetta. Not and keep their respect!"

Brasednewic just stood there, his eyes on the ground,
fists clenched at his sides. Then, without another word,

he turned his back on Grayson and strode from the group.
Grayson started to call after him, but Montido held up
his hand. "Let him go, Captain. One of us'll talk to him
later. It'll be better that way."

Dace nodded. "Meanwhile, what are your orders,
Captain?"

Later, in the dark and near-chill of Verthandi's predawn, Lori found a favorite rock among the trees beyond
the plantation clearing. The Li Plantation lay at the top
of the Basin Rim, amid a straggling of jungle growth that
had climbed the slopes from the Silvan Basin and spread
across the Bluesward. BattleMechs, their black shapes
strange under the ragged cloaks of camouflage they wore
among the jungle trees, loomed against a starry sky.
Verthandi-Alpha had long since set.

The dream had come again, and she had decided to
walk off some of the horror's edge. Listening to chirimsims keening and shrieking in the jungle basin below,
she hugged herself and closed her eyes, willing the
dream's terror to fade.

She loved Grayson. She was certain of that now, but
somehow, somewhere deep within, she still could not
trust him. That conflict in her feelings for the young
BattleMech commander were tearing her apart. She had
learned to override her own fears—even her terror of
fire—during battle, but she had not yet managed to come
to grips with the storm of her own emotions. She had
been a MechWarrior long enough to know that such a
tearing of mind and will would sooner or later be fatal.
The time would come when she would make a mistake,
and . . .

The dream had put her in a black mood. Would death
be so unwelcome, after all? Beyond the men and women
of the Legion, she had no family. Certainly she had had
no romantic relationships since her closeness with Grayson on Trellwan. Somehow, every man in the Legion
knew she was the Captain's woman. She laughed aloud
at that. The Captain's woman!

In the weeks since Sue Ellen's rescue, the two women
had become friends. Recognizing each other's loneliness, they took comfort in one another. Lori knew that

Sue Ellen's loneliness was so much worse. Her man was dead.

She opened her eyes, trying to shake off these thoughts of despair and death. In the darkness and pale starlight, it was difficult to make out who they were, but she could see a man and a woman approach the clearing from another path in the distance. It was some moments before she recognized one of the Verthandian women rescued weeks before. What was her name? Janice, was it? Walking beside her, the man had his arm around her waist.

So, if Janice Taylor had found companionship among the men of the Gray Death Legion, why couldn't she? The man had both arms around the woman now. As Lori watched them embrace, then kiss, her own loneliness became suddenly overwhelming. She wondered what Grayson was doing right now. If he were awake, would he want her to come to him?

The couple drew apart after a final kiss. Janice turned then, and started across the clearing toward what was now the women's barracks on the Li Plantation. When the man turned, Lori finally saw his face clearly, too.

It was Grayson.

He saw her at the same moment. He seemed to hesitate, then started toward her. She rose from her seat on the rock and turned to pass him.

"Lori . . ."

"Good evening, Captain." At that moment, she felt more mixed up than ever. Was this betrayal that she was feeling? Was it jealousy? Or was it simple anger at her own confusion and distress?

"Lori, what is it . . . ?"

"Nothing, Captain. Nothing at all. Good night."

It was all she could manage to walk back toward the womens' barracks without breaking into a run.

The Captain's woman, indeed!

Not many more weeks passed before it became clear that the Second Battle of Fox Island had been an important turning point in the war. Duke Hassid Ricol had departed for his starship the *Huntress*, leaving Governor General Nagumo still in command. After all, Ricol admitted, the idea of attacking Fox Island had been his own, and Nagumo had deployed the two Light Recon lances with skill and dispatch during the desperate fighting outside the University walls. The rebels had been within meters of winning through the gates and into the University courtyard when the two lances and the sentry *Crusader* had arrived and forced their withdrawal. The destruction of one of the rebel 'Mechs was a decided plus, for the rebels would be hard-pressed to replace their BattleMech losses.

Ricol was more than willing to call the battle a victory and leave Nagumo in charge. His alternatives were either to place the incompetent Admiral Kobo in command or to remain on Verthandi himself to take charge personally, neither of which the Red Duke was prepared to do. He was scheduled for an audience with Lord Kurita himself on Luthien in another two weeks. Besides, if he took command, he would have to produce a victory. At this point, Ricol wondered privately if victory were ever going to be possible on Verthandi.

He had seen the faces of the people of Regis as they watched the passage of his entourage. The Loyalists were grim and reserved, already fearful that their Kurita allies would depart, leaving them at the mercy of the rebels. Sheer, open hatred was on the faces of the rest.

For the Combine, victory might well consist of escaping Verthandi with a whole skin.

In the wake of the fiasco at Fox Island, patrols now departed less and less frequently from Regis or the other Kurita strongholds to sweep the countryside or probe the hills for rebel supply caches. The battle at the airfield had destroyed two AeroSpace Fighters completely and the third would be crippled and useless for at least three months. The remaining fighters on Verthandi-Alpha had been loaded aboard Ricol's DropShip, along with DEST 4. If it turned out that Nagumo would be unable to pacify Verthandi, at least those valuable units would not be lost. Of course, that meant Nagumo was left without their services in tracking rebels or providing air cover.

The Kurita 'Mechs and the Regis Blues never entered the jungle anymore. To do so invited attack and annihilation.

Within a few weeks, the Kurita presence on Verthandi had dwindled to Regis itself, a handful of mines in the southern desert, and a scattering of fire bases and supply depots guarding the principal government routes of supply and communication. What was left of the 44th Line and the Light Recon regiments remained within Regis itself, while the others were deployed in garrisons at the mines and elsewhere. At any given time, a quarter of the Kurita 'Mechs were down and under maintenance, their pilots on leave at the base on Verthandi-Alpha. For the first time in nearly a decade, most of the countryside and smaller towns were not under the shadow of the Kurita 'Mechs.

Nagumo dared not risk a major confrontation with the rebels, not with their numbers growing explosively every day, with rebel attack growing fiercer and more daring with each incident. In one day alone, eight Verthandian astechs, five Regis Blues, and three Kurita soldiers had vanished in downtown Regis in broad daylight. Their heads appeared later, artfully arranged on the steps of the University, and no one would admit having seen who'd left them.

Nagumo may have won a victory at the walls of the University, but he was beginning to feel like a man with a noose around his neck. There were no more riots in the streets, but the air was charged as if by an approaching storm.

In the countryside, Grayson and the Gray Death continued to work informally with rebel bands, taking the best recruits and training them in anti-Mech commando tactics, then taking the best of those and training them to operate the growing army of captured Verthandian 'Mechs. By this time, most of the old AgroMechs had either been destroyed in battle or been cannibalized for parts, but more than enough Kurita 'Mechs had been captured to replace them. The ranks of the Free Verthandi Rangers' conventional infantry had swelled so much and so fast that Grayson's most urgent problem was providing food, shelter, and weapons for the mob of new recruits. Raids were mounted week by week, then day by day, to secure the food, ammunition, shelter kits, medical supplies, weapons, and clothing for an army that numbered now in the tens of thousands.

Very quickly, Grayson found that he could not begin to cope with the logistical nightmare by himself. He reorganized the army under local commanders, men and women who had already learned what the Gray Death had to teach and who had proven themselves in combat against the enemy. These commanders took their own units, organized as short battalions, to hiding places throughout the Silvan Forest, while friendly plantation owners and farmers diverted most of the food tagged for delivery to Regis to the rebel camps. When questioned by the Regis Blues, the standing answer was "The rebels took it! I had no choice!"

In the end, Nagumo had over a hundred BattleMechs and elements of eight separate infantry regiments tied to a score of towns, villages, cities, mines, and transport sites, while the rebels held near-absolute control over every other habitable part of the planet. The Governor General could not allow this state of affairs to continue much longer. Not if he wished to keep his head when the Red Duke returned.

As the rebel raids continued, it became painfully clear to him that the rebels were drawing their supplies from one source only: the supply dumps established by Nagumo's own troops. Such depots were necessary if Nagumo's forces were to operate with any kind of freedom outside the walls of Regis, but they invited attack and were difficult to defend. After all, there were so many sites to protect, and only so many operational 'Mechs at any given time . . .

With that realization, Nagumo's eyes had widened, and his fist had come down on the palm of his other hand with a smack. The mercenaries were the key to the rebels' success. They always had been. Perhaps it was not too late to destroy the rebels by striking down those mercs. And if he could capture Grayson Carlyle himself . . .

Nagumo was sure he had the answer now, and those supply dumps were going to be the key.

33

Seven BattleMechs worked their way through the light woods. No longer did any practical distinction exist between mercenary or Free Verthandian unit. When Grayson gave the commands, the other six 'Mechs spread out in a line behind the low ridge above the Kurita supply depot.

As he called off the names, each responded in turn. McCall in his battered *Rifleman* and Clay in his *Wolverine* were the only other representatives of the Gray Death present in the column. The others were lighter Battle-Mechs of the Free Verthandi Rangers: Vikki Traxen's *Locust*, Collin Dace's *Phoenix Hawk*, Olin Sonovarro's *Wasp*, and Nadine Cheka's *Stinger*. An eighth member of the raiding party, Lori Kalmar, had been posted in her *Locust* on a hill three kilometers back. Once the supply dump was secured, she would lead in the main body of the rebel hover transports to fill up on needed provisions and ammo.

"Move to your assault positions," Grayson said over the combat frequency. "And stand by. Transmit when you're in position."

Grayson fingered the controls on his cockpit vision devices, enlarging the image displayed on his main screen. The dump was peaceful enough, a typical collection of drab, military-style quonset huts and stack upon stack of crates, tanks, and boxes. There was a light fence around the perimeter of the base, and Grayson could see sentries—conventional infantry—pacing just outside. In the distance was the village of Blackjack, partly hidden by the trees. A farmer from Blackjack had arrived at the main rebel camp in the Silvan forest only a week before with word that this Kurita supply dump was being constructed.

He smiled to himself. More and more of the native Verthandians had been making contact with rebel forces across the planet's northern hemisphere, asking to join the Free Verthandian Legion, offering weapons, help, or shelter, offering information about Kurita movements, garrisons, and plans. Janice had been instrumental in that.

His smile grew wider. He liked Janice. It was fun to be with her and fun to talk to her. Their late-night walks had become less frequent in recent weeks, though, because she had joined the Free Verthandian Legion and begun training under Ramage's battery of instructors.

Grayson wished that Lori understood. He'd seen little of her since that evening at the Li Plantation. The memory was still painful. Why, though, did he feel guilty when she had made it so abundantly clear that a relationship with him was no longer of interest? Besides, the most important aspect of his relationship with Janice had nothing to do with evening walks or tender kisses among Verthandi's jungles. Janice was proving to be a treasure trove of information about Verthandi beliefs, attitudes, hopes, and passions. This was especially crucial now that Verthandians in the villages and towns and even those living in the shadow of the towers of Regis University had left the middle ground and become solid supporters of the rebellion. More and more Blues were deserting, and Nagumo's officers found fewer and fewer Loyalist families to give them information on rebel activities or positions.

Urgent voices suddenly interrupted Grayson's thoughts.

"David, in position."

"Sonovarro, ready."

"McCall, aye."

The others checked in quickly, one after another.

"Right," Grayson said. "Ladies and gentlemen, our supply officer is waiting."

The rebels had come to refer to Nagumo almost affectionately as their supply officer, but for several weeks now, supply dumps and depots had dried up. It was almost as though Nagumo had finally realized that his equipment and stores were subsidizing the rebel army. This new depot was going to be a big help to the rebels.

He gave the area one last long, hard look. There was no sign of enemy forces, of 'Mechs or gun emplacements or troops. When he'd first heard about this single supply base, far out in the central expanse of the Southern Highlands, hundreds of kilometers from Regis or the Silvan Basin, it had made him suspicious of a trap. He was still uneasy.

Why had Nagumo put the dump here? There were no mines close enough to draw on the supplies, no airfields or spaceports, no BattleMech maintenance centers or any other thing of enough value to warrant a BattleMech guard. Grayson had nearly decided to leave it alone. What with three more rebel MechWarriors ready to be assigned machines, and those machines needed long- and short-ranged missiles, autocannon rounds, 15 mm machine-gun ammo, tanks of coolant fluid, he had little choice. This base would have those supplies. He could see the coolant fluid tanks from where his *Shadow Hawk* crouched under the shadow of the trees along the ridge, and the ammunition he needed was stocked at every base catering to BattleMechs.

No, this base was too important to pass up. The farmer had reported only two BattleMechs in the area, a pair of battle-gouged *Centurion*s, and those were often out on patrol. There was no sign of them now. In fact, it looked too peaceful, too easy.

"Wha' d'ye see, Captain?" McCall asked over the private circuit.

"Not a bloody thing."

"And tha's worryin' ye." McCall knew Grayson well enough now to read his moods.

"It is. What's a base like that doing way out here, anyway?"

Clay had been listening in. "We may learn that when we take it, Captain. They may be planning something in these parts, where they think we don't patrol."

"Possibly." It was so quiet. He changed frequencies. "Lori?"

"Here, Captain."

"Your people all set?"

"We're set, Captain. Just give the word."

"I want to make this a fast one, in and get-the-hell out fast. To coin a cliche, it's too quiet, and I don't like it one bit."

"We'll be there the moment you say, Captain." There was a pause. "And Gray . . ."

"Yes?"

"Be careful." What did he hear in her voice? Regret, perhaps? He wished he could talk to her, but there was no time. They had to move *now*. Time enough for talk later, when they were safely back in camp.

"Always am, Lori. You know me. Keep your circuit open. I'll be calling."

He gave the order, and the 'Mechs moved forward.

The sentries at the supply dump fence saw the rebel 'Mechs as soon as they appeared above the crest of the ridge. There were scattered shots, and a machine gun began hammering from the cover of a low pile of sandbags and dirt off to the right. Grayson could see men scattering off into the woods and brush that surrounded the base.

"McCall!"

"Aye, Cap'n."

"Mount guard here and give us cover." The *Rifleman* had the heaviest firepower of the raiding party. "The rest of you, hit the fence."

Traxen's *Locust* reached the perimeter fence first, crumpling the wire mesh flat with one huge metal foot. As the other 'Mechs rushed through onto the poured ferrocrete slab, the hammering machine gun abruptly went silent.

The base was deserted, its workers and astechs fled into the brush. Much of the land in this part of the Southern Highlands was swampy, fed by the broad and sluggish Vorma River to the north. Grayson wondered how many of the Loyalists would die in those swamps. Except for that, it looked as though this raid would be remarkably bloodless.

"Lori!"

"Here, Captain."

"We're secure here . . . but I don't like it." Considering it was the only Kurita supply dump they'd found anywhere outside of Regis itself for weeks, the place was too lightly guarded. "Get your boys and girls in here, but don't plan on staying long."

He eyed the horizon. How long would it take a force of Kurita 'Mechs to arrive from the nearest government outpost? He knew there were no 'Mechs in the village of Blackjack itself. Rebel scouts had been watching it ever since they'd learned of the supply dump's existence. Indeed, there was no armor in the area except for a pair of *Centurions*, and even those weren't in evidence today. If there were 'Mechs at Tyssedal, 50 kilometers to the northeast, they would need at least forty minutes to reach Blackjack, even if they had a strike force ready to go on an instant's notice.

Where were those *Centurions*? On patrol, evidently . . . but partrolling what?

Clay's *Wolverine* and the rebel 'Mechs with hands began moving among the piles of supplies, stacking up what could be easily loaded and carried away aboard the hover transports. Whatever they could not carry, they would destroy.

Grayson's external pick-ups shrilled with the whistle of an incoming missile. It landed close beside Dace's *Phoenix Hawk*, smashing a wooden crate in a whirl of splinters. Grayson checked his *Hawk*'s instrumentation almost before realizing they were under attack. The sonic scanners traced the incoming LRM from the south, but his Magnetic Anomaly Detector showed distinct traces of movement to both the east and the north.

The *Phoenix Hawk* dropped the heavy canister of coolant fluid it was carrying and brought its heavy laser up to the ready. Traxen lowered her *Locust* into a deadly crouch, the barrel of her laser protruding from beneath her 'Mech's cockpit like the snout of a cornered animal.

"Heads up!" Grayson barked. "MAD traces north and east! Make that north, east, and south! We've got company, and lots of it!"

The first Kurita *Archer* broke through the underbrush three hundred meters from the eastern edge of the base perimeter. A second followed close behind. Grayson's MAD readouts were giving fragmented warnings now, so rapidly were they picking up approaching masses of fusion-driven armor.

An *Archer* weighed 70 tons, ten tons more than the

heaviest of Grayson's 'Mechs. It mounted 20 long-range missile tubes in each of two enormous launcher packs set over its shoulders, and carried a medium laser in each arm as well. Two more lasers were set into its torso, directed toward the heavy 'Mech's rear to protect it from attacks from behind. The *Archer* was an old BattleMech design, but it was a highly respected one, valued for its ability to lay down sustained, long-range bombardments.

Grayson counted four *Archer*'s in sight so far, two to the east, one in the north, one in the southeast. Those monsters could pound his tiny raiding party into fragments before any rebel 'Mechs could get close enough to be certain of scoring a hit.

Grayson thought fast. It was obvious now that the supply dump had been bait for a trap. The arming of the trap was less obvious. His guess was that the Kurita 'Mechs had been carefully hidden in the woods and swamps around the Blackjack site *before* the establishment of the supply dump, so that they would go unnoticed by rebel scouts. He punched up a computer map projection on his main console screen. Data was spotty for this area, but he could see large patches of swamp in every direction. Those *Archer*'s may even have been submerged in the swamps, with nothing showing but their flat heads and missile bins. Rotating crews outs of the supply base or from Blackjack could have kept them constantly manned and ready, certain that the rebels would attack this base sooner or later. It was a neat trap, and it showed every sign of working perfectly.

Grayson's mind raced. His force of light and medium 'Mechs would not last long in a sluggish match with *Archer*s. He directed his 'Mech's computer to overlay the map with MAD readings and the four *Archer*s that were already in sight. The display showed a ragged ring of amber lights three-quarters of the way around the cluster of lights marking his own command. There was an empty space to the west, but the ridge they'd been hiding behind was in that direction and could well be shielding the approach of enemy 'Mechs.

He and his men were being herded toward the west.

Missiles were flashing and banging throughout the supply dump now, but so far with little effect. The only option other than staying put was to fight off the closing of the ring. If he ordered his raiders to scatter toward the west, they might escape the *Archers*' inexorable advance.

If this was a trap, the trappers would have foreseen that move. Grayson's mind flashed across the various intelligence reports he'd read, the statements taken from enemy prisoners and Verthandians who had deserted the Regis Blues to join the rebels. There weren't that many *Archers* on Verthandi. He knew of one company— Company A of the 3rd Strike Regiment—that had four of them. Four *Archers* were what he could see right now.

Company A, First Battalion of the 3rd regiment was a typical mix of light and heavy 'Mechs. Grayson put himself in the enemy commander's boots. If he were laying a tray like this, he would hold his heavy machines somewhere where they wouldn't be seen right away, then make noise everywhere else to drive the prey into the waiting heavies' grasp.

The ridge. Those *Archers* were herding his raiders toward the ridge. The enemy heavies must have moved up behind it while the rebels were advancing into the supply dump. They'd be waiting there now for the rebel machines to come up the exposed eastern face of the ridge.

"All units!" he shouted. "Move south! Stay tight, and watch your flanks!"

Dace protested. "I'm getting heavy MAD readings that way, Captain! It's clear to the west!"

"Yeah . . . that's what they want us to think! Now . . . *move!*" He switched frequencies. "Lori! Are you there?"

'We're here. What's the matter?"

"It's a trap . . . an ambush. We're breaking out. Tell the hovercraft to scatter . . . and you take off with them. We'll rendezvous at Point Delta!"

"Can I . . ."

"You can't! We're facing heavies! Run for it, now!" The thought of Lori's 20-ton *Locust* facing *Archers* or the other heavies of the 3rd was chilling.

Grayson, Clay, and McCall formed their three 'Mechs into a wedge with Grayson's *Shadow Hawk* at the point, the *Rifleman* behind and to his left, and the *Wolverine* on his right. The rebel 'Mechs clustered behind the three Gray Death machines, moving south in a shambling run punctuated by the bursts and mushrooming pillars of smoke marking the fall of incoming missiles. Dace's

Phoenix Hawk took an LRM hit in one arm, and Sono-varro's *Wasp* was limping. The wedge slowed to allow Sonovarro to keep up.

Something moved in the woods dead ahead. Grayson triggered a burst of autocannon fire, shredding trees and tearing up great clumps of ground vegetation. It was a *Crusader,* the same one they'd faced that day below the walls of the University. Grayson recognized the patches of new armor where his autocannon fire had hit the enemy machine in the earlier battle.

The Kurita 'Mech blocked the way to the south.

"Keep moving!" Grayson shouted. The *Crusader* could only stop one of them if they all kept moving. A quick glance at his scanner readouts showed that the *Archer*s to the north and east had closed in and were at the supply dump now. There were MAD readings from the ridge to the west, too—big ones. Grayson's computer identified a *Marauder* and a *Warhammer* at the crest of the ridge.

He fired his laser, smashing and clawing at the *Crusader*'s upper torso. McCall's *Rifleman* added a hail of laser and autocannon fire to the volley. The Kurita 'Mech staggered back a step under the assault, but recovered quickly. Short-range missiles cleaved the air, smashing into Grayson's 'Mech with savage accuracy. Next, the enemy 'Mech's arms came up, and laser bolts hammered into Clay's *Wolverine*. The rebel 'Mechs behind them wavered, their pilots uncertain. Warning lights rippled across Grayson's instrument boards.

The *Archer*s were closing rapidly from behind, and it would be only moments before the failed ambush at the ridge would re-form and sweep down on the struggling rebel band. At the moment, though, the three Gray Death 'Mechs outweighed the *Crusader* with a combined 170 tons against its 65. If they hesitated, they were all doomed. If they forged ahead . . .

"All units!" Grayson yelled. *"Charge!"*

Autocannon fire chopped and shredded at the *Crusader*'s torso. Laser pulses flashed across the narrowing range and seemed to sink into thirsty metal. Grayson triggered a salvo of five LRMs and saw four of the five shriek into the heavy 'Mech's midsection.

All seven rebel 'Mechs were running at full speed now.

McCall yelled something unintelligible, a Scots curse or battle yell, Grayson guessed. His own head sang with battle thrill, an exultation that overrode his fear in a blinding surge. He triggered his *Hawk*'s jump jets and vaulted the final 50 meters to the *Crusader*, landing with a momentum that hurtled him squarely into the *Crusader* at full speed.

The roar of colliding tons of metal momentarily drowned out the crash of explosions. The *Crusader*, already off balance in the withering fire from its opponents, went over backward in an ungainly sprawl. Unable and unwilling to check his *Shadow Hawk*'s charge, Grayson went down on top of it in a tangle of metal limbs and weapons.

Grayson's *Hawk* was on its feet first, but he was too close to use his own weapons effectively. Instead, he kicked savagely with his 'Mech's right leg as the *Crusader* struggled to rise. The heavier 'Mech fell back once more. Grayson had an instant's warning as he saw the SRM pack covers set into the *Crusader*'s legs pop open. He twisted aside as twelve SRMs streaked into the sky, narrowly missing him. Missile reloads dropped home into the empty tubes, but Grayson was already bringing his hand down on his *Hawk*'s jump jet controls. Backpack rockets fired, a throaty roar arrested almost before it had begun as Grayson chopped off the power as quickly as he'd cut it on. The *Shadow Hawk* rose three meters, seemed to stagger in mid-flight, then dropped from the sky, a 55-ton sledgehammer that caught the prostrate *Crusader* squarely in its already gouged and cratered chest.

Coolant fluid exploded in mist and steam. Miniature lightnings arced and stabbed from shorted circuitry cables and power leads. Armor tore, peeling back like shredded metal foil as he extracted the *Hawk*'s legs from the ruin of the larger 'Mech's torso.

The other rebel 'Mechs arrived at that moment, still running. Grayson brought his 'Mech's leg back a second time. "For Piter," he said, and the leg snapped forward. From the looks of the *Crusader*'s ruined head, he had no doubt that the pilot was already dead.

The rebel 'Mechs were outside the closing ring of ambushers now, racing south. Grayson's move had caught the enemy by surprise, and they seemed to be in confusion. The jaws of the trap had snapped shut—on thin air.

Grayson rapidly gave his orders. There was only desert to the south, untold thousands of hectares of Verthandi's most inhospitable terrain. They would have to work their way to the west and then north to make it to the rendezvous. The enemy did not seem to be pursuing them. Perhaps they could cut through the woods behind the ridge above Blackjack. The Kurita forces would not expect them to cut so close to the site of the failed trap. If there were other enemy units in those woods and swamps, they would be looking farther afield.

Clay called Grayson's attention to a rising column of smoke well to the west of the supply dump's location. "Trouble, Captain. That could be our hovercraft convoy."

Cold fear took Grayson's heart, replacing the exultation that had gripped him during the hand-to-hand fight with the *Crusader. Lori!* He urged his *Hawk* into a lurching run, ignoring the heat overload lights already beginning to wink and flicker on his board.

Lori must have been trying to shield the hovercraft in her charge when the Kurita 'Mechs had burst down on her out of the woods to the east. Grayson saw the flaming wrecks of a trio of hover transports scattered across the clearing, but no sign of the others. Perhaps they'd made good their escape.

Lori's *Locust* was on a low knoll, crouched hull down, its laser spraying the woods eighty meters away. The *Locust* was hideously damaged, the left leg smashed and twisted, the radio antennae reduced to tangled wiring and blackened scars in the cockpit armor. Four Kurita 'Mechs advanced from the east, a *Griffin,* a *Stinger,* a *Phoenix Hawk,* and a *Wasp.* Those four were the recon lance for the 3rd Strike Regiment's A Company. While swinging west from the failed ambush to try to block the raiding force's retreat to the north, they must have stumbled into Lori and the hovercraft convoy.

Grayson hit his autocannon controls once, then savagely hit them again. A red indicator glared back at him from his console with baleful urgency. The autocannon was jammed in its mount, possibly destroyed. Whether the damage was the result of enemy fire or his collision with the *Crusader*, he couldn't tell. The loading mechanism stubbornly refused to feed. He checked his LRM packs, then triggered the controls, which slammed in his reload for the long-range tubes.

"Quick time!" He struggled to keep the desperation out of his voice. "McCall, Clay! Rush them!"

Lori's *Locust* was still six hundred meters away and the Kurita 'Mechs slightly further. Grayson felt as though he were trapped in the horror of a slow-motion dream. Step after lumbering step brought his *Shadow Hawk* no closer to the tableau of Lori's BattleMech, crippled and alone as she exchanged fire with the four Kurita 'Mechs.

The 55-ton *Griffin* was in a half-crouch, its right arm heavy PPC leveled at the light scout 'Mech. Blue lightning blasted through the space between them, and Grayson saw fragmented control packs and the power leads to the *Locust's* medium laser scatter in flaming wreckage across the knoll.

Five hundred meters.

He triggered a salvo of LRMs and watched the missiles arc into the enemy *Griffin*. The *Griffin* took no notice of this new attack, but continued firing bolt after searing bolt into Lori's 'Mech. The *Locust* was burning now, black, oily smoke coiling into a sky already darkened by the funeral pyres of the wrecked hover transports.

"Eject, Lori! Eject!" With her reception antennae shattered, he knew she wouldn't hear him, but Grayson found himself willing her to blast the escape hatch clear and to eject from the burning hulk. Perhaps it was already too late. Perhaps the ejection mechanism had fouled. Perhaps the *Locust's* power was dead. Perhaps Lori was already dead . . .

Four hundred meters.

There was a flash, and metal panels hurtled away from the burning 'Mech. Before the fragments hit the ground, another flash sent Lori's control chair rocketing into the sky on flaming thrusters.

Missiles arrowed through the trees, exploding in front of the charging rebel 'Mechs. Grayson's 'Mech stumbled as craters opened in the ground ahead. He checked the *Shadow Hawk's* charge and turned to face a Kurita *Marauder* smashing through the trees two hundred meters to his right. An enemy *Warhammer* and a pair of *Archer*'s now stepped into the clearing between him and the battle around Lori's 'Mech.

His last salvo of LRMs snapped into their tubes in the *Hawk*'s right torso. Ignoring heat overload warnings and the rattling impact of shrapnel against his 'Mech, he brought the HUD crosshairs of his sights onto the enemy *Marauder* and triggered the missile controls. He had no doubt at all that he had the enemy Regimental commander in his sights. Missiles slammed into the *Marauder*. One struck the egg-shaped hull squarely where the cockpit screen mated to armor. The enemy 'Mech froze in position. A hit! A hard one!

With rage, grief, and frustration boiling in him, Grayson started forward. A metal-armored hand on his *Hawk*'s arm stopped him. "This way, Captain," Clay said, without emotion. "We've got to retreat! There's nothing we can do for her now."

Through a haze of tears and anguish, Grayson could see brown and orange-clad foot soldiers closing on the spot where Lori's ejection seat had landed, not far from the shattered, blazing wreckage of her *Locust*.

The *Rifleman* staggered under the impact of a pair of LRMs from one of the *Archer*s. More enemy 'Mechs were arriving, rushing past the immobile form of the *Marauder*. He'd crippled the leader, but the fact brought no relief or thrill of victory. *Lori!*

"Pull back." Grayson scarcely recognized his own voice. "Scatter to the west, and rendezvous."

But Clay and McCall stayed with him as they broke free of the ambush and made their way west and north. Behind them, the smoke from Lori's shattered machine continued to stain the sky.

34

A Regis Blues deserter told Grayson that the Dracos had taken Lori alive, but under close guard, to the University's Central Tower the next day. The Kurita high command was jubilant, having immediately realized that they'd managed to take one of the offworlder mercs who had transformed the rebel army into a combat-experienced, efficient fighting machine.

The deserter could say nothing more about her, save that Nagumo's Special Branch was to question her closely. The man had drawn guard duty once in the bowels of the University Tower where the Special Branch worked. His descriptions of the sights, sounds, and dark rumors about Room 6 left Grayson feeling ill and shaken.

Lori . . .

Grayson met Tollen Brasednewic by the mouth of the Fox Island cave late that evening. He had been dreading this talk, but knew it must be done. Brasednewic had surprised Grayson by remaining with the rebel army after the incident on the day of the airfield raid. Many rebel troopers felt that their first loyalty was to Brasednewic himself, and so Grayson was grateful that the man had chosen to remain in the fight. Tollen spoke little, and his eyes bore a haunted look, but he'd fought with valor and determination in half a dozen raids and battles since his abdication from the rebel army's command.

He'd not been along on the Blackjack raid, but he'd learned of Lori's capture when Grayson's party had returned to camp. To his credit, he'd been among the first to tell Grayson how sorry he was.

That didn't make Grayson's problem any easier.

"We're running a raid against the University, Tollen,"

Grayson said, without preamble. "A sneak commando strike might get our people out."

Brasednewic's eyebrows crawled up his forehead. "This is a rather sudden turn-about, isn't it, Captain? Last I heard, we were to stay clear of that place. *All* of us."

Grayson nodded. "You also heard me say that you'd risked the whole strike force by changing plans at the last minute, in the middle of the action."

"It's different when *you* tell us to change plans, is that it? One thing for the high and mighty MechWarrior, something else entirely for the peasants in the ranks! Is *that* it?"

"Dammit, no!" Grayson closed his eyes. How was he going to carry this off? He'd known Brasednewic's ego was bruised, that he would have trouble convincing the man to help, but had not been able to come up with an approach that might soften his resistance. "This operation will be planned from the start, not made up as we go along! But we have to get Lori out of there. If Carlotta's alive, we'll get her, too, and any of the rest of our people we can find."

"Look, I can sympathize with you having lost your woman, Carlyle, but if you're asking me to bring my people in on this, forget it."

"She's not 'my woman', as you put it. But she *is* one of us."

"So was Carlotta."

"We don't even know that she's alive, Colonel!"

"We don't know a damned thing more about Lori Kalmar . . . except that she's in there and due for questioning!"

"Exactly! And you know as well as I do that when they start questioning her, they'll find a way to break her. Anyone can be broken . . . and that's a specialty of Kurita. They'll break her . . . and find out about the *Phobos* and where it's hidden."

"So?"

How could the man be so blind? "So . . . the ship will be destroyed, and with her all of the machine shops and casting equipment and electronics repair facilities that've kept us going these past few months! Maybe you foot soldiers don't realize what's needed to maintain a

BattleMech unit, but when Nagumo took the heavy equipment from Fox Island, he left us the *Phobos* and the people and equipment aboard her! If they locate and destroy our DropShip, the Gray Death and the Free Verthandi Rangers are finished, too!''

Brasednewic looked at Grayson with dull eyes, his face stiff and unexpressive. "I . . . can't, Carlyle. It's . . . a point of honor.''

"Honor? What does honor have to do with it? The honorable thing would be to drop that wounded pride of yours and help us!''

"Your own views seem to have changed somewhat since our last meeting.''

"What do you mean?''

"You weren't willing to sacrifice the whole group for one person. Now you are.''

"Don't you see? Whatever my own personal feelings in the matter, we've got to break in there and get Lori out . . . get her out, or . . . or . . .''

"Or what?''

Grayson had not let himself face the question until now, and the reality made him feel wrenchingly sick. "Or we'll have to kill her ourselves. We can't let Nagumo find out about the *Phobos.*''

Brasednewic's face worked against some cold silent, inner battle. "Why are you telling *me* all this?''

"Because we need to work together on this operation . . . the Free Rangers and the Gray Death. Every rebel soldier in the Silvan Basin must know by now that I took you down that day for going in against the University without orders, and every one of them must know why you did it. How can I give the order for them to do the exact same thing, unless you're willing to help? Ramage's commandos will follow my lead, I think. For this to work, we need to throw in everything we have, the whole Free Verthandian army. I *need* you, Tollen. I need your help . . . and your influence with your troops.''

There was a flicker of something behind Brasednewic's eyes, but Grayson saw that something die as he watched. The rebel turned away. "No, Captain . . . no.''

"Good god, man, why?''

"You have the gall to stand there and ask me to send

my people to certain death . . . after what you did to me
. . . *in front of my own people?''*

"Look, you'll have your command back. You didn't
have to walk away from it in the first place. We could
have worked something out.''

"It's too late for that, Carlyle. You embarrassed me in
front of my people. You think they'd follow me . . .
now?''

"I don't see why not,'' Grayson said evenly. *''My* people are following me.''

"Maybe it's different for mercenaries. Pay them
enough, and—''

"Dammit, what does that have to do with it? Look . . .''

"Carlyle, I don't think you understand. I've got a
handful of people—ones who were with me before you
came—who might still follow me. The rest . . . I don't
know. Maybe they would, but that bond of trust just isn't
there anymore. You broke that, Carlyle. You did. Well,
I can still fight Nagumo, but in my own way. In my own
time.''

"Tollen, everything we've built here in the past
months, the cooperation between the different rebel
bands, between your people and mine . . . we can't let
that be torn down.''

"It already has been.'' He shook his head. "Most Verthandians wouldn't follow me . . . anymore than they'd
follow you if you turned around the way you're asking
me to do for you. It'll be better this way. I won't stand
in your way, Captain, or interfere with your plans. But
I'm taking everyone who will follow me back to the Uppsala Mountains, above my old home. We'll raid and harry
the Dracos from there.''

"That's not the way, Tollen. We have to work together.
Your people *know* you. They'll follow you.''

"While I follow you? No Captain, I can't do that. I
can't ask my people to do that.''

"I don't understand.''

"No? Then maybe you're not the leader I thought you
were, Carlyle. Hell, you may be some kind of tactical
wizard, but you've got a lot to learn about people.'' He
turned and strode away, leaving Grayson standing there
alone.

And Grayson knew Brasednewic was right.

* * *

Nagumo nodded at Vlade's image in the intercom screen. "You think she might know something, then?"

"I'm certain of it, my Lord. We got extremely specific responses over the monitors when I questioned her about where the rebels had the heavy support equipment and repair facilities for their 'Mechs. She was lying, of course, but some of her answers suggest that the mercenaries have a secret base or facility hidden somewhere."

Nagumo's pulse quickened. "Did you ask her about their ship? Was it lost in a storm as everyone supposed?"

Vlade showed his teeth. "She said the DropShip was lost in the storm. I calculate an 80 percent probability that she is lying on that point as well and that the ship is intact, somewhere in the Silvan Basin."

"That would explain a very great deal. What else did you learn?"

"I found her weak point, my Lord. I have the lever with which to break her."

"Oh?"

"I don't know the details, of course. What I suspect is that at some time in her past, Kalmar suffered a terrible loss . . . and that loss is associated with fire."

"Ah . . ."

"Exactly, my Lord. She showed no more than the usual response to statements designed to evoke images of death or pain or imprisonment, of wealth, of any of the usual stimuli. But she appears to be terrified of death by fire. A very unusual . . . very *gratifying* response to that particular stimulus."

Nagumo closed his eyes and controlled his reaction. He would not let Vlade see his feelings.

The man's enthusiasm for his work had always repelled the Governor-General. Nagumo had not realized how much he actually loathed the man and his eager smile until now. He wondered if he had grown softer in the past months, for the interrogator to grate at his nerves so.

"Then I can count on you to . . . to use that response, to get me the information I need."

"Of course. Would you like to come down and participate? It should be interesting."

"No." *Dammit, man, I've got other things to do than*

make myself ill watching you play! "I leave it in your hands. And when you're through, be sure I get a complete report."

"Of course, my Lord," Vlade said, and Nagumo could tell how anxious he was to get back to his gruesome task.

Under the circumstances, it was the best plan they could come up with. A volunteer commando team of fifty Verthandians followed Grayson and Sergeant Ramage, picking their way through the dark. They wore black from head to toe. Their faces were smeared with black dye, and their weapons and every piece of equipment were carefully wrapped and taped to keep metal from clinking against stone or other metal. Ramage had told Grayson privately they were the best unit he'd ever worked with. For months, he'd been training them in special, small-unit operations.

Not all of the commandos were Verthandians. One of them, unrecognizable in her night vision goggles and black face paint was Sue Ellen Klein, fighter pilot turned commando.

Grayson had found her sitting on a rock, sharpening a knife with long, slow strokes across a whetstone. "What are you doing with this bunch?" he'd asked.

"I volunteered, Captain." Her voice was soft, but very steady.

He'd had little opportunity to talk with her since her rescue several months before. Her captivity among the Dracos seemed to have left her little more than a hollow shell for some time, and the new light in her eyes surprised Grayson.

"I wonder if it's a good idea for you to go in there," he said. "If you're looking for a chance to get even with someone . . ."

"I'll do my job, Captain." She snapped the knife into her boot sheath, and added in a quieter voice, "I'll do what I have to do."

The answer had not entirely satisfied Grayson. He had lived long enough with the fiery coals of vengeance inside his own gut to recognize it in another. Her hate focused on someone else besides him now, someone within the Kurita camp. He could read that in the deliberate way she stroked her knife against the stone.

She looked up at him and smiled strangely, her teeth gleaming through the mask of black stain. "You needn't worry about me, Captain. It took time, but . . . I'm all right now. Thanks to Lori."

She read the question in his eyes and smiled. "It seems we were both pretty lonely, Captain. We began talking. It's so easy to talk to her, you know. She . . . she helped me pull through a pretty rough time. Lori . . . Lori was *my* friend, too."

He had no answer for that. Besides, the time had come to move out.

Grayson peered ahead through his night vision goggles, then nodded to Ramage at his side. The factory entrance was just ahead.

The unit accepted the reason for going in without comment or surprise. They were volunteers, of course, but they followed because the man who had trained and fought with them said he needed them. If anyone resented that they were about to do what Tollen Brasednewic had been ordered not to do, no one showed it. Grayson knew, however, that it would be different for most of the regular line troops.

The operation, as he, Ramage, and the other Gray Death MechWarriors had worked it out, required the commando team to slip into the University grounds. They were fairly certain they could get as far as the Courtyard, because of the broad, high-ceilinged passageway that ran between factory and University Courtyard. This was the old avenue for students on work-teaching programs or for AgroMechs to travel to 'Mech demonstrations in the Courtyard. That passageway still existed, and Grayson knew where it was from Thorvald's maps. It would be guarded, certainly, but that was work for the commandos.

In the darkness behind them, in the dry gully that led by winding ways back to the Basin Rim, three of the four remaining BattleMechs of the Gray Death lay hidden, awaiting Grayson's signal. There had been some last-moment reshuffling. Khaled now piloted Grayson's *Shadow Hawk* instead of his *Stinger*. All had agreed that in the fight to come, they would need the *Hawk*'s firepower, and Khaled had readily agreed to switch to the larger machine. As for Grayson, he would have preferred to be at the controls of a BattleMech—*any* BattleMech—but Brasednewic's words still burned.

He would not ask of his own people something he would not do himself. The chancy part of this operation would be the initial penetration. Once the team was inside, the BattleMechs would lay down a diversion to distract the Kurita troops from the true nature of the assault within their walls. The diversion would be necessary if the commandos—and Grayson and Lori, if he could find her—were to make good their escape.

Grayson carefully refused to think about what would happen if he found Lori but was unable to get her out of the University. His mind went no farther than the certainty that either he and Lori would make it out of the University . . . or that neither of them would.

The Ericksson-Agro factory was deserted, a place of dust and shadows and bare ferrocrete floors and walls. The streets outside were deserted, too, save for a solitary Regis Blue sentry on a roving patrol. The commandos had watched the man go, then slipped across the street behind his back. Guided by their infrared goggles, they slipped through the factory to an unguarded stairwell, then made their way to a lower level to the yawning mouth of the tunnel they sought.

The gate was padlocked, but the lock yielded to a hand torch wielded by one of the Verthandian raiders. Every man took that moment to check his weapons and gear. Grayson carried a TK assault rifle cradled in his arms and a 12 mm automatic pistol holstered on his right hip. Three grenades, including a pair of smoke grenades, were clipped to his harness. In various pouches, he carried spare magazines for the TK and the pistol and a spare battery clip for the stunner. A combat knife was sheathed and fastened at his right ankle outside his boot. A single-channel combat communicator was clipped to his throat and his ear, though he could use it to talk to his comrades only across very short ranges. It would not penetrate the walls of the University at all. To reach the BattleMechs outside, he had a more powerful hand transceiver fixed to a pouch at the small of his back.

The door opened, rusty mountings creaking and booming protest into the dark. Anxious eyes probed this way and that through the dark, but no sentry appeared, no voice shouted challenge. In single file, the commandos plunged into the Stygian black of the underground passageway. The tunnel extended through blackness absolute for two hundred meters, then slanted upward along a flat-sloped ramp. There was another steel door at this end, and a brief inspection showed Grayson why the tunnel was not better guarded. The door was welded shut.

Ramage looked at Grayson, who nodded. Ramage gestured, and a pair of Verthandi Rangers dashed up, slipping heavy canvas pouches from their shoulders. One examined the welded door and grinned through the dark at Grayson. "Five minutes, Captain. Better have everyone move back up the tunnel a bit."

Waiting in the darkness, Grayson was startled by a light touch on his shoulder. He turned and found himself staring into a blackened face that was recognizable—just barely—as the face of a young woman. "Don't worry, Captain. We'll do it."

"Eh?"

"I'm sorry," she whispered, her voice carrying no further than the two of them. "But the expression on your face. Even through those goggles, you looked so . . . so *intense*. I just . . . just wanted to let you know that we're with you."

"Did I look that afraid?"

"Not afraid. More like you were going to go through that door without waiting for the guys to blow it."

Grayson peered at her face but couldn't recognize her. For a moment, seeing the glint of almost savage purpose in her eyes, he thought it might be Sue Ellen. This woman was taller, her hair longer when he saw it escaping from under her cap. "Uh . . . do we know each other?"

Her teeth showed through the blacking. "Janice Taylor, First Squad, Special Commando, Free Verthandi Rangers," she recited with matter-of-fact crispness. "Just one of your new recruits."

"Janice!" Then the darkness exploded in flame and thunder, and he had no time to think about anything more at all.

35

Governor-General Nagumo heard the dull, hollow boom and briefly wondered if someone had dropped a heavy section of armor in the maintenance area across the courtyard. Then the piercing ululation of the emergency siren keened warning the attack.

A light flashed at his intercom. He stabbed the accept switch. "What is it?"

"This is Gordoyev, my Lord, Captain of the Guard!" There was no picture with the voice, which was pitched high with shock or fear. "I'm on Level Two and . . . and . . . rebel troops, General, in the lower levels! They're pouring through a hole blasted through from an abandoned tunnel!"

"You have a guard. Use it!"

"Yes, my Lord! We'll hold them as long as we can, but . . ."

"But what?"

"My Lord, there are hundreds of them down here! We need reinforcements!"

"Help is coming. Hold where you are!"

He opened a channel to the barracks and found that the alert had already roused the city's garrison commanders. Between elements of four infantry regiments, there were close to two thousand Kurita troops in Regis, not counting the unreliable Regis Blues. He did not for a moment believe Gordoyev's assessment of "hundreds of troops," but it was always better to overreact to such a threat than to respond with half-measures. He relayed orders to the Third Strike Regiment. Companies A and B were both just outside the University, stationed in the streets of central Regis. They would be in the courtyard in moments.

What could be the purpose of this raid . . . for a raid was all it possibly could be. It was inconceivable that a large enemy force could worm its way into the University grounds through whatever forgotten gateway or tunnel they might have found. It must be a small force, probably a highly trained commando unit with some specific target.

Target? He pulled at his lip, the fingers trembling ever so slightly. The rebels could well be after him, the Governor General. His death would not mean the end of Kurita rule on Verthandi, of course, but it would mean that that idiot Kodo would take command. If the rebels knew about the Kurita chain of command on this world, they might believe having Admiral Kodo in charge would give them a better chance at some planned coup or assault.

He opened a desk drawer and pulled out a small, deadly Sunbeam-Electric laser pistol, checked its power pack, and tucked it into the waistband of his uniform. Then he opened another channel on the intercom and summoned his personal guard.

Grayson stepped across the sprawled, wide-eyed body of a blue-clad Loyalist trooper, checked the man's belt and pouches for keys or security devices, then moved with light-footed haste further into the warren of passageways ahead. He was under the main University Tower now, he knew. The descriptions provided him by Regis Blue deserters and liberated Verthandian prisoners were proving accurate so far.

Gunshots and explosions echoed behind him. According to plan, forty of the commandos were launching their attack on the enemy's BattleMech maintenance area, not far from where the forgotten tunnel opened into the courtyard.

Outside the University walls, the Gray Death 'Mechs would be moving toward the Ericksson-Argo factory, firing at anything that moved along the walls above them, and preparing to take up defensive positions to cover the retreat of the raiders when they reappeared from the tunnel.

Those two distractions ought to keep the Dracos and

their Verthandian allies quite busy, for a few minutes anyway. Grayson and the ten remaining commandos had penetrated the underground levels of the central University Tower. Those levels were a maze of interconnecting rooms and passageways that the Dracos had converted from storage of records and supplies. The eleven had separated and spread out to better their chances of finding Lori quickly. Grayson was alone.

He hurried on through the semi-darkness, following courses drawn and redrawn countless times on paper and in his head since he'd learned them from people who had already travelled these corridors. The cells for special prisoners were supposed to be down one level and to the right. The stairway down ought to be . . . there!

A man in a blue uniform appeared, a heavy automatic rifle slung across his shoulder. Grayson brought up his TK and fought the bucking, flashing muzzle as high-speed 3 mm slivers burned through the air to shred cloth and flesh in a fine mist of blood. The soldier was kicked up and back, then plunged headfirst down the stairs behind him with an unholy clatter of equipment and weapon. Grayson followed a moment later, somewhat more quietly.

The lower passageway was well-lit and mercifully deserted. He shoved his IR goggles back on his head and checked the soldier's body. A small, black rectangle—a plastic security card—rested inside a breast pocket. Grayson retrieved it, then straightened, glancing about. That way!

He found the cell doors, but there was no way of knowing who was in which cell. He picked the first door he came to, inserted the plastic card into a slot in an otherwise featureless box mounted on the stone wall beside the entrance, and stepped back as the door slid open. Inside the narrow, stone-walled cell was a woman, but his initial surge of elation faded when he realized it was not Lori.

She blinked against the sudden light. "Who . . . are you?"

"Cavalry to the rescue," Grayson said lightly. Where was Lori being held? "Quick! Come out of there!"

The woman stumbled out into the passageway. Grayson was already at the next cell, fumbling with the card.

That room held ten Verthandians, one-time students or teachers crowded into a three by four meter space stinking of sweat, excrement, and fear. The next cell held the same . . . and the next . . . and the next.

A pair of soldiers in Kurita uniforms interrupted Grayson as he opened the cell after that. Someone yelled warning, and Grayson twisted his TK up and chopped the pair down before they could unholster their weapons. Their uniforms yielded two more security cards and weapons for two of the newly freed prisoners.

With a small army unexpectedly on his hands, Grayson had to take time to organize them. He sent one party off with one of the guards' pistols to search for more weapons. The body by the stairway would yield at least one automatic rifle, and there were bound to be weapons lockers elsewhere in this warren. The rest of the ex-prisoners he divided into two groups, gave a security card to each group, and sent them in opposite directions with orders to open every cell they came to. The Verthandians scattered amid shouts and ragged cheers. Grayson thought to warn them to remain quiet, then decided there was no use. A fierce determination seemed to have seized every one of those dirty, ragged men and women, a determination to close with their Kurita captors and settle some longstanding scores.

Confusion was spreading throughout the lower levels. The other commandos were finding and releasing prisoners as well. Soon, these levels and those above would be filled with freed Verthandians looking for Kurita blood.

He skidded to a stop, his rifle up. The shadow he'd seen moving up ahead resolved itself into the black-clad form of another commando.

He recognized her. "Sue Ellen! What the hell are *you* doing here?" He was aware of the odd light in her eyes, aware that the sight of these corridors must be bringing back memories of horror. He'd not known that she was among the ten who had volunteered to come down into these chambers. He'd thought she was with Ramage, on the surface.

She laughed, an unpleasant sound. "Still worried about me, Captain?"

He shook his head, ashamed of the lie. "Have you found anything yet?"

"No. I don't think she's here."

"Where, then?" He knew the answer, but had been denying it to himself. At the same time, a growing dread was urging him to hurry, to race through the passageways to the place Sue Ellen had described after her rescue.

"Room 6, of course. Where they took me a time or two."

The interrogation chamber was in the lowest level of all. The team's assault plan called for each of the commandos to close on Room 6 as they systematically checked the cells in the levels above. During the planning sessions for this raid, they had decided that sending a team straight to the lowest level would not be practical. There were not enough troops available to do that and to also check the rooms above. Anyway, it seemed more likely that they would find Lori in one of the cells. Now, though, Grayson felt a cold and growing horror in the pit of his stomach telling him that Room 6 was exactly where Lori was at this moment.

"Will . . . will you lead the way?" He watched Sue Ellen carefully as he suggested it. On the one hand, he didn't want to rekindle the horror for her any more than it already was. On the other, he was suddenly afraid to have her out of his sight.

"No, Captain. There's something else I have to do." She took a step toward him, and for a moment Grayson thought she meant to attack him. Her rifle was slung from her shoulder, but she held her combat knife in one hand.

"We're going to take care of them, Sue Ellen. And you can help."

She laughed, and the sound turned Grayson cold. "Help? I've helped you, Captain. The place you want is down that corridor, then to your left, then to your right. Room 6. There will be sentries outside the door."

"Sue Ellen! What's . . . what's wrong with you? Come on . . ."

"No, Captain. I'm not going there." She hurried past him, moving in the other direction.

"Sue Ellen! What about Lori? You said . . . she was your friend . . ."

She paused next to the still form of a Kurita guard,

stooped quickly, and retrieved a sonic stun pistol. As she tucked it into her combat harness, she looked back across her shoulder. "She was my friend, Captain. And . . . I think you were, too. You accepted me, even after . . . after what I'd done. But I can't help you any more. Or *her*.

"Of course you can . . ."

"No, Captain. But . . . thanks anyway, for trying. There's something else I have to see about. Someone I have to see."

Almost, he called to her again, but the look in her eyes burned through to the marrow of his bones. He would have to try to track down Sue Ellen later.

The sentries were where Sue Ellen had said they would be, a pair of grim-faced Kurita troops flanking a door marked Room 6. They shifted the black and vicious-looking automatic weapons in their hands to aim at Grayson as he stepped around the corner and into the main passageway.

Grayson's TK spat fire first, hammering one of the sentries back against the wall. The second man returned the fire, the roar of his subgun murderously loud in the narrow space between the dank stone walls. Grayson was already on the floor and rolling to the opposite side of the passageway. The TK bucked and yammered again, then cut off with a silence as deafening as its roar, the chamber clicking empty.

But the sentry was dead, his body sliding to the floor, leaving a heavy trail of blood smeared down across the stone wall at his back.

The door to Room 6 swung open, and Grayson plunged through into a scene of horror.

Sergeant Ramage crouched low behind the crumbled pile of stone facing as submachine gun bullets ricocheted against unyielding stone, spraying him with tiny fragments of powdered rock. He touched his throat mike and yelled to be heard above the battle's roar. "Jared! Three o'clock from my position! You see him?"

"Got him!" a tinny voice confirmed in his hear. "Wait one . . ."

There was a thump from the darkness behind and above Ramage's position, followed by a crashing blast of noise from the doorway thirty meters to his right. The subgun's chatter was chopped short by the scattering shrapnel of the 20 mm grenade from Jared's launcher.

A chorus of shouts and yells sounded from straight ahead, through the archway under the main tower. Ramage brought his laser rifle up, then froze, his finger still off the trigger. It was another wave of freed Verthandian prisoners, ragged in the gray uniforms they'd been given by their captors, haggard but still defiant. There were about thirty in this group. Many brandished weapons wrested from now-dead guards and chance-encountered Kurita troops. Ramage stood, shouted, and waved his own weapon until the band saw him. It was risky, but he thought his black night-fighter's garb set him apart enough from the usual denizens of the citadel that he would not be shot out of hand.

Shot by accident, maybe, he thought, but out of hand, no . . .

The prisoners surged toward his position with a cheer. Ramage's eyes widened as he recognized one of the faces, owlish behind the thick glasses he still somehow wore.

"Citizen Erudin!"

The former rebel council member grinned. "Hello, Sergeant. It's good to see you again!"

"It's good to see you, sir. We . . . we thought all of you were dead."

"If you mean the Council members . . ." His mouth twisted. "They shot poor Ericksson. They were keeping the rest of us alive, though, in case they needed us for a public hanging." He glanced past Ramage to where a blue uniform showed beside a fallen mass of stone. He stepped over to the body, stooped, and pried a submachine gun from stiffening fingers. "Are you in charge of this show?"

"I am up here. Didn't the Captain let you out?"

"Some of my fellow guests in this hotel let me out, Sergeant. I couldn't quite make out how they had been freed. Captain Carlyle's behind all this, then?"

Ramage grinned. "Afraid so, sir. He makes a mess when he sets his mind to it, don't he?"

"A glorious mess, Sergeant. I'm glad to see I didn't make a mistake choosing him . . . and you . . . after all."

"Well, recriminations later, Citizen. How about you take charge of your people. Round 'em up. Get them under cover over there. Any that have guns, send 'em along to that entrance over there . . . see it? Through there, fifty meters, then down. There's a tunnel that leads out of the University and into the factory next door."

"Ericksson's AgroMech plant. I know."

"Some of our 'Mechs are waiting out there. They'll get your people to safety."

"Right." Erudin turned, and began shouting orders.

Altogether, Ramage estimated that there must be a hundred or so freed prisoners in the Courtyard already, with more arriving from the passageways leading under the main University Tower every moment. One large party had consisted of prisoners who had not burst into the courtyard, waving guns or shouting. They had shambled out, men and women led by the hand of their fellows, eyes staring but unseeing, their faces etched with shock, pain, or a blind emptiness. Some showed the scars or bruises or bloodied bandages of rough usage in those hell pits under the tower. All showed evidence of more serious scars somewhere behind their eyes. Ramage had taken time to give directions to the people guiding these walking wounded. He wasn't sure how the rebel army was going to take care of them without permanent facilities in the jungle, but he knew he had to get them away from these walls.

A dull, low, booming thunder sounded from the main courtyard gate, the one to the south, leading to the downtown center of Regis.

He touched his throat mike. "Kev? Can you see into the street?"

"Kev's bought it, Sergeant," a woman's voice answered. "This is Greta. There're BattleMechs out there, coming up the main street. A *Warhammer* just fired a round at the main gate."

"O.K. Keep your head down, but watch 'em for me! Vince?"

"Here, Sarge."

"Company. Round up any anti-'Mech teams you can find, and bring 'em up here, fast!"

"We're on our way."

Hurry up, Captain, Ramage thought as he stared across the barrel of his gun at the courtyard gates. *We can't stay here much longer!*

═══ 36 ═══

As Grayson burst through the doors to Room 6, he took in the scene as isolated and unrelated fragments, with the unreality of a dream. He saw Lori—alive! *Alive!* He shouted in triumph at the sight of her, and she shrieked his name in answer. She was stretched out, bound at wrists and ankles and strapped to a hellish-looking steel table that had been tilted up to bring her face to face with her captors.

There were three of these, a pair of brawny types in Kurita uniforms with pistols at their belts. In their midst was a smaller figure in a stained white smock. The one with the smock was just pulling a rod tipped with tightly wrapped rags from a shallow basin set on a tripod in the center of the room. The basin held some liquid that had been ignited, as well as a chilling array of sinister-looking, long-handled tools. The fire danced and flared halfway to the high, vaulted ceiling, casting weirdly distorted shadows on walls and floors, along the massive wooden beams that supported the ceiling, and across the stacks of crates and kegs that lined the room.

The rags fixed to the end of the rod took fire from the basin as the man with the smock looked up, eyes wide and glittered in the light of the basin's flames. The guards fumbled at their holsters for their guns.

Grayson's TK was empty. His rush at the door had carried him through almost before he'd realized the weapon had stopped firing. He continued his rush now, crossing the five steps from the door to the nearest Kurita soldier in a pell-mell charge, swinging the butt of the rifle up and into the man's jaw with the final step.

The second guard had his pistol out, was yanking the

slide back to chamber a round. Grayson swung the TK again with a roundhouse stroke that shattered the rifle's plastic stock against the man's temple.

"Gray!" Lori's shriek rang from stone walls, stark with fear. "Behind you!"

He stepped forward and ducked as something burning hot whooshed through the air just above his head. Grayson sidestepped as the torch swung again. He groped at his belt for his pistol, dragged it free, then felt a stinging shock as the torch snickered back and smashed against his wrist. Flames billowed in his face as his pistol clattered across stone to the far end of the room. The interrogator advanced with deadly purpose, his smock flapping. The torch in his hands roared as he swung it a fourth time, missed, recovered, and brought it around again. With each swing of his arm, the flaming rags on the torch were fanned into a blazing meteor of fire.

Grayson dropped and rolled. The torch smashed into the stone where his head had been an instant before, and sparks and shreds of burning rag skittered across the stone. The Kurita interrogator brought the torch up again, holding it spear-like in a clawed, white-knuckled death's grip. Grayson watched the burning end of the torch with a horrid fascination as the attacker advanced step . . . by step . . .

He needed a weapon. His pistol was gone, the guards' weapons were out of reach, and even his knife was out of reach on his boot. A grenade would kill everyone in the room, himself and Lori included. That was one way out, but . . .

His hand closed on one of the three grenades on his vest. His attacker's eyes widened above the light of the torch, then narrowed with a fanatic's determination. The interrogator lunged forward, thrusting the fire at Grayson's face. Grayson twisted and backed away, smashing the back of his head against the wall behind him.

Head ringing, he lunged to one side as the torch stabbed at him again. The flaming rags ground against stone, leaving a furiously burning patch where the liquid in the cloth was splattered against the wall. The grenade came free from Grayson's vest as he stepped back once more. His attacker swung around, the torch ready for another swing.

Grayson hurled the grenade without pulling the pin to arm it. It hit the interrogator squarely in the mouth, sending him tumbling backward into a table set with utensils of horror. The torch dropped guttering to the floor. Grayson's opponent scrabbled among blades, clamps, and other nightmarish objects that glittered as his fingers reached for the long, deadly wand of a neural whip.

Grayson stepped inside the slender blade, his left hand closing on the man's throat. He felt savage, keening agony in his side as the neural whip raked across his ribs, but the light jacket he wore shielded him from the worst of the weapon's charge. His right hand smashed forward, the heel of his hand ramming into the jaw of his enemy. The man's head snapped back, the whip falling from nerveless fingers.

Gasping, Grayson limped over to the table where Lori remained bound. Wincing against the pain of the whip's burn, he drew his knife and sawed at the leather straps that held her.

"Gray . . . you're here . . ."

He took her in his arms. "Easy there, Lori. I couldn't go misplacing my own best first officer, now could I?"

She was shivering, unable to say more. He shrugged out of his combat vest, then stripped off his lightweight black jacket and pulled it around her shoulders. He then took a moment to check his side. There were no marks, but it burned like fire when he pulled his tactical vest back into place over his undershirt.

Lori's boots lay on the floor nearby, next to an empty liter cask of azelwax. Grayson brought them to her. "Think you can walk?"

She nodded as she pulled the lightweight boots onto her bare feet. Grayson stooped to retrieve his automatic pistol from where he'd dropped it and pulled another one from the grasp of a fallen Kurita soldier. He handed one to her, and tucked the other into his trousers.

"O.K., we're going to get out of here now. Everything will be . . ."

Lori threw herself against him with a scream, knocking him to the side. The neural whip sang past his ear and whanged against the empty steel table. The white-smocked Draco interrogator was on his feet again, stag-

gering forward, his lower face a bloody mask where
Grayson's blow had broken teeth.

Lori swung her pistol up, but their attacker had already
stepped between her and Grayson. She froze, unable to
get a clear shot. Grayson grappled with the man, his fingers groping for a hold on his wrist to keep the deadly
blade of the neural whip away from his face. Slick with
sweat, Grayson's fingers lost their hold. The blade descended and rang loudly against the steel table as he
twisted away from the blow. The neural whip described
a flashing circle as the interrogator snapped it around for
another lunge.

Grayson stepped forward, blocking the blade with his
left arm as he brought his fist back for a punch. The
neural whip scribed white fire down Grayson's left arm
and tore a agonized, uncontrollable scream from his
throat. He sagged back against the table, helpless. The
attacker smiled through a bloody mask, the neural whip
blade levelling, weaving centimeters from Grayson's eyes.

The torch kindled to new, blazing life as it whipped
through the air, smashing into the interrogator's bloodied
face from the side. The blow snapped the man up and
back, arms flailing, as the torch dropped clattering from
Lori's hands.

The flames in the basin on the tripod had subsided
somewhat during the wild battle through the room, but
the liquid burned still with flickering yellow flames. The
interrogator fell against the tripod, shrieking as the liquid
splashed, soaking his smock. Flames roared, licking at
the ceiling. Grayson stepped past the drunkenly staggering human torch, turned Lori away from the horror, and
shoved her out toward the passageway.

He pulled his pistol free and whirled, ready to deliver
a mercy shot, but white heat clawed at his face as flames
raced across the room. He heard screams, weaker now
. . . but he could no longer see his target. The cries were
swallowed by the roar of the fire.

Lori's face held dull shock. "I killed him . . ."

"And I'm very glad you did." He held his still tingling
arm across his chest. "You probably just saved us both."

He looked at her carefully. After all she'd been
through, she looked . . . stronger somehow.

Lori raised her eyes to Grayson and managed a smile. "I'm . . . O.K."

"I know you are." He pointed back to where smoke was curling out from under the door to Room 6, between the sprawled forms of the two sentries. "They'll send someone down to see to that fire any minute now. Let's move!"

Hurrying through dimly lit corridors, they found an elevator guarded by mangled bodies in Kurita uniforms, but Grayson did not trust the building to continue providing power for long. They kept hunting until they found a stairway leading up. On the next level, they heard the rattle of gunfire and the dull, flat crack of exploding rockets. Cautious now, they moved toward the sound with pistols held ready. They found more dead, here a trio of men in prisoner's rags splattered with blood, there a Kurita soldier beaten into grisly horror, his weapons gone.

They came to a vast, open room enclosed by shadows and menacing shapes. It was a BattleMech maintenance facility. There were stacks of shells and armor plate along the walls between twelve-meter high skeletal frameworks of work gantries. Two of the gantries were occupied, and Grayson recognized both 'Mechs. The one on the right was the *Crusader* he'd faced twice already. The other was the *Marauder* that he knew belonged to the Kurita senior 'Mech regimental commander.

Across the room, a huddle of men moved behind a hastily thrown-up barricade of carts and armor plate. At first, they were only moving shapes against the light from outside. Grayson's eyes adjusted to the light in the same instant that one of them turned away from the firing line. It was a Kurita soldier.

The man shouted and raised his submachine gun. Bullets sang and chittered overhead as Grayson and Lori ducked down among the stacked arrays of BattleMech treasure. That armor plate would protect them from any weapon those soldiers could carry, but he could hear the shouts and running footsteps of troops spreading out to both sides. It wouldn't be long before he and Lori were pinned down and killed.

Grayson raised his head far enough to cast his eye over the two BattleMechs. The *Crusader* was closer, but its torso had been opened to reveal tangles of power cables and actuator circuitry that hung from it like an obscene parody of disembowelment. The *Crusader* had been badly damaged in its last fight and was in the racks for extensive repairs.

The *Marauder* looked untouched, however, its weapons gleaming, its cockpit hatch invitingly open. That was deceiving, Grayson knew. He had hit the *Marauder,* and critically. Had the damage already been repaired?

Bullets snapped overhead and Grayson dropped behind the armor plate. Lori was finishing with the fasteners of her borrowed jacket. She pushed a tangle of stray blonde out of her face and gave Grayson a weak smile. "Lovely day for a last stand, isn't it, Gray?"

"It's not time for that yet. How'd you like to try for that *Marauder* over there?"

She glanced in the direction he'd indicated with his thumb. "I'd love to. How do we get past those . . . people?"

"Like this. Be ready to run."

He pulled two grenades from his tactical vest. Each of the dull, squat canisters bore the legend "WH SMK." He handed one to Lori.

"I only have two of these, so make it count. You put yours over there," he said, pointing. "Mine will go on the other side. Count ten, and we'll go."

She nodded and took a firmer grip on the canister, the index finger of her other hand looped through the arming pin. Grayson held down the arming lever of his own grenade, yanked the firing pin, then waited while Lori did the same with hers. Then he nodded out a silent three-count and hurled the canister with a stiff-armed swing.

The two grenades clattered among the stacked supplies and exploded with dull thuds. White smoke boiled up from two widely spaced spots in the room. There were wild shots and yells of alarm. Grayson counted ten, then stood and slipped over the sheltering pile of armor. Lori was close behind.

The smoke was a gray and impenetrable fog. Grayson and Lori held hands to keep from being separated as they sprinted across the open area that Grayson had noted in his brief inspection. Once a shadow moved across their path just ahead, but it was swallowed by the smoke as quickly as it appeared. Smoke rasped harsh and scratchy in Grayson's throat. He tried to take shallow breaths but he found he was holding his breath by the time they reached the far wall. When he finally let the breath out, the exertion of his run forced him to draw in a deep breath at the same moment. The whole routine nearly doubled him over in a gasping fit of coughing.

"Take shallow breaths," Lori said, but Grayson had neither breath nor strength to answer. They had reached a wall of stack equipment crates, which Grayson had re-membered seeing piled on either side of the two 'Mechs. Now, was he to the left or the right of the *Marauder?*

He decided they were between the two 'Mechs, and just to the right of the *Marauder.* They turned left and hurried. The smoke was thinning rapidly. Already, he could see shadows running through the fog meters away, charging back toward the way they had just come. Just ahead, he saw the shadow of the *Marauder.*

The BattleMech's ladder was not down, but there was a ladder on the gantry framework that held it. Lori handed him her pistol and started up first. He tucked both pistols into his combat belt, gave her a moment's head start, then scrambled up after her.

A high-pitched whining puzzled him as they climbed. It took him a moment to place the sound. Large fans set into ventilators in the walls or ceilings had been turned on. Such fans were standard equipment in 'Mech repair areas, where poisonous fumes or the smoke from smol-dering battle damage could accumulate. Once they were turned on, the smoke began clearing rapidly.

Too rapidly. There was a shout, a crack, and a bullet howled off the side of the ladder ten centimeters below his right hand. The vast and echoing room rang with the chatter of a submachine gun, and rounds spanged and chirred through the steel framework around him.

He twisted around, pulling one of the pistols from his belt, thumbing the safety off. He was eight meters above the ferrocrete now, and the figures of the Kurita soldiers below him were made small by the distance. He clung with one arm to the ladder, pointed the pistol almost straight down, and squeezed the trigger. The gun snapped in his hand, and spent brass flicked through the air and down toward the soldiers suddenly scattering in every direction for cover. He fired again . . . again . . . again.

He hit no more, but his targets showed a sudden reluctance to remain in his line of sight.

Glancing up, he saw Lori's long legs flash in the gloom as she swung off the ladder and dashed across a metal walkway to the *Marauder*'s open hatch. Grayson swarmed up after her as shots from below began potting through the air in his direction.

The *Marauder*'s cockpit was big enough for the two of them—just barely. Up close, the damage from Grayson's lucky LRM shot into the heavy 'Mech's head was still evident. The cockpit screen had been breached, and jagged fingers of metal and plastic pointed inward where fragments had broken through. Blood stained the control seat, and Grayson wondered what had happened to the 'Mech's pilot. Had it been Kevlavic? Probably. On an ambush as important as that one, he would have been there. He must have been seriously wounded at least, though he'd managed to con his machine back to Regis. Wondering if Kevlavic were still alive, Grayson swung the canopy down into place and dogged it tight.

"Maybe this isn't the time to bring it up," Lori said from behind the control seat, "but I've never piloted one of these things."

"Don't worry," Grayson said as he clicked the pistol's safety back on and tucked the weapon back into his belt. "I have." He didn't tell her that his experience with *Marauder*s was limited to time spent in the simulators of his father's unit. Why worry her? It *should* be the same . . .

The shouts outside were louder now. Bullets whanged and keened off the *Marauder*'s armor. Those Techs would know of the damage to the forward screen, would be telling marksmen where to aim. A high-powered rifle bullet expending energy as it bounced back and forth inside the narrow cockpit could chew both of them to bloody rags in a few horrible seconds.

He sat in the seat, ignoring the stains. Two major hurdles remained. He ran his fingers across the instrument panel, depressing plastic touch plates and flicking switches to "on." Somewhere deep in the bowels of the huge machine, powers woke and uncoiled, grumbling. Green readouts winked on in uneven patterns across the board. They had crossed the first hurdle. The *Marauder*'s power systems were operational.

He hesitated a moment, then reached for the neuro-helmet suspended overhead by its webbing of power feeds and circuitry. This was the big hurdle. If the *Marauder* was still keyed to Kevlavic's brain waves, it would be impossible to steal the machine. Grayson knew, though, that BattleMechs hanging in the racks for repair generally had the coded sequences in their computer interlocks opened so that the Techs and astechs could run test programs and check the operational controls and circuit overrides. He'd been able to steal his own *Shadow Hawk* from a Kurita repair facility on Trellwan because the Techs had not yet recoded the 'Mech's computer. That's what he was counting on now.

A bullet sang off the cockpit's outer armor, a hand's breadth from the jagged hole. Another struck, close by the first.

He brought the helmet down onto his head, taking the cushioned yoke onto his shoulders. He hesitated again as he checked the power readouts on his panel. It was possible to booby-trap a BattleMech against would-be thieves, as well as to lock it up with codes. Several thousand volts searing through the brain would abruptly end any thoughts of hijacking someone else's 'Mech.

There was only one way to find out. He reached out and opened the 'Mech's helmet-computer interface.

Dizziness twisted at his head and stomach, and strange sensations tugged at his inner ears, but the protective charge of high-voltage current did not flow. His hands gently eased vernier dials, as oddly doubled waveforms on an oscilloscope blended, merged, then steadied into a single trace. The dizziness vanished, and Grayson was one with the machine.

He did a rapid check of circuits and weaponry. As near as he could tell, the only damage to the 'Mech was the hole in the forward screen. There could be additional, unmarked damage to some vital circuit or lead, but there was no quick or simple way to check that out. Grayson brought the visor down across his eyes, and told Lori to grab hold of something solid where she stood behind him. Then he brought his hands down on the primary controls.

The computer interface took advantage of Grayson's own sense of balance. It read the signals relayed to his brain from his own inner ear and translated them into gentle surges of power to selected actuators, transforming the 'Mech's motion from the stiffness of an automaton to the fluid moves of a living being. Feedback from sensors located at points across the 'Mech's legs and torso were fed back through Grayson's inner ear, replacing his own sense of balance with that of his 75-ton mount. In no sense did the BattleMech become his body, but man and machine did blend in the same way a horse and rider team might have done in an earlier, less bloodstained era.

The *Marauder* straightened against the binding constraints of the gantry framework. Steel pipe and titanium-vanadium alloy struts snapped free of mountings, spitting sheared bolts across the room like high-powered rifle bullets. Part of the structure collapsed with a resounding clang, and the *Marauder* stepped forward, scattering the gantry's skeleton like a windblasted house of cards.

Machine gun fire from the 'Mech service area across the courtyard had ceased moments before, though Ramage could still hear shouts and racketing gunfire from inside the building in that direction. He wasn't sure what was happening, but perhaps the mixed force of commandos and armed ex-captives could use the diversion, whatever it was, to pull back from their positions and withdraw to the tunnel.

If only Grayson would show up. Ramage didn't want to leave without him, but the Verthandian prisoners had stopped coming out of the tower's sublevels ten minutes before, and none of them had seen the Gray Death's commander.

Ramage didn't want to believe that the young man who had built the Gray Death from rags and odd ends on Trellwan was dead. At the moment, however, he didn't see what else *to* believe.

He looked about him. The commandos had seized most of the courtyard and still held it, but half of their number were dead or wounded. The command would not survive another determined assault. Curiously, the enemy 'Mechs at the courtyard gates had departed. He eyed the massive steel gates uncertainly. It *could* be that the 'Mechs had been unable to break through, but one of the commandos had told him that the Combine 'Mechs had swept those gates aside like cardboard during the University riots.

If that were so, why hadn't they attacked? What else could they be planning?

A chirruping from the transceiver at his belt interrupted his circling thoughts. He snatched the device to his mouth and opened the channel. "Ramage."

"Clay here, Sergeant. We're coming in."

"What? What do you mean?"

"We've got a full company of Kurita 'Mechs, pretty near! They've circled around the AgroMech factory and are moving in fast! There's no way to go but . . . down the tunnel!"

Ramage digested this bit of information. So, that was where the 'Mechs had gone. They must have suspected that the Gray Death BattleMechs were waiting outside, and so had circled about to catch them in a trap. Those 'Mechs were more important targets than a few dozen commandos trapped in the rubble of the University courtyard—especially when 'Mechs and commandos could be dispatched at one time with a little patience and a well-timed maneuver.

"Clay! This is Ramage! If you come in here, you'll be trapped!" He couldn't believe that the enemy 'Mechs had left the courtyard gate unguarded. More Kurita 'Mechs would be out there, perhaps unseen in the tangle of Regis' streets, but ready to rush the gates when the time came. "Do you hear me? Don't come in! Scatter north, and save yourselves!"

"Too late," Clay replied. "They came down on us from three directions at once and hemmed us in. If we show ourselves outside the factory, we're dead meat." The transmission was garbled by the hiss of a nearby explosion. "*Archer*s," he said. "They're starting to shell the factory! We're coming through before we're trapped in the rubble. Maybe we can figure things out once we're inside!"

"Right. Come on through!" Ramage opened his combat transmitter and spread the word. He didn't want an anti-'Mech team burning down friendly BattleMechs as they emerged unexpectedly from the tunnel.

"Sergeant!" A soldier tugged at his sleeve, pointing

across the rubble barricade. "Something's coming out of the service area!"

He twisted around to see, and fought the panic that rose gibbering at the back of his throat. Lumbering from the dark cavern of the repair facility it was a *Marauder*, 70 tons of deadly fighting steel.

"God," he said, "They've been holding back in there, waiting for us! That monster is going to trap our 'Mechs as they come up out of the tunnel!"

Hurriedly, he opened his combat channel. "Anti-'Mechs! I've got a target for you, a big one! Get up here!"

A moment later, three black-clad youngsters scrambled through the rubble to Ramage's side. Two of them carried satchel charges. The third cradled the squat, bulky shape of a portable inferno launcher.

Inferno launchers were among the deadliest of soldier-carried anti-'Mech weaponry. They were twin-barreled, over-under projectors that fired 20 mm shells containing CSC or another highly flammable compound designed to ignite moments after it left the muzzle of the launcher. Liquid fire, like napalm but hotter and more viscous, sprayed in a ravening sheet across armor, circuitry, and heat sinks.

Grayson had captured a light 'Mech singlehandedly on Trellwan merely by threatening it with a portable inferno launcher. That was how he'd first met Lori Kalmar, when her *Locust* had been on the other side. Even monsters like a MAD-3R *Marauder* could be fried by a trooper with good aim and a steady hand.

Ramage had picked and trained this assault team himself. He gave the orders, pointing out the damage he'd noted on the BattleMech's cockpit. If white-hot inferno streams could be directed at that opening, they'd fry the Kurita pilot before he even knew what had happened.

The *Marauder* lumbered closer. Ramage opened his throat mike. "Now, boys! Take him!"

37

Grayson saw the black-suited commando team roll across the rubble barricade, lugging their satchels and the deadly, twin-tubed shape of the inferno launcher after them.

'Lori, quick! Undog the canopy!''

"Huh? But . . .''

"Do it, or we're dead!'' She squeezed past the control seat, reaching past the instrument consoles to twist the hatch lugs. The *Marauder* mounted several hatches in its flattened, egg-shaped hull, one up to topside, another in the belly between the legs. The canopy was designed to open as well, making it easier to repair or replace circuitry in the instrumentation. It also gave *Marauder* pilots cramped in the stifling heat of their enclosed cabin an opportunity to let in a bit of cool air.

Lori hauled at the hatch release. It didn't move.

"Grayson, I can't budge it! It's stuck!''

From his control seat, Grayson could not reach the hatch release without disconnecting from the neurohelmet, a process that would take a number of seconds that they simply did not have. He could see one of the commando bringing the inferno launcher to his shoulder.

Desperately, Grayson scanned the control board. Somewhere in that maze of instrumentation was the switch to the *Marauder*'s outside hailer, but he couldn't decide which of a dozen controls it might be. Simulators taught the use of basic controls and suggested the feel of a particular machine, but they could never teach the arrangement of secondary controls, which often differed from 'Mech to 'Mech.

And it was useless to try the radio. Each BattleMech

and infantry unit had microprocessor-monitored guards on all transceivers. Those simple-minded computers used a programmed code to scramble and unscramble all communications within the unit. The result was that enemy units who happened upon the right radio frequency might hear a battle transmission before or during combat, but they would never figure out what was being said unless they had access to the same computer transceiver program. Grayson knew what frequency the commandos were using, but they would hear only electronic gibberish when he spoke.

His own throat mike was gone, knocked away and lost during his scramble with the Kurita interrogator. The *Marauder*'s radio was useless until it could be reprogrammed to translate the Gray Death's battlecodes.

Grayson gave no thought to any of this. In his mind's eye, he could see the commando's finger tightening on the trigger.

Lori pulled again on the stubborn hatch release. As she hauled back, she looked up, saw the shapes ahead, and gasped.

"Down, Lori! Down flat!" When she didn't move, he swept a booted foot out, knocking her ankles from under her. She fell, bringing her arms up over her head. Grayson brought his hand down on the emergency eject controls, slapped off the arming switch cover, and stabbed the bright red button exposed underneath.

Explosive bolts banged on the outer hull, and the canopy split over their heads, its two halves falling away to either side in the sudden gush of fresh air that spilled in from a green sky. Grayson was already on his feet. Though encumbered by the tangle of cables spilling from his neurohelmet to their connectors behind his seat, he was plain in the sight of the commandos twenty meters in front of him.

Then Ramage was on his feet, waving and shouting, and the trooper with the inferno lowered his weapon with the reluctance of a professional denied the chance to demonstrate his craft.

Grayson sank back in his seat, suddenly drained. "It's all right, Lori," he said as she levered herself up to her knees using the seat's armrest for support. His voice cracked, and he felt a strange sensation in his hands.

Looking down at them, he realized they were trembling. Death by fire had brushed close by them both. To be trapped, helpless, consumed in agony . . .

It took him a second more to control his voice. "I think I finally know what you've been feeling all this time."

Governor General Nagumo motioned to his body-guards and turned from the communications center. Kodo had been alerted to the situation and would arrive with reinforcements from Verthandi-Alpha in a few hours.

Not that he really needed Kodo's presence, but Na-gumo did not believe in doing things by half measures. The DropShips landing outside Regis would serve to warn the Verthandians in the city to keep the peace in the wake of the pitched battle in and about the University grounds. With luck, the landings would trap some of the rebel soldiers who'd been reported in the fields outside the city proper.

Somewhere in the distance, a fire alarm was wailing. A blaze was out of control in the lower levels of the Tower, and gunfire or some other cause had wrecked the automatic sprinklers built into the University ceilings. The fire control crews were all Loyalist Verthandians, but most of them had already fled, abandoning their Ku-rita masters to their fate. According to the building mon-itors, that fire was spreading with ferocious speed through the lower sections. The Tower's remaining staff would have to evacuate very soon.

There was still time to win the battle in the courtyard and to crush the rebel forces outside the city as well. If the reports were accurate, most of the mercenary BattleMechs were inside the walls of the University now, trapped by the sudden redeployment he'd ordered from the Tower a few moments before. From his vantage point, Nagumo could see the Courtyard spread out like a sand-table battle at the Luthien Military Academy, could look beyond the main gate and see his own forces massing for their assault. It had taken only a moment to consult com-puter records and find the forgotten passageway. That rebel woman, Helgameyer, had spoken of the tunnel dur-ing her questioning.

The tunnel would be part of Nagumo's trap now. Once

the mercenary BattleMechs had been herded through it and into the courtyard, Nagumo's 'Mechs would close in, Company A of the 3rd Strike Regiment through the main courtyard gate, Company B through the tunnel itself. Eighteen 'Mechs would be more than enough to finish the four 'Mechs that had been reported outside the walls.

The Gray Death would die at his feet in the courtyard below.

He hurried to his office, noting the empty passageways. Many of the building's workers had already fled. News of the fire in the Tower sublevels had spread quickly.

"Wait here," he told his guards, and he stepped through into his office. A strange drama was unfolding in the courtyard below his window. A *Marauder*—Kevlavic's *Marauder*—was emerging from the repair facility and advancing on the enemy commandos' perimeter.

Strange. The Colonel was in the hospital, still recovering from the amputation of his arm. Had one of the Techs powered up the machine in an attempt to rush the commando defenses?

The door hissed open behind him. He turned, a puzzled scowl forming on his face. "What do you . . ."

He stopped, open-mouthed. The girl who stood there held a stun pistol in one hand, a long, keen-bladed combat dagger in the other. She stepped past the senseless forms of the two bodyguards, her face an expressionless mask. She wore a form-hugging black outfit and combat harness, and her face was smeared with black camouflage paint.

"Who the devil are you?" he demanded with a scowl, though she looked familiar somehow. "Do I know you?"

"Don't mind me, General," she said. There was a strange light in her eyes, a touch of wildness. "I'm just one of the things you . . . *used* once."

"Now wait a minute. Put that thing down! Look, I've got money. I can make you . . ."

She continued speaking, her voice honey-sweet. "You really should be more careful of your toys, General. Sometimes they can turn on you, just when you're least expecting it."

She had stepped closer. Desperate now, he grabbed for

the stunner in her hand. Her fighter pilot's reflexes proved
faster, and her finger tightened on the trigger.

She had reset the stunner for a light charge after she'd
used it to dispatch the guards outside. Nagumo was quite
conscious when she tied him to his chair, conscious and
fully aware of what was happening. His stunned nervous
system simply had no control over his muscles.

For some time after, he couldn't even muster the mus-
cular control that his throat and diaphragm needed to
scream.

Moments later, the Gray Death BattleMechs plunged
into the slanting, early morning light in the courtyard.
Khaled, the last one through the tunnel, reported that
enemy 'Mechs had been breaking into the factory compound just as his borrowed *Shadow Hawk* had ducked
into the passageway entrance.

They were surprised at the sight of the *Marauder*
standing there among the battle-haggard commandos, but
Ramage was explaining as they stepped through into the
light. Lori used a lightweight line to haul a combat transceiver up into the cockpit of the captured 'Mech.

"Good morning, Sergeant! What's the situation?" she
asked, once the unit was in place, clipped to her ear with
the thin pick-up extended in front of her lips.

"Lori! It's good to have you back!"

"It's very good to be back." Her voice was unsteady,
and the adrenalin pumped into her system at the sight of
that inferno launcher still had her trembling. She kept
her voice light, though, hoping Ramage wouldn't notice.
She knew that Grayson already had, but she didn't mind
that. "I'm relaying for the Captain," she continued.
"What's happening?"

"They boxed us. They swung something like a company of 'Mechs around outside and caught our people
against the factory wall. Now they're out there and we're
in here . . . and I expect something to be coming through
that main gate, too, any minute now."

She paused to relay the information to Grayson, then
reopened the channel. "O.K., Sergeant. Orders from the
chief. Get clear of the tunnel. We'll take care of that.
You all deploy to cover the main gate. Clay? McCall?
Khaled? You all copy that?"

There was a chorus of assents. The *Marauder*, its canopy still hanging open, made its way toward the archway through which the Gray Death BattleMechs had just emerged. A short way into the shadows, a ramp opened, leading down one level. Beyond that, the tunnel entrance yawned, twelve meters tall and ten meters wide to accommodate the lumbering AgroMechs that had passed that way in more peaceful times.

Lori looked back at Grayson, hunched forward in the control seat.

"Careful of the control panel, Lori," he said. "Remember, our eject system is armed. One touch, and . . . whoosh!"

She glanced up at the cracked gray plaster of the ceiling, half a meter above the autocannon extending just over their heads.

"Just watch what buttons you push," she replied.

"Hold it . . . quiet a moment." He appeared to be straining at the darkness, listening.

"They're coming," he said at last. "Slow and cautious, but they're coming. It's a good thing there's no way to make a twenty-ton metal monster silent. I can hear a BattleMech's leg joint down that tunnel creaking and popping like a rusty old door."

Lori could hear the sounds, too, a far-off, hollow echo of metal scraping against ferrocrete. The *Marauder* positioned itself close beside the mouth of the tunnel.

"Okay, Lori. When it goes down, I want *you* down, flat to the deck. With the canopy open, we won't have any protection from the dazzle or the UV bleed from the PPCs."

Her eyes widened. "You're going to unleash those things in *here?*"

"None other. *They* won't be expecting it, either."

"That's one way to look at it."

A long moment crawled past. Then Grayson spoke quietly. "Right, Lori. Dig yourself a hole in the deck."

Somewhere on that alien control panel there was a switch for the *Marauder*'s floodlights, twin lenses under the canopy chin that could have bathed the black tunnel with the radiance of a sunny day. There was no time to find that switch right now. Instead, Grayson waited until

he guessed the enemy 'Mechs would be close, then
stepped across the tunnel entrance.

The particle projection cannons mounted in each of the
Marauder's forearm heavy weapon mounts had been
charged for several minutes already. He triggered the
right arm cannon first, squinting through the dark visor
of his helmet with one eye only, the other squeezed tightly
shut.

Man-made lightning glared with intolerable brilliance,
starkly illuminating the clustered band of BattleMechs in
blue-white radiance. For the split second of its existence,
the beam of charged particles burned low across the left
torso of the *Centurion* that led the pack. The beam
snapped off, plunging the tunnel back into darkness
again, leaving the eyes and optic systems of the Kurita
'Mech pilots momentarily dazzled by the PPC's glare.

Grayson opened his left eye, the one he had held
closed, and peering into the darkness. Then he squeezed
the eye shut again. His right eye still danced and watered
with the green and purple disks planted there by the
beam's brilliant discharge, but had cleared enough for
him to place his second shot. The *Marauder*'s left arm
fired, and again lightning seared through the narrow tunnel. The shot was higher this time and more toward the
center. It caught the *Centurion* squarely in the chest.
LRMs in the 'Mech's chest pack rocketed into the startled darkness, trailing fire. Explosions sent fireworks
flashing down the length of the tunnel, lighting up the
company of 'Mechs in sharp relief.

The *Marauder* discharged both arm lasers in a quick
one-two shot that scattered burning fragments of armor
through the passageway. A *Phoenix Hawk* behind the
Centurion also opened fire with its heavy laser, but the
bolt went wide, scoring the ferrocrete wall across the passageway from the *Marauder*.

Both PPCs fired again. One bolt caught the *Phoenix
Hawk*, shearing away an arm in flaming chunks of debris.
The other drilled the *Centurion* high in the torso a second
time. The unfortunate *Centurion* pitched backward, flame
and molten gobbets of metal and plastic spewing from a
gaping crater in its chest.

The *Marauder* stepped back away from the tunnel
mouth. Bolts spit and burned from the tunnel mouth,

followed by a pair of missiles that exploded against the far wall. Smoke was pouring from the tunnel opening now, and something burning in the passageway lit the darkness.

Grayson swung the *Marauder*'s right arm into the tunnel mouth, exposing only as much of the heavy machine as he needed to make the shot. The enemy 'Mechs were caught in complete confusion behind the flaring light of the burning *Centurion*. Grayson triggered the PPC and the laser together. An *Archer* took both hits, one in an arm, the other in the torso. Considering the thickness of the big 'Mech's armor, the damage was minor, but the *Archer* collided with a *Stinger* as its pilot attempted to back out of the line of fire.

Lori rolled over on the *Marauder*'s deck and looked up at him. "Gray! Ramage is calling! They're coming through the front gate!"

"Damn," Grayson replied. "Do we hold here, or go help?"

"He says the gates have been blown clear off their hinges. He says that there are at least eight 'Mechs coming through the gap, and that he sure could use our firepower."

"I guess that's the answer. Flatten down again, Lori." The *Marauder* stepped fully into the opening again, ignoring the wildly aimed bolts and missiles that whirled down the tunnel at them. Both PPCs triggered together. Blue light engulfed the struggling *Archer*, which still had not disentangled itself from the *Stinger*. In the dying light of the burning *Centurion*, Grayson fired his lasers into the tangle, watched the *Archer* stagger and topple in flailing metal limbs, dragging the *Stinger* down with it. The tunnel was blocked, at least for the moment. It would take a concentrated effort to get the passageway clear enough for BattleMechs to squeeze through.

With the surviving 'Mechs in full retreat down the sheltering darkness of the tunnel behind them, Grayson didn't think they were going to make that concentrated effort very soon. He had Lori suggest that Ramage post an anti-'Mech team to watch this route into the courtyard, and then took the *Marauder* thundering up the ramp to the upper level.

An explosion rocked the tunnel behind them as a damaged 'Mech exploded, bringing chunks of rock and ferrocrete down in dust-spewing ruin.

That was our way out, Grayson thought, grimly. With the tunnel closed, the Gray Death was trapped within the University Courtyard.

38

Smoke wreathed the Courtyard, providing some slight cover for the black-clad men crouching behind their barricades. The Courtyard grounds were still shadowed by the surrounding walls and buildings, but slanting, red-gold rays of Norn sliced through the rising smoke and dust clouds. The Courtyard gate had been blasted open, the cast steel warped and blackened by satchel charges packed with high explosives.

The smoke was heavier in the street beyond, where several vague shapes moved against a background of gray fog. Blue-white bolts of lightning flickered and probed out of the murk, shattering craters in the masonry above and behind the defenders, showering them with a powdery avalanche of crumbled stone. McCall had planted his beloved *Bannockburn* just behind the main barricade, and the *Rifleman*'s quad weapons swung back and forth in tiny arcs across the opening. A shadow moved, and the 'Mech's autocannons barked, spent casings trailing streamers of smoke as they spun away from the furiously cycling guns.

As the *Wolverine* was crouched in an enfilading position across the Courtyard on the east side, in a position where it could catch the enemy in a crossfire as he came through the gate, Khaled had Grayson's *Shadow Hawk* high up on the roof of a two-story building along the western side of the court.

The *Marauder* emerged from the deep shadows of the ramp to the lower level, Grayson had Lori call Ramage on her combat transceiver.

"He says they rushed the gate about a minute ago, but

pulled back when McCall opened up. He think's they're still testing us."

Grayson raised his visor on his neurohelmet and wiped at the sweat pooling above his eyebrows. "That won't last long. They'll be along any . . ."

His words were chopped off by the shrieking hiss of incoming rockets, arcing on white contrails over the Courtyard walls and erupting in volcanic fury amid rubble piles, buildings, and crouching men. The barrage ended as suddenly as it began, enfolding the courtyard in an unnatural silence.

Grayson guided the *Marauder* into the light and close alongside a three-story building. "End of the ride, Lori," he said.

Seeing argument in her eyes, a protest forming on her lips, he shook his head. "Quickly! I can't close the canopy on this thing, which is going to make this open cockpit a target! Now get off, if you don't want me to throw you off!"

Conflicting emotions struggled in Lori's face. "You need someone on the radio."

"Not anymore."

"What's the point, then?" Her face was flushed, her eyes bright. "We're trapped in here! Do you think I'm going to leave you now?"

Grayson hesitated, surprised. Then he smiled. "Look at it this way, Lori. Here I am, all set to eject if I get in trouble. But I can't very well punch out with you squeezed in next to the chair thrusters now, can I?"

Again, Lori's face revealed her inner struggle at this strange piece of logic. At last, she only nodded, then bent forward to kiss him, a deep, hungry but brief joining. "I love you," she said.

He held her for a moment, searching her eyes. He saw the love there, and his own spirit soared. Grayson nodded, squeezing her shoulders tightly. "I love you, too, Lori. Now git. And mind the hot metal."

She climbed out of the cockpit onto the open hatch panel that extended from the hull like a stubby wing. From there, it was a short leap across and down to the roof of the building. Their eyes met as she looked back at him from the rooftop, and then she was on her feet and sprinting toward the safety of an open doorway.

The next flight of missiles volleyed into the Courtyard an instant later, their detonation filling the enclosed space with light, thunder, and hurtling clots of debris. Close behind the missiles, a pair of vast and threatening shapes pressed up against the open Courtyard gate. Grayson recognized the squat, massive silhouettes against the battle fog. They were *Archer*s rushing forward in a close assault role.

The Kurita command must be anxious to finish this, he thought. *They could stand off and shell us into submission if they had the patience. What's their hurry?*

He checked his weapons. Both PPCs were at full charge. His hands closed over the firing controls, and computer-generated characters on his console screens spoke of power levels, target locks, and combat-ready status. The PPCs fired together, twin beams arrowing into the first *Archer* as it strode through the swirling dust. The impact staggered the heavy 'Mech, caught it off balance, and sent it lurching into one of the warped Courtyard gates.

Grayson hit the recharge and triggered his lasers. White-hot, minor suns flared into radiance close together, high up on the stricken *Archer*'s torso, close by the cockpit. The *Rifleman* fired lasers and autocannons together at the same instant, and gouts of flame marked the detonation of autocannon shells in partly molten slabs of armor.

The second *Archer* crowded past the first, LRMs rocketing on flat trajectories into the black wall of the central University tower behind the *Rifleman*. Chunks of shattered ferrocrete and stone rained onto the barricades in a steaming, smoking avalanche that sent the commandos there scattering for deeper cover. The Courtyard had become a blazing hell where unprotected humans could not hope to survive for more than a few seconds.

The *Wolverine* opened up from its corner alongside the gateway wall, autocannon fire hosing across the second *Archer*. The *Shadow Hawk* joined in from its position on the rooftop opposite. Three streams of high-explosive mayhem converged on the 70-ton BattleMech, transfixing it in fire and the stuttering flash of explosions.

The *Marauder*'s autocannon was empty, but Grayson could still join in the litany of destruction with his lasers.

A green light winked readiness on the charge for his PPCs. He fired them again, the searing bolts closely spaced. Fragments of white hot metal erupted from the *Archer*'s flat snout as the 'Mech's cockpit took a direct hit. In an agonizing parody of slow motion, the stricken *Archer* twisted slowly, then toppled. It slammed into the ground with the shattering impact of a crashing aircraft, trailing an arc of black smoke from its smashed-in cockpit screen. Flames licked from the wreckage.

The first *Archer* remained on its feet, crouched back by the open gate, missiles rocketing into the Courtyard buildings. The machine was too close to its target to take effective aim with its LRMs, but it could and did shower thundering chaos through the smoking ruin of the court. Lasers burned white, their paths dazzling against the particles of dust and smoke that choked the air. Khaled nailed the damaged *Archer* with a spray of autocannon fire that sent the heavy 'Mech staggering back out the gate in retreat.

More shapes surged into the gateway and stopped, hesitating behind the obstacle of the fallen, second *Archer*. A *Griffin* was in the lead, closely followed by a *Wasp* and a *Stinger*. The *Griffin*'s PPC stabbed flaring lightning against the barricade. The *Rifleman* staggered back a step, struck full in the chest by the blow.

Clay fired a spread of SRMs at the *Griffin*, three of the missiles striking the Kurita 'Mech in the arm. The *Griffin* spun and returned the fire, PPC bolts slapping into the *Wolverine*'s armor. Grayson crouched low in the exposed seat of his *Marauder* and urged the captured 'Mech forward. The *Griffin*'s PPCs were threatening to take out all four of the defending 'Mechs.

The *Griffin* turned at Grayson's approach and hesitated. With a surge of triumph, Grayson realized that the *Griffin*'s commander must be confused. The enemy 'Mech's unit markings read Company A, 3rd Strike Regiment . . . the same unit as the captured *Marauder*. The Kurita MechWarrior would be looking through the smoke and confusion of the firefight and be seeing his own regimental commander's BattleMech. And that stayed the Draco pilot's hand for the critical second Grayson needed.

Twin PPC bolts lanced out from the heavy forearms of the advancing *Marauder*, striking close together in the heavy armor of the *Griffin*'s chest. Exposed circuitry sparked and flashed behind the pump and gush of green coolant fluid. Twin laser beams arrowed through the ruin, flashing plastic and tender wiring into superheated steam. The *Griffin* tried to turn, but actuators failed and power failed. The deep-set, spherical head split open like a blossoming flower. For an instant, the enemy Mech-Warrior was visible, hunched forward in his control seat. Then ejection thrusters fired and the seat rocketed into the sky, leaving the *Griffin* frozen in place, a dead hulk.

Grayson swung the *Marauder* for a shot at the next advancing 'Mech and held his fire. A black-clad figure was dropping away from the *Stinger*'s foot as it swung up to scramble across the fallen *Archer*. The satchel charge behind its knee exploded in a fine spray of jagged fragments and coolant mist. The leg came down, the savaged knee buckled, and the *Stinger* collapsed across the wreckage of the *Archer*.

The *Wasp* standing in the gateway swung an arm up and around, as though pointing out the scattering figures of the commandos. Machine gun fire flickered and yammered, chopping miniature geysers of dust in zigzags across the ground. Another black-clad figure rose from the debris nearby, and held its ground in the face of the hail of machine gun fire as it took aim with the weapon at its shoulder. The weapon thumped, and liquid fire sleeted across the *Wasp*'s torso. The 'Mech stood transfixed, a pillar of raging fire. Grayson found himself willing the pilot to eject, but it didn't happen. The inferno's white heat must have overloaded the emergency power to the eject circuits.

The blazing *Wasp* and the tangle of wrecked 'Mechs blocked the gateway completely. Grayson took advantage of the sudden lull to check his instruments. Except for the obvious problem of the open canopy, his 'Mech was undamaged so far. The heat build-up from his use of the PPCs was extreme, but not critical. He'd not been moving the heavy 'Mech much, and that helped. He eased his machine back into the shade of the veranda lining the Court.

He couldn't tell for sure without radio communications, but the other Gray Death 'Mechs did not seem badly damaged. So far the Courtyard battle was all in their favor, with four enemy 'Mechs destroyed or seriously damaged at the gateway, and at least two more out of action in the tunnel underground. Grayson knew, though, that there was no way their luck could last much longer.

Shapes moved through the wreathing smoke in the gateway. Armored hands smashed the burning wreckage of the *Wasp* to the side, clearing the way for another BattleMech charge. An *Archer* loomed through the smoke, but Grayson couldn't tell if it were the damaged one returned or a new one. Autocannon fire and laser beams lanced across the Courtyard, clawing at the massive shadow. The *Archer* did not return the fire, but bent to the task of dragging the wreckage of the destroyed *Archer* to one side.

Grayson opened up with his PPCs and lasers, but directed his fire to one side of the struggling monster. Craters gaped and cracked in the stone wall beside it. The archway over the gate shivered and flexed. Blocks of stone showered onto the Kurita 'Mech, but without apparent effect. The entire gateway began to crumble as the *Shadow Hawk* and *Wolverine* added their autocannon fire to the effort. The *Rifleman* kept its weapons trained on the *Archer,* burning chunks from its arm and side, flaying open raw patches of twisted armor.

Smoke, dust, and falling rubble were so thick that Grayson could hardly see past the death-choked gateway. Another shadow appeared, looming squat and powerful as it shouldered past the *Archer.* With those long, heavy PPC cannon barrels that made up the 'Mech's forearms, there was no mistaking that silhouette.

A *Warhammer!*

39

Lori hurried through passageways heavy with writhing smoke, trembling to the thunderous blasts from outside. The corridor twisted back through the building, leading, she was sure, into the Administrative Complex, the cluster of buildings around the base of the University's Central Tower. The smoke grew thicker as she ran deeper into the complex. There were no other people here, save the occasional still and bloody forms of Kurita soldiers or Regis Blues caught by mobs of freed prisoners.

She stopped, sagging against a wall, coughing hard. Which way? A moan and the sound of someone else coughing attracted her attention. She hurried forward and saw a woman on hands and knees, struggling through smoke so thick it burned the eyes and turned throat and lungs to fire. A nearby wooden door burst open, and flames exploded into the corridor just beyond the woman. Lori almost turned away, but the woman's struggles were growing weaker, more aimless. Lori was caught, frozen for an instant's struggle within her. Then she moved forward. She *had* to help.

And she found that she could. The confrontation with the Kurita interrogator had broken through some barrier within her. She'd recognized that when her feelings for Grayson had welled up in her in a way that had not been possible until now. And that was the key.

It seemed that she had feared, not the fire, but that sense of helplessness she'd first known the night her parents had died. Helplessness, not fire . . . and not Grayson himself, had been the barrier that made her a stranger to herself. Her helplessness had been acted out in all too vivid a fashion when Nagumo's interrogators had strapped her to that table, had kindled a torch and advanced on her, leering . . . But Grayson had come . . . and she had joined him in the fight. The barrier, like prison gates flung wide, was gone now.

Breathing in shallow gasps, Lori rushed to the woman's side as flames roared close. She pulled one of the woman's arms across her own shoulders and half-carried, half-dragged the limp form, backing away from the fire. After awhile, the smoke grew so heavy that Lori dropped to hands and knees herself, pulled the woman across her back, and crawled in the direction that instinct told her was the way outside. The smoke was not so thick close to the ground.

Instinct proved correct. A door led to a veranda where Lori could sprawl against a mound of rubble, gulping down air. The woman lying beside her recovered slowly. It was Sue Ellen Klein, apparently unhurt, but haggard and dazed. Her uniform was torn, and her arms and hands stained with blood.

Beyond the rubble barrier, the clash of armored giants continued, their weapons like lightning and thunder and hell's own fury.

Powerful, confident, undamaged thus far in the struggle, the *Warhammer* of the Command Lance, Company A, First Battalion, 3rd Strike Regiment, strode past the blocking wreckage and into the center of the Court. The *Bannockburn* fired round after burning round into the advancing monster's chest. Clay's *Wolverine* opened up from behind, pouring white fire into the *Warhammer*'s flank. The rest of the company's 'Mechs crowded through behind it—another *Archer*, lasers flaring, a *Phoenix Hawk*, another *Wasp*.

A deafening explosion smashed Grayson forward in his control seat, and blue fire scalded his bare left arm. He spun the *Marauder* and faced a new threat. Another *Archer*, the odd, forward-thrusting shape of a *Jenner*, and a pair of *Stinger*s were crowding through the entrance to the lower level. A *Wasp* limped heavily, showing where an anti-'Mech commando had struck it with a satchel charge, but the tunnel's defenders had not been able to withstand this new rush.

He fired, PPC lightning flickering across the *Archer*

and the *Jenner*. Machine gun fire rattled across the open cockpit panels, and Grayson backpedaled the *Marauder* out of the line of fire and into the Courtyard proper. The *Warhammer* targeted him at once. Twin PPC bolts splashed across the *Marauder*'s legs, and Grayson screamed as his face burned in the light. He returned the fire, still screaming, saw his bolts striking home in coruscating flashes of fire and glittering fragments of metal.

The Courtyard was filled now with BattleMechs struggling in the smoke. An *Archer* battled hand-to-hand with Clay's *Wolverine*. Grayson's captured *Marauder* and McCall's *Rifleman* stood back to back atop the burning ruin of the Courtyard barricade, as the enemy Battle-Mechs advanced from two directions. The *Shadow Hawk* joined them, firing bolt after point-blank bolt into the torn and broken armor of the advancing *Warhammer*'s torso.

A new roar crashed and rumbled from overhead, and something heavy smashed into Grayson's open cockpit. He looked up, startled. The Central Tower of the University was wreathed in fire, and smoke was billowing from open windows halfway up its height.

More debris fell, splashing into the Courtyard. *The fire,* Grayson thought. *The fire in the lower levels! It must have spread! There was enough wood in the framework, under all that stone, that the whole tower must be in flames by now. The place was burning down over our heads and we didn't even notice!*

The Kurita 'Mechs closed in.

Tollen Brasednewic had planned to lead the hundred-odd men of his original band to the Uppsala Mountains to continue the fight, but he never left the Fox Island camp. Instead, he listened to the growing thunder in the distance, a thunder barely audible above the keening of the jungle chirimsims. The words he'd exchanged with Grayson Carlyle still burned . . . the humiliation still burned . . . But what was right?

He'd painted his refusal to help as a matter of honor as well as practicality. The rebel army—those men and women beyond his original small band—would no longer follow him, not after that mercenary offworlder had publicly criticized him. Inside, though, Tollen wondered if he were more enraged by the fact that his relationship with Carlotta had become public. With that, Old Family and Immigrant alike would be reluctant to follow him now.

Wouldn't they? And was it honor or pride . . . or his own unreasoning fears that kept him from finding out? The truth of the matter was that he didn't *know* if any in the Verthandian rebel army would follow if he gave the order to attack Regis.

Somehow, his anger against Grayson Carlyle had become a smaller thing. As the sounds of battle rising from the capital became more urgent, he gathered his original band and gave orders to saddle up a company of hover transports and move out. They would travel south, toward Regis, not to the west.

The main body of the rebel army had been waiting in some confusion ever since word of the Gray Death's commando raid had spread among them. Individual company commanders had been uncertain what to do. Even the Verthandian 'Mech lance, led by Rolf Montido, had done no more than gather along the edge of the Bluesward at the crest of the Basin Rim. With neither orders nor clear leaders, they'd been helpless.

When Brasednewic swept past them in the lead hover transport, Montido's *Dervish* relayed the signal. *All units . . . follow!* And the Free Verthandi Rangers had swept down on Regis.

By the time they reached the outskirts of the city, the Gray Death 'Mechs that had been arrayed outside the walls of the AgroMech factory had been driven back into the University Compound. Brasednewic had barked orders over the rebels' combat frequency. They couldn't afford to get pinned down in a firefight outside the University. Instead, the column split, each side swinging toward a different gate in the city wall. With luck, at least one column might be able to force its way through to join the fighting inside.

Montido's *Dervish* smashed through the gate Brasednewic had targeted with his group, scattering Blues and Brownjackets with its sudden rush.

"The way's open!" Brasednewic yelled above the battle roar. "Gun it!"

With a keening whine, the hovercraft angled toward the door. Through billowing smoke, Brasednewic glimpsed struggling throngs of people and uniformed soldiers beyond.

Grayson's PPC savaged the *Warhammer* twice more, stopping its advance in mid-stride. Khaled joined the *Shadow Hawk*'s laser fire, shearing away smoking chunks of white-hot armor plate. The 70-ton Kurita 'Mech hesitated, one PPC raised to fire directly into Grayson's cockpit from fifteen meters away.

Sparks danced and jittered along the battle scars in the *Warhammer*'s torso. The Draco pilot couldn't fire! His weapon circuitry had been destroyed, and he couldn't fire! The enemy's PPC resumed its upward swing, and the heavy 'Mech took another step forward, its deadly purpose starkly clear. It was going to use one of those heavy forearm cannons as a club.

Desperate, his head reeling from pain and loss of blood, Grayson triggered both PPCs under the enemy heavy's upraised arm. Lightning flared and crashed. A fireball rolled up from the *Warhammer*'s shattered chest, and the armored giant staggered backward, collapsing in a blazing, twisted tangle of BattleMech junk.

Grayson whooped victory through scalding air that seared his lungs, but the triumph died in his throat as he glanced at the shattered main gate. Another BattleMech force with Kurita markings, a full company at least, was pounding through and into the Courtyard, each machine fresh, undamaged, and combat-ready.

One of them, a *Jenner,* fired. A missile burst on the *Marauder*'s hull. Grayson ducked low as hot shrapnel seared into the cockpit. He looked down in surprise and saw blood drenching his left arm and side. At that moment, Grayson wished he had a working radio. It would be nice to say, "This is it," or "It's been good fighting at your side," or any one of the other cliches that a MechWarrior might utter at a time like this. He wished that he might see Lori again, too. She'd said she loved him! He wished . . .

A trio of missiles burned low above his shattered cockpit. A fourth impacted on his *Marauder*'s leg. The stricken machine lurched wildly. He twisted at the *Marauder*'s controls, but the heavy machine failed to respond. Sparks spat and flared across the instrument panel, and red lights warned of heat overload, of circuit cards melting, of weapons system failure . . .

Throughout the city, the Verthandians were joining the fight. For ten years, they had remained helpless and voiceless as the Kurita fist tightened on their world and on their city. Now, though, the savage battle gutting the centuries-old heart of the University had brought them out in a rising tide of fury that would not be stemmed. Wild-eyed Blues threw down their weapons and ran in the face of that onrushing crowd. Kurita Brownjackets did the same, or else opened fire with a hopeless, desperate ferocity before they were overrun and torn to shreds.

Weapons were scooped from the pavement or torn from the grip of bloodied hands. A lance of Kurita Battle-Mechs pressing toward the University paused as the mob swept around the University Plaza and surged toward Kurita positions south of the University Gate. When the lance turned and opened fire with machine guns and lasers, they opened bloody gashes in the mob's body. Hundreds, thousands of shrieking civilians continued to press forward, vaulting infantry barricades and rushing past the feet of the helpless metal giants.

Everywhere, Kurita soldiers found themselves isolated in small, struggling knots as the Loyalist militia melted away and the numbers of frenzied civilians storming through the streets swelled. Bottles filled with oil and gasoline and stoppered shut with rags took flame and arced smoking through the air. Clots of flame and black smoke wreathed BattleMech limbs and lower torsos. The four embattled 'Mechs reversed course and began moving away from the University. To a half-screamed demand for information over the Kurita combat net, they reported that the streets of Regis were lost, that they were falling back.

In the streets two blocks to the east, the four Kurita 'Mechs encountered rebel 'Mechs smashing through the city gates. Three of the four pilots decided that the cause of House Kurita could best be served on Verthandi if they took up positions outside the city . . . considerably outside the city. The fourth pilot remained where he was, his *Orion* wreathed in flames, his dead hands still clutching the controls.

Throughout the city of Regis, Kurita 'Mechs and men began retreating. BattleMechs are never at their best within the confines of buildings and narrow streets, and now the civilian mobs were threatening to slaughter every Kurita Brownjacket in Regis.

The tide was turning.

The Courtyard was strangely quiet. For a moment, Grayson wondered if he'd gone deaf, exposed as he was to the crash and thunder of heavy weapons. Then, gradually, he became aware of the roar of flames gnawing at the vitals of the broken *Warhammer* a few meters in front of him. The *Jenner* and the other fresh Draco 'Mechs were still there, but they had stopped their charge, had turned . . . They were retreating!

Why?

He reached out to hit an override panel and caught sight of his own arm, blood-crusted and blistered. He was becoming aware of the heat now, wafting off the hot metal of the *Marauder*, crowding its way into his lungs, sending shrieking agony across the exposed parts of his skin that were already horribly burned. Then shock, long held at bay, rose in a comforting, black embrace, drowning the pain, sending him hurtling forward into darkness.

Ramage helped pull him from the *Marauder* minutes later. At his side, smoke-blackened and victorious, was Tollen Brasednewic.

The Free Verthandi Rangers had arrived, quite literally in the nick of time.

40

Hours after the battle in the streets of Regis had ended, two Kurita *Leopard* Class DropShips landed at the spaceport ten kilometers north of the city. There was little the rebel forces could do to stop the landing, for the spaceport was still protected by several Kurita 'Mech companies and by a large number of ground troops. In the days following the Battle of Regis, tens of thousands of additional Kurita troops trickled into the spaceport area from towns and outposts all over the Verthandian Highlands. A tent city of refugee troops sprang up along the landing pad area, and grim-faced Kurita soldiers lined the entrenchments and hastily constructed fortifications of the spaceport perimeter.

There were Kurita BattleMechs everywhere. The Draconis Combine 'Mechs on Verthandi still outnumbered the rebel 'Mech forces. No one doubted for a moment that a determined thrust by the Kurita 'Mechs could lay utter and complete waste to Regis, the entire Bluesward, and to every town, village, and mine between the Silvan Basin and the Southern Desert. Yet, the Combine forces made no move. The entire planet had turned against them, and both their line troops and MechWarriors were afraid to leave the crowded huddle of the narrow spaceport perimeter.

Nor were the outnumbered Verthandian forces prepared to assault the spaceport. Though victorious, the rebel forces were still scattered, poorly equipped, often poorly fed and leaderless. More, they were exultant with the victorious climax of a hard-fought campaign that had lasted for two Verthandian years. There was a natural tendency to view further combat as something of an anticlimax.

Not one of the young men and women hemming in the encircled Kurita veterans was willing to die *now*, with final victory in sight. If they could rid themselves of the hated invader through negotiation rather than combat, so much the better. If negotiations failed, the Kurita invaders could sit where they were and die of the starvation and disease that had already begun to stalk their ranks. If that death didn't appeal to them, they could charge the Free Verthandi lines instead, and die under the rebel guns surrounding them.

"Fight to the death" is a grand-sounding phrase, but in reality, war rarely comes to that. Sooner or later, the two sides usually decide to talk rather than fight.

Several days after the DropShip landings, one of the *Leopard*s lifted on roaring belly thrusters and shaped orbit for Verthandi-Alpha. When it returned, it carried Admiral Kodo himself, the new military commander of the Kurita forces on Verthandi. In name at least, he was also the new Governor General of the planet, until some trace could be found of the vanished Nagumo.

Verthandi seemed to have a new importance as a crossroads for galactic traffic. Three days after Kodo's arrival, a fleet materialized out of hyperspace at Norn's zenith point. Hurried radio consultations quickly identified the newcomer's identity. It was the First Tamar Fleet, warships, DropShips, and two battle-ready regiments of 'Mechs in the service of the Lyran Commonwealth.

In the van of the fleet was the jump freighter *Invidious*. Its DropShip *Deimos* set down at the airfield close by the walls of the city. Captain Renfred Tor was on board with five more BattleMechs and a small army of recruits for the Gray Death Legion.

Grayson's arms were heavily wrapped and bandaged, but he was well enough to meet Tor when he stepped off the DropShip ramp in the shadow of the University's fire-ruined Tower. Tor restrained himself in greeting Grayson for fear of causing him further injury, but he made up for it in his enthusiasm at seeing Lori and Sergeant Ramage again.

"It went just like you suggested in your message," he told Grayson, his face split by a broad grin. "It took some doing, but I finally interested Ambassador Steiner-Reese in what was going on here. The vanadium samples didn't impress him much at first, but I eventually convinced him.''

''Steiner-Reese?'' Ramage's eyebrows clawed toward his hairline. ''That wouldn't be a relative of . . .''

Tor's smile grew wider. ''That he is. He managed to cut quite a nice swath through the red tape, and even shepherded me clear through to Tharkad itself!''

Grayson whistled. Tharkad was the Lyran capital, and he'd never dared to hope that his message would carry so far.

''Tharkad . . .'' Grayson said. ''You made it to the Lyran capital?''

''Yep. I had an audience with the Archon herself.''

''You met Katrina Steiner?'' Lori said, equally dumbfounded.

''I had dinner with her,'' Tor said with a wink. ''Well, there were a few thousand other guests present at the time, but I had a quiet talk with her and her High Council afterward. I told them what you said in your message, Gray . . . that the Verthandians had a fighting chance of winning their independence, but that they needed outside help to pull it off. When I gave them your analysis of the mining potential of this place, they rushed off to wherever it is that government types go to talk a subject to death. It took them three weeks, but they finally decided to put together a fleet. The First Tamar Fleet is station-keeping at the zenith point now. I'll bet those Combine troops over yonder are getting a mite nervous, now that they know the Lyrans are there.''

''Their military commander landed three days ago,'' Grayson said. ''I imagine the presence of the Lyran fleet will . . . ah . . . influence the peace talks a bit.''

''Peace talks?'' Tor said. ''The Verthandians are talking peace with the Dracos?''

''They've had enough war, Ren, and they're not anxious to charge the Kurita encampment to force them out.'' He shrugged and looked off toward the north. ''I've seen the defenses up there. I can't say that I blame them.''

Tor shook his head. ''I just remember how determined that Rebel Council fellow was not to settle with the Dracos. What was his name?''

"Devic Erudin." Ramage laughed. "Believe it or not, he's on the negotiating team. It should be interesting to see what they hammer out."

Grayson smiled. "Interesting? I guess that's the word for it. Anyway, whatever happens, it's out of our hands now."

Epilogue

The band of the newly organized Free Verthandi Legion played a crashing martial march, as troops in new and glistening uniforms snapped to attention and rifles came to crisp, military salutes. Behind the ranks of men were ranks of BattleMechs. Though cleaned up now and with battle scars repaired, those 'Mechs still showed more pain and hard use than the fresh-faced youngsters lining the Scandia Way from the University's Gate of Heroes to the airfield. Two Gray Death DropShips waited there, ramps extended, to take their final passengers aboard.

The parades, the speeches, the presentations of medals and honors had lasted most of the previous day, much of the evening, and most of the present morning. Grayson was resplendent in the new gray uniform presented him by a group of Regis citizens, the ornate golden Star of Verthandi heavy against his chest. He felt that his arm would fall off if he were forced to return one more salute. The dressings had been removed from his arms only a week before, and the skin was still raw and tender.

The elite commandos whom Ramage had trained were the last unit to pass in review. The crowd was still applauding the Verthandi Rangers when Tollen Brasednewic and his wife separated themselves from the crowd that lined the reviewing stand and made their way toward Grayson. Trailing them was another small parade of their assistants, council staff, and secretaries. Though the couple wore civilian dress, Grayson felt they rated a proper salute as members of Verthandi's new Citizens' Council.

"Councilman," he said formally, with a smile, then turned and bowed ceremoneously to Carlotta Brasednewic. "Carlotta. Your husband appears to have made the transition from rebel general to head-of-state quite nicely. I credit you with whatever political expertise he has developed.''

Carlotta smiled softly, and Grayson caught himself watching her eyes for the haunted look that had been there during the past weeks. They had found her among the worst of the horror-numbed prisoners during the Battle of the University, so deeply in shock it was feared she would never recover. Time spent with Tollen Brasednewic seemed to have gone a long way toward healing her, but traces of the pain were still there in her expression. Grayson was glad to see that there was warmth as well. Perhaps, even a measure of peace.

''We are grateful to you, Captain,'' Tollen said. ''Our offer stands. You could remain here to build our army. We need people like you and your unit.''

Grayson shook his head. ''You've been doing that yourself, Tollen.'' He nodded toward the ranks of one-time rebel veterans, near-children still. Only their eyes were old.

He caught sight of one face in the Verthandians' front rank. Sue Ellen Klein, at least, had found her place here. She'd refused to talk about what had happened after she'd left Grayson in the tower, and Grayson felt she still carried some black, inner pain. Unable to talk with Grayson, she had discussed her decision to remain with Lori. At Lori's urging, Grayson had released Sue Ellen from her contract to the Gray Death. He still didn't know what her secret was, but he trusted Lori's judgement.

Sue Ellen had immediately accepted a commission with the Free Verthandi Navy. They had no ships, as yet, but the purchase of a pair of aging Lyran freighters was about to change that. Sue Ellen had happily accepted the task of organizing the new Verthandian fleet arm. Grayson was glad for her.

''Your battle now is a political one,'' Grayson continued. ''All I'll say is . . . remember what I told you last night. You could easily find yourself giving away at the conference table what you've already won on the battlefield.''

''I'll remember,'' Brasednewic said, but Grayson wondered if anything he'd said would make any difference.

Admiral Kodo had sued for peace. There was not much else the vacillating little man could do, with his troops down to quarter-rations and disease already gnawing at the ranks of men who had obviously lost the will to fight. The garrison regiments on Verthandi had been badly handled. Grayson wondered how long it would be before they were in fighting shape again. He knew that combat could ruin a man in ways more subtle and more devastating than a physical wound or maiming.

Only two days later, things became really complicated when Duke Hassid Ricol's flagship *Huntress* appeared at the zenith point, accompanied by the Draconis Combine Fifth Fleet.

Combat between jumpships is rare in this era because starships are a resource too rare and too fragile to risk in combat. With the situation on Verthandi in doubt, the two fleets hovered at the jump point on gently pulsing thrusters and kept a wary armed truce. After all, there was no current state of war between Luthien and Tharkad. Ricol conferred with Admiral Kodo, but the result was already a foregone conclusion. Unless Ricol wanted to initiate a whole new invasion of Verthandi—this time with a Lyran fleet facing him at the jump point and Lyran BattleMech regiments waiting for him on the ground— he would have to accept the negotiated peace Kodo had signed. In time, that is just what he did.

Once the peace talks were ended, the Kurita troops began boarding the DropShips that had arrived to ferry them offworld. Verthandi was once again a free and independent planet.

Independence had not brought peace, however. The Dracos had refused to take any Verthandian Loyalists with them. They had, in fact, abandoned them. As far as the rebels were concerned, the ceasefire of their talks with Kodo had never applied to Loyalists and Regis Blues. The massacres continued in scattered villages, forest patches, and hill country across the planet, a bloody, fratricidal civil war that no one seemed able or willing to end. Listening to Brasednewic tell of the slaughter, seeing the pain in a face grown markedly older within just the past weeks, Grayson suddenly remembered that the big rebel's brother had been a Loyalist. It looked as though this part of the Verthandian war might never end.

The talks continued, however, between Verthandi and the offworlders. The Lyrans had arrived because Grayson had sent word that their intervention might win them a contract for Verthandian heavy metals—the same precious ones that the Draconis Combine had coveted. The arrival of the Lyran fleet had been the telling factor in Duke Ricol's decision that further military intervention on Verthandi would be foolish. Ambassador Steiner-Reese, the Lyran representative aboard the flagship, felt that the new Verthandian government owed the Commonwealth certain concessions in the mines of the Southern Desert.

Ricol and his warfleet remained as well. Though the Duke had conceded Verthandi's independence from Draconis rule, he was quick to point out that the mines and machinery of the Southern Desert sites belonged largely to the Draconis Combine, and that their appropriation was an act of war. After all, the Verthandians themselves had shown scant interest in the various heavy metals and rare earths present on their world. Surely something could be worked out to a mutual advantage, he said.

Also on the bargaining table was the Kurita naval base on Verthandi-Alpha, an expensive investment that Luthien was not about to turn over to an upstart independent world with absolutely no space navy of its own! How could the Verthandians possibly claim that their sovereignty extended to their own planetary satellite when they had no way of enforcing—or even manifesting—that claim?

To which the Lyrans responded that they would be more than willing to help Verthandi develop her spaceflight technology. For a price, that is. Rights and concessions to the Skovde Mine would do for a starter . . .

Grayson didn't explain to Brasednewic his real reason for wishing to leave Verthandi, however. He now feared that the new Verthandi government was about to trade away its hard-won independence while drunk with the intoxicating wine of power bloc politics. The men and women who had fought and died at Fox Island, the Basin Rim, and the Battle of Regis could too easily be forgotten as Free Verthandi came under the sway of one or the

other of the two major powers in the region: the Lyran
Commonwealth or the Draconis Combine.

Whichever interstellar power was to become Verthandi's master, Grayson didn't want to know. The blood of
too many people he'd cared for—Piter, Jaleg, and heroic
Verthandian freedom fighters too numerous to mention—
lay heavy on his heart. Better to watch the parades, receive the honors and medals, give the politicians and
fellow warriors one last salute, and then up ship and away
for . . . wherever.

"It's time for us to boost, Tollen."

Brasednewic extended his hand. "We appreciate what
you've done for us, Captain. We owe you . . . everything."

Carlotta nodded solemnly. "That's right, Grayson. If
you ever change your mind . . ."

He smiled. "I'll remember. I wish you . . . and your
world . . . well." When he saluted again, the band leader
took that as a cue to crash into yet another rendition of
the march, already ancient, that Verthandi had chosen as
its anthem. He strode down the reviewing stand ramp.
Ahead was the *Phobos*, now ready for flight after a refit
and jury-rigged repairs in the Regisport yards. She waited
close by the *Deimos*, her boarding ramp extended. Captain Tor had returned to the *Invidious* days before to prepare the ship for jump, and both DropShips had been
busy shuttling men and women and material back to the
Invidious during the past weeks. All of the Gray Death's
Techs, warriors, and BattleMechs had already returned
to the starship, or waited now aboard the *Phobos*.

The Gray Death's order of battle had grown. There
were volunteers from among the Verthandian forces, including a young commando, Janice Taylor, who had resigned from the Free Rangers in order to join the Gray
Death Legion. Too, Grayson's Techs had taken aboard a
number of BattleMechs, machines captured from the
Draco forces, repaired in the field, and officially transferred to the mercenaries by a grateful Verthandian Citizens' Council. Grayson's *Marauder* was fully operable
now, its ejection hatch repaired. Lori's *Locust* had been
replaced by a refurbished and re-armed *Shadow Hawk*,
the same 'Mech that Grayson had used since he'd captured it on Trellwan.

"After all," he'd joked to her, "I can't have my own Executive Officer running around without a BattleMech now, can I? That would be indecent!"

Lori and Ramage were waiting for him at the bottom on the reviewing stand steps. Lori touched the Star of Verthandi on his chest and smiled. Ramage saluted, then pounded his back in congratulations. Grayson took one last look around at the uniforms and the determined young faces and sent them a silent prayer that they would be able to hold on to what they'd won.

Then Lori slipped her arm through his, and the three of them strode side by side toward the *Phobos*. Grayson knew that he would hold onto what he had won. Always.

CRUSADER

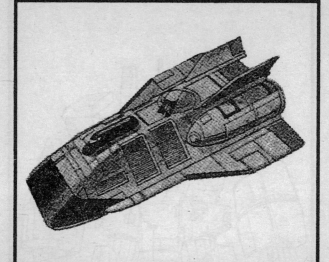

LEOPARD CLASS DROPSHIP

UNION CLASS DROPSHIP

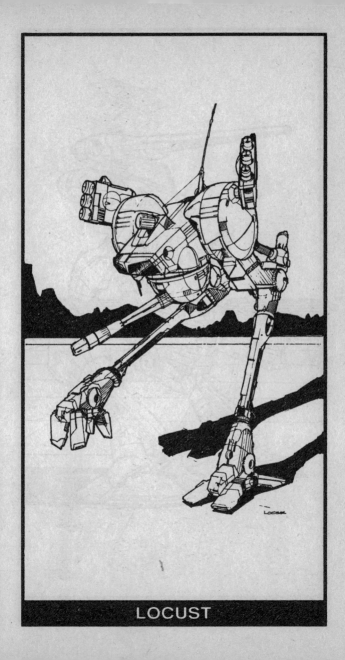

LOCUST

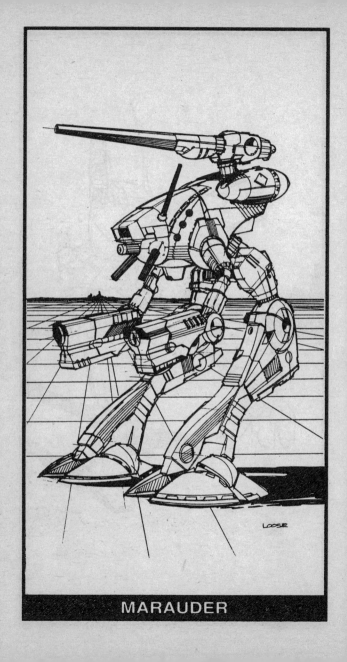

MARAUDER

PHOENIX HAWK

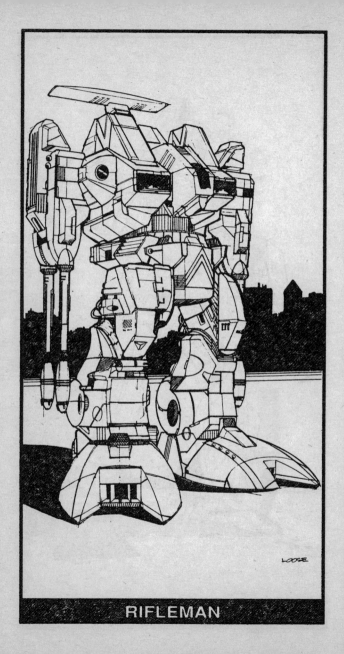

RIFLEMAN

SHADOW HAWK

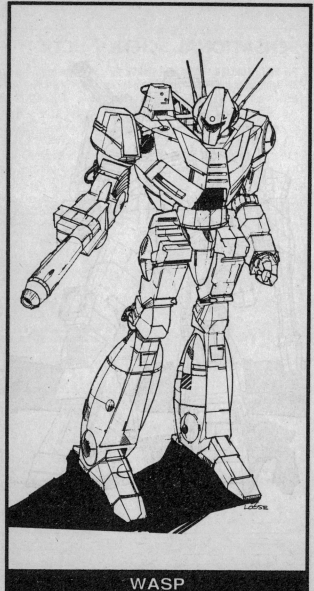

WASP

SENSATIONAL SCIENCE FICTION

THE FUTURE IS UPON US . . .

If you and/or a friend would like to receive the *ROC Advance*, a bimonthly newsletter featuring all the newest and hottest ROC books and authors, on a complimentary basis, please fill out this form and return it to:

ROC Books/Penguin USA
375 Hudson Street
New York, NY 10014

Your Address

Name _____

Street _____ Apt. # _____

City _____ State _____ Zip _____

Friend's Address

Name _____

Street _____ Apt. # _____

City _____ State _____ Zip _____